REBECCA BRANDEWYNE

is a bestselling author of historical novels. Her stories consistently place on the bestseller lists, including the *New York Times* and *Publishers Weekly* lists. She was inducted into the *Romantic Times* Hall of Fame in 1988, and is the recipient of the *Romantic Times* Career Achievement Award (1991), *Affaire de Coeur*'s Golden Quill Award for Best Historical Romance and the Silver Pen Award. You can visit her at www.brandewyne.com.

GINNA GRAY

A native Texan, Ginna Gray lived in Houston all her life until 1993, when she and her husband, Brad, built their "dream home" and moved to the mountains of Colorado. Coming from a large, Irish/American family, in which spinning colorful yarns was commonplace, made writing a natural career choice for Ginna. "I grew up hearing so many fascinating tales, I was eleven or twelve before I realized that not everyone made up stories," Ginna says. She sold her first novel in 1983 and has been working as a full-time writer ever since. She has also given many lectures and writing workshops and has judged in writing contests. The mother of two grown daughters, Ginna also enjoys other creative activities, such as oil painting, sewing, sketching, knitting and needlepoint.

JOAN HOHL

is the bestselling author of almost three dozen books. She has received numerous awards for her work, including the Romance Writers of America's Golden Medallion Award. In addition to contemporary romance, this prolific author also writes historical and time-travel romances. Joan lives in eastern Pennsylvania with her husband and family.

ANN MAJOR

loves writing romance novels as much as she loves reading them. She is a proud mother of three grown children. She lists hiking in the Colorado mountains with her husband, playing tennis, sailing, enjoying her cats and playing the piano among her favorite activities. Readers can contact her through www.eHarlequin.com or her own author site www.annmajor.com.

REBECCA BRANDEWYNE

GINNA GRAY
JOAN HOHL
ANN MAJOR

Winter Nights

Published by Silhouette Books
America's Publisher of Contemporary Romance

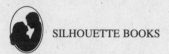 SILHOUETTE BOOKS

WINTER NIGHTS

Copyright © 2002 by Harlequin Books S.A.

ISBN 0-373-21802-8

The publisher acknowledges the copyright holders
of the individual works as follows:

THE ICE DANCERS
Copyright © 1996 by Rebecca Brandewyne

SEASON OF MIRACLES
Copyright © 1987 by Virginia Gray

HOLIDAY HOMECOMING
Copyright © 1993 by Joan Hohl

SANTA'S SPECIAL MIRACLE
Copyright © 1990 by Ann Major

This edition published by arrangement with Harlequin Books S.A.

® and TM are trademarks of Harlequin Books S.A., used under license.
Trademarks indicated with ® are registered in the United States Patent
and Trademark Office, the Canadian Trade Marks Office and in other
countries.

Visit Silhouette at www.eHarlequin.com

Printed in U.S.A.

CONTENTS

THE ICE DANCERS   11
by Rebecca Brandewyne

SEASON OF MIRACLES   89
by Ginna Gray

HOLIDAY HOMECOMING   159
by Joan Hohl

SANTA'S SPECIAL MIRACLE   227
by Ann Major

THE ICE DANCERS

Rebecca Brandewyne

For Suzi, for wilder days and happy endings.
With love.

Dear Reader,

I hope you enjoy this novella, "The Ice Dancers." Ice-skating is one of my favorite sports, and since I can't ice-skate myself, I really admire those who can—not to mention that it's simply one of the most beautiful sports in existence. Something I will always remember is being one of the judges of the Miss USA 1990 pageant, for which Olympic ice-skater Robin Cousins was also a judge. It was such fun for me to chat with him and get a glimpse of an insider's viewpoint of the sport.

At my house, Christmas is always a very special time of the year, spent with family and close friends. We have four Christmas trees, each with its own theme, and every year we choose a different tree to put up in our house. Sometimes, depending on how much time we have that year, we put up more than one. Since my husband, John, is from England, we celebrate both American and British traditions, with a mixture of American and British foods, which John and I cook together. My mother and I always make quite a bit of candy and other yummy treats, too (John had never seen a candy cane before coming to America—and he wanted to know why a man was putting a lighted walking stick in his front yard!). Stockings are hung by the chimney with care, and both Santa Claus and Father Christmas leave appropriate goodies in them (unlike Santa Claus, the British Father Christmas doesn't leave ashes, switches and lumps of coal for naughty children!). We attend midnight mass on Christmas Eve, open our gifts on Christmas Day and celebrate Boxing Day, the day after Christmas, which is a holiday in Britain.

Mariah and Alek were in my head for a long time. I'm so glad I had this opportunity to introduce them to you! Please visit my virtual home, Ravenscroft Castle, and sign up for my readers' newsletter at http://www.brandewyne.com. Send e-mails to me at rebecca@brandewyne.com.

Happy holidays!

Rebecca Brandewyne

The Ice Dancers

Like a phoenix, love rises from the ashes
Of an old but not forgotten flame.
It begins again, with "Do you remember when
You whispered low my name
And held me close in the darkness—"
Which one of us was to blame?
It seems so unimportant now.
We are changed, no longer the same.

So come to me urgently in silence.
On this wintry night, we will start anew;
And when all of the old memories awaken,
As they are bound to do,
We'll bury the worst in the past,
Keeping only the best, we two.
So, came, love. Dance forever with me.
We are changed; still, this ice isn't new.

We have trodden it before, you and I.
We know each rut that e'er led us to grieve,
And every fragile patch along the perilous path.
So this time, do not leave.
It is only the lucky ones who are given
A second chance, a reprieve.
And sometimes, dreams really do come true.
We are changed—if only you believe.

Chapter 1

An Old Flame

"I thought I told you never to mention her name to me again." Alek Khazan's voice, while low, contained an underlying note that warned of his anger. A muscle flexed in his set jaw, as well, a sure sign of the turbulent emotions he held in check with difficulty. Anybody else in the world of figure skating would have backed off at this point, Alek's black Russian rages being notorious. But Jules Straetham was not just anybody.

"Alek, be reasonable." The former Olympic gold medalist turned coach exhibited not the least sign of fear in the face of his protégé's wicked temper and ill mood, having himself equally strong emotions and an equally imposing, well-muscled physique, despite the fact that the older man was more than twice Alek's age. "Although I wish Cissy nothing but happiness, her quitting ice dancing to get married *does* leave you without a partner. And no matter how you feel about it, the fact remains that the only one available to you at the moment is Mariah."

Alek winced again as he heard the name of his former ice-dancing partner—and former fiancée. *Mariah!* For his own sanity and self-preservation, he had tried determinedly, desperately, to forget her. Despite all his efforts, he had never gotten over her. She still haunted him.

It had not helped that, with both of them being ice dancers, albeit skating now with different partners, they had inevitably run into each other at competitions during the more than two years since their highly publicized professional and personal breakup. Whenever they met, mindful of the watchful cameras of the media, they nodded and greeted each other politely, as though they were practically strangers. But every time, Alek was seized inwardly with a fierce, wild desire to snatch Mariah up, to carry her away to the nearest private place and to fling her down and make endless passionate love to her, as he had used to do.

He was drawn irresistibly to watch her performances on the ice—in the arms of another partner—and he was consumed with jealousy at the sight. Until the automobile accident that claimed the life of Mariah's new ice-dancing partner, Worth Deverell, Alek had longed to throttle him, even though Worth had been a friend, and not responsible for taking Mariah away from him. No, if anyone was to blame for their breakup, it had been Alek himself. He had driven Mariah away, pure and simple. Deep down inside, he knew that, although he was unwilling even now to admit it to himself.

"I can't skate with Mariah," Alek instead insisted stubbornly to his skating coach. "Even if we didn't have a personal history between us, she's just not willing professionally to devote the necessary time and practice to her ice dancing."

Jules snorted scornfully to demonstrate just what he thought of this remark.

"That's terribly unfair, Alek—and, what's more, you know it! With the exception of you, there's nobody harder-working or more devoted to her art than Mariah. Cissy, for all that she's sweet and talented, isn't half the skater Mariah is. Yet you were never as tough on Cissy as you were on Mariah. The truth is, you allowed your personal feelings for Mariah to interfere with your professional relationship, Alek. And I must shoulder a portion of the blame for that, as well, because I saw what was happening, and I didn't put a halt to it. Like you, I wanted Mariah to be not just the best, but perfection personified on the ice. It was too much to ask of anyone—and you *demanded* it, Alek, as you demand it of yourself. But Mariah wasn't you. She wasn't me. We should have realized that...realized, too, that she wanted, that she was *entitled to,* a life beyond her work. You pushed her too hard, and I let you do it. But we won't make that mistake this time around, will we?''

''No, because I'm not going to skate with her again—and nothing you say or do is going to change my mind about that, Jules.''

''Then you must have plans of which I'm unaware, Alek.'' Jules's craggy, handsome face went suddenly still. ''Are you thinking of quitting ice dancing, too, then, like Cissy? Of...of *retiring?*''

''You must know that if I were, I would have informed you of that fact,'' Alek said stiffly, the muscle in his jaw still throbbing ominously.

''Well, then, have you discovered some fresh, unknown talent you've invited to be your new partner?''

''If I had, I would have told you about that, too, Jules.''

''So...you're not retiring, and you don't have a new partner I don't know about. I have to confess you've got me stumped, then, Alek.'' Jules scratched his head, as though purely puzzled. ''Just how are you going to ice-dance without a partner? Have you bought one of those inflatable dummies, maybe? Do you plan on tying its feet to your ice skates or something, and hoping the judges won't notice your partner's not exactly too lively?''

''No.'' Alek's mouth turned down sourly at the sarcastic humor. The more Jules hammered at him, the more Alek realized how unreasonable he was being. If he wanted to continue ice dancing—and he did—he had to have a new partner. And whether he liked it or not, Mariah Nichols was the only one available at the moment. Still, he made one last-ditch effort to squelch the idea. ''She won't skate with me,'' he declared flatly.

''How do you know?'' Jules pasted on his best poker face, so that his excitement and triumph would not show. He had won. He knew it. Still, Alek was just volatile and unpredictable enough to get in a huff, to quit ice dancing altogether and to stamp out of the rink forever, if he spied his skating coach openly gloating. "Have you asked her?"

"Don't be ridiculous!" Alek's tone was sharper than he had intended, and he had to force himself to modulate it. "Except for the polite inanities we've exchanged for the benefit of the media's cameras, Mariah and I haven't spoken to each other in years."

"Then how do you know she won't skate with you?" Jules paused for a moment to allow his question to sink in. Then he continued. "Look, Alek, she's had a hard time and a tough break—one a hell of a lot worse than losing her skating partner to the dingdong of wedding bells. It's only by the grace of God she wasn't killed in that accident, along with Worth and Richard. At least neither your partner nor your coach is lying dead and buried in a cemetery. And you haven't spent some weeks in a hospital, recovering from such a traumatic experience."

"I know...I know..." Alek replied softly, running one hand raggedly through his shoulder-length black hair. He had been stricken when he heard about the fatal automobile accident. For a moment, he had felt as though his own heart had stopped. It was only when he learned Mariah, although injured, was alive that he had become aware of his heart lurching to life again, of its beating in his chest, albeit far too hard and quickly. He had sent flowers to Mariah at the hospital, along with an awkward letter that did not even begin to express his innermost feelings. Mariah's choreographer, Lanie Prescott, had responded with a short but courteous note, thanking him on Mariah's behalf for the flowers and reporting, to his relief, that Mariah, while not yet up to speed, was expected to make a full recovery.

"I almost went to visit her at the hospital, you know," Alek confessed. "But then I decided she...she probably wouldn't want to see me. And even though we both need a partner, Jules, my gut instinct still tells me Mariah won't want to skate with me again, either."

"Well, your gut instinct is wrong, Alek," Jules announced bluntly, playing his trump card. "I've talked to Lanie several times, including late last night. It seems Mariah is willing to give your professional relationship another chance, provided you're willing, too. If you agree, I'll coach you both, of course, and Lanie will come on board as the team's choreographer. So, what do you say, Alek? Shall I call Lanie back and give her the go-ahead...or not?''

The question hung in the silence of the rink, and in that moment, Alek had a strange, nebulous impression that he was standing at a crossroads in his life, uncertain of which path to take. Before his dark, handsome face, his breath formed tiny clouds in the air, and he had an unreal sensation that he could see Mariah in the mist, a miniature figure turning and gliding like a fairy princess across a frozen pond, so small that he could have held it in his palms. Her long black hair was loose, falling nearly to her waist, and she was dressed in the white feathered costume she had worn for the program they had once danced together to music from *Swan Lake*. She was beautiful—and he was honest enough to acknowledge the fact that, despite everything, he still wanted her.

"Yes," he at last uttered slowly, huskily. "Tell Lanie to tell Mariah I said yes."

After that, Alek removed the blade protectors from his skates, then stepped out onto the ice. The rink was cold, as always, so he kept on his heavy sweater and gloves while he warmed up, then began his practice session, executing chassés and mohawks and other movements fluidly. But the fact that, more than once, Alek missed a more intricate step informed Jules that his protégé's mind was not on his skating, for it was unlike Alek to make a string of careless mistakes. Normally, Jules would have been pounding his fist on the rail of the rink, shouting rebukes and instructions. Today, however, the older man was compelled to hide a grin of satisfaction. Abruptly he strode from the rink into the corridor beyond. On his cellular telephone, he dialed Lanie Prescott's number, a victorious smile lighting up his face.

Chapter 2

It Begins Again

She was going to skate with Alek Khazan again. As she gazed at herself in the mirrors of Lanie's dance studio, Mariah Nichols could not believe she had agreed to such a thing. She must have been out of her mind, she thought as she stretched her slender body out over one long, graceful leg, which was positioned on the bar that ran along one wall. She grabbed her foot, holding the pose for several long counts and remembering to breathe normally as she did so. There was still, now and then, an occasional twinge of pain when she forced her leg muscles to respond. But, for the most part, she had fully recovered from the automobile accident that had left her hospitalized for several weeks and had killed her ice-dancing partner, Worth Deverell, as well as their skating coach, Richard Underwood.

The three of them had been returning home late one night after a skating performance when their car was struck by a drunk driver. Even now, months later, Mariah had only vague, horrifying memories of the accident. It had been raining, and the car's wipers had made a squishing sound against the windshield. Wisps of mist had drifted across the road, and the wet highway had shimmered in the glare of their car's headlights.

At first, Mariah and the others had thought it must be some

trick of that same mist and headlights that made it appear as though the oncoming pickup truck had veered from its own lane into theirs. Too late had they grasped their peril. Richard, cursing with rage, fear and disbelief, had tried frantically to steer their car out of the truck's path, onto the shoulder of the road—to no avail. The impact had been sudden and violent, the brutal crunching of glass and metal sickening. Richard had been killed instantly. Worth had died in the ambulance en route to the hospital. In the curious, ironic way of things, the drunken driver of the pickup had walked away without a scratch.

Over and over, as she had lain in her hospital bed, not knowing if she would ever walk again, much less ice-dance, Mariah had replayed the deadly accident in her mind. She had wondered endlessly whether there had been any chance of avoiding it, although she had known deep down inside that Richard had done everything humanly possible to attempt to prevent the terrible collision. There had simply been no escaping from the wildly speeding, weaving truck that barreled toward them. She saw it still—in her dreams.

More than once since the accident, she had awakened from a deep sleep, screaming and feeling the cool rain drizzling down on her as the paramedics had worked frantically to save her life, and then the ambulance attendants had lifted her onto a gurney to transport her to the hospital. Only after her heart had slowed and her mind had oriented itself following the nightmare did Mariah realize she was lying in her own bed, that the wetness on her face was tears, not rain.

In addition to the nightmares, she still experienced moments of unexpected shock, dazedness and panic. She thought it must have been during one of these times that she agreed to ice-dance again with Alek Khazan. Mariah could not explain her having consented to their reunion, otherwise. She didn't *want* to skate with him. She did not even want to *see* him! He had pushed her professionally with a single-mindedness that bordered on monomania, sacrificing their personal relationship in the process. He had broken her heart. That its shattered pieces still ached for him was all the more reason to avoid him.

"Earth to Mariah...Earth to Mariah..." Lanie Prescott's

voice, followed by her soft, musical laughter, rang in Mariah's ears. "Sweetie, if you stay bent over like that much longer, you're liable to freeze in that position. Are you regretting your decision already? Is that why your mind isn't on your work this morning?"

"Yes," Mariah admitted reluctantly, with a rueful smile, as she rose and changed legs, continuing to stretch her muscles. If it weren't for the fact that her and Alek's first performance together would be a Christmas Eve benefit for the Letters to Angels program for the All-Children's Hospital, she'd have had Lanie call Jules Straetham back and tell him she'd changed her mind about skating with Alek. "But how can I refuse to help a program I believe in so strongly, Lanie? A fact I'm sure you counted on when you proposed this match made in hell!" Mariah shot her choreographer and dance coach a knowing, accusatory glance that spoke volumes.

"As I recall, it used to be a match made in heaven—or so the press always claimed. Nichols and Khazan were the dream team of the decade, the American hope for Olympic gold, Mariah— and, what's more, you know it! Oh, you and Worth skated well together, yes. But let's face it, the two of you never achieved on the ice that indefinable quality you and Alek shared. You and Alek had something special together, Mariah. You had *magic!* A magic each of you lost when you started skating with Worth and Cissy."

"Worth was a marvelous ice dancer!" Mariah protested, stung.

"Oh, sweetie, I know he was." Lanie's eyes, like Mariah's own, were abruptly shadowed with grief. "But the two of you were only good friends, not lovers...and so the chemistry was just missing from the mix—not to mention the fact that Worth's style was as different from Alek's as yours is from Cissy Howland's. The pairings produced competent, professional performances, yes. There's no doubt about that. But the heart and soul that elevate the excellent to the magical just wasn't there, Mariah—for you *or* Alek. And *that's* what makes a performance outstanding and memorable, what brings the audience to its feet and prompts the judges to hand out sixes. Because it's so rare to see that. Only a handful of ice dancers have brought it to the rink—Torvil and Dean, and Klimova and Ponomarenko among them.''

Mariah sighed at the mention of these fellow ice dancers, because of all the competition she and Alek had faced during their time together, she had always known that these couples, especially, set the standards for everybody else in the past decade or so, elevating the art with their dramatic and innovative performances. Marina Klimova and Sergei Ponomarenko, especially, were Mariah's idols.

"Much as I hate to admit it, I know you're right, Lanie. If you want to know the truth, I always felt in my heart that Worth should have been paired with Cissy. Still, that doesn't make the prospect of skating with Alek again any easier. Despite everything, I still have…feelings for him, Lanie—and I'm not sure if I can sort out all my emotions and tuck them into neat little compartments for the sake of my art. But I'm not going to back out of the commitment now, if that's what you're worrying about. Letters to Angels is a wonderful program to benefit an extremely worthy cause, and, of course, it goes without saying that the All-Children's Hospital is something I'm proud and glad to support.''

"Good,'' Lanie said briskly. "Then, if you feel like you're warmed up, why don't we get to work?''

Because of Alek's Russian heritage, he and Mariah had developed a practice routine that relied almost as heavily on dance—ballet, especially—as it did upon their actual skating. As a result, after their breakup, Mariah had continued to spend nearly as many hours in the dance studio as she did upon the ice. It was not enough just to learn a dance or program. It took weeks, months, of development, training and refinement to bring a performance to its peak. Although ice dancing lacked the jumps that characterized both individual and pairs skating, it was in other respects more difficult than either, requiring extremely precise footwork and exceptional grace of movement. Ice dancers also had to conform to the regulation that required them not to be physically separated for more than very brief intervals on the ice.

Of course, in a benefit performance such as she and Alek would be doing for the All-Children's Hospital, they could skate any kind of program they wished. Even so, it would be a good place to try out routines they planned to skate later on in competition. So today she and Lanie were going to work on a few ideas to propose to Alek and Jules tomorrow morning, when the four of them were to have their first meeting.

Mariah's heart pounded at the thought of seeing Alek again, of skating with him. The prospect so unsettled her that she flubbed several steps in a row. She could not understand why Lanie merely shook her head and smiled. Lanie had said Alek had agreed to the proposed pairing, but Mariah knew nothing about the telephone conversation her choreographer had had earlier that morning with Jules Straetham—during which he had related to Lanie that the normally cool, arrogant Alek Khazan had just taken a most uncharacteristic spill on the ice, landing flat on his backside.

But even if Mariah *had* known that, she would not have believed it. In the world of figure skating, Alek was frequently referred to behind his back as the Ice Man, because nothing ever unnerved him. Nothing at all. He was as cold as the ice he skated on. As a result, it was absurd that just the thought of him should make her feel so strangely hot and flushed, as though she were melting inside. Absolutely absurd.

Chapter 3

Memories Awaken

It was in the dark, predawn hours that Mariah and Lanie made their way to the local ice rink where Mariah, Alek and various other well-known skaters, both amateur and professional, regularly practiced. Both Mariah and Alek had always preferred the quiet of the early dawn to begin working. It was one of the things that had drawn them together initially as ice-dancing partners, and that was something Mariah could not help thinking about as Lanie pulled the car to a halt in the still-lit parking lot and shut off the engine and headlights.

"Are you ready, sweetie?" Lanie asked, glancing over at Mariah. Wisely, the choreographer had neither chattered like the proverbial magpie nor remained absolutely mute during the drive to the rink. Instead, she had carried on a perfectly normal conversation, speaking when she had had something to say, while at the same time not rushing to fill natural silences.

Mariah nodded, slowly unfastening her seat belt. The fact that she was wearing her seat belt the night of the automobile accident had, she knew without a doubt, saved her life. Neither Worth nor Richard had taken the time to buckle up on that fatal night. Now, even if she were going no more than a block, Mariah always fastened her seat belt, as did Lanie.

Outside, the early-winter air was cool and crisp, with a hint of rain. Dead leaves blown by the wind from the deciduous trees into the parking lot crunched beneath Mariah's feet as, after retrieving their gear bags from the trunk of the car, she and Lanie walked to the building that housed the rink. As Lanie opened the door, Mariah took a deep breath, trying to quell the racing of her heart, the jumping of her nerves. She thought yet again that she had been crazy to agree to this professional reunion of her and Alek. It was all she could do not to turn around and run back to the car, insisting Lanie drive her home. Despite the cold, Mariah's palms, clenched into fists inside the pockets of her bright down ski jacket, were sweating.

Inside, the rink was hushed, its lighting dim, its ice empty. She and Alek were to have the place all to themselves this morning. Mariah marveled that, after this and all the other arrangements had been made, word had not yet leaked to the press. She had expected a horde of media cameras in the parking lot. Instead only Alek and Jules were at the rink. Alek had clearly completed his stretching and other preliminary warm-up exercises, and he was in the process of lacing up his ice skates. At the sight of him, Mariah felt her mouth go abruptly dry and her heart begin to throb deafeningly in her ears. Impossibly, he looked even handsomer, sexier and more potently masculine than ever. He was tall, dark, lean, and superbly muscled, like some sleek, predatory animal, and as she glanced at him, she could not prevent the rush of memory that assailed her, the memory of how those sinuous, hard muscles had felt, bunching and rippling against her naked, sweating skin. To cover her sudden confusion, Mariah turned to Jules Straetham, who had been her own skating coach, as well as Alek's.

"Hello, Jules," she said quietly, holding out her hand. "It's good to see you again."

"Mariah!" The older man's voice boomed as, smiling broadly, he flung out both arms warmly in welcome. "Now, surely, you're not going to stand on ceremony with me!" Then he grabbed her and gave her a big bear hug that, had she been a smaller, less physically fit woman, would doubtless have crushed her.

Against his broad chest, Mariah could feel tears stinging her eyes. She had always liked Jules tremendously and had been very sorry to lose him when she and Alek parted ways. Although she had also liked Richard Underwood, he had been Worth's coach before becoming hers, and she had never felt she and Richard meshed the way she and Jules always had. Grateful Jules held no hard feelings toward her, she hugged him back fervently until he finally released her.

"You're looking as beautiful as ever, Mariah," he declared. Then, as though he sensed Mariah and Alek would prefer to exchange their greetings more privately, he turned to Lanie, standing to one side. "And you, Lanie! You're a sight for sore eyes!"

"Jules, you old rascal, you!" Lanie exclaimed in response.

As though by mutual, unspoken consent, the two coaches strolled away toward the rink, leaving Mariah alone with Alek— despite her urgent, pleading glance in Lanie's direction. Mariah had no choice then but to address Alek himself. Having finished lacing up his ice skates, he had risen to his feet. The blades made him even taller, so that, even though she was a tall woman, he appeared to tower over her, reminding her somehow of a panther poised to spring, animal magnetism and menace seeming to emanate almost tangibly from him.

He had his long, glossy jet-black hair tied back in a ponytail, as he had always worn it at practice, exposing the tiny diamond stud earring in his left ear. His startlingly green eyes glinted like fiery emeralds when caught by the diffuse light, contrasting sharply with the dark stubble of beard that shadowed his face and that Mariah could remember grazing her skin when they had used to make love. The cable-knit sweater he wore matched his eyes, and his black practice pants hugged his legs tightly, emphasizing the superior, powerful muscles that corded his thighs and calves. Despite herself, Mariah could not help but think about how those strong legs had once entangled with her own as he had taken her to the heights of rapture and back.

"Hello, Alek." She nodded in his direction, not offering her hand, wanting to postpone as long as possible the moment when he would touch her again. Her pulse was jerking erratically at the memory of the warmth of his hands, of his skin, of his breath. She could feel a blush creeping into her cheeks as she wondered whether Alek guessed what she was thinking. Somehow, he had always been able to tell.

To hide her discomfiture, Mariah sat down on a bench and shrugged off her ski jacket. Then she bent over the bag in which she carried her gear. Unzipping it, she removed her ice skates and gloves, which she set to one side. After that, she began her stretching and other preliminary warm-up exercises, telling herself it was only these that made her breath come fast, her heart beat too quickly in her breast.

"Hello, Mariah." Alek's voice was low, serrated by emotion he could not quite conceal. Seeing her again, being so close to her again, had affected him deeply. She was, as Jules had noted, as beautiful as ever, he thought as he watched her stretch and bend her body, loosening up her muscles.

Mariah had the figure of a classic ballerina—tall, willowy, with small, high, round breasts and long, graceful arms and legs. In sharp contrast to her gorgeous blue-black hair, her skin was very white and luminescent, like fine porcelain, so her large, liquid midnight-blue eyes seemed to dominate the delicate planes and angles of her face. On the ice, she could appear like spun sugar, like a fairy princess gliding or a swan floating over a still, serene, misted pond—qualities she and Alek had always capitalized on when they had skated together. They had made an extraordinarily striking couple.

Today, Mariah had her long hair twisted up in a French knot, exposing her swanlike nape and throat, to which Alek used to press hot, impassioned kisses. At the remembrance, it was all he could do to prevent himself from bending over her and planting kisses there now as, finished with her exercises, she began to tug on her ice skates.

"I want you to know how sorry I was to hear about your automobile accident, Mariah, about Worth and Richard," he stated awkwardly, instead. "I...wanted to come visit you while you were in the hospital. But I—I thought that perhaps you wouldn't want to see me.''

''I didn't want to see anybody, actually,'' Mariah confessed, her head bent as she pretended to concentrate on lacing up her ice skates—a task that did, indeed, require close attention. Improperly laced ice skates would not only provide inadequate support on the ice, but could also prove dangerous, since a dangling lace or strap could get caught under a blade, sending a skater sprawling. ''It was a very difficult time for me. But I—I appreciated the flowers and note you sent, Alek.'' She did not add that, upon receiving them, she had wondered if, deep down inside, he still harbored some feelings for her, as she did for him.

Finished lacing up her ice skates, she at last glanced up at him, her breath catching in her throat at the intensity of his gaze. For a long moment, silence stretched between them, taut, expectant, fraught with significance.

''Hey, you two!'' Jules shouted, abruptly breaking the hush, the tension. ''Are you going to gab all morning over there, or arc we going to get some work done here? We only have the rink for so long, you know, and time's a-wasting.''

Alek cleared his throat. ''Well, I guess we'd better get going, or else Jules is liable to have one of his infamous conniption fits,'' he said.

''How well I remember those!'' Mariah managed a small laugh as she got rather shakily to her feet. ''More than once, I went home in tears after a day of Jules's tirades.'' She paused briefly, remembering. Then she continued. ''But I've been through a lot since then, and I'm no longer the woman I was then. I'm much stronger now, Alek,'' she asserted, looking him straight in the eye, putting him on notice that neither he nor Jules would find it so easy to intimidate her these days.

But, to her surprise, Alek did not take up the gauntlet she had cast down between them.

''Good. I'm glad to hear that,'' he replied shortly instead. ''You were always much too sensitive, Mariah, too easily hurt, because you took things so much to heart. And in this business, as you know, you've got to be tough to survive. Still, I do hope that, in the process of becoming strong, you've not grown hard, as well. Your femininity, your softness around the edges, was always one of your most appealing qualities.''

For an instant, he did not trouble to conceal the heat in his eyes when he gazed at her, and Mariah felt her heart turn over in her breast. Oh, God, she had been such a fool to agree to this reunion, when she knew in her heart that she could not trust herself to keep her emotions under control when it came to Alek Khazan. Just one look from him—and she already felt as though she were melting into a puddle at his feet! So much for the strength of which she had boasted only minutes before! With difficulty, she forced herself to gather her wits and composure.

''Jules and Lanie are waiting,'' she reminded him, a trifle breathlessly, as, pulling on her gloves, she stood and walked toward the rink.

Slipping off her blade protectors and laying them aside, Mariah stepped out onto the ice, briefly testing it with a few movements that sent her sailing gracefully across its hard surface. It was not new ice, for which she was inordinately grateful. New ice was brittle, prone to rutting from the sharp blades—after which it was all too easy to hit a rut or catch a blade in one. And one thing she did not want to do this morning was fall flat on her posterior in front of Alek Khazan. Presently, he joined her on the ice, his own movements strong and clean.

''Okay, why don't the two of you get warmed up?'' Jules directed as he watched them. ''After that, the first thing I want to do this morning is run through some of the technical programs. We'll do the Starlight Waltz and a couple of others…see if you remember any of your old programs together. Then we'll discuss new routines. You're going to need at least two for the benefit. Lanie, I know, already has some great ideas.''

''Yes, I do,'' the choreographer confirmed.

Mariah and Alek spent several minutes warming up on the ice, skating individually for the time being, for which Mariah was grateful. Since the accident, she had developed a fear she had previously lacked: that her legs would give out under her, that she would slip and fall on the ice especially during a performance. It was an irrational fear, she knew. Now that she was fully recovered, her legs were as strong as ever, despite the occasional twinge of pain—and even those were increasingly few and far between. Besides which, all skaters fell; it was part of the price of the sport. And even though it was extremely unusual for an ice dancer to fall during a performance, it still happened. In ice dancing, more than a matter of score deductions or losing a competition, it brought a feeling of having failed your partner. And since Mariah had always striven to do her best, she loathed the thought of giving any less than that.

Alek, of course, was so single-mindedly driven that, at times in the past, his ambition and determination had frightened her. Now, having worked with Worth, she understood Alek's purposefulness better, because deep down inside she'd known Worth lacked that fine, sharp cutting edge that separated the good from the best, the best from the brilliant.

"All right, Alek…Mariah…" Jules clapped his hands together to get the two skaters' attention. "Lanie's finally all set up now, so let's try the Starlight Waltz, shall we?"

This was the moment Mariah had been dreading—and yet perversely awaiting, too—the moment when Alek would touch her again, when they would skate together again. As always, it was cold upon the ice. Still, she felt heated after her warm-up— although that was not the only reason. All the while she had been skating, she had been all too aware of Alek's proximity on the ice. Now, he was moving toward her—taking her in his arms, in preparation for the Starlight Waltz. He could feel the tension in her body. She knew that when he spoke.

"Relax, Mariah. I'm not going to bite you."

His words did not help, because, of course, there had been a time when he had bitten her, nipped lovingly at her ear, her nape, her shoulder.…

"I *am* relaxed," she insisted, although she knew her words for a lie. "Or at least, if I'm nervous, it's got nothing to do with you, Alek! I haven't skated with a partner in a while—or had you forgotten that?"

"No. Yes. Sorry," he said tersely.

A muscle pulsed in Alek's set jaw. His hand tightened involuntarily upon Mariah's waist, so she was aware of his sudden anger at himself. For a moment, holding her in his arms again, he *had* forgotten the accident. All he could remember was the feel of her.

As the opening strains of the waltz drifted over the ice, Mariah felt as though she had somehow been transported back in time, as though she and Alek were once more dancing this technical program in a competition.

Alek was as masterful on the ice as he was on a dance floor, leaving his partner in no doubt as to who was leading whom. As though it were only yesterday, the moves came flooding back to both him and Mariah, as they executed the chassés and mohawks that formed the basis of the Starlight Waltz, following the prescribed pattern, from which there could be no deviation. Even so, each couple had its own individual style, movements and lifts, and Mariah and Alek were no exception to that rule. It was these they now remembered, as though the two of them had never been separated as partners, as though Worth and Cissy had never been.

Watching Mariah and Alek, Jules sighed deeply with satisfaction. Whatever "it" had been—rapport, telepathy, chemistry, magic—the two of them still had it together. They had not lost it, as he had half feared.

"They still look like the couple on top of a wedding cake," Lanie observed softly, echoing aloud the skating coach's thoughts. "Oh, Jules... This is a good thing you've done. I do think that if you hadn't called me to propose this reunion, Mariah might have given up ice dancing altogether—and it would have been such a pity, such a crime to deprive the world of her talent. She and Alek together have the ability to rank right up there with the very best in the sport. It's not too late."

"No, it's not too late," Jules agreed softly. "We've got a few years to prepare for the next Winter Olympics. Meanwhile, the benefit is an excellent place to begin."

"And I've got some good ideas for choreography, as well as for music and costumes." The music for the Starlight Waltz at last faded to a halt, and Lanie inserted another cassette. On the ice, at Jules's direction, Mariah and Alek started the technical program to this particular music.

As they went on skating fluidly together, Mariah's confidence in her performance, at least, grew steadily. She had until now, she realized, almost forgotten what it was like to skate with Alek, having been compelled these past few years to accustom herself to Worth's style instead. Now she recognized how Worth's affable, easygoing nature, his "Hey, we'll be great, babe" attitude toward his skating, had subtly affected her own performances, eroding her sharpness, her assertiveness, making her as nervous as Worth himself had always been underneath all his bravado. Subconsciously Mariah had always been half-afraid Worth would accidentally drop her during a lift—even though he never had, and had never even given her good cause to suspect he might.

There was just something about Alek's own self-confidence, however, that seemed to communicate itself to her. More than one reporter had remarked that Alek had nerves of pure steel, not to mention incredible strength and stamina. Like Elvis Stojko, Alek had a background in the martial arts, which made him extraordinarily focused when it came to his skating.

But although her confidence in her performance had increased, Mariah's faith in herself had not. Pairs skating and ice dancing were, in many respects, extremely intimate, the male's hands often on his female partner's body in ways and places otherwise familiar only to her husband or lover. Every time Alek's arm brushed her breasts or his hand clasped the inside of her thigh during a lift, she remembered how he had touched her when he had made love to her, and her pulse jerked, deeply unsettling her. She wondered if he, too, was assailed by memories of them lying naked and sweating together, their hearts pounding as one. But she could not bring herself to ask. If she meant nothing to him now, Mariah did not want to know.

For his part, Alek put the slight tension he continued to feel in Mariah's body down to the fact that, as she had reminded him, she had not skated with a partner for a while. Even so, that did not quell the wild desire he had to run his hands over her body in ways that had nothing to do with the technical program the two of them were currently skating together.

Once, late one night after practice, when the rink was dim and deserted, they had made love together on the ice. It had been a mad thing to do—cold, wet and awkward, with both of them shivering, freezing and laughing until, grabbing up her discarded clothes, Mariah finally leaped to her feet and fled, with Alek in hot pursuit. They had wound up in the women's locker room, which had at least been infinitely more comfortable than the ice. But, despite his memory of how chilly the ice had been against their nude skin, Alek was still seized by an urge to throw Mariah down upon it and make love to her then and there.

So it was with both annoyance and relief that he heard the music come to an end at last, and Jules's voice ordering the two of them to take a break. Jules and Lanie were, it seemed, ready to discuss future routines, music and costumes.

"Good skate, Mariah," Alek commented as they left the ice.

"Thank you. It's…very kind of you to say so, Alek—especially since I felt rather wobbly at first."

"That's understandable, I think. You've…had a hard time, a tough break—and I know it can't be easy for you, working with me again, either. I'll be honest with you, Mariah. I wasn't certain how I felt about our skating together again myself. Frankly, I'm still not sure—although, obviously, since we're both here, we're at least willing to give it a try." He paused for a moment, collecting his thoughts. Then he continued. "Earlier, you said you've grown stronger. Now, I'd like to tell you I hope I've grown…more tolerant. Since it looks as though we're going to be spending a lot of time together, I just wanted you to know that. I realize I was perhaps…too demanding in the past, that maybe I pushed you too hard, too fast. I, ah, don't want to make that mistake again, Mariah. I'd like us to build a good relationship, professionally at least. We had a chance before at Olympic gold, and now, we might have that chance again. So if at any time you feel I'm asking too much of you, I hope you'll let me know."

Mariah was momentarily caught off guard by his words. She had not expected to hear them. The Alek she had known in the past would not have spoken them.

"I…don't know what to say, Alek—except that I hope you didn't say all that out of…out of some misguided sense of pity for me. Because I couldn't bear that. I don't want pity, yours or anybody else's. I've got no reason for anyone, least of all you, to feel sorry for me, do you understand? I was the one who survived, remember?''

"Yes, I do—and believe me, what I feel toward you isn't pity. I just wanted to get a few things straight between us right from the start, that's all. There's no real reason why we shouldn't work together, why we *can't* work together, just so long as we understand each other and we're not each at the other's throat all the time. I simply thought things would be easier for us both if we laid out some ground rules, right up front.''

"You're right. Of course, you're right,'' Mariah replied at last as, reaching the edge of the rink, she picked up her blade protectors and slipped them onto the blades of her ice skates. Sitting down on the bench she had used before, she withdrew a towel from her gear bag, wiping off her face and throat before slinging the towel around her neck. She tugged off her gloves, and took a drink of mineral water. "It's the sensible course of action.''

"And that surprises you?'' Alek, too, had opted for the bottled water over the coffee Lanie had offered him. Upending the container, he emptied it in three long swallows.

"A little,'' Mariah admitted. "The Alek Khazan I used to know wasn't particularly concerned about whether or not he trampled on other people's feelings. He was always more interested in taking first place.''

"I suppose I deserved that.''

"No, you didn't, actually—and I was sorry I said it the moment the words left my mouth. It was a low blow, uncalled-for under the circumstances. I guess I'm still slightly on edge and, to be honest, kind of thrown for a loop by your behavior, Alek. It's...not what I expected. We hardly parted friends.''

"No, we didn't. But we can hardly go on being enemies if we're going to work together. So, what do you say to our letting bygones be bygones and starting afresh?''

"I say that's a deal.''

"Are you two done yakking over there and ready to pay attention?'' Jules asked gruffly, interrupting their conversation. "It's like I keep telling you, we've got work to do!''

"That we do, Coach,'' Alek agreed as he sprawled in his seat, stretching out his long, muscular legs and crossing them at the ankles.

"Yes, let's get back to work," Mariah urged. "Tell us what you and Jules have in mind, Lanie."

"Okay." After putting on her reading glasses, Lanie produced a sheaf of notes she had made to herself. "You'll be doing two numbers at the benefit, and since this will be your first appearance together following your reunion, I believe people are going to want to see if the two of you still have 'that old black magic' together. Jules agrees with me. Neither of us feels a program to music that's peppy and popular is going to be particularly conducive to proving that. On the other hand, since Letters to Angels *is* a program to benefit children, we don't want something classical or operatic, either. It might win points with the judges, but it's not going to be particularly appealing to children. We have an additional problem in that we've got a lot of ground to cover, a lot of work to make up since your separation, so we really can't afford to waste time developing programs you might only skate once or twice." Lanie paused, shuffling her papers, and, with a pencil she took from behind her ear, made additional notes to herself on them. Then she continued.

"I've got two possible songs and a third song I believe we definitely ought to use. The first two are both Whitney Houston songs, slow and emotional enough that we can put together the type of dramatic routine the two of you used to skate together and that I think people will be expecting. One is 'The Greatest Love of All,' the other is 'One Moment in Time,' and personally, I'm inclined toward it. It's a very inspirational number from the '88 Summer Olympics. Might remind people of your Olympic potential." Lanie grinned. "The third tune is entitled—appropriately enough—'Mariah.' It's an old country-western song, but it can be reworked with a hint of blues, perhaps."

Again Lanie paused to jot down notes on her papers. Then she went on. "Now, as to costumes...I'm open to suggestions for the Whitney Houston number. I do, however, have definite ideas about the costumes for the 'Mariah' routine. Alek, I'd like to see you dressed totally in black. We might use some bugle beads on your shirt and down the sides of your pants, put a bandanna around your neck to give you a 'lethal gun-slinger' appearance. Since you, Mariah, will obviously be the wind they call Mariah in this number, I see you dressed totally in white...something light, airy and flowing. I'd like your hair to be loose, too, so we can really give the impression that you're a wild, western wind and that Alek is the only man brave enough to attempt to tame you.''

"Well, I like the sound of that," Alek drawled insolently, glancing speculatively from beneath lazily hooded lids at Mariah, by his side. His green eyes glinted, as though twin flames burned in their depths, as his gaze raked her slowly, lingering on her mouth, her breasts.

To her dismay, she could prevent neither the blush that crept up to stain her cheeks, nor the strange, electric tingle that coursed through her body at his appraisal. Surely he could not think that, just because she had agreed to work with him again, she would also consent to sharing his bed once more! Earlier, he had addressed only their professional relationship. He had not mentioned their personal one. And no matter what her feelings toward Alek Khazan were, Mariah had no intention of becoming involved with him again. He had broken her heart once. She was not going to give him an opportunity to do that a second time!

"I agree the tune has good dramatic possibilities, Lanie," Mariah said to cover her confusion. "But shouldn't the wind triumph in the end? I mean, after all, the wind is far stronger than any mere man." She allowed her words, with their underlying meaning, to speak for her to Alek.

"I think we need to see some of the choreography Lanie has in mind for the number before we make any concrete decisions about just how it will play and just who will prevail over whom," Jules declared tactfully. "So, why don't we do this...you and Alek get together, Mariah, and decide which one of the Whitney Houston songs you like best. Also, I'll want to hear both theme and costume ideas from you, once you've picked one of those two tunes. Meanwhile, since it seems we're all in agreement that we will do the 'Mariah' routine, why don't we meet at Lanie's dance studio tomorrow morning, and she can show us exactly what she has in mind for it."

"Excellent suggestions, Jules. Are we done for today, then?" Alek asked, slowly straightening in his seat, his hands already moving to the lacings on his ice skates.

The older man nodded. "Yes, we're done."

"Then why don't you have Lanie run you home, Jules, and I'll take Mariah with me. We can grab some breakfast somewhere, listen to those two songs together, and start working up some ideas to present to the two of you tomorrow morning. I can drop Mariah by her place later, when we're done. If that's all right with you, Mariah?" Alek turned to her inquiringly.

She knew him too well, however, to be fooled by his seeming innocence. How cleverly and smoothly he had maneuvered things so that he could get her alone with him. But did she truly have cause to be suspicious of his motives? she wondered. Perhaps, because of her past experience with him, she was reading more into the situation than was warranted. After all, following their breakup, Alek had kept his distance from her; he had not sought to pursue her again. And how on earth was she planning on working with him if she insisted on having a third party present whenever they were together? That was just plain foolish. It was not as though she were afraid of Alek…not exactly. She just did not know if she was indeed strong enough to resist him if he turned the full force of his devilish, sexy charm on her again—especially if, as it appeared from his words earlier, he had changed in ways she had always hoped and wished for.

"Sure, that'll be just fine, Alek," Mariah answered his question at last, forcing herself to speak casually, and shrugging her shoulders slightly to show she could not have cared less, one way or another, what the car-pool arrangements were. "We have to start somewhere, sometime, and I guess it might as well be here and now. We don't have that much time. If the benefit is to be broadcast on TV on Christmas Eve, I assume we'll be taping before then."

"Well, get your ice skates off, then, and let's hit the locker rooms." Alek was already putting his own ice skates into his gear bag. "Lanie, Jules, we'll see you two later. Oh, and, Lanie, don't forget to leave us those two tapes."

Lanie handed them to Alek. "Mariah, sweetie, why don't you give me a call when you get home?"

"Will do," Mariah said.

Gathering up all their paraphernalia, Lanie and Jules departed, so that all too soon, Mariah was left alone with Alek in the dim, deserted building. Just as she had been on the ice, she was acutely aware of him, even though he was not now touching her. Once she grew accustomed to being around him again, she was sure, the sensation would pass. He was just a man, like any other—except that, for her, there was no other and had been no other for more than two years. Well, she would just have to get over him, that was all. Resolutely she put her ice skates in her gear bag, then zipped it shut and slung it over her shoulder. At her abrupt action, Alek, too, stood and, without speaking, they headed for the locker rooms.

Chapter 4

This Ice Isn't New

In the past two years, when she entered the women's locker room at the rink, Mariah had only occasionally thought about the night she and Alek had made love here. But this morning that memory, like her others of Alek, was uppermost in her mind. As she stripped and showered, she recalled standing naked with him beneath the warm spray of the shower head, after they had made love, and how they had laughed together and soaped each other leisurely, becoming aroused again, and he had taken her once more, this time against the shower wall.

Mariah wanted to wash away those memories. Still, they came, flooding over her like the water that streamed from the shower head. She had a mental image of Alek in the men's locker room, standing in the men's shower, nude and separated from her only by the tiled wall between them. When she closed her eyes against the spray, she could see every plane and angle of his tall, dark bare body, sleek and powerful with hard muscle, his broad chest dusted with fine black hair, his flat, firm belly, his lean hips and buttocks, his corded thighs and calves. She wondered if he was even now picturing her as she was him, and her breath caught in her throat at the thought. What would she do if he suddenly came striding into the women's locker room, naked and dripping wet, to press her against the shower wall again?

She simply *must* stop thinking about him like this! Mariah told herself, silently but sharply. It was over between them—and even if they were ice dancing together professionally once more, she could not, *would* not, let herself get involved with him on a personal level again!

Stepping from the shower, she toweled herself dry, then dressed in fresh clothes, rolling up her practice garments and stuffing them in her gear bag. When she exited the women's locker room, she saw that Alek was already waiting for her in the corridor beyond.

"I thought we'd go to the Irish Coffeehouse," he told her. "You always liked their Top of the Morning breakfast, and one of those sounds pretty good to me right now, too, after the workout Jules gave us."

"That...that would be fine, Alek," Mariah replied reluctantly as they left the building and started toward his car in the parking lot. She would have preferred to go somewhere else, someplace that did not hold so many memories. She wished Alek was not being so courteous, that he did not recall her favorite breakfast— or anything else about her, either. It would be easier—much easier—to hold him at arm's length that way, to tamp down the emotions and longings roiling inside her, to tell herself he had never truly cared for her, that they would never have made it together as husband and wife. But if she suggested the two of them eat breakfast elsewhere, Alek would surely suspect why she did not want to go to the Irish Coffeehouse. Perhaps he was even testing her again, trying to determine her feelings toward him. "I could use a cup of hot coffee, too, right about now." She forced herself to speak casually.

"Good." Taking his key ring from the pocket of the black wool topcoat he now wore, Alek popped open the trunk of his British-racing-green Jaguar XJ6, stowing his gear bag and Mariah's own. Then he slammed shut the lid and opened the passenger door for her.

Even his car evoked memories for her, she thought as she slid into the rich buckskin-leather seat, drawing the seat belt across her body and fastening it. She had ridden in the Jaguar countless times before now, in the days when she and Alek were an "item" in the world of figure skating, and even before then, when they were involved only on a professional level. They had been friends before becoming lovers. She remembered that, too, as he opened the driver's door and slipped into the seat beside her. That had been one of the most devastating things for her when they had parted ways: She had not only had her heart broken, she had also lost her best friend.

Inserting his key into the ignition, Alek started up the car and pulled away from the parking lot, which was no longer so deserted, now that other skaters were arriving. Mariah had to quell the sudden, wild urge she had to crouch down in the seat, so that nobody would observe her and Alek together.

"It's only a matter of time until everybody knows about our professional reunion, Mariah," Alek remarked, somehow reading her mind, as he always had.

"Was I cringing that obviously?" She laughed softly, ruefully, trying to make light of the uncanny intuition it seemed he still possessed where she was concerned.

"No, not really. It's just that I haven't forgotten, either, what it was like for us. Living under the telescopic lenses of the media. Always having to be 'on' for the cameras. These days a relationship is difficult enough, without that added strain. I suppose it's no wonder so many marriages between celebrities fail."

His implication was that their own marriage, had it gone forward, would have failed, too, sooner or later. Mariah wondered if this were his way of hinting that, even if he might be interested in sleeping with her again, he would not have marriage in mind.

"Yes, I suppose so," she agreed slowly, after a moment. "But then, I believe that any two individuals these days, whether celebrities or not, have to be very much in love, very strong and committed, to make a marriage work." She knew there was a wealth of underlying meaning and rebuke in her words. But somehow, Mariah could not make herself stop speaking. "Life itself has become a competition, Alek, and the pressure is tremendous, with much more than an Olympic gold medal at stake.

It's hard to be friends, much less lovers, if all the hours of all your days are taken up with trying to be the king rat in a race that has no finish line. If at night you're so tired that all you want to do is fall into bed and sleep forever. And if when you think of your partner at all, you feel guilty for thinking of him or her so little.

"I know it sounds like a cliché, but there really *is* something to be said for taking time to smell the flowers while you have the chance. Because, otherwise, you're bound to wake up one morning and realize it's too late. And I feel certain that, when you finally *do* come to understand that, all you've achieved is outweighed by your regrets. Worse, not taking that time somehow seems like a sin, when you think of all the people who never have that time allotted to them. Kids, especially, like so many of those at the All-Children's Hospital. Kids who are dying before they've ever even had the chance to live. Kids who will never know what it means to grow old with someone they love—" Mariah broke off abruptly, tears unexpectedly stinging her eyes and a lump rising in her throat, choking her. Pretending to have suddenly spotted something of interest out the window, she quickly turned her head away so that Alek would not spy her tears. She wished she had her hair down, loose, so that she could hide behind it, so that he could not see her face, even in profile.

Not only had she revealed too much of her own feelings toward Alek, her own regrets about their failed relationship, but she absolutely hated and deeply mourned the fact that any child should die. Life was short enough as it was—and so terribly unfair. Death was for those who were too old and too tired to care about living anymore—not for children, who were young and vibrant and eager to live.

"Each of us does what he or she can, Mariah," Alek said quietly. To spare her embarrassment, he spoke as though the thought of the kids at the All-Children's Hospital alone were the cause of her tears, although, deep down inside, he knew that it was not, that he had hurt her deeply. How he regretted that— now, when it was perhaps too late for them. "With our ice dancing, we'll not only be entertaining those children, but also raising money to benefit them. The Letters to Angels program will make some of those children's dreams come true, at least.''

Mariah nodded. ''It's such a wonderful program…and so thought-provoking sometimes, to learn what the children have wished for in their letters to their 'angels.''' She was glad her voice quavered only a little as she strove to speak normally, to recover her composure. ''A lot of them want only to go to Disney World before they die. But some of them ask for a horse and a pasture to ride it in, or a fishing hole in a little woods, or a vacant lot with a baseball diamond on it. When I hear all those kids' dreams, I can't help but wonder what those boys and girls might have become if they hadn't been stricken with a terminal disease…whether they would have grown up to become scientists or politicians, artists or builders. And I wonder what the world has lost because those children will never reach adulthood.'' Mariah paused for a minute, dwelling on the terrible tragedy of that loss. Then she continued. ''I'd like for our Whitney Houston number to be something really special for those kids, Alek. Do you have those two cassettes Lanie gave you?''

''Yes, I do.'' Reaching into his coat's inside pocket, he withdrew the two tapes. ''Why don't we go ahead and give them a listen?'' he suggested. ''We've got some time before we get to the Irish Coffeehouse, seeing as how we seem to have caught the tail end of the morning rush-hour traffic.'' He grimaced wryly as he nosed the Jaguar forward, down one of the town's busy main streets.

Mariah put the first tape in, and within moments, the strains Whitney Houston's beautiful voice filled the car as she sang about the greatest love of all. Alek and Mariah did not talk while the tune played, each of them instead listening intently to the slowly building music, envisioning the way in which they might ice-dance to it. When it had ended, Mariah removed the tape and popped the second one into the cassette player. The minute she heard this song—''One Moment in Time''—she knew her choreographer's instincts were right on target, that this was the one she and Alek should dance to. Not only was it a powerful melody, but the lyrics just seemed inordinately appropriate, since they were all about wanting just one moment in time, when dreams were only a heartbeat away and you were the best you could be. After all, that was really what the Letters to Angels program was all about, Mariah thought, giving those kids just that one moment in time when their dreams came true and they were on top of the world.

"That's it. That's the one," she declared firmly.

"I think so, too," Alek agreed as he pulled the Jaguar into an empty space in the parking lot of the Irish Coffeehouse. "So let's eat—and talk about costumes, why don't we?"

Open twenty-four hours a day, the Irish Coffeehouse, decorated with lots of hanging plants, brass pots and Irish paraphernalia, was a popular restaurant. But since the workday had finally begun, the place was largely empty now. Mariah and Alek waited briefly until a table by the large windows that flanked three sides of the building was cleaned. Then the hostess led them to the cheerful dark green vinyl booth, handing them each a plastic-encased menu. Mariah barely glanced at hers before she laid it aside. Moments later, Alek tossed his menu on top of hers.

"So...what thoughts do you have about costumes?" he inquired as he shrugged off his topcoat and folded it up beside him on the seat.

"I'm not sure, really." Mariah slipped off her ski jacket and laid it aside. "Two ideas came to mind while we were listening to the song. The first is that we wear something really bright and jazzy, in a fabric with swirls of color that make it look like a rainbow. I think that would be appealing to the children, at any rate."

"Yes, very appealing, I should imagine." Alek nodded. "But do you really think rainbows suit the tempo and mood of the song? They always make me think of cotton-candy clouds and wizened leprechauns, of four-leaf clovers and pots of gold."

"True. But then, pursuing dreams can also be thought of as chasing rainbows," she reminded him. Like the dream she had years ago that one day she and Alek would be married. Dreaming that *was* like chasing a rainbow—only there was no pot of gold at the end of it for her. No, maybe bright rainbow colors wasn't the way to go, after all. "I have another idea."

"Which is?"

"We're both in midnight-blue costumes, with small gold suns, moons and stars. You know, going after your dreams can also be called reaching for the stars. That way, the costumes would be much more dramatic—and as I recall, one of the playrooms at the All-Children's Hospital has a dark blue ceiling with tiny stars scattered all over it, so it looks like a midnight sky."

"You know, I think you're right about that. I like that idea. Midnight blue it is, then."

Before they could talk further, one of the waitresses appeared at their booth. She was plainly frazzled from her busy morning, tendrils of dusky-brown hair escaping from beneath the cap of her uniform and her apron slightly askew around her waist. Still, she was young and bubbly enough to make light of her day so far, blowing her fringe of too-long bangs up out of her eyes and then wrinkling the pert nose on her Pollyanna face as she smiled at Mariah and Alek. Mariah could not refrain from smiling back when she noted that, ironically, the name tag on the waitress's blouse actually read Polly.

"What a day! I swear, my poor feet are swollen up like a couple of fat old toads this morning!" the girl announced artlessly. "What'll you have, folks?"

"Two Top of the Morning breakfasts, and lots of hot black coffee," Alek told her.

"Coming right up." True to her word, Polly reappeared moments later with their coffee.

Mariah also noticed how, from beneath her lashes, the waitress eyed Alek admiringly. As she poured the coffee, she stole glances at Alek and smiled openly at him. Women were seldom immune to Alek's good looks and charm, and Polly's flirting really didn't bother Mariah. She knew that, since her breakup with him, there had been no one to speak of in his life. Like her, he had had the occasional casual date, but there was nobody about whom he was serious. Mostly he had thrown himself into his work, as she had her own. Only now, this morning, was Mariah willing to admit for the first time that, as much as she loved ice dancing, her total dedication to it for the past two years had been as much to try to forget Alek as it had been to hone her craft. And, to some extent, her devotion had worked. There had been long blocks of time during her days when she had not thought about Alek Khazan at all.

It had been during her nights that he haunted her. Although, during her practice sessions, she had driven herself to the point of exhaustion to ensure that she would fall asleep the moment her head hit her pillow, the attempt had proved futile. No matter how tired, she had lain awake at night instead, tossing and turning, thinking of him, missing him, and wondering just where and when their relationship had gone so wrong. Mariah had found no easy answers; she had known that, in some respects, she had been as much to blame as Alek for their breakup.

She sipped her black coffee gratefully. It was steaming-hot, and took the chill from her bones. Because she spent so much time on the ice, she did not seem to be as susceptible to the cold as most people. She had, she thought, somehow become acclimated to it. Still, winter had come early this year and threatened to be bitter. The wind outside, although not strong, was sharp and crisp. From the gray clouds in the sky, a drizzle had begun that promised sleet or snow in the hours to come.

"Well, now that we've got the costumes settled, what about ideas for the program itself?" Mariah asked, turning from the bleak, wintry view afforded by the wide windows to resume the conversation that had been interrupted by the waitress's arrival. "Lanie and Jules both seemed very keen on something dramatic."

"Yes, well, those always *were* the most effective routines for us, Mariah, the ones we skated best together," Alek pointed out. "And since this is a comeback for us, I think you'd also agree we want our first program to make the unmistakable statement that not only are we back together professionally, but we're better than ever. After all, it never hurts to shake the competition up a little, does it?" He grinned at her—the beautiful, familiar grin that had always made her heart turn over in her breast.

To Mariah's dismay, this morning was no exception. Her heart began to thud so loudly that she thought Alek must surely hear it. To hide her sudden consternation and confusion, she took another long swallow of her coffee before replying.

"Naturally, it always helps to have a psychological edge over the competition—especially those who have a tendency to crumble under pressure."

They both knew that, over the years, the sport had seen its fair share of skaters who gave way under the enormous strain of competition, skaters known for their erratic performances, skaters who excelled at the Olympics, only to fall apart at the World Championships, and vice versa. It took a special breed of athlete to compete successfully in any sport, to endure the rigors of training, of performing, and the harsh glare of the media's spotlights. Not every athlete, no matter how he or she excelled at his or her chosen sport, was cut out for all the things that accompanied it. Like any good team, Alek and Mariah knew that, and they had capitalized on it in the past, as they would again in the future. It was one of the things that helped to set the best apart from all the rest, and the competition Alek and Mariah faced as ice dancers was stiff.

"So it would appear we have a consensus," Alek noted, nudging Mariah from her reverie. "We'll want to make the two routines totally different, while retaining their drama. Since 'Mariah' is going to be about a man attempting to tame a wild wind and will have an underlying western flavor, I vote we go with a much more classical routine for 'One Moment in Time,' something spiritual and uplifting, to suit the music's lyrics."

"Yes, that's what I think, too." Mariah was surprised to discover how easily she and Alek were reaching agreements this morning. In the past, it had been common for the two of them to argue about just about everything, from costumes to the interpretation of their music. Maybe Alek had indeed changed; equally as startling was the thought that maybe *she* had changed, too.

A few minutes later, Polly appeared with their breakfasts.

"I feel so stupid," she announced as she set their plates in front of them. "I thought the two of you looked familiar. But it took me a while to figure it out. You're Alek Khazan and Mariah Nichols, the ice dancers, aren't you?" At their nods of confirmation, she rushed on. "Wow! Is my mom ever going to be impressed when she finds out I waited on you two this morning!

She's been a big fan of skating for years, long before the Tonya Harding–Nancy Kerrigan fiasco.'' The waitress pulled her order pad from the pocket of her apron and tore off a sheet. "Would it be a terrible imposition to get your autographs for her? Her name's Helen...Helen Edwards.''

"We'd be happy to sign an autograph for her," Mariah said, taking the pen Polly handed her. After addressing a little note to Polly's mother, Mariah signed her name with a flourish before passing the pen and paper to Alek. "It's always nice to hear the public enjoys figure skating as much as we do. It didn't used to be such a popular and well-known sport. In fact, it never ceases to amaze me that, despite all the great skaters in the past—skaters like Peggy Fleming and Dorothy Hamill, for example—it was the Tonya Harding–Nancy Kerrigan feud that really focused a spotlight on the world of figure skating. Unfortunately, that did more to bolster our ratings than all the brilliant spins and fabulous jumps in history.''

"Well, you certainly do see a lot more of figure skating on TV these days," Polly declared. "My mom's glued to her set every other week, it seems. Why, I honestly believe she'd run off with that Philippe Candeloro!''

"So would a lot of other women." Mariah smiled. Philippe was quite handsome, and extremely popular with the female fans of the sport. "Instead of bouquets and stuffed animals, I always half expect to see undergarments and hotel keys tossed out onto the ice following one of Philippe's performances.''

Polly grinned. "Wow! That must be something, knowing all those other skaters! Are you friends with any of them? I mean...how *can* you be, when they're your competition and all?''

"Well, we don't compete against *all* of them." Alek spoke up as he handed Polly her pen and paper back. "Only the other ice dancers. And some of those we used to compete against have turned professional in recent years, although it's possible these days to have your amateur status reinstated, even so. But really, despite the fact that they're competitors, many skaters are good friends. It's such a consuming sport that you don't have a whole lot of time for a social life beyond it, so you tend to be drawn to other skaters who know what it's like on the circuit.''

"Yeah, that makes sense, I guess." Polly nodded her understanding. "Well, I guess I've taken up enough of your time. Thank you so much for the autographs! Mom'll just be thrilled! You two enjoy your breakfast now, and give me a holler if you need anything else.''

When Polly had gone, Alek picked up a slice of toast and, after opening a small plastic container of grape jelly, began to spread it with a knife on the buttery toast. "I never before realized you found Philippe Candeloro so attractive." His tone was casual, but Mariah was not deceived.

She knew him so well that her pulse leaped with sudden excitement. Why, he was jealous! Of course, with both Alek and Philippe being so good-looking, there had always been something of a rivalry between them. But, surely, for Alek to express interest in her thoughts about Philippe could only mean he still had feelings for her. For a moment, although she knew Philippe only to speak to at competitions, she was tempted to insinuate that the two of them were more than just friends. But she couldn't.

"I hardly know him, actually. I was just stating my observations about him. Why?''

"Oh, no real reason." Alek shrugged nonchalantly as he concentrated on his breakfast. "Just curious, I guess.''

But, of course, he would not have been curious if he had no interest in her, Mariah told herself again. Still, she would be foolish to get her hopes up, based on an offhand question. Foolish to become involved with him again at all, she reminded herself stringently.

So what if, despite everything, she still found Alek Khazan one of the handsomest, sexiest, most masculine men alive, and all her old feelings for him had rushed up to engulf her this morning? There was no future in loving him. She had already learned that the hard way. She did not want or need a second lesson.

Chapter 5

Do You Remember When?

In the days and then weeks that passed, Mariah was to remind herself more than once of her conviction that morning at the Irish Coffeehouse. Because, despite all her determination, it was not easy for her to avoid being drawn to Alek again. No matter how hard she fought her feelings for him, it seemed that, at every turn, her resolve weakened. He watched her every move with a fierce, hungry intensity that both frightened and excited her. In the past, such glances had led eventually to his impassioned love-making, which had left her breathless, exhausted and exhilarated. Especially difficult were practice sessions at the dance studio, at which Lanie was not always present to defuse tensions. At those times, Mariah was acutely aware of Alek's strong hands moving on her body, of his and her reflections in the mirrors that lined the dance studio's walls. The two of them were tall, black-haired, elegant, and striking together. They danced together as though they were performing some elaborate mating ritual—chassés, mohawks, lifts and spins all a prelude to something much more sensuous and serious, something that made Mariah's heart beat fast and Alek's voice grow hoarse as he called out the moves.

"Lay back," he uttered huskily now, his hands beneath her body, holding her as she bent deeply backward.

Once in position, performing what Lanie referred to as "snake arms," Mariah brought her hands up, only to bring them rippling slowly, sinuously, downward. The movement was made even more exquisite by the fact that, while she did it, she brought the thumbs and middle fingers of her hands together lightly, a small trick Lanie had taught her for giving the hands a more graceful appearance.

"Very good, Mariah," Alek uttered softly.

He was bent over her, his powerful legs spread, his hands holding her waist firmly. In this particular pose, his dark, handsome face was almost pressed against her breasts, which swelled above the V neckline of her black leotard. Mariah could feel his breath, warm and harsh against her skin, which was glistening with sweat from their practice session, and gradually she became conscious of the fact that her nipples had hardened, of their own accord, at the erotic sensation. They strained so rigidly against the fabric of her leotard that Alek could not help but be aware of them.

In the next moment, she knew it was so, as her midnight-blue eyes met his brilliant green ones, the intensity of his gaze taking away her breath. She had seen that look on his hard, lean visage in the past, a look that said he wanted her, had to have her—now. Both she and he froze in place. Silence seemed to stretch interminably between them, fraught with tension and expectation. Mariah could hear her heart beating so loudly in her ears that the sound deafened her. A small gasp escaped from her lips as, without warning, Alek's eyes darkened with desire. Then he abruptly buried his face between her breasts, his hands sliding roughly, urgently, up her body, tightening on her rib cage, his thumbs circling and caressing her nipples lightly.

"Mariah," he groaned, low against her skin. "Mariah."

She was vividly conscious of his swift, sudden arousal—and of her own response, the abrupt rush of heat that flooded her entire being. Her common sense told her to pull away from him before it was too late. But her heart cried out otherwise, and of their own volition, her arms wound around Alek's neck as his mouth descended to claim hers. In that instant, it was as though more than two years had not passed since he had last kissed her—while, at the same time, those years of separation imbued the kiss with a fierceness, passion and longing that spoke more eloquently than words could have of his desire for her. His lips moved on hers, devouring her hungrily, as he clasped her to him, pulling her upright and spinning her around to press her against the mirrored wall. His tongue outlined her mouth, then boldly insinuated itself inside, tasting, savoring, setting Mariah's heart to pounding even harder and faster than before. The chemistry between them was as hot and explosive as it had ever been, as though, during their time apart, it had not died, but instead had smoldered like embers, waiting for this moment, when it would again be fanned to flame.

Fingers tense and splayed, her hands framed Alek's face, combed back the strands of his hair that had come loose from his ponytail and that now, glossy and damp with sweat, tangled around his dark visage. Mariah could feel his hands roaming over her body ardently as he kissed her. The rough stubble of his beard grazed her skin, arousing her wildly. She opened her lips to his, sighing into his mouth as he swallowed her breath. Her tongue darted forth to tease and twine with his. All the old familiar feelings she had tried so hard to keep at bay now broke down the walls she had erected around her heart. In some dark corner of her mind, Mariah knew she had never stopped loving Alek Khazan. He had only to take her in his arms again and she melted like ice beneath a spring sun, her bones dissolving, leaving her weak and pliant against him, wanting him.

She was only dimly aware of his hands at her shoulders, sensuously sliding the sleeves of her leotard down to bare her braless breasts. His palms cupped them possessively. "Champagne breasts," he had always called them, insisting they would fill a champagne glass to perfection. Circles of delight radiated from their centers as he touched and stroked them eagerly, tearing his lips from hers to envelop one firm, flushed nipple. His mouth was hot, greedy, as he suckled her, his tongue licking and laving the stiff peak, before moving to its twin. Mariah's fingers burrowed convulsively through his hair, drawing him even nearer to her.

"Mariah...oh, Mariah..." Alek murmured against her breasts, his breath brushing her nipples enticingly. "How I've missed you...ached for you..."

Fervidly his lips seared their way up her slender throat, back to her mouth, his tongue plunging deep. Mariah moaned low against his lips as he kissed her, his hands continuing to caress her breasts, to stimulate their rosy crests. No one had ever stirred her as Alek did, made her feel as though her entire body were being consumed by flames, growing molten, becoming a mass of liquid fire and sensation. She burned at the very core of her being, ached for him to lay her down upon the hardwood floor and make love to her. Still, realistically, she knew that if he did, she would once more be swept away by him, would lose herself to him—only to have her heart broken again. And so, now, at last, reason prevailed, and she wrenched her mouth from his.

"Stop, Alek. Please...stop..." she whispered breathlessly, pressing one trembling hand to her lips and the other against his chest, holding him at bay.

"Mariah...why? You want this as much as I do. I can feel that in every fiber of your being, in the way you respond to me. And it's not as though this is something new for us. We were lovers before."

"Yes, but we're not now, and I—I don't know where this will lead, what it is you want from me. I don't want to sleep with you just because there are still...feelings of attraction between us, Alek. I *won't* do that. I'm just not the one-night-stand type. I never have been."

"Don't you think I know that?" He stared down at her sharply for a minute. Then, muttering an imprecation, he turned away from her, running one hand raggedly through his hair. A muscle flexed in his set jaw, visible evidence of the emotions that roiled within him. "I promised myself I wouldn't start anything like this. I don't know what I was thinking just now—except that I wanted you. There's been no one since you, Mariah. I've missed you. Sometimes I think I was the world's biggest fool ever to let you get away from me."

"What...what is it you're saying, Alek?" she asked, drawing her leotard up to cover her nakedness, not daring to hope he wished to renew their engagement, not knowing how she would answer if he did—because how could she risk her heart again?

"That I want you back in my life, Mariah." Alek paused for a moment, considering, gathering his thoughts. Then he continued. "Look, maybe I was only fooling myself, but I believed we could work together professionally without becoming involved together personally once more. But these passing weeks have made it clear to me that's not what I want—and I don't think you want that, either. We belong together, Mariah. I feel that so strongly inside, and I believe you feel it, too. We made a mistake before. But it's not too late for us."

"Yet you were willing enough before to call off our marriage, Alek," she replied defensively, playing for time. "At least, you didn't protest when I returned the engagement ring you bought for me. Now it seems you would have us pick up exactly where we left off—as though more than two years haven't come and gone. I just don't know if I can do that, Alek. In all honesty, I don't know if I'm strong enough to go through all that pain again, if things don't work out between us. And why should this time be any different from before?"

"Because we've both changed?" he suggested. "Because we're both older, wiser, more experienced, better equipped to handle the stress and strain of our careers combined with our personal lives?"

"That's not exactly what you said that first day of our reunion, on our way to the Irish Coffeehouse. You said then that marriages between celebrities are apt to fail—and you implied that would have been the fate of our own marriage, had we gone through with it."

"Yes, well, maybe I've decided I was wrong about that."

"Maybe so," Mariah agreed slowly. "But you see, Alek, I can't be certain whether it was your heart or your hormones that led you to this new conclusion, and neither can you. And I'm afraid that, when it comes to my own heart, I'm not nearly as strong as I claimed that first day, but...terribly vulnerable."

"I know I hurt you before. But you must believe me when I

say I would never hurt you again, Mariah,'' Alek insisted softly. "I'm not a fool who can't—or won't—learn from his mistakes. I know you've been through a lot these past few years. And despite how I've tried to fight my feelings for you, I also know— and *you* must know—that I still love you.''

"Do you, Alek?" she asked quietly, her heart at once soaring with joy and clenching with pain at his words. It seemed she had waited forever to hear him speak those words once more. Yet, now that he had, she was not sure she could set aside the past, commit herself to him again: "Do you really?"

"Yes, I do. I never stopped loving you. Our breakup was as painful for me as it was for you, Mariah. Why do you think there's been no one else in my life since then?" He fell silent once more, allowing her to absorb his words. Then he spoke. "If I give you back the engagement ring you returned to me, will you wear it again?"

"You mean you still have it?" She was surprised and touched by the admission. She would have guessed he had thrown the ring away in a fit of temper and hurt. The fact that he had kept it, instead, spoke volumes.

"Oh, Mariah." Alek's voice was low and contained an underlying note of anguish. "Of course I still have it. How could you think otherwise? What can I do to prove myself to you?"

"Be my friend, as you used to be. That was one of the things that hurt the most about our breakup, you know. I not only lost my lover, but also my best friend. There were so many times when I wanted to call you, to cry on your shoulder. But I couldn't—because *you* were the man I wanted to talk about, to be consoled about." She gave a small, wry, tremulous laugh at the irony of it, blinking back tears at the memory. "So, please don't press me for a decision right now. Give me some time to think about all this, Alek."

"I understand, and it's all right, Mariah. Really, it is. If that's the way you want it, then that's the way it will be. I'm willing to give our personal relationship the time you're asking for, however long it may take, and to go slowly, to get it right this time." After a moment, he gave her a crooked smile. "So, back to the old grindstone, then. Where were we?"

"Ah...at the layback," Mariah reminded him, even though she knew from the sudden deviltry that danced in his eyes, the manner in which his grin widened on his face, that he remembered as well as she. "But perhaps we should just forget that part and go on from there."

"Too bad. It would have been nice to practice that move all afternoon. But...so much for that idea. Do you want to run the tape back, or shall I?"

"I'll do it." Glad of an excuse to move away from him for a minute, Mariah walked over to the boom box that sat on the floor and punched the rewind button.

If she was honest with herself, she'd admit that, ever since consenting to their reunion, she'd harbored the hope that she and Alek would get back together not only professionally, but also personally. Still, she had never expected him to make the first move in that direction, to declare himself so openly, to confess he still loved her. *He still loved her!* Her heart thrilled at that knowledge. It was only her doubts and fear that caused her to tread cautiously, to hang back, when she yearned to fling herself into his arms.

The music started again, its powerful, soaring strains filling the dance studio. Despite herself, the beautiful notes were like wings beneath Mariah's heart as she laid her hand in Alek's own and they began to move together as one, turning, twining, oblivious of all but each other as they danced.

Chapter 6

On This Wintry Night

Mariah had a fear of flying, but in her profession, airplane travel was a prerequisite of the job. So over the years she had managed to grow accustomed to it, even if she had never truly conquered her fright. Upon disembarking from a flight, she never failed to feel as though she had barely escaped from the jaws of death, and now was no exception. Alek knew this, and he patted Mariah's hand reassuringly before they unfastened their seat belts, now that the airplane that had flown them from their hometown to the city that was home to the All-Children's Hospital had landed. Both of them stood, Alek ducking to avoid hitting the cargo space. Flipping open the hatch, he dragged forth their coats and carry-ons, slinging the straps of the garment and duffel bags over his shoulders.

"Here. I can take my stuff." Mariah pulled on the bright down ski jacket he had handed her.

"No, that's okay. I've got it." Alek motioned her forward, his hand at her elbow to steady her as, trying not to bump into other people in the crowded airplane, Mariah started down the narrow aisle, he, Lanie and Jules following close behind.

Presently, they were through the chilly jetway and into the

warmer terminal. At the baggage claim, they collected the rest of their luggage, then proceeded to a rental agency to pick up the car Jules had hired. Armed with a city map, Jules drove them to the hotel, Lanie up front, beside him. Alek and Mariah rode in the back, she settling gratefully into the curve of the strong arm he wrapped around her. Besides her fear about flying, she found airplane travel dehydrating and exhausting. Physically, she felt as though she had been on a grueling three-month tour, and she yearned for a long, hot bath and bed. She would be glad when they reached the hotel.

Winter's early dusk had already fallen. The streetlamps shone with a soft glow along the highways that led from the airport into the heart of the city, illuminating the powdery snow that fell from the dark sky, making it glitter like diamond dust. Downtown, the bright lights of holiday decorations were ablaze in a multitude of colors. Angels, snowmen, Santa Clauses, sleighs and reindeer, Christmas trees and candy canes gleamed like a kaleidoscope. The bare branches of the trees in front of the buildings sparkled with tiny white lights, so the entire city appeared like some wondrous fairyland.

As Jules at last pulled the car to a stop before the hotel and they all stepped out into the cold night air, Mariah smelled the crisp wintry scent of smoke from burning fireplaces. When the hotel doors were opened by the doorman and bellboy, the fragrance of evergreens and holly wafted from the lobby. In its opulent center stood a towering pine tree, beautifully decorated and surrounded by a huge pile of gaily wrapped boxes.

To Mariah's relief, Jules and Lanie always handled the business details, so there was nothing for her to do but trail along after the bellboy hauling their luggage toward the bank of elevators. Soon she was installed in her suite, where a hospitality basket filled with local goodies sat upon a table.

"Do you need anything else, Mariah? Do you want some ice or something?" Alek inquired as he turned from speaking to the bellboy, who had finished pointing out the suite's amenities.

"Yes, please. I'm very thirsty from the flight."

"We'd like a couple of buckets of ice, too." Alek handed the bellboy a generous tip. Then he turned back to Mariah. "I know you're probably too tired to go out for dinner, so why don't I order room service for us?''

"That would be wonderful, Alek," Mariah replied, touched by his thoughtfulness.

"Great. I'll leave you to get unpacked, then, and call you when supper is served. I'll have them set it up in my suite. Meanwhile, if there's anything else I can do, just knock." He indicated the twin doors that joined his suite to hers.

"I will—and, Alek, thanks. I appreciate…well, everything, actually. Your caring, your patience, your understanding, your willingness just to be there for me, to give me the time I've needed. Despite the pressures of putting together the two new routines, these past several weeks have been some of the very best of my life. Almost like old times—but without all the bitter arguments that spoiled it all before. To be honest, I didn't think you could change, Alek. But you have.''

"Yes, I have," he agreed, his face sober. "I lost something, some*one,* very important to me before. And I don't want to lose you again, Mariah. Whatever it takes, I mean to hang on to you forever this time around. See you at supper—and be sure to lock this door behind me,'' he reminded her as he left the suite.

He was very conscious of her safety, not just because she was a woman, but also because, these days, any kind of celebrity was a potential target of stalkers and other crazies. From past experience, Mariah knew Alek would stand in the hallway until he heard her turning the dead bolt and fastening the extra security latch in place, so she did both. Then she began to unpack her clothes, hanging some in the closet, putting others away in the dresser. All the while, her mind dwelled on Alek. What she had told him was true: The past several weeks with him *had* been heavenly, despite all the long, hard hours the two of them had worked.

Even when they were not training, there had been reams of videotape for them to watch, cassettes not only of their competitors' previous performances, but also of pairs' and individual skaters' programs. They'd studied Scott Hamilton's footwork and the innovative routines of the top ice dancers.

Still, to her surprise, Alek not only had insisted they take at

least some evenings off here and there, but Jules and Lanie had
also agreed. It was almost as though the older couple were con-
spiring with Alek, Mariah had thought. Because on those nights,
Alek had proceeded to court her. The word seemed old-fashioned
in this day and age, but she could think of no other term that
suited. He had taken her to supper, to the movies, dancing, even
to an arcade once or twice. And during these romantic evenings
out together, he had made it clear to her that he both loved and
desired her. Even so, he had not pressed her for more than a few
kisses and caresses, which had left her aching, unsatisfied, and
wondering why she continued to hold him at arm's length, when
she wanted nothing more than to surrender to him.

She loved him. Only her fear of having her heart broken again
caused her to hang back. But surely Alek had done everything
in his power to convince her he had changed, that he wanted her
back—this time forever—that he would not hurt her a second
time, driving her to break off their engagement again.

When her ice arrived, Mariah poured a cold glass of fruit juice
from the small refrigerator in her suite. Sipping her drink, she
drew herself a bath.

Sooner or later, she was going to have to come to grips with
her tumultuous emotions toward Alek, she thought as she
stepped into the fragranced water. She could not keep putting
him off. She had to make a decision. She must either trust him—
or not. She sighed, feeling torn. It would all have been so simple—if only this were the first time around for them.

She had just stepped out from the bathtub and was pulling on
a fluffy, terry-cloth robe emblazoned with the hotel's crest when
she heard Alek knocking on the adjoining door.

"Just a minute," she called, tying the robe tightly as she left
the bathroom. There was a moment's delay while she fumbled
at the latch on the door. Then she pulled it back to find Alek
lounging against the doorjamb. "I'm sorry I took so long. I just
finished my bath."

"So I see." Alek's intense green eyes roamed over her slowly,
taking in the loose, damp tendrils of hair that had escaped from
her French comb and now curled about her nape, his glance
continuing to her bare legs and feet. Beneath his smoldering

gaze, Mariah flushed as she became abruptly conscious of her nakedness beneath the robe. Despite her having tugged it around her body as closely as she could, the robe had still loosened, gaping open to reveal the valley between her breasts. Reaching out in the sudden, taut silence, Alek slid his fingers beneath the garment's wide lapel, drawing the back of his hand lingeringly down her soft, nude skin. "Supper is served," he noted huskily, nodding toward the table that had been rolled into his suite, which was covered with dishes. "However, I'd be amenable to skipping it and going straight to dessert."

As he stroked her bare skin, Alek moved in very close, invading her personal space. Now, she was backed up against her open door, with no place left to retreat. She was acutely aware of his size, his strength. He seemed to tower over her, magnetic, dangerously masculine, potent and predatory. Instinctively she felt a woman's age-old desire to submit to a superior male. Her heart hammered with both fright and anticipation. Her breath came quickly, shallowly. Reason urged her to protest against him, but somehow, the words stuck in her throat, and before she could force them past her lips, Alek's mouth captured hers. Mariah moaned low in her throat at the contact, at the feel of his lips moving upon her own, his tongue parting them, shooting deep, stabbing her with its heat.

His hands had spread open her robe, slipped beneath the thick terry cloth to cup her breasts. His palms glided erotically over her sensitive nipples, teasing them to taut, hard peaks. Waves of pleasurable sensation rippled from their centers, coursed through her entire body. She trembled against him, wanting him to stop, wanting him to continue. In some dark corner of her mind, she wondered if she had subconsciously wished to incite him by appearing before him dressed only in her robe, obviously naked beneath it. Perhaps she had. But in her heart, she knew she was still not certain she was emotionally ready for this, no matter how her body responded to him, burned for him.

"Alek, no," she murmured as his mouth scalded her throat, her breasts, his beard stubble grazing her skin. His lips closed over her nipple. He sucked it into his mouth, laved it with his tongue, sending a rapturous thrill through her. His fingers were at the knot of the belt that bound her robe, untying it. "No, Alek," she whispered again. "I'm—I'm not ready."

Her robe fell completely open, exposing the length of her nude body to his hungry eyes. His hand slipped between her quivering thighs, caressed her warm, wet mound.

"You're ready," he muttered thickly, pressing against her so that she could feel the hard evidence of his desire for her, feel his harsh, labored breath upon her skin.

"Yes...no... I mean, I'm—I'm still not sure. I—I need more time. Please, Alek."

"Go." He jerked back from her, his hands in the air. "Go get dressed before I forget I'm a gentleman and do something we might both regret."

Her heart pounding fiercely, Mariah fled. She snatched her clothes, then ran into the bathroom to dress. They'd come too close this time. She was playing with fire to think she could kiss Alek without wanting to make love to him. Once she was in his arms, self-control took a back seat to passion. And she knew it was the same for him, too.

When she finally worked up enough nerve she entered Alek's suite. He was seated at the supper table, waiting for her. To the casual eye, he would have appeared relaxed and composed. But Mariah was not deceived. He was as tightly coiled as the proverbial spring. The muscle still worked in his jaw. His brilliant green eyes glittered like a panther's. She felt guilty and ashamed. Her subconscious longing for him had driven her into subtly provoking him, and then she had drawn back, afraid, still uncertain. She would not blame him if he were angry with her.

Instead, with a low, rueful, mocking laugh, he observed, "Good thing we spend so much time on the ice. Otherwise, I'd be taking a lot of long, cold showers."

"If it's any consolation, I *am* sorry, Alek," Mariah replied softly as she sat down across from him at the table. "I just...got cold feet. Maybe if we can just get through the benefit, my emotions won't be in such a turmoil afterward...."

"Hey, no problem. I promised not to rush you, and perhaps I was out of line. It was just that...seeing you standing there, in that robe, brought back so many memories that I guess I got a little carried away.'' Taking up the wine bottle, he poured them each a glass. ''So, what do you say we eat before our dinner gets totally stone cold? Then I thought we'd go over the itinerary together, make sure we have enough practice time. There's also the tour of the All-Children's Hospital. That's tomorrow morning, as I recall.''

''Yes.'' Mariah's voice was solemn, because her emotions toward the forthcoming tour were mixed. It wrenched her heart to visit the hospital, even though she knew how much the children enjoyed meeting all the figure skaters. ''We don't want to forget our new publicity photos. The kids love getting autographed pictures.''

''I'll make a note to myself. How's your wine?''

''Good.'' She sipped the fine Chablis appreciatively.

''And the food?''

''A little cold—but then, that's not the hotel's fault.''

''No.'' Alek's eyes met hers meaningfully, causing Mariah to blush and lower her gaze.

Butterflies churned in her stomach, making her feel more nervous than she ever had before any performance. She could barely choke down her supper—and she drank far too much wine, wondering all the while if Alek hoped to get her drunk and seduce her. That image, too, held great, if unsettling, appeal. But after they had finished their supper and he had walked her to the doors that adjoined their suites, he only kissed her lightly on the forehead and bade her good-night. Mariah closed her door and latched it, but she heard no corresponding sounds from the opposite side, so she knew Alek had left his own door standing invitingly open. After undressing and pulling on her negligee, she slipped into bed, vividly conscious of the fact that only a thin wall—and her own insecurities—lay between her and him.

Chapter 7

And Sometimes, Dreams

The All-Children's Hospital was a huge, sprawling redbrick complex several stories high and comprised of a number of different buildings and wings. It had begun life in the late 1800s as an orphanage. Since, in those days, many of the children who wound up in its wards had been from poor backgrounds, suffering from malnutrition and the effects of laboring in sweatshops, it had gradually evolved into a small hospital. Eventually, over the years, it grew into the vast structure it was today. The original edifice still stood, now serving as the lobby and general information and admissions areas. It was through this building that Mr. Fielding, the director of the Letters to Angels program, led Mariah and Alek and the other skaters when they stepped down from the bus that had brought them here.

Having skated in a previous Letters to Angels program to benefit the hospital, Mariah had been on this tour before. So she knew what to expect, and it was therefore with a mixture of gladness, hopefulness and sadness that she passed through the wide glass doors of the All-Children's Hospital and into the entrance lobby. Inside, a large gilt-framed painting of the hospital's founder hung on one wall, beneath which was prominently displayed a gold plaque engraved with the hospital's motto: Caring For Children Today, Because They Are The Hope Of Tomorrow. Unfortunately, as Mariah knew, despite the research that continued to be done, the advances that continued to be made, for many of the children at the hospital, there was no hope. There would be no tomorrow for them. The thought brought tears to her eyes, tears she knew were but the first of many she would experience before the tour ended.

"Mariah, are you sure you want to do this?" Alek took her hand. "If you don't feel up to it, I—"

"No." She shook her head. "I'll be all right. It's just that the children… When you see them, you just wish you could do more to help. You feel so guilty at giving nothing more than a few hours of your time to skate a couple of numbers you were probably going to use in competition anyway."

"I know exactly what you mean, Mariah. But the money we'll raise by our skating will do some real good. Who knows, maybe it'll make one child's dream come true."

"I know you're right. But in my heart, I still feel I could do more, that I *should* do more!"

It was a feeling that only increased as Mr. Fielding led the group of skaters through the various wings, his voice pleasant but passionate.

Through it all, what tore at Mariah more than anything was how brave and cheerful the children were. Those who could, greeted their visitors with a bold brightness or a shy gaiety that made her long to find a private place where she could cry her eyes out. She felt deeply ashamed of how she had lain in her hospitable bed morosely, turning away visitors and pitying herself after the accident. Instead of feeling sorry for themselves, these indomitable youngsters talked and laughed and cracked jokes with the skaters, who signed endless autographs on publicity pictures and in scrapbooks, on plaster casts and even on hospital gowns.

In yet another unit, Mariah approached the bed of a beautiful little girl who, before the group's appearance in the hallway beyond her ward, had been bent over a coloring book lying on the hospital table before her, her soft blond hair falling carelessly over one eye, an expression of intense concentration on her piquant face. The child looked to be about seven years old, and although Mariah could not have explained why, she felt strangely, irresistibly drawn to the little girl.

"Hello, there," Mariah said quietly as she entered the ward and neared the child's bed. "I'm Mariah Nichols. I'm with the group that's touring the hospital today."

"I know," the little girl replied, politely, only her big brown eyes speaking of her excitement. "You're an ice dancer, and you skate with Alek Khazan. He's been your partner twice now."

Mariah was genuinely surprised by the child's statements, because unlike the more popular sports, such as football and basketball, figure skating did not really have any stars the caliber of a Joe Montana or a Michael Jordan, the type of sports heroes with whom most children tended to identify and whose pictures were regularly featured on trading cards. And while the youngsters at the hospital were aware that the skaters were celebrities in their own right and begged them for pictures and autographs, Mariah knew most of the kids would not have known Oksana Bayul from Nancy Kerrigan. Further, ice dancers tended to be the least well-known of figure skaters; it was usually the individual skaters who received the lion's share of publicity and the spotlight.

"Now, how do you know all that?" Mariah asked lightly, genuinely puzzled.

"I know because you and Mr. Khazan are two of my heroes," the little girl confided, a trifle breathlessly. "When I grow up, I want to be an ice dancer just like you!"

"You do? Well, I'm extremely flattered, Miss...?" Mariah's voice trailed off as she realized she did not know the child's name. "You know, you haven't told me your name, so even though you know mine, we haven't really been properly introduced yet."

"I'm Bethany. Bethany Thacker."

"Well, as I was saying, Miss Thacker, I'm quite flattered to be numbered among your heroes. Would you like to have an autographed picture of me and Mr. Khazan?"

Bethany nodded shyly, her eyes shining with pleasure. Even

so, for the first time, Mariah noticed the shadows of grief in their depths, the same shadows she had seen in her own eyes for months after Worth and Richard were killed. It was a different darkness from that in the eyes of the other youngsters—the ones who were burn victims and terminal cases. Bethany was not going to die or be scarred for life; this was the wing for crippled children. At that realization, Mariah glanced down involuntarily at the little girl's legs, but they were concealed beneath the sheets and blanket on the bed. Was it possible that this child who longed so fervently to become an ice dancer couldn't walk... would never walk? Mariah's heart went out to the little girl. Mariah knew what it was like to lie in a hospital bed, longing to ice dance—and wondering if she would ever even be able to walk again.

"You know what? I seem to have run out of pictures," she lied as she opened her leather portfolio a crack. "Wait right here. I'll be back in a jiffy, I promise—and I'll bring Mr. Khazan with me. Okay?"

"Okay," Bethany agreed, trying her best to conceal her disappointment and fear that Mariah might not really return.

But it was not in search of Alek that Mariah went—at least not initially. Instead, she made her way to the nurses' station down the hall.

She greeted the three nurses on duty as they glanced up at her inquiringly. "I'm Mariah Nichols. I'm with the figure skaters who are doing the Letters to Angels benefit, and I was wondering if you could tell me about one of your patients in this unit. Her name's Bethany Thacker. She's in a ward just down the hall."

"Oh, yes," the head nurse responded. "Such a sweet little girl. She's here for an operation."

"Can you tell me what for? I mean...I realize I'm not a relative or anything, and so it's probably against hospital regulations or something to give me any information about her condition. But, well, the thing is, she actually recognized me. I mean, she knew who I was, even before I told her. She's seen me and my partner, Alek Khazan, skate, and she told me she wants to be an ice dancer just like us when she grows up. I was...I was just wondering what her chances of that really are.

Because if she's truly serious, there are classes for children at most ice rinks, and I could help her get started. But I...I don't want to say the wrong thing, to give her any false hope...."

"That was very considerate of you, Ms. Nichols." The head nurse's voice was kind but sober. "Because the odds for the success of Bethany's operation aren't too good, I'm afraid. In all probability, she'll be in a wheelchair for the rest of her life."

"Oh, no," Mariah murmured. "Is it at all possible there's— there's been some terrible mistake? I mean...I know the staff here is excellent, but doctors are human, after all. Even the best of them sometimes make mistakes." Mariah remembered herself again, lying in a hospital bed—her legs paralyzed from the sheer trauma of the automobile accident and Worth's and Richard's deaths, and her fear that her career, her life's ambition, had ended in one fell swoop.

Although they had not found any evidence to support their theory, the physicians who examined her initially had believed there must be some as-yet-undiscovered injury to her spine...which had resulted in the paralysis of her legs. The horrifying misdiagnosis—however understandable under the circumstances—had compounded her shock and terror, so her hysterical paralysis had continued until a specialist was called in for consultation and finally recognized that her mind was playing tricks on her body, that there was, in reality, nothing truly wrong with her legs at all, other than some traumatized muscles and ligaments.

"We'd all like to think every youngster here has been misdiagnosed, Ms. Nichols," the head nurse declared, with both sympathy and understanding. "Unfortunately, for Bethany that's not the case. Her injuries are the result of an automobile accident in which she also lost both her parents. Their car was struck by a drunk driver. She hadn't any other relatives, so she's an orphan now, too, poor little kid. And since adoptive parents who want an older child rather than an infant—particularly a crippled child—are very few and far between, I'm afraid it's quite likely Bethany will wind up growing up in a series of foster homes."

"Oh, no," Mariah uttered softly again, instantly grasping the parallels between her own case and Bethany's—and the terrible differences, as well. "How sad, how horrible for her. She's such a lovely child and seems so bright, so intelligent...."

"She is, Ms. Nichols—and she really *does* love ice skating, especially the ice dancers, like you and Mr. Khazan," the head nurse said. "She's been so excited ever since she learned all of you were coming here to visit. It's the first time she's really shown any interest in anything since her parents were killed. That's part of the reason the doctors have held off on the surgery. They'd like to see her emotionally stable first, before doing the surgery. But just meeting you has done wonders for her, I'm sure."

A thoughtful expression knitted Mariah's brow as she walked back toward Bethany's room. She ran into Alek in the hall and explained to him about Bethany, then led him to the little girl. Bethany's face lit up at the sight of them.

"Hello, Bethany." Alek withdrew a publicity picture and set it next to the coloring book on the table before her. "I understand you're a big fan."

"Oh, yes...yes, I am!" Bethany cried softly, her enthusiasm obvious. Then she turned to Mariah. "I was afraid you weren't really going to come back, but you did—and you really *did* bring Mr. Khazan with you!"

"Of course, I did. How could you doubt I would?" Mariah forced herself to adopt a teasing, lighthearted tone. "I'll have you know I always keep my promises, young lady."

"Always?" Bethany queried.

"Always."

Mariah and Alek both signed their photograph for Bethany, chatting with her for several more minutes, during which time Mariah again observed how very good Alek was with children. He would make a wonderful father, she realized, feeling her heart fill suddenly with tenderness and yearning at the thought. Why had she ever held him at arm's length? she wondered. Why had she let her doubts and fear overshadow her love for him? He *had* changed. Could she not find the courage within herself to believe that?

Mr. Fielding appeared in the doorway, interrupting her reverie. "Skaters, could I have your attention, please. I hate to break up

your visits, but it really *is* time we were moving on,'' Mr. Fielding announced, causing the youngsters to groan and boo him
loudly. ''I'm sorry, children. But we need to complete our tour.''

''Yes, of course, Mr. Fielding. We'll be right with you,'' Alek
called to him. Then he turned back to Bethany. ''Well, Bethany,
it looks as though duty calls, so I'm afraid Mariah and I have
to go now. But I'll tell you what— We'll come back to visit you
again, if you'd like.''

''Do you mean it? Really and truly?''

''Cross my heart.'' Alek made the age-old childhood gesture
that accompanied a sworn promise.

''Me too.'' Mariah did the same.

As she waved goodbye to Bethany, she couldn't help but wonder what would become of the little girl. Would her future really
be as bleak as the nurse had painted it?

During the days that followed, that question haunted and tormented Mariah endlessly. True to their word, she and Alek vis-
ited Bethany faithfully. In fact, they were encouraged by Bethany's doctors, who insisted their visits were doing wonders for
the child's spirits. While Mariah herself could see that this was
indeed the case, she still could not help but worry whether she
and Alek were doing more harm than good. In just a short time,
they had grown inordinately attached to Bethany and she to
them. And, although they did their best not to give her any false
hope that she would eventually walk and ice-dance, the thought
occupied Bethany's mind constantly. When she wrote her ''letter
to an angel,'' in which she described what she wanted most in
all the world, she wished simply for a pair of ice skates.

''Oh, Alek,'' Mariah murmured as they left the hospital. ''I
just can't bear the thought that Bethany's operation might fail,
that she might never walk again, much less be able to learn to
skate.''

''I know.''

As he escorted her through the garage to their rental car, Alek
slipped his arm comfortingly around her slender waist, as he had
in the days when they were lovers and engaged. Strangely, it felt
so natural and right for him to do this that it did not even occur
to Mariah to pull away from him, that she was once more low-

ering her defenses against him, letting him get too close to her. In fact, she unconsciously laid her head against his shoulder, grateful for the warmth of his body and how he shielded her against the winter wind. His arm tightened around her, and there was a peculiar expression on his dark visage when he glanced down at her.

He *did* love her, Alek thought, not for the first time since their reunion. He had never stopped loving her. And he knew suddenly that if someone was to hand him a pen and paper and tell him to write a "letter to an angel" so that his dream of a lifetime might come true, he would wish for Mariah, as his lover...as his bride. She was everything he had ever wanted in a woman, in a wife. Seeing her with Bethany these past several days had only emphasized that fact. He did not know how he could ever have permitted Mariah to get away from him, to walk out of his life. And now that she was back in it on a full-time professional and a more limited personal basis, he knew with certainty that that was not enough for him, that he wanted her in the most personal, intimate ways...forever.

He wanted to awaken every morning for the rest of his life and see her lying in bed beside him. He wanted to share her dreams, her successes, her fears, her failures. He wanted to sit with her before the fire on a winter's eve, sipping wine and talking, to have the right to touch her, hold her and make love to her whenever he wished. Still, Mariah held him at bay, unsure of herself, of him. Nevertheless, Alek refused to give up hope that he could win her back in time.

"Somehow, I have faith that everything will turn out well for Bethany." Much as he longed to, Alek did not add, "And for us."

"What makes you say that?" Mariah wanted his reassurance, and yet was afraid to believe him, for fear her hopes would be dashed in the end.

"It's the holiday season." Alek told her. "It's a time of miracles—if only you believe."

Chapter 8

Dance Forever with Me

The rehearsals had ended. Tonight was the big show and the arena was packed from floor to ceiling with spectators, whose ticket money would go to the Letters to Angels program to benefit the All-Children's Hospital. The media were present, too, along with the camera crew that would be recording the show for the national broadcast scheduled for Christmas Eve.

Backstage, Mariah was keyed up more than was usual for her before a performance. This would be her first time before a live audience since Worth and Richard had been killed. Even though this was not a competition and there were no judges present to hand out scores, she paced restlessly, her fists jammed into the pockets of her warm-up jacket.

"Relax, Mariah. It's wearing me out just to watch you," Alek declared from the stairstepper machine he was working out on, off to one side of the backstage corridor that led from the dressing rooms to the rink.

"I told her! I told her that myself, not more than two minutes ago!" Jules gestured volatilely with his hands to emphasize his words. "But did she listen to me? No, she did not!"

"Hush, Jules! None of us wants to hear one of your tirades

right now." Lanie grimaced at him sternly. "The way you're behaving, a body'd think this was the Olympics or the World Championships."

"Oh, for heaven's sake! It's the debut of the reunion of Nichols and Khazan, woman! The entire figure-skating world—not to mention the media—is watching!" Jules insisted fiercely, practically shouting. "I just—" At the sight of Lanie's raised eyebrows, he broke off abruptly. Then, lowering his voice, he continued. "I just want everything to go well, that's all," he ended gruffly.

"It will," Lanie assured him. "Now, come away, Jules." She tugged firmly on his arm. "Unless I miss my guess, you're making Mariah even more nervous than she already is!" Over his protests, she led him away, casting a sympathetic smile over her shoulder at Mariah.

"Thanks, Lanie." Mariah mouthed the words behind Jules's back.

Alek vacated the stairstepper machine and grabbed his towel. He wiped off his face, then slid his arm around Mariah's waist.

"Time to get suited up and warmed up on the ice."

"Finally!" she said with relief. "It's the waiting, you know, that unsettles me."

"It always was."

Presently, all the skaters were flying over the ice, the individual and pairs skaters practicing their jumps, the ice dancers reviewing lifts and spins. Mariah and Alek had numbers in both the first and second halves of the show. They had chosen to perform their "Mariah" program first, so Alek was dressed in his black gunslinger costume, his flowing-sleeved satin shirt open at the collar, revealing a sexy portion of his broad chest dusted with fine black hair. His long black hair was loose, damp and tangling about his face emphasizing his dark attraction. Every time he neared the boards emblazoned with the names of the commercial sponsors for the Letters to Angels show, which walled the rink, the women in the audience went crazy, shouting and screaming, calling out his name and waving bouquets in his direction. Now and then, he paused to sign autographs. And once, when Philippe Candeloro, handsomely decked out in his

Godfather costume, skated past, performing a triple toe-loop in the process, Alek glided into a jump of his own—a triple axel.

"You been practicing that move long?" Mariah asked, unable to repress her smile as she remembered that morning at the Irish Coffeehouse, and Alek's jealousy when he had thought she might be attracted to Philippe. It was obvious to her that Alek had been showing off for her benefit, a display of male rivalry that both flattered and amused her.

"Long enough to get it right," he replied smugly. "Just because I'm an ice dancer doesn't mean I can't do the jumps. I just happen to like to dance."

"You'll get no argument from me. Oh, look! There's Bethany!" Spotting the little girl, Mariah smiled and waved. "Come on, Alek. Let's go see her!" Her hand in his, Alek's arm around her waist, they skated across the rink to where the excited child was seated with a group of other youngsters from the hospital. "Bethany, I hoped you were going to be here tonight," Mariah said. "I'm so glad you were able to come."

"So am I," the little girl announced shyly, her face beaming. "Dr. Parkinson said it was all right, though. He even carried me inside here to my seat. I hoped I'd see you. I brought you both something." She held out a bouquet, along with a stuffed teddy bear that was dressed up to resemble a martial artist. "The flowers are for you, Mariah, and the bear is for Alek."

"Why, thank you, Bethany." Mariah was genuinely touched. "You know what, this white rose goes beautifully with the costume I'm wearing, and that amber mum will match the blue-and-gold outfit I'll be dressed in for our second number. So I'll put those flowers in my hair, I promise."

"And this little guy will make a perfect good-luck charm for my spot in the dressing rooms," Alek asserted, making the bear appear as though it were ice dancing, much to Bethany's delight. "The show's going to start, so Mariah and I have to go now. But we'll be back to see you again later."

"All right. Break a leg!" the child called after them enthusiastically as they skated away.

Their "Mariah" number was midway through the first half of the show. Still, all too soon, it seemed to Mariah, she heard the

announcer introducing them to the applauding crowd. Then she
and Alek were actually on the ice, beneath the bright spotlights
that always made skaters' programs more difficult than usual,
since it was, among other things, harder to gauge distances in
the semidarkness. Her heart pounding, adrenaline rushing furiously through her body, she assumed her pose in Alek's arms,
waiting tensely for the music to start.

The initial eerie, solitary notes of their bluesy version of "Mariah" drifted over the ice, followed by the fuller opening strains.
At those, Mariah and Alek began to dance. Earlier, she had at-
tempted to steel herself against her nerves, even while she had
prepared herself to be a little shaky at first. But right from the
start, as she began to move, Mariah suddenly knew that this was
going to be one of those rare and fabulous nights when she was
wonderfully, incredibly "on." Equally elating was the fact that
she could sense the same in Alek.

Heated   chemistry—sexual   and   exciting—seemed   without
warning to explode between them, an almost tangible thing the
audience also felt. The arena, except for the music and the scrape
of Mariah's and Alek's sharp blades on the ice, had been silent,
as though the crowd were holding its collecting breath, waiting
to see if Nichols and Khazan still were magic together. Now, the
spectators went mad, hollering, whistling and clapping as Alek
set out determinedly to conquer the wind that was Mariah. And
she herself danced and spun as though she had wings instead of
blades upon her feet, teasing and taunting him tantalizingly, alternately as shy as a gentle breeze and then as bold as an unbridled storm.

Her cloud of long blue-black hair and the diaphanous folds of
her ethereal white costume floated and flew about her face and
body as the saxophone wailed like the wind she had become,
and the lead guitar moaned and keened in intricate counterpoint.
Alek's own black hair was a sheeny, unkempt mane. His green
eyes held a predatory glitter in the spotlights as he moved with
her, the subtle swagger of his hips and the provocative thrust of
his pelvis sinuous, sensual, like some lethal animal on the prowl,
in search of a mate. He tossed his proud, dark head arrogantly,
challengingly. His powerful arm snaked out as though he were

cracking a whip. Then he abruptly caught hold of her wrist and yanked her to him, his hands forcefully propelling her upward in a beautiful, complex lift that had taken them hours and hours of training to perfect.

Mariah twined and twisted, wrapping herself lithely around his hard, lean body as he lowered her back to the ice. His strong hands were now at her waist, supporting her as he spun her while she lay back, arms imploring, beckoning, then holding him at bay. The throbbing beat of the drums had grown progressively louder, wilder, and more savage. Now, in keeping with the music, she and Alek executed a serious of complicated steps and moves, followed by another stunningly involved lift. They ended their performance precisely on the music's final note, with a triumphant Alek standing with his corded legs spread, his right fist skyward, his left hand snarled in Mariah's hair as she, now tamed, half lay at his feet, her face upturned to him breathlessly.

The arena rang deafeningly with applause, the audience on its collective feet in a thunderous standing ovation that seemed to continue interminably. His sensual mouth curved in a smile of satisfaction and appreciation at the crowd's response, Alek drew Mariah to her feet so that they could take their bows. Then they skated around the rink together, collecting as many of the bouquets and stuffed animals as they could. They made a special point of halting to speak to Bethany, whose eyes were huge with wonder and shining with excitement.

"Mariah, you *did* wear my rose!" the little girl cried, gazing raptly at the white flower Mariah had earlier stripped of thorns, threading the stem through a black French comb she had fastened in her hair, over one ear.

"I promised I would, didn't I?"

After that, Mariah did not think the night could get any better. But whereas the "Mariah" number had been wild, fierce and passionate, the routine to Whitney Houston's "One Moment in Time" was beautifully, unbelievably dramatic and spiritually uplifting. It was as though, before when they had danced, Mariah and Alek had been raw, earthy, primeval creatures, and now, transcended, they were become eternally exalted, heavenly beings. This time, when the music ended, Alek held Mariah herself skyward. Her head was thrown back joyfully; her arms were spread wide like the wings of an angel, her fingers tense and splayed, as though she were reaching out to grasp the very stars in the firmament.

For a full minute after the program was finished, the stadium was silent with awe. Then, suddenly, people everywhere began leaping to their feet, cheering and applauding furiously, causing the entire arena to reverberate. After he had slowly lowered her back down to the ice, Alek tilted Mariah's face up to his and kissed her tenderly and deeply, full on the lips, before he released her so that the two of them could take their bows.

Later, when she watched the videotape of the show, Mariah would hear the commentators declaring to one another that she and Alek had fallen in love again that night, right there on the ice, in front of thousands of wildly shouting and clapping spectators. And she would know it was not so, that she had given her heart away to him long ago and somehow had never gotten it back. But she would also know it was in that one moment of time that she had admitted to herself, finally and forever, that she did not, after all, want her heart back, that she intended to leave it safe in Alek's keeping for always.

"I love you," she whispered to him just before they turned to face the audience.

"And I love you, Mariah," Alek answered quietly, seriously, his eyes kissing hers. "I always have, and I always will."

Afterward, not only at the cast party that followed the performance, but also for years to come, people who had witnessed the Letters to Angels show insisted something special had happened on the ice that night. But it was young Bethany who summed it up best of all. When asked by one of the commentators what she had thought of the program, she said simply, "It was magic."

Chapter 9

Urgently in Silence

"Would you—would you...like to come in for a nightcap, Alek?" Mariah inquired, her heart thudding, as she glanced up at him in the hallway just beyond her hotel suite, to which they had now returned following the Letters to Angels show and cast party.

"Is it just a nightcap you're inviting me in for, Mariah—or something more?" Alek's voice was low, seductive. His green eyes gleamed speculatively, expectantly, as they locked on her blue ones mesmerizingly. Slowly he reached out, smoothing her hair back from her face before he cupped her chin, drawing the pad of his thumb lingeringly across her moist lower lip. "I mean, I'd just kind of like to know the ground rules before I agree to come inside. You see, as much as I'd like to, I don't want to...start anything again that you aren't willing to finish. I'm afraid my self-control where you're concerned has grown volatilely, perilously thin, especially after tonight."

There was no misunderstanding him. He wanted her. She had seen this side of him before, knew how tightly wound he was— especially after a performance—how it was only with the greatest of difficulty that he restrained himself, continued to play the part of a gentleman. He stood very close to her, so close that she could actually feel the heat that emanated from his tall, lean, powerful body. Without warning, a wild, atavistic tremor shot through her, setting her aquiver, aflame. A blush crept up to color her cheeks, and she found she could no longer go on meeting his eyes. She swallowed hard.

"Come inside, Alek." Was that really her own voice, so soft, so husky with emotion and desire? "I'm not going to ask you to leave, not this time, not tonight."

His sudden, sharply indrawn breath made Mariah shake so badly that she could not insert the electronic key into the door's lock. She did not have to look at him to know his eyes had darkened, now smoldered with passion. Wordlessly he wrapped his hand around hers, guided the plastic card into the slot, then quickly withdrew it, turning the knob as the green light flashed to admit them.

Inside, he flicked on the light switch beside the door. A single lamp flared to life, dimly illuminating the darkness, which was fragrant with the lush perfume of the flowers he had had delivered to her suite earlier, to wish her good luck in the show. The gorgeous bouquet sat in a heavy crystal vase on the table; beneath, a tiny shower of fallen petals strewed the carpet, like stars across the night sky. In the silence, Mariah felt Alek's strong hands at her shoulders, tugging off her fur-trimmed wool cape before he pressed his mouth to the curve of her bare nape, causing her breath to catch in her throat as an uncontrollable shudder of longing and need ran through her. Then, turning away, opening the closet, he draped the cape carefully around a hanger before he shrugged off his long topcoat and hung it up, too.

"What would you like to drink, Mariah?" he asked.

"A—a brandy, please."

As Alek prepared her drink, Mariah was unable to watch him. She was too nervous. After all, it had been more than two years since she and Alek had made love together. Rubbing her arms as though she were cold, she moved to the bank of windows on the far side of the suite. The curtains were drawn back, revealing the snowy city that seemed to spread out infinitely below, aglow with streetlamps haloed with mist in the darkness, amber beacons amid the bright colored lights of the holiday decorations. The scene was beautiful, magical, like something in a movie.

From behind her, she could hear the sounds of Alek pouring the brandy into glasses. Even without turning to gaze at him, she could see him, she realized. His image was reflected by the inky windows she faced. Somehow, he had always reminded her of a panther, with his brilliant green eyes, his mane of glossy black hair and his long, supple, muscular body. His every movement was cool and elegant, yet tinged with some intangible thing that invariably made her think of animal magnetism and menace. Perhaps it was his training in the martial arts, specifically Kung Fu, which drew much of its style from the animal kingdom, from tigers and other wild creatures. It gave him a dangerous edge, made him exciting.

But Alek had never scared her, nor would he. It was her own agitation and anticipation that had her so keyed up, Mariah knew. Despite how much she loved him, he *had* broken her heart once before. It was so difficult for her to trust him a second time, even though he had done everything possible to reassure her that he had changed, that their relationship would be different this time around. Still, she had made her decision at last, and now she would stick by it. After tonight, she just could no longer believe he would hurt her again.

Behind her, Alek switched on the radio. Briefly the suite was filled with the strains of Christmas music. Then he adjusted the dial, and a slow, sensuous blues song began to play. Somehow, strangely, it suited the wintry night. If the suite had contained a fireplace, a crackling hearth would have made the setting perfect. But the powdery snow that swirled outside, beyond the windows, reflecting the amber glow of the streetlamps, was perhaps not a bad substitute.

"Here's your brandy." Alek handed her one of the glasses. Then he lifted his own in a toast. "To us, Mariah," he murmured.

"To us," she echoed, raising her own glass.

Together they drank, in a silence broken only by the strains of low music. The amber liquor was warm and mellow. It seemed to melt upon Mariah's tongue, as she felt herself melting inside, to burn down her throat, as she burned at the core of her being. She trembled with expectancy and rising passion as, after a long moment, Alek gently but deliberately took her glass away, setting it and his own aside.

"You are so beautiful." He reached out, pulling the French combs from her upswept hair, so that the glorious blue-black mass tumbled down in shimmering waves about her. His fingers ensnared the strands at her temples, turning her face up to his own. For a fleeting eternity, he gazed down at her, in his intense eyes the certain knowledge that, soon, very soon now, she would be lying naked beneath him, that he would be a part of her, as he had been before. Mariah's breath caught in her throat at the sight. Her eyes fell beneath Alek's as his thumbs traced tiny, erotic circles on her cheeks. "You know I'm going to make love to you, don't you?" His voice held a hoarse, thick note that made her shiver as she nodded. "Tell me you're sure, Mariah," he demanded softly. "Tell me it's what you want."

"I'm sure, Alek. It *is* what I want," she whispered.

Between them, then, there was an interminable moment, as highly charged as the atmosphere before a wild, winter storm. Alek inhaled sharply, his eyes glittering with triumph, before his mouth descended to seize possession of Mariah's own. He kissed her once, twice, lightly and tenderly, before he gave way to his blind hunger for her, his lips growing urgent, insistent, against hers. His tongue parted her lips, drove hotly between them as she yielded pliantly to his fierce onslaught, her hands creeping up to twine about his neck, her fingers burrowing through his own loose hair.

He seemed to kiss her forever, his mouth devouring her, before at last, with a low groan, he swept her up in his powerful arms. Striding to the bed, he laid her down, bending over her, his lips and hands moving on her feverishly. He slipped off her shoes, dropping them heedlessly to the floor. He kissed her ankle, the back of her knee, the inside of her thigh, as his palms slid lingeringly, electrifyingly, up one black-stockinged leg.

"Did you wear this for me?" he asked as he tugged with satisfaction and pleasure at one strap of her lacy garter belt.

"Yes," she breathed.

"You'd better have," he growled, his eyes dancing devilishly as he glanced up at her, "because I warn you, Mariah—I am a very jealous man where you are concerned."

He took her mouth again, his tongue plunging deep, wreathing her own until she gasped for breath against him. She was only dimly aware of the fact that he had somehow unzipped the back of the black cocktail dress she had worn to the cast party, and that its bodice now tangled around her waist, baring her braless breasts to him. His lips left hers, scorched their way across her cheek to her temple, her ear. He nibbled her earlobe, his harsh breath warm and enticing against her skin, sending a wild thrill coursing through her.

In response, her rosy nipples puckered, hardened, straining eagerly against Alek's palms as he cupped her breasts. Her fingers shook as she pulled and fumbled impatiently at his shirt, wanting, *needing,* to feel his naked flesh against her own. He raised up to help her, sitting back on his haunches, his thighs imprisoning hers. His eyes were riveted on her face as he swiftly unbuttoned his shirt and cast it aside to reveal his dark, broad chest, heavily layered with muscle, and his strong, corded arms. Sweat sheened the fine black hair that matted his chest and trailed invitingly down his firm, flat belly to disappear into his trousers.

He looked like some pagan warrior as he knelt over her, drawing her dress down languidly over her hips, so that the silken material rubbed sensuously along her stockings, before he tossed it to the floor as carelessly as he had her shoes minutes ago. He unhooked her garter belt, which went the way of its predecessors. Then he slowly peeled away her stockings and lacy French-cut panties, so that she lay naked beneath him. And all the while he undressed her, he kissed and caressed her, honing her desire for him to a keen edge. Then, at last, his hand moved to his leather belt, unbuckling it, and presently, his bare skin, slick with sweat, covered her own.

"Oh, Mariah," Alek muttered in her ear, his teeth nipping her earlobe once more, his mouth and tongue wreaking havoc upon her senses. "You don't know how good it feels to hold you again like this. I've missed you. God, how I've missed you!"

He found her lips once more; kissed her deeply, ardently, before his mouth scalded her throat. His tongue flicked out to tease the sensitive place on her nape, causing a jolt of excitement to shoot through her body. Mariah gasped aloud, her breath catching raggedly in her throat. Her hands on his back spurred him on as his lips fastened upon her nipple. His tongue rasped across the stiff, flushed peak, teasing, taunting, making her moan and writhe helplessly against him. She could feel his powerful muscles rippling and bunching in his back as he clasped her to him, his hard sex nudging her belly, speaking wordlessly of his desire for her. At the heart of her womanhood, a hollow, burning ache seized her savagely, so that she longed instinctively, desperately, for assuagement.

"Alek, please. I need you inside me."

"No." He denied her maddeningly, his voice a long, low sigh. "Not yet." Still, his knees pushed her pale white thighs wide. His palm cupped her dark, moist, downy mound, exploring the soft, burgeoning folds that trembled and opened to him like an unfurling bud bursting into bloom. Slowly, torturously, he slid two fingers into her deeply, momentarily easing her frantic yearning as she arched her hips imploringly against his hand. He murmured her name huskily as he stroked her, spreading musky heat, flicking the tiny, throbbing nub at the heart of her, bringing her to the brink of climax again and yet again, only to stop. He was driving her wild.

Mariah whimpered with passion and need, her head thrashing as she bucked against him.

"Please, Alek," she begged again. "Please."

Unable to restrain himself any longer, he took her then, his body moving exigently to claim her own, his hands ensnaring her hair roughly as she arched her hips to meet the swift, forceful thrust that pierced her to the very core. Gripping his wrists tightly, she cried out softly, a low moan of surrender, of gratitude, of rapture. It had been so long since he had possessed her. Too long.

"Does it feel good, love?" Alek held himself poised above her, deliberately prolonging the moment of his entry, gazing down at her intently in the semidarkness, his eyes like twin flames.

"Yes...yes..."

"There's been no one else but me, has there?"

"No."

Triumph and satisfaction flared in his eyes at that. Then, groaning her name, his mouth abruptly seizing hers again, he began at last to move inside her, plunging hard and deep, faster and faster, as he lost what little control he had somehow managed to retain. Mariah's blood roared in her ears as she strained against him, wrapped her long, graceful legs around him and lifted her hips to meet each strong thrust. Her climax was so powerful that it took her breath away, leaving her gasping and shaking in his embrace as the tremors exploded within her, seeming to go on forever. Alek rapidly followed her. His hands tightened on her body fiercely, as though he would never let her go. He threw his head back, his breathing harsh and labored, as his primal release came. Shuddering long and hard against her, he spilled himself inside her.

After a while, he slowly withdrew, pulling her into his arms, kissing her deeply and cradling her head against his shoulder. Beneath her palm, his heart thudded as furiously as her own. The rasp of their breathing filled the air. In the quiet afterglow, his hand stroked her damp, hair, her silky skin, glistening with sweat from their lovemaking.

"I have something for you," Alek said finally in the stillness, which was broken only by the low strains of bluesy music that still drifted from the radio.

"I thought you just gave it to me," Mariah teased gently, smiling up at him lovingly, her heart in her eyes.

"Besides that, I mean." He smiled back at her sexily, his eyes appraising her lazily, appreciatively, from beneath drowsy lids. "*That* I plan to give you again and yet again before this night is through. No, this is something else." Bending to reach the floor, he picked up the trousers he had discarded earlier, searching one pocket, from which he withdrew a small velvet box. Then, after tossing aside his pants, he snapped open the lid to remove the diamond engagement ring nestled inside. Grasping

Mariah's left hand in his, he slid the ring onto her finger. "Don't ever take that off again. Because if you do, I'm warning you right now that, this time, I will protest so long and violently that the media will be showing film at eleven of my holding you hostage until you agree to marry me."

At the sight of the engagement ring she had worn once before, Mariah's heart filled to overflowing with love for him.

"I promise you I'll never take it off again, Alek," she replied quietly, soberly, tears of deep emotion stinging her eyes. "Never. I *do* love you, you know—with all my heart."

"And I you. Now, there is one thing more."

"What's that?"

"There's a beautiful little girl at the All-Children's Hospital who's become very precious to us both, and who could very much use a couple of loving parents. I know that, before, we hadn't planned on having a family anytime soon. But I was wondering if perhaps you'd changed your mind about that, if you'd like for us to adopt Bethany?"

"Are you—are you serious, Alek?" Mariah was both touched and stunned. "Do you mean it? Regardless of the outcome of her surgery?" The child's operation was scheduled for the day after tomorrow, and the results would be known by Christmas Day.

"Yes and yes and yes. So, what do you say? Shall we have her come live with us?"

"Oh, Alek. Yes...yes! Oh, I can't wait to see Bethany's face when we tell her! Do you think she'll be happy at this news, that she'll *want* us to adopt her?"

"I believe so, or I would never have suggested it. I'll check into all the details first thing tomorrow morning, I promise you. But now, the night is young..."

"The night is late—"

"The night is young," Alek reiterated firmly, aroused again, intoxicated by her very nearness. He pressed her down upon the bed, his body moving determinedly to cover hers once more, his leg riding between her thighs, opening her. His hand tugged gently at her moist, fleecy curls; his fingers slid slowly, provocatively, down the delicate seam of her. "And we have more than two years of lost time to make up, so we're going to have to practice endlessly.''

"Somehow, I don't think this qualifies as an Olympic sport," Mariah insisted with false solemnity, her eyes dancing, laughter bubbling in her throat as he kissed the corner of her lips.

"Too bad. I would have awarded you a gold medal," he declared huskily, before, his eyes darkening again with renewed passion, he silenced her with his mouth, once more taking her to the heights of ecstasy and back.

Chapter 10

If Only You Believe

"Well, go on. It's yours. Open it, sweetie," Mariah urged as she smiled at Bethany tenderly. It was Christmas morning, and the little girl sat in her bed at the All-Children's Hospital, a big, gaily wrapped box on the hospital table in front of her. It was her present from Mariah and Alek, who stood to one side, both of them nearly as expectant and excited as the child herself.

"What is it?" Bethany asked, her eyes shining, her cheeks flushed.

"I don't know. Open it and find out." Alek added his own words of encouragement to Mariah's.

Slowly, holding her breath, as though scarcely daring to believe something wonderful might be inside the box, Bethany untied the huge red bow and carefully lifted the lid. At the sight of what lay within, she gasped with amazement and incredulity, tears of joy filling her eyes.

"Ice skates," she whispered worshipfully. "A pair of ice skates all my own! Oh, Mariah, does this—does this mean my operation was a success? Will I walk again?"

"Walk!" Mariah exclaimed, her own tears of happiness spilling down her cheeks as she hugged the child tightly. "Oh, Bethany, honey, you're not only going to walk! You're going to skip and run and play just like other kids. You're going to ice-dance, if that's what you want.''

"And what's more—'' Alek spoke again ''—Mariah and I are going to be married. Very soon.'' From beneath hooded eyes, he shot his bride-to-be a heated glance that made her heart leap in her breast and that informed her wordlessly just how impatient he was for their wedding day—and night. "And while we know no one can ever take the place of your parents, we'd like very much to adopt you, for you to come and live with us after you get out of the hospital.''

"You mean…forever? That I wouldn't ever be alone anymore? That I'd be—I'd be *your* little girl always, and never have to go live in a foster home?'' On Bethany's face was such a mixture of hope, longing and disbelief that it wrenched Mariah's heart.

"No, never,'' she responded quietly, fiercely. "You'd be ours for always, and we would love you very much, Bethany. I promise.''

"And you always *do* keep your promises, just like you said. Oh, Mariah, my angel really *did* answer my letter! It is a miracle!'' the child cried, her delight and agreement plain.

"Yes.'' A hard lump of emotion rising in his throat, Alek reached out to take one each of Mariah's and Bethany's hands in his, squeezing them tightly. "Sometimes they *do* happen—if only you believe.''

"*I* believe,'' Bethany announced firmly.

"And so do I,'' Mariah declared softly as Alek kissed the little girl lightly on the forehead before drawing his bride-to-be into his arms and kissing her on the mouth—deeply, passionately, with all the love he felt in his heart for her.

The Ice Man had melted.

From outside, the joyful ringing of church bells somewhere in the distance reached Mariah's ears. And just as she and Alek had earlier that morning, on the solidly frozen pond in the park beyond the All-Children's Hospital, lovers and other skaters danced and dreamed in the falling snow.

*　*　*　*　*

SEASON OF MIRACLES
Ginna Gray

Dear Reader,

For me, Christmas is the most wonderful time of the year—a time for family and friends, a time for sharing and love. A time for miracles. I come from a large, boisterous Irish/American family, and getting together on holidays is a treat that we all cherish.

When I was asked to write a Christmas story it occurred to me that not everyone is as blessed as my family. I began to wonder what it would be like to be all alone in the world with Christmas bearing down on you? What if you had loved only one man in your entire life, and he had married someone else, never knowing of your feelings? What if you had longed for children, but life had passed you by, and now you feel it is too late?

Merely thinking up this scenario made my heart ache, and I knew that I had to wave my writer's "magic wand" and conjure up a miracle. The result—this story, which is one of my all-time favorites. I hope it will be one of yours.

So make yourself a cup of hot chocolate, curl up before the fire and lose yourself in the magic of the holidays.

Christmas, after all, is the "Season of Miracles."

Happy reading,

Ginna Gray

Chapter 1

Kathryn's spirits were as gray as the overcast Texas sky.

It was the approaching holidays, of course, she told herself as she tussled with the old lock on her back door. They were wonderful for business—already the shop's daily receipts were climbing, and it was only the first of November—but for her, the holidays were a time to be endured, a sharp annual reminder of dreams unfulfilled and the emptiness of her life.

In years past she had tried to adopt a festive attitude, putting up a tree and decorating the house, cooking a feast with all the trimmings, but somehow, with just her and her father to share it, it had never seemed like much of a celebration. Now that he was gone, she knew that this year she would not even bother to make the effort, and that saddened her even more.

Impatient with her maudlin mood, Kathryn gave the key a hard twist. The lock clicked and she opened the door, shoving the self-pitying thoughts away as she stepped inside. Following her routine by rote, she turned on the radio to fill the silence and switched on the coffeemaker. As it brewed she flipped through the day's mail.

A few minutes later the rumble of an engine drew her attention. Leaning forward, she peered out the window over the kitchen sink, her eyes lighting when she saw Daniel Westwood climb from his pickup and head for her back door.

Quickly, she bent and checked her reflection in the gleaming surface of the toaster, but she barely had time to fluff her hair and inspect her lipstick before his knock sounded. The next instant the door opened and Dan poked his tawny head inside.

"Hi, Kath. You busy?"

"No, not at all." Even if she had been, it wouldn't have mattered. She was never too busy for Dan. Smiling, she fluttered a hand toward the coffeemaker. "I just got home and was about to unwind with a cup of coffee. Would you like some?"

"Sounds good."

Dan shrugged out of his sheepskin-lined coat and hung it and his Stetson on the rack beside the back door. He joined her at the counter, lounging back with his lean hips against the edge, his long legs outstretched and crossed at the ankles. When she handed him the steaming mug of coffee, he accepted it with a wink and a smile.

Blustery winds had tousled the sun-streaked hair that grew just a shade too long over his ears. The fresh crispness of the outdoors clung to his skin, mingling with his scent and the delicious aroma of freshly brewed coffee. Kathryn's senses tingled, and a soft smile curved her mouth as she looked at him. He dominated her blue-and-white kitchen with his size, his tough maleness, that vital sensuality that was so much a part of him.

"Hmm. You always did make the best coffee in Boley," he said, swigging down nearly half the scalding brew in one swallow.

She merely smiled and sipped her own, content for the moment simply to be near him.

Something was bothering him, Kathryn thought as she focused on the pulsing vein in his temple. She had known Dan all her life, and, despite his casual air, she could tell when he had something on his mind. She waited, knowing he would tell her when he was ready.

"So, how are the children?" she asked after a moment.

Dan gave a snort and shot her a wry look. "Susan creeps around the house like a little ghost, Joey sucks his thumb and whines all the time and Carla bursts into tears at the drop of a hat. I never know what I'm going to say to set her off."

"It's just the age, Dan. Fourteen is very a difficult time for a girl."

"Yeah. Especially for one without a mother."

He looked tired and dispirited, and Kathryn's tender heart went out to him. Since his wife's death three years earlier, Dan had struggled to be both mother and father to his children. Between his large veterinary practice and the demands of his family, he was run ragged most of the time.

She placed her hand on his forearm. "I know it's difficult, Dan, but you're doing a wonderful job. Really."

He took another swig of coffee and shook his head. "Lord knows I try, Kath, but those kids need more than I can give them. They deserve more. And I've made up my mind to do something about it."

Kathryn felt as though her chest were being squeezed by a giant fist. Dear Lord. Had he come to tell her he was getting married again?

Swirling the brown liquid remaining in his cup, Dan stared at it. "That's why I'm here, Kath." He looked at her then, his hazel eyes dark and serious. "I have to talk to you."

She braced herself, her free hand clenched so tightly that her nails were digging into her palm. "All right."

"I've been giving this a lot of thought, and, well...I think it would be a good idea—for both of us—if we got married."

She stared, not quite believing she had heard him right.

The cup she was holding began to rattle against the saucer, and she carefully placed it on the counter.

"You...you want to marry me?"

"I want a mother for my children, Kath," he said bluntly. "They need a woman in their life, someone gentle and understanding who'll be there for them, care for them, listen to their troubles—someone they can tell all those things that they can't tell a dad."

He could have no idea how much his proposal hurt her. She had loved Dan since she was sixteen, had dreamed of him asking her to marry him in a thousand different ways...but not like this. Never like this.

She wanted to lash out, to pummel his chest and shriek at him for trampling on her feelings, but of course she wouldn't. He didn't know of her feelings. She had taken great care to hide them from him—and from everyone else. She was simply his friend, someone who was always there, ready with a cup of coffee and a sympathetic ear when he was down and needed to talk.

"Dan, I know you love your children, but that's not a good enough reason to marry," she said in a voice that was not quite steady.

"I can't think of a better one."

Her blue eyes widened in astonishment. "What about love?"

"Aw, Kath, honey, I can't wait around for love. My kids need a mother now. And I need a wife." Startled, Kathryn blinked, and he gave a little laugh. "My reasons for wanting to marry aren't altogether selfless, I'll admit. To tell you the truth, I'm damned tired of sleeping alone in a cold bed."

Kathryn blushed hotly, her body tingling at the thought of sleeping with Dan. How would it be, lying in his arms, holding him, loving him? Oh, God, she'd dreamed of it so often!

Grinning, he touched his forefinger to her warm cheek. "What's the matter, Kath; did I shock you? I'm a man, honey, with a man's needs, and I'm tired of having to go to Amarillo every time I want to satisfy them. After nineteen years of marriage I guess I'm too domesticated to enjoy playing the part of a young stud. I prefer one woman to a string of one-night stands."

The fist around Kathryn's chest squeezed tighter. She pulled back from his touch and took three jerky steps away, wrapping her arms around her middle. She didn't want to hear this. All those years she had tried not to think of him in bed with his wife, making love to her, holding her in the sweet, warm darkness. It had been too painful to bear. Since Barbara's death she had naively assumed, or maybe she had just pretended, that he led the same solitary existence as she. The thought of him sharing intimacies with another woman, a string of other women, brought a vicious, slashing pain.

She looked at him over her shoulder. "Why pick me?" she asked, her eyes unconsciously pleading for something more, some small hope that he desired her for herself.

"When I decided that marriage was the answer, you were the first one I thought of."

Then he saw the hurt in her eyes. He put down his empty mug and came to her, placing his hands on her shoulders and looking at her contritely. "Ah, Kath, I'm sorry. I didn't mean to hurt you or upset you. It's just that I thought…hell, I still think…that it would be the perfect solution for both of us."

"Solution?" For some strange reason she had an insane desire to giggle.

"Kath, you're all alone now that your dad is gone, and I know you've always wanted a family. I can give you that." His mouth quirked up in a lopsided, half-apologetic smile. "A ready-made one, true, but it's better than nothing."

And at forty, your chances of having any other kind are slim. Dan was too kind to come out and say it, but the implication was there. That it was true didn't make it any easier to accept or the pain any less.

Not that she hadn't had offers. Only two months ago Greg Richards had asked her to marry him. She had been flattered, but she'd had to refuse. Even if he weren't too young for her, she didn't love him.

Mutely, quivering with hurt pride and fighting the ache in her throat, she stared at the second button on Dan's shirt.

He placed a finger beneath her chin and tipped it up. Tenderness softened his rough-hewn features. "Do you find the idea of being married to me distasteful?" he asked softly.

Distasteful! She had to stifle a sob of hysterical laughter. Oh, God, if he only knew! Marriage to Dan, loving him, sharing his life, mothering his children it was all she had ever wanted, more than she had ever hoped to have. But…she had wanted it to be for love, not for such cold, practical reasons.

Even so, to her disgust, she could not quite bring herself to reject the offer. That was how weak she was where Dan was concerned. She closed her eyes. "No. No, of course I don't."

"Is there someone else? Someone I don't know about? I know you date several men, but I didn't think you were serious about any of them."

"No, it's not that. There's no one special. But, Dan, I—"

"We could make it work, Kath," he insisted. "In fact, I think we could have a damned good marriage. We're old friends, so we're not likely to be in for any nasty surprises. We have mutual admiration and respect going for us. The kids like you, and I think you're fond of them."

"Of course I am, but—"

"And..." He cupped his hand around her cheek and looked into her eyes, giving her a teasing smile. "...I happen to think you're one fine-looking woman, Kathryn Talmidge. Believe me, honey, I won't find marriage to you a hardship."

Kathryn's heart thumped. As compliments went, it wasn't terrific, but it was the most intimate thing he had ever said to her. Just knowing that he found her attractive made her feel weak and warm inside. Foolishly hopeful.

"So, what do you say, Kath?" He gave her a coaxing smile and cocked his head to one side. "Will you marry me?"

"Dan, I...I can't give you an answer just yet. I have to have some time to think it through. This...this is all so new."

He frowned, obviously not pleased with her answer, but after a moment he nodded and released her, stepping away. "All right, you think it over," he said, taking his coat from the rack and shrugging into it. With his hand on the doorknob he paused and settled his Stetson on his head. From beneath its broad brim he gave her a piercing look. "Just don't take too long, Kath. I made myself a promise that my children were not going to go through another holiday season without a mother."

With that, he left. In a daze, Kathryn slipped her hands into the deep pockets of her skirt and moved across the kitchen to the door. Night had fallen while they talked, and she watched him stride to his pickup, his broad-shouldered form barely visible in the dim light that spilled from the windows.

Long after he had gone she remained where she was. Her chest was tight with a tumult of conflicting emotions; joy, anger, sadness and hope roiled within her.

Focusing on her reflection in the windowpane, she touched her cheek with her fingertips. What did Dan see when he looked at her? she wondered. She was forty years old, but that was not such a great age, and the years had been kind. Except for a few fine lines about her eyes, her skin was smooth and clear, and as yet no gray had appeared in her shoulder-length sable hair. She was slender, maybe a bit on the thin side, but that was fashionable these days. She was no ravishing beauty or cuddly sexpot, but, with all due modesty, Kathryn knew she was attractive.

With a sigh, she turned away from the window and wandered aimlessly through the house. Whether she was attractive or not, everyone thought of her as the town spinster. If she married Dan, they would think she had done it out of desperation, an old maid taking on the responsibility of another woman's children just so she would finally have a husband.

An ironic smile tilted her mouth. All this time, she had hidden her feelings so well she doubted anyone even suspected that she had been in love with Dan since her sophomore year in high school.

He had graduated that year and gone away to college, and she had lived for those times when he came home for visits. It had been during Christmas holidays, two years later, that she had asked him if he would take her to her senior prom in the spring. Grinning, Dan had ruffled her hair and said, "Sure, Kath. It's a date."

They never kept that date, Kathryn recalled sadly as she curled up in her father's favorite, leather easy chair before the fireplace. When Dan had come home during spring break, he had brought his bride with him.

She had spent her first year at college trying to forget him, dating dozens of young men and eventually entering into an affair. It had not lasted long; Kathryn had quickly realized that sex without love was not for her. And she loved Dan. Eventually, she'd had to accept that she always would.

Maybe if she hadn't come back to Boley to live, she would have gotten over him, but Kathryn never had the chance to find out. Her parents had been middle-aged when she was born, and by the time she'd finished college her father was a widower and in uncertain health. So Kathryn had come home to stay, and, mainly to have something to fill her days, she'd opened her dress shop.

Kathryn knew what people said about her. "Kathryn Talmidge? Oh, my, such a sweet, unselfish little thing. Devoted her whole life to taking care of her elderly father. That's why she never married, you know.''

It wasn't true. Kathryn had loved her father and would have taken care of him in any case, but he was not the cause of her single state. She'd had proposals. Several of them. She hadn't married because she couldn't have Dan.

But you can have him now. You might not have his love, but you can share his life and his children.

Kathryn sighed. It wasn't much, but it was so much closer to her dreams than she had ever thought to come.

She was torn between logic and longing, and in the end, longing won out. She could well be letting herself in for more heartache, but she had no choice. If she did not marry Dan, he'd find another woman to mother his children and warm his bed, and she simply could not go through that again.

Chapter 2

When Dan made up his mind to do something, he did it.

Kathryn called him that same evening with her answer, and four days later, in his parents' living room, with only a few friends and his family present, they were married.

It wasn't that he was an impulsive man, given to rash actions. He had devoted a lot of thought to his situation, but once he had decided to marry, he had seen no reason to delay. Plus, he admitted to himself, there had been that uneasy, half-formed feeling that if he gave Kathryn too much time to think it over, she might change her mind.

Dan sipped champagne and gazed across the room at his bride of fifteen minutes. She had been the first woman he'd thought of. Which was curious, considering he'd never dated her, had never even kissed her before that brief, surprising exchange at the end of the ceremony.

He knew a lot of single women, both in Boley and Amarillo. Most were younger than Kathryn. Some were prettier. Well…as pretty, anyway, he amended as he took in the lovely picture she made in the pale blue dress, with her dark hair piled on top of her head.

A few of the women he'd considered asking had been widowed or divorced, experienced in marriage and child rearing.

Yet his thoughts had kept returning to Kath. He wasn't sure just why.

Probably because you're so comfortable with her, he told himself as he watched her smile at something Ivy Thompson said. The minister's wife was a vague woman who could drive a saint crazy with her meaningless chatter, but Kathryn's attention never wavered.

There was a serenity about her, a quiet strength that soothed and reassured. It had drawn him to her countless times over the years. Whenever he had felt discouraged or angry or worried about something, he had always dropped by Kathryn's for a cup of her coffee and a chat. She would listen, really listen, her soft blue eyes filled with understanding and fastened on you as though what you were saying was the most important thing in the world.

Oftentimes he had thought that those visits with Kath had saved his marriage. Barbara had been a fiery, exciting woman, both in bed and out, and he had loved her, but she'd had little patience with—or for that matter, interest in—any problem that did not affect her or her precious quarter horses. So he had talked to Kath.

Now he realized suddenly that he had been so determined to marry Kathryn because he wanted—needed—all that warmth and caring. For himself _and_ for his children.

Regardless of his reasons, he'd made the right choice. He was sure of it. There was a feeling of...rightness about the whole thing.

He only wished the kids would show more enthusiasm. Recalling their reactions when he had told them the news, Dan grimaced. Susan had withdrawn even more into her shell, and the way Carla had carried on, you would have thought Kathryn was the Wicked Witch of the West.

Only Joey had seemed to like the idea of having a new mother. He had asked hundreds of questions in the past four days, and since they had arrived for the wedding he hadn't let Kath out of his sight. Even now, he was practically hanging on to her skirt.

"Where are you going to take Kathryn for a honeymoon?"

Dan turned his head and looked at his father, surprised by the question. "We're not taking a honeymoon."

"Why not?" Charles Westwood demanded, his white eyebrows drawn together in a disapproving frown. "Kathryn is a lovely woman, and this is her first and only marriage. It seems to me that the least you can do is make it special for her. Things like a honeymoon are important to women."

"Dad, Kath and I are old friends who married for very practical reasons. It's not as though this is a love match."

Charles subjected his son to a long, intent look. "Then more fool you," he said with patent disgust.

Dan's eyebrows arched skyward as he watched his father stalk away, but before he had a chance to question the comment, someone else claimed his attention.

It did not take Dan long to circulate among the few guests, and once the cake had been cut and eaten, the champagne drunk and well-wishes received, it was time to go.

As Dan and Kathryn were saying their goodbyes, Carla, Susan and Joey appeared, all buttoned up in their coats. "We're ready, Dad," Carla announced flatly.

"Wait a minute, you three," Nora Westwood intervened with a chuckle. "You're not going. You're going to stay here with Granddad and me tonight."

The two younger children looked uncertainly from their grandmother to their father, but Carla's eyes flashed defiance. She lifted her chin, her face growing even more sullen. "We can't. We didn't bring any clothes with us."

Nora sent her son an exasperated look that told him exactly what she thought of his lack of sensitivity and planning, but when she turned to her recalcitrant granddaughter she smiled. "Nonsense. That's no problem. There are plenty of your clothes here." She put her arm around Carla's stiff shoulders and gave her a squeeze. "We'll make some popcorn and watch movies. It'll be fun."

"No thanks, Gran. We'd rather go home."

"All the same, I think it would be better if you stayed," Nora said, and this time there was a note of steel in her voice that said she would brook no argument.

"Why? So Dad can be alone with *her?*" Carla flared, glaring at Kathryn. "I can't see what difference it makes. Everybody knows what they're going to—"

"Carla!" Dan thundered. "That will be enough!"

"If you loved my mother you wouldn't ha—"

"I did love your mother, Carla. Very much. But she's gone. I'm married to Kathryn now, and as my wife she at least deserves your respect. Now, I want you to apologize to her at once."

"Dan, no, please—"

"Yes," he insisted, cutting off Kathryn's protest. "I won't have her behaving this way toward you."

An uncomfortable silence fell. Susan edged to the back of the group. Clinging to his grandmother, Joey buried his face against her thigh and began to whimper.

After a tense moment, Carla muttered a surly, "I'm sorry," not quite meeting Kathryn's eyes.

"That's all right, dear. I understand," she replied, but the statement merely earned her a narrow-eyed look of intense dislike.

Nora and Charles stepped into the breach, smoothing over the awkward moment with hugs and well-wishes, and soon everyone joined in. They opened the door to blustering winds and sleet, and as Dan and Kathryn made a dash for the car they were peppered with rice and boisterous shouts of congratulations.

When they had pulled away from the curb and were heading for Dan's place on the outskirts of town, he slanted her an apologetic glance. "Sorry about that, Kath."

"About what? The send-off, or Carla's outburst?"

"Both, I guess." He reached over and gave her hand a squeeze. "But look, about Carla—please don't take it personally. It's just that...well...she was very close to her mother, and it's hard for her to accept someone else—anyone else—in her place. But she's always liked you, Kath; she'll come around eventually."

"I hope you're right."

"I am. You'll see. As you said, fourteen is a difficult age."

Kathryn gave him a wan smile and leaned her head back on the seat.

Dan glanced at her delicate profile and knew again that warm feeling he'd been experiencing ever since he had asked her to marry him.

They rode in silence, each lost in thought. The only sounds were the swish of tires on the wet paving, the rhythmic thump of the wipers, the soft whir of the heater. As it filled the car interior with warmth, Dan caught a whiff of Kathryn's subtle perfume. To his surprise, he realized that he was acutely aware of her—her warmth, her nearness, the allure of the soft feminine curves beneath the enveloping coat.

Ironically, until Carla's outburst he hadn't given all that much thought to the physical side of this marriage. He'd been too busy rushing around making the arrangements. Plus, he simply wasn't used to thinking of Kathryn in a sexual way. Not that he hadn't had a stray erotic thought about her now and then. After all, he was a normal male, and she was a beautiful woman. But, besides the fact that he believed in being a faithful husband, their friendship had always meant too much to him to risk jeopardizing it.

Now, however, he found he was looking forward to making love to her. Already he felt a stirring rush of heat in his loins as his body tightened in anticipation.

Of course, he didn't expect fireworks or steamy passion. Kathryn was a soothing woman—gentle, quiet, giving. Easy on the nerves as well as the eyes. And she was exactly what he needed. Her tender heart would make her a good mother and a pleasant companion, and she would bring order and peace to his life with that sweet calm of hers.

At that moment, Kathryn was feeling anything but calm. She had not had a calm moment in four days.

They had passed in a blur of activity and turbulent emotion, fear and doubt, hope and anticipation all churning within her. And today—today she had been a bundle of raw nerves. Everything had seemed like a dream—the music, the flowers, floating down the stairs on Charles's arm, Dan waiting for her,

Reverend Thompson's mellifluous voice saying those words she had never thought to hear.

Do you, Kathryn Ann Talmidge, take this man, Daniel Roman Westwood, to be your lawful wedded husband? To have and to hold from this day forward, for better or for worse, for richer or for poorer, in sickness and in health, as long as you both shall live?

Kathryn had been quaking inside, her heart filled with such sweet pressure that she'd thought it would surely burst. She had barely been able to whisper "I do." If it had been possible to die from joy, she would have at that moment.

Dan had made the same reply in his strong, sure voice, and they were pronounced husband and wife. He had gathered her in his arms then, and for the first time, their lips met in a slow, soft, stunningly sensual kiss that surpassed every dream she'd ever had. She had almost shattered with delight, her heart booming, her body going weak and warm, melting against him as his hard arms supported her.

Even now, just thinking about it made her giddy.

Surreptitiously, Kathryn extended her left hand and gazed at the wide gold band on her finger. It gleamed in the dim light from the dash. *Kathryn Westwood. Mrs. Daniel Westwood.*

She closed her eyes again, a tiny smile curving her mouth. Those few precious moments would stay sharply etched in her memory forever, even if she lived to be a hundred.

Carla's tantrum had been the only sour note. It had added to Kathryn's doubts and briefly made her wonder if she had done the right thing in marrying Dan. But it was too late to turn back now, and in any case, she doubted that she could have mustered the strength to refuse him.

It did not take long to reach Dan's home. The rambling old house had been built in the previous century by a local rancher, and though it was of no particular period, it had charm and character. Dan and Barbara had purchased it ten years ago, along with the surrounding hundred acres of land, but the locals still referred to it as the Ebersole place.

Since childhood Kathryn had been enchanted by the house. It was built with quality and craftsmanship, full of interesting nooks and crannies, lovely hand-carved wood and molding and extravagant decorative flourishes from a bygone era.

After parking the car in the garage, Dan took her small case from the back seat, then grabbed her hand, and they sprinted through the blowing sleet and rain to the back veranda.

"Well, this is it. Welcome to your new home, Kath," Dan said, unlocking the door.

Kathryn hesitated, hoping he would carry her over the threshold, but when he pushed the door open and gestured for her to precede him, she swallowed her disappointment and stepped into the old-fashioned kitchen.

As he led her through the downstairs she was surprised and faintly dismayed. The house had stood vacant for a few years before he had bought it, and in those days Kathryn had fantasized about living there, what she would do to spruce it up and return it to its former glory. She assumed that Barbara had done all that, but the interior was just as forlorn and shabby as it had been ten years ago.

The wallpaper was darkened with age and buckling in spots, the dull oak floors had not seen a coat of wax in years, and ancient, heavy curtains hung in limp folds over the windows. The house was clean and fairly neat, but there was no sign of a woman's touch anywhere.

Kathryn knew that Dan's wife had been a tomboy, more interested in the quarter horses she raised than in decorating or fashion or any of the other things most women enjoyed. Still, it surprised her that Barbara had not bothered to put her personal stamp on the home she had lived in for so long.

It was yet another stark reminder of the differences between herself and Dan's first wife. Depressed, Kathryn wondered, as she had so many times before, if she was even remotely Dan's type. Certainly she was nothing like Barbara. Never had two women been more different, in looks, personality and style.

"Sorry about the house, Kath," Dan said beside her, and she looked at him, blushing as she realized that her dismay had shown on her face. "It needs a lot of work, I know, but...well, Barb just never took any interest in that sort of thing."

"Oh, Dan, I'm sorry. I didn't mean to be rude. I just—"

"That's all right, honey. I've grown used to it like this, but I know it's a mess." Putting an arm around her shoulders, he hugged her to him and smiled. "But at least this way, starting from scratch, you'll be able to decorate it as you please."

Surprise raised her eyebrows. "You wouldn't mind?"

"Mind! Honey, I'm hoping you'll turn this moldy old barn into a home." He leaned down and kissed her, and Kathryn felt the bottom drop out of her stomach. When he raised his head his gaze roamed over her face, surprise glittering in his hazel eyes, along with something darker, more intense, that sent shivers up Kathryn's spine. "This family needs you, Kath," he said in a husky murmur. "I need you."

Kathryn's heart boomed like a kettledrum. He didn't love her, but surely need was the next thing to it. And in time... maybe...

Her mind shied away from completing the thought, but it was there all the same, a small kernel of hope to which her heart clung fiercely.

He kissed her again, his tongue slipping between her lips to touch the tip of hers. The contact sent fire streaking through her, and she shivered within his embrace.

When their lips parted Dan drew back and cupped her cheek with his palm, his expression tender. "Are you nervous, Kath?"

"I...a little," she admitted.

"There's no reason to be. We'll still be friends. Just more...intimate friends." He brushed his thumb over her lower lip, his eyes growing dark and heavy lidded as he watched it tremble. "Friends...and lovers," he whispered as he slipped his arm around her and led her up the massive oak stairway.

In the master bedroom he placed her case on the bed. "I've cleared some space in the closet and the dresser. The bath is right through there," he said, pointing to the door in the far wall. "I'll use the one across the hall." He kissed her quickly and left.

Standing in the middle of the room, quivering with almost unbearable excitement, Kathryn stared after him.

A short while later, Dan lay propped up in bed, waiting. As

he listened to the soft sounds coming from the bathroom he was both amused and amazed at how eager he was for Kathryn to join him.

Eager. He shook his head, giving a rueful chuckle at the understatement. Since leaving his parents' house, he'd been in a constant state of arousal. It was beginning to hit him that along with the change in their relationship, his feelings for Kathryn had shifted subtly. How, he wasn't quite sure yet, except that he was aware of her in ways he never had been before.

The bathroom door opened, and Dan's breath caught. Kathryn stood in the doorway wearing a delicate confection of rose silk and cream lace, and for a moment, backlit by the bright light from the bathroom, her shapely curves were visible through the sheer gown. Except for two thin straps, her shoulders were bare, and her shining hair tumbled against her skin like dark silk.

Kathryn turned out the light and took a hesitant step, then stopped. She gazed at him, her soft blue eyes wide and vulnerable and filled with uncertainty, and Dan felt his heart turn over.

Throwing back the covers, he rose from the bed and went to her. He forgot that she was his lifelong friend and confidante. He forgot that he had asked her to marry him for the most practical and prosaic of reasons. He forgot that he was naked.

He stalked toward her, drawn by her alluring, fragile beauty. Kathryn gasped. Her eyes grew round as they slid over his large muscular body, but he didn't notice her discomfort.

Stopping in front of her, he framed her face with his hands, his long, blunt fingers threading into the hair at her temples. "Oh, Kath." Her name was a sigh on his lips, breathy and full of wonder. His thumbs brushed the hollows beneath her cheekbones as he gazed into her wide, startled eyes. "Sweetheart, you're so beautiful."

The steam rolling from the bathroom was redolent with the feminine scents of bubble bath, floral soap and talc. They clung to her skin, but mixed with them was her enchanting woman smell, which made their effect all the more potent. Dan breathed deeply, delighted, intoxicated.

With utmost tenderness, he kissed her forehead, and when her eyes fluttered shut he pressed his lips to first one satiny lid, then the other. Making a tiny sound of pleasure, Kathryn swayed and grasped his waist for support.

The feel of those small soft hands on him drew a low groan from Dan, and his mouth found hers, rocking, rubbing, nipping with barely restrained hunger.

Blindly, Kathryn sought to deepen the kiss, pressing closer, her mouth open, seeking. A wild, almost unbearable pleasure shuddered through her, making her heart pound and her knees turn to water.

Feeling her quivering reaction, Dan wrapped his arms around her, molding her to him as the kiss became hot and hungry and urgent. His hands smoothed over her, sliding downward to fondle her waist, the enticing rounded hips, before grasping her buttocks and pressing her against his aroused body with a slow, undulating rhythm.

The explosion of pleasure was almost more than Kathryn could bear. Years of longing surged to the surface, and she wrapped her arms around him, her hands moving restlessly, her fingers digging into the hard, flat muscles that banded his broad back.

Plastered together, their mouths still joined in feverish passion, Dan eased them toward the bed, sinking with her onto the wide mattress. He lay half over her, his hand beneath the plunging bodice of her gown cupping her breast, his callused palm rotating against the engorged nipple. His crooked knee pressed between her legs.

Kathryn writhed beneath him, crying out at the tension building inside her, so sweet and hot it was almost pain.

"Easy, sweetheart. Easy," Dan crooned, feeling his control slipping perilously. He was stunned and delighted by her response, but her innocent movements were pushing him over the edge. He wanted to draw it out, to ensure her pleasure, too. It surprised him, but he also wanted to see that lovely, gentle face flushed with passion, feel her going wild beneath him. "This is new ground for us, Kath," he whispered, stringing kisses along her arched neck. "We can take it slow and easy. There's no need to rush."

Kathryn was too caught up in the spiraling need to heed his words. And she had waited years already.

She reached for him, her hands frantic, her expression rapt. She touched him everywhere, his ears, his shoulders, the hollow at the base of his throat, lightly raking his nipples with her nails, threading her fingers through the mat of hair on his chest.

"Love me, Dan," she urged. "Love me."

With a helpless groan, Dan shoved aside her gown and bent his head. Kathryn cried out and arched her back when he took her nipple into the warmth of his mouth. As he drew on her with a slow, sweet suction, his hand slipped under the lower edge of her gown and glided up her silky inner thigh to stroke and caress the moist petals of her womanhood.

In a frenzy of need, Kathryn's exploring hands followed the narrowing path of chest hair downward to his flat, quivering belly. Sucking in his breath, Dan went perfectly still, his jaw clenched, but when he felt her intimate touch he shuddered violently and his restraint snapped. "Oh, God, yes. Yes!"

With swift, desperate motions, he stripped the gown from her, tossing it aside to flutter soundlessly to the floor, and he moved into position between her thighs. Braced above her, he looked into her slumberous eyes, stunned anew by her ardency, the rapturous expression on her face. His hesitation lasted only a moment, for his aroused body demanded satisfaction. Following the urging of her soft hands, he thrust into her, slowly, deeply, the intense pleasure of it taking their breath away.

The sensuous rhythm caught them, carrying them quickly beyond reason, beyond all but the exquisite pleasure they shared.

Long moments later Dan braced up on his forearms and smiled at her. "You amaze me, Kathryn Westwood," he said, but there was deep satisfaction in his voice. "All these years I had no idea there was a passionate woman hiding behind that serene exterior."

He was the first to call Kathryn by her new name, and the sound of it on his lips thrilled her. She slid her hands up his arms and over his shoulders, giving him a beguiling look. "Are you complaining?"

"Hardly." Chuckling, he rolled from her and pulled her close, tucking her head against his shoulder. "Just surprised." With a hand under her chin, he tipped her face up and looked at her, his expression tender and serious. "And pleased. Though I should have known we'd be good together; we've always been compatible." He brushed her mouth with a soft kiss, then settled her head back on his shoulder. "We're going to have a good marriage, Kath. I'm going to do my damnedest to make you happy."

Kathryn snuggled closer, and he reached out and turned off the lamp. In the darkness he absently rubbed his jaw against her temple and stared at the window, where tiny pieces of ice clicked against the pane.

She hadn't been a virgin. That surprised him, and because it had, he felt like a ridiculous fool. In truth, he'd never really given a thought to whether or not Kathryn had had any sexual experience, but, he supposed, like everyone else in town, he had assumed she had not. Which was absurd. She was forty years old, a vibrant, lovely, normal woman, not some neurotic old maid. It was to be expected that at some point in her life she had cared enough for some man to make love with him.

Dan wondered who the man was. It had probably happened a long time ago, and he was sure it couldn't have been anyone in town, or he would have heard about it. In a town the size of Boley it was impossible to keep something like that a secret.

It was normal, Dan told himself. Natural.

Still, though he silently chided himself for it, somehow the thought of Kath lying in the arms of some nameless, faceless man made him feel like punching something.

Unaware of the trend of her new husband's thoughts, Kathryn sighed, blissfully content. She closed her eyes and smiled, absorbing the feel of his warm flesh pressed against hers. Lord, she loved him so! At that moment Kathryn was happier than she had ever been in her life.

The only way she could be happier would be if she had his

love. Still, she wouldn't be greedy. For now she would concentrate on their marriage, on making him happy. To do that
she was going to have to win over the children, especially
Carla. And she would. Somehow.

In time he might even come to love her. Already, by some
miracle, she was his wife. Who knew how many more miracles
were in store?

Chapter 3

The next morning Kathryn was disappointed when she awoke alone.

"What did you expect?" she chided herself as she slid out of bed and headed for the bathroom. "An early morning cuddle session? Did you really think that one night of lovemaking would make Dan fall head over heels for you? That he would want to linger in bed like a besotted bridegroom?" She bent over the old-fashioned pedestal sink and splashed icy water in her face, then grimaced at her reflection in the mirror as she patted her skin dry with a towel. "Don't be a fool, Kathryn."

Over and over, as she dressed and made her way downstairs, she reminded herself that Dan had married her for practical reasons. He had been open and honest about that, and she had no right to expect more.

She knew that Dan felt affection for her. He would honor her, care for her, be a thoughtful companion. She vowed that she would not be greedy, that if that was all the future offered, then she would be happy with it.

Her spirits took another nose dive, however, when she stepped into the kitchen and discovered that it, too, was empty. Then she spotted the note on the table, anchored beneath the sugar bowl. Reluctantly, she picked it up.

Sorry, Kath, but I got an early call. Colby's prize mare is about to foal, and she's in trouble. I'll be back as soon as I can.

That he had gone out on a call on this particular morning told Kathryn exactly how little sentiment he attached to their marriage. Dan's practice was large and demanding, but there were two other vets in the clinic, and either would have covered for him if he had bothered to ask.

She allowed herself a moment of self-pity, standing there in the middle of the kitchen, her shoulders drooping, feeling hurt and abandoned. But only a moment. With quiet determination, Kathryn squared her shoulders and shook off the mood, reminding herself of her earlier vow.

Deciding there were better ways to spend her time than moping around waiting for Dan to return, she located the keys to his car and drove to her house. Everything had happened so quickly, she had not had time to move her things or even decide what to keep and what to get rid of, and now was as good a time as any to start on that chore.

Two hours later she was bent over, dragging a box that she'd filled with shoes and purses from her closet, when a pair of hard, masculine hands cupped her bottom.

"Hmm, Mrs. Westwood, I presume."

Kathryn let out a shriek, straightened and whirled around. "Dan!" Weak with relief, she sagged against his chest, and his arms closed around her.

"Who else were you expecting?" he asked with a chuckle.

"No one. Least of all you," she mumbled into his shirt.

She had not meant it to sound like an accusation, but apparently it had. He grew still, and his strong arms tensed around her. "Kath." He said her name hesitantly, his voice touched with wariness and regret. "I'm sorry about this morning."

Kathryn pulled free of his embrace. Their wedding night had been wonderful, marvelous, and she loved Dan to the depth of her soul, but suddenly, recalling the passion, the intimacies, her own abandoned response, she felt self-conscious and ill at ease. And despite the bracing lecture she'd given herself, she harbored some residual hurt and anger over his cavalier treatment. "Oh, don't worry about it," she said. "I understand." She went to the dresser and snatched out items willy-nilly, then added them to the suitcases spread out on the four-poster bed.

Frowning, Dan watched her agitated movements. "I didn't have a choice, Kath," he said quietly. "We're shorthanded at the clinic. Bob is out with the flu, which is why he didn't make it to the wedding. Eli is on call this weekend, but when Colby phoned this morning he was already out on an emergency, so I had to go."

Kathryn looked up, hope she was powerless to hide lighting her eyes. "Really?"

Dan came around to her side of the bed and cupped her face between his palms. "Kath, did you really think I would leave you alone, today of all days, unless I had to?" he asked softly. She bit her lower lip and stared at him, her eyes filled with uncertainty, and he shook his head. "Honey, I may not be the most sensitive guy in the world, but I wouldn't leave my bride of less than twelve hours unless I had no choice. This marriage is important to me, Kath," he stressed in a low, husky voice. "*You're* important to me."

He lowered his head and kissed her, and because she wanted to believe him, *needed* to believe him, she melted into his embrace and let her doubts slip away.

His lips were warm and soft on hers, exquisitely arousing, and Kathryn trembled beneath the tender assault. When he raised his head she blushed. She wasn't used to Dan kissing her, touching her so intimately, and though she loved it, she was terrified of giving herself away.

A teasing glint entered his eyes, and he touched her warm cheek with one finger but made no comment.

To hide her embarrassment Kathryn stepped away from him and bent over one of the open cases on the bed. Sliding his fingers, palms out, into the back pockets of his jeans, Dan looked around with interest. "So this is your room."

"Yes." It had been hers since the day she was born. During the past forty years it had sported everything from a child's clowns and teddy bears to a young girl's frills and flounces to a teenager's posters, mobiles and assorted junk, but for the past eighteen it had looked as it did now, with delicate blue floral wallpaper, graceful period furniture and her mother's plush cream and pale blue Oriental rug covering most of the polished oak floor.

"You know, I've probably been in this house a thousand times over the years, but I've never been upstairs before," Dan mused as he took in the antique bed with its lacy, hand-crocheted canopy and the graceful Philadelphia highboy. He looked at her and smiled. "It looks like you—peaceful, in good taste and elegantly beautiful."

Kathryn was both warmed and flustered by the compliment, but before she could reply, Dan calmly shut the suitcases and set them on the floor. Her eyes widened as he tossed back the candlewick bedspread. "What are you doing?"

"I'm going to make love to my wife." He walked toward her. The weak light filtering in through the lace curtains struck his face, and Kathryn's heart began to thud when she saw his intent look, the heavy-lidded eyes that were fixed on her with blatant desire. Her body grew warm, and a trembling started deep inside her. It was a fantasy come true, one she'd had countless times over the years, seeing that hunger and heat in Dan...for her.

He stopped in front of her. "I want you, Kath," he said in a velvety murmur. "Right here. Right now. In this lovely room." Reaching out, he slowly unbuttoned her blouse. "For hours."

So excited she could scarcely breathe, Kathryn stood docilely and allowed him to strip her. When he eased her onto the bed and stepped back to remove his own clothes, she lay watching him, fascinated by his male beauty, the lithe perfection of his hard, fit body. Enthralled as she was, she even forgot about guarding her emotions.

Smiling, Dan lay down beside her and gathered her to him, and Kathryn gave a helpless little moan as he pulled her into his heat. He kissed her temple, her cheek, her arching neck. "You, my sweet Kath, are like an addicting drug," he whispered in her ear. "One taste, and I can't get enough."

*   *   *

Winter's early darkness was already settling in when they returned home hours later. Feeling sated and smug and filled with soaring hope, Kathryn drove Dan's car, and he followed in the pickup, both vehicles loaded with her belongings.

Those hours of passion had been delicious. Dan might not love her, but he desired her. She didn't know how the miracle had come about, but she accepted her good fortune gratefully. Feminine instinct told her that desire that strong could eventually lead to love. If they could make the transition from friends to lovers, surely anything was possible.

As they drove through town, Kathryn noticed that already the merchants were getting into the holiday spirit. A few shops had Thanksgiving decorations in the windows—cornucopias, pilgrims, cardboard turkeys with fanned out crepe paper tails—but most had bypassed that holiday in favor of the glitter and tinsel of Christmas. The bay window of Janine's Hobby Shop boasted a display of handmade ornaments and wreaths, and the bakery, the drugstore and Pruit's Shoe Emporium were all decked out in blinking lights. Sprayed in artificial snow on the plate-glass window of Bowden's Hardware on the corner of Main and Pine was a sign that read Pre-Christmas Sale! Soon, Kathryn thought, the city fathers would hang those huge silver bells tied with red velvet bows to the town's three traffic lights and string gold garlands from lamppost to lamppost, as they did every year.

The decorations, the thought of Christmas, brought home to Kathryn that she no longer had any reason to dread the holidays, and her heart swelled with elation. This year, and for all the years to come, she had a family with whom to share it. A husband. She had Dan.

When they reached the house Dan unloaded her things, then left to pick up the children while Kathryn prepared dinner.

It was the first meal Kathryn had ever cooked for her family, and she wanted it to be special, but she soon discovered that the kitchen was stocked with only the most basic ingredients. Either Dan was not much of a cook or they were all accustomed to very plain fare, indeed.

Making a mental note to grocery shop the next day, Kathryn made do with what she could find and managed to put together a chicken Florentine of sorts, rice pilaf, a salad, rolls and a cherry pie made from canned filling.

She was setting the table in the kitchen when the back door flew open and Joey came barreling in. At the sight of Kathryn he stopped short, relief, then joy chasing across his babyish face. "You're here. Just like Daddy said you'd be. I wanted to come home this morning to see, but Gran wouldn't bring us."

The innocent words revealed a world of fear and wrung Kathryn's tender heart. She put down the silverware and ruffled his tawny hair. He looked so much like his father, she thought, smiling into the dark-fringed hazel eyes gazing up at her with adoration. "Yes, I'm here, Joey," she reassured him softly. "I live here now."

"And you'll be here every day when I get home from kindergarten? Just like a real mommie?" he asked hopefully.

"I..." Until that moment Kathryn had not given a thought to making any drastic changes regarding her business, but Joey's expression caused her to rearrange her entire work schedule without a second thought. Kneeling in front of him, she took both his hands in hers. They were soft and warm, still pudgy with baby fat, and slightly sticky. "Yes, Joey. I'll be here."

She would cut back on her hours and work mornings only, make Sarah, her one full-time clerk, store manager, and get her part-time helper to come in more, she decided quickly. It would mean smaller profits, but Joey's needs came first.

"And I can call you Mommie?" he asked eagerly.

"She's not your mommie," Carla snapped from behind him.

Kathryn looked up to see the girl standing just inside the door, glaring at her with undisguised dislike, her stout young body rigid with fury. Susan stood behind her, staring at the floor and twisting one blond braid around and around her fingers.

"Is, too!" Joey insisted, whirling on his sister. "Daddy said so!"

"Just because she married Dad doesn't mean—"

"That's enough, Carla." Dan's stern voice cut across his daughter's. "If Joey wants to call Kathryn Mommie, he can, provided it's all right with her."

Four pairs of eyes turned on Kathryn. Dan's were bland and

noncommittal, Joey's bright with expectancy. Susan clasped her hands behind her back and shuffled her feet, but every few seconds she risked a wary, curious glance at the woman kneeling before her baby brother. Carla's brown eyes burned with resentment.

Kathryn looked back at Dan in silent censure for putting her on the spot, but when her gaze once again encountered Joey's she knew she was going to have to risk Carla's ire; there was no way she could resist the plea in those big hazel eyes. Nor did she want to.

With a gentle smile, she touched his cheek and pushed the unruly sun-streaked curls off his forehead. "Of course it's all right with me," she said softly. "I've always wanted a little boy."

Before the words were out of her mouth Joey gave a delighted cry and flung himself against her, his chubby arms clamping about her neck in a strangling hug.

Kathryn wrapped her arms around his warm little body and cuddled him close. She could scarcely breathe for the lump in her throat. Over his shoulder, her eyes met Dan's. His smile held approval and gratitude. Emotion quivered through Kathryn. Her chin wobbled and her throat ached, and she closed her eyes against the sudden rush of tears.

"Hey, sport, if you want to eat, you're going to have to let go of her," Dan said, untangling his son from her arms.

The child relinquished his hold with reluctance, but as Kathryn rose to her feet she silently thanked Dan for saving her from making a complete fool of herself; in another minute she would have been weeping.

When they sat down to dinner, Carla took one look at the meal and announced that she didn't like any of it.

"How do you know?" Dan inquired. "You've never had it before."

"I just know, that's all."

He frowned when Carla rose and headed for the pantry. "What are you doing?"

"I'm going to make a sandwich."

"You'll do no such thing. You're going to eat the meal Kathryn cooked for you."

"Daaad!" Carla wailed.

"Dan, I don't think you should—"

"Don't interfere, Kath," he snapped, never taking his eyes from his daughter's petulant face. "I will not tolerate rudeness."

Kathryn felt as though she'd been slapped. Carla sent her a smirking look of triumph, but it faded quickly into anger when her father ordered her to return to the table. With a furious toss of her blond hair, she flounced back across the room and threw herself into her chair.

The first meal with her new family turned out nothing at all the way Kathryn had envisioned. Dan and the girls ate in silence, while Joey, oblivious to the tension in the air, dug into his dinner with gusto, keeping up a cheerful barrage of chatter between bites. Quivering with hurt, Kathryn kept her eyes downcast and did little more than rearrange the food on her plate.

Pleasure moved through Dan as he watched Kathryn. Wearing only a towel knotted about his lean hips, he stood in the bathroom doorway, a shoulder propped against the jamb.

She was sitting at the antique dressing table, which he'd carried upstairs just a few hours ago, her head tilted to one side, methodically brushing her hair. It crackled about the brush and shimmered in the lamplight.

She was a beautiful, desirable woman. Why had it taken him so long to notice? No, that wasn't quite right. He'd noticed. But now...now he was seeing her from a different perspective. Now she was his. His wife. Dan smiled, the thought pleasing him.

Her rose silk gown was cut in a deep V all the way to her waist, and as his gaze tracked the elegant curve of her spine he felt a hot surge of desire. His mouth quirked. Considering the hours they'd spent twined together in her delicate four-poster bed, he hadn't expected to want her again quite so soon.

He'd enjoyed making love to her in that exquisitely feminine room where he was absolutely certain no other man had ever been. There had been something erotic about it, something deeply satisfying.

And she had surprised him, last night and again this afternoon, with all that flaming passion. He was still having a difficult time relating soft, sweet, serene Kathryn Talmidge with that sensual woman who'd caught fire in his arms. He shook his head. Still waters.

He pushed away from the door and crossed the room to stand behind her. When his hands settled on her shoulders she jumped and stiffened.

"What's the matter, honey?" he asked, grinning as he rotated his thumbs over her shoulder blades. "You're as tense as a fiddle string. Don't tell me you're still shy."

Her somber gaze met his in the mirror, and gradually his teasing look faded into a frown. His voice deepened with concern. "What is it, Kath? What's wrong?"

"Before we go any further, Dan, I want to know exactly what it is you expect of me."

His frown deepened. "What do you mean?"

"You told me you wanted a mother for your children, yet whenever I open my mouth you shut me up, tell me not to interfere."

"For Pete's sake, Kath, are you still fretting about that scene at the table? Carla was behaving like a rude, obnoxious brat, and I put a stop to it. That's it. It's over. Settled."

Kathryn rose and faced him, her arms folded over her midriff. "Dan, you can't *make* her like me, and forcing the issue is only going to make things worse."

"So what am I supposed to do? I told you, I won't have her treating you that way."

"Give her time. Let her get to know me. Once she sees that I'm no threat, either to her mother's memory or to her, everything will be fine." She stepped close and put her hand on his chest. Her eyes were soft and beseeching. "Let us work out our relationship on our own, Dan. Please."

Dan cupped his hand around the back of his neck and sighed. "All right. I guess I've had them by myself so long that I'm just not used to sharing the responsibility," he said wearily. "But the next time Carla gets into one of her snits, I promise, I'll let you deal with her."

"Good." A wistful smile wavered about Kathryn's lips. "After all, that's why you married me."

Dan frowned. He didn't like that. Yet…he couldn't dispute it. Feeling somehow at fault, he watched Kathryn walk to the bed and slip beneath the covers. Thoughtfully, he followed.

In the darkness he reached for her, and Kathryn came willingly into his arms, her sweet, soft body pliant against him. This time he took her powerfully, a little roughly, driven by a compulsive need he didn't understand.

A long while later, as Kathryn slept at his side, Dan lay staring at the darkened ceiling, filled with disquiet and a vague sense of guilt.

Chapter 4

Kathryn did not expect miracles. She could only wait and hope that Dan and his children would eventually open their hearts to her.

Because Carla, Susan and Joey were his, she loved them, but she knew it would take time for them to accept her.

She didn't push, didn't make any overt attempts to win them over. Kathryn was simply herself. With patience, understanding and gentle determination, she eased herself into their lives, quietly doing the hundred and one things that wives and mothers do and families take for granted.

Whether or not they noticed, under Kathryn's hand the household ran more smoothly. Suddenly the refrigerator and pantry were always stocked with delicious things to eat, there were always fresh towels in the bathrooms, clean linens on the beds, pressed clothes in the closets, neatly folded underwear in the drawers. The beds were always made, the kitchen always spotless. The stacks of old newspapers and magazines had disappeared from the living room, and fresh flowers and leafy plants were scattered throughout the house.

The children came home to a warm house and were greeted by delicious smells wafting from the kitchen and the sweet scent of potpourri that Kathryn had placed everywhere in little jars and dishes. She was always there to meet them with a smile and a soft word. Caring was in her eyes, and implicit in her manner was the silent offer of support and love—if they wanted it.

Joey, of course, had been her devoted slave from the first, and Kathryn doted on him. He was a bright, affectionate child, as starved for a mother's love as she was to give it. She adored it when he climbed into her lap and cuddled close, and at night when she tucked him into bed and he clamped his chubby little arms around her neck and gave her a wet, smacking kiss she never failed to get a lump in her throat. She even found bath time delightful. Amid the squeals and giggles and splashing she usually ended up as wet as Joey, but it was worth it. When he clambered from the tub for her to dry him, his sturdy little body all warm and rosy and smelling of soap and his wonderful little-boy smell, his hazel eyes gleeful, she knew a happiness beyond measure.

The girls were a different story. Kathryn's overtures of friendship were met with resentment from Carla and skittish withdrawal from Susan. It was distressing, but she bore it with equanimity and forbearance and kept right on trying. Time and patience. Kathryn knew they were her best weapons.

News of their marriage spread through Boley like a prairie fire in the wind. All of Kathryn and Dan's friends and acquaintances called to wish them well. People she barely knew and some she didn't know at all stopped by the shop to offer their congratulations and comments. Kathryn suspected, from the women's giggling comments and sidelong glances, that most had come out of curiosity, wondering how on earth the town's old maid had snagged its most eligible male.

A week after the wedding, Kathryn was in the shop during the noon hour when an attractive woman in her early thirties came in. She paused just inside the door and looked around. When she spotted Kathryn she headed straight for her.

Sighing, Kathryn braced herself for more gushing comments and probing stares and stepped forward to greet the woman. "Hello. May I help you?"

"Yes, I hope so. You are Kathryn Westwood, aren't you? Dr. Dan Westwood's new wife?"

Kathryn willed her smile to remain in place. "Yes, I am."

"Oh, good." At first the woman looked uncomfortable, but she drew a deep breath and began determinedly, "Mrs. Westwood, I'm Lucille Bates. Susan's teacher. I wonder if I might have a word with you."

Alarm widened Kathryn's eyes. "Is something wrong? Is Susan ill?"

"No, no. Nothing like that. It's just that…well…I was wondering if you were planning on being at school this afternoon."

"At school?"

"For the spelling bee." Kathryn gave her a blank look, and Ms. Bates's face registered surprise. "You mean you don't know that Susan had made the semifinals? She didn't tell you?"

"She didn't even mention that she had entered the competition."

"My goodness. I wonder why. I know it's very important to her. She's been studying for months, and she's very excited. You see, today's winner will go on to the district competition."

"I see."

"That's why I'm here. Mrs. Westwood, I hope you don't think I'm interfering, but…well…I think it would mean a lot to Susan if someone from her family were there. She's never had anyone to support her at these sorts of things in the past. Her father tries, but the poor man is always so busy that he seldom can make it. That's why I was so delighted to hear that he'd remarried. My first thought was, now Susan will have someone to root for her."

"Thank you so much for telling me, Ms. Bates. I assure you, I'll be there. And I'll try to reach my husband, too." Kathryn felt a little thrill as she said the words. She still could hardly believe that she and Dan were married.

"Oh, good. It will be held at two o'clock in the school auditorium." Lucille Bates glanced at her watch. "I really must run now. I'm on my lunch break, and if I don't hurry, I'm going to be late." At the door, however, she paused with her hand on the knob and turned back to Kathryn with a speculative look. "I wonder…would you consider becoming a room mother? All you'd have to do is help out with school parties, act as chaperon on field trips—that sort of thing."

Amusement glittered in Kathryn's eyes. Susan's teacher obviously thought she'd found a soft touch. Smart woman, Ms. Bates. "I'll think about it and let you know. Thank you for asking me."

As soon as the door closed behind the woman, Kathryn rushed to the phone and called the veterinary clinic. Dan was out on a call and not expected back for hours, but she left a message, anyway.

Kathryn arrived at the school early and got a seat in the third row. At precisely two o'clock the principal, the teacher who was conducting the spelling bee and the semifinalists filed onto the stage. Susan's gaze made a cursory sweep over the audience, sliding past the third row without a flicker, then stopped and flew back. Kathryn smiled and waved as she watched her step-daughter's eyes grow round.

When Susan's first time up came her voice was shaky, and Kathryn began to worry that perhaps her presence was making the child nervous.

The initial few rounds brought no casualties, but after a while, one by one, contestants were eliminated. Each time Susan was given a word, she first glanced at her stepmother, who smiled and gave her a thumbs-up signal, then slowly spelled it. And each time Kathryn heard that quivering little voice, her heart swelled with pride, and tension knotted her stomach.

At the end, only Susan and a boy named Mike Sanders were left standing. There followed five more perfect rounds. Through them Kathryn sat forward in her seat with all her fingers crossed, gnawing her lower lip, her gaze fastened on Susan.

Then Mike missed a word.

Kathryn held her breath. When Susan spelled the word correctly the breath came out in a whooshing sigh, and she clapped so hard and so long that when the applause ended her palms were red.

"You came," Susan said when she joined Kathryn afterward. Amazement widened her eyes and made her voice a wisp of sound.

"Of course I came. I wouldn't have missed it for anything. Oh, Susan, I'm so proud of you."

"But how did you know?"

"Ms. Bates told me. Sweetheart, why didn't you tell us? If you had, I'm sure your father would've arranged his schedule so that he could have been here."

"I...I knew Daddy would be busy."

"You could have told me."

"I thought you'd be busy, too. Besides..." Susan fingered one braid, stared at the toe of her scuffed shoe and mumbled, "I didn't think you'd be interested."

"Oh, Susan." Kathryn placed her fingers beneath the girl's chin and tipped her face up. She smiled gravely, her blue eyes soft with gentle reprimand. "I'm interested in *you*. Don't you know that?"

Susan licked her lips and swallowed hard. She stared searchingly, her expression a mixture of wariness and hope, and Kathryn felt her heart constrict at the stark vulnerability in that thin, painfully young face. "R-really?" she finally managed.

Kathryn wanted to hug the child to her breast and tell her what was in her heart, but she resisted the temptation. Not yet. Not yet, her common sense urged. It's too soon.

"Yes, really." Striving for a lighter mood, she gave Susan's braid a teasing tug, put her arm around her shoulders and led her toward the auditorium doors. "Come on. Let's go find your brother before he gets on the school bus, and I'll give you both a ride home."

Susan acquiesced without a word, her expression thoughtful. As they walked down the hall toward Joey's kindergarten class Kathryn glanced at her and said, "By the way, your teacher asked me if I would be a room mother."

The girl's head jerked up, her startled gaze flying to Kathryn's face. "Are you gonna?"

"I thought I would." Casting her a sidelong look, she cocked one brow. "Unless, of course, you'd rather I didn't."

"No, I'd li—" Susan stopped. Schooling her features, she gave an elaborately casual shrug and replied, "Makes no difference to me."

"Then it's settled," Kathryn said, fighting back a smile.

* * *

Taking Dan at his word, Kathryn started right away on redoing the house. The entire project was going to take months, but she was determined to have at least the living room, dining room and entry hall finished in time for Christmas. Having known for years exactly what she would do with each room, she was able to skip the planning stage and plunge right in.

She hired Jake Riley, the local handyman, to do the work. He walked through the house with her as she explained what she wanted done, and he made up a list of supplies he would need. Armed with the tally, Kathryn drove into Amarillo, where she rented a floor sander and bought varnish, solvent, paint, wallpaper and various tools. Two days after Susan's spelling bee, work began.

The children arrived home from school that afternoon to chaos. All the furniture had been removed from the living room, dining room and foyer; the floors were littered with shreds of wallpaper that had been stripped from the walls; the air was thick with dust and reeked of old paste, age and the pungent fumes of varnish remover. In the center of the living-room floor, two sawhorses with a sheet of plywood over them formed a work surface, and scaffolding was set up along the walls. Standing on the raised platform, wearing a cap on his bald head and paint-spattered white coveralls that hung on his lanky frame like wet wash on a windless day, Jake Riley was slopping solvent onto the ceiling molding. Dressed in faded jeans and one of Dan's old shirts, with a bandanna tied over her hair, Kathryn watched him from below.

As usual, the children burst into the house in a storm of clattering footsteps and boisterous chatter, but as soon as the door slammed behind them absolute silence fell.

Surprised, Kathryn glanced at her watch, then spun around and stepped to the doorway. "Hi, kids. My goodness, I had no idea it was so late."

They were standing stock-still, their expressions dumbfounded, looking around at the bare walls and the mess littering the floor. Carla's gaze, angry and accusing, turned on Kathryn. "What are you doing?" she demanded.

"I've started redecorating. I know it looks awful now, but just wait. It's going to be beautiful when—"

"You have no right! No right!"

"Carla, please, listen to me. It will be lovely when I'm through, I promise you. I'm sure you'll like it. And think how pretty it will be for the holidays to have it all fixed up."

"No! I'll hate it! I hate it already. How dare you come in here and start changing everything! This is my mother's house, and we like it just the way it is." With a sob, she bolted for the stairs, taking them two at a time, the anguished cry trailing behind her.

They heard her footsteps pounding down the upstairs hall; then a door slammed. In the uncomfortable silence, Kathryn looked back at the other two and found that Joey was biting his lip, his eyes round as saucers, and Susan was watching her uncertainly. Kathryn recalled how happy the child had been after the spelling bee, how last night and again this morning she had seemed to draw tentatively closer. And now this.

Kathryn sighed. "Perhaps you'd better go up and make sure she's okay," she suggested, and Susan nodded and flitted up the stairs like a wraith.

"Why's Carla crying? What's she mad about?" Joey asked in a quavering little voice.

"She's just upset, Joey, but it's nothing for you to worry about. Now, why don't you run out to the kitchen and get some cookies while I talk to Mr. Riley. I'll be there in a few minutes."

"Okay," he muttered as he trudged away through the litter toward the door at the end of the hall, glancing back over his shoulder at her every few steps.

When Kathryn reentered the living room, Jake paused in the act of dipping his brush into the can of solvent and looked at her with his bushy eyebrows raised. "You want I should stop?"

"No, of course not. It's too late for that now, anyway."

"Just wondered. That little gal was shore upset." He spit a stream of brown tobacco juice into the empty can sitting on the end of the scaffolding and wiped his mouth with the back of his hand. "But then, I reckon she'll get over it," he said, picking up the brush again.

"I'm sure she will."

Kathryn folded her arms around her middle and looked sadly

at the stairs. It seemed that for every step forward, she took another back.

Dan's reaction to the remodeling was not much better than Carla's.

Due to an emergency he had to work late that night, and sometime after eleven Kathryn was awakened from a sound sleep by a tremendous crash, followed by a string of curses. Without taking time to put on her robe or slippers, she dashed downstairs to find Dan standing in the middle of the hall, his booted feet braced wide, fists propped on his hips, scowling at the mess. Jake's extension ladder lay drunkenly across the floor, one end tilted up on the bottom step of the stairs.

"Dan! What happened?"

His furious gaze turned on Kathryn, where she hovered halfway up the stairs, one hand on the rail, the other curled into a fist and pressed against her chest. "I knocked the damned ladder over," he said in a grating voice. "Now, would you mind telling me just what in the name of hell is going on here?"

Kathryn shifted uneasily from one bare foot to the other. "I, uh...I hired Jake to do the renovating and redecorating. He started today."

"You what!"

"You told me to fix the place up."

"Good Lord, Kathryn, I didn't mean right now! It's less than six weeks until Christmas! And Thanksgiving is just nine days away. How are we supposed to enjoy either one in this mess?"

Hurt pierced her. In all the years she'd known him, Dan had never talked to her in that tone of voice before. Nevertheless, she lifted her chin and replied, "We can have Thanksgiving at my house. And Jake assured me that he'll be finished in four weeks. Five at the most."

"Uh-huh, sure." Dan jerked up the ladder and propped it against the wall, then started to climb the stairs.

"Dan, please." Kathryn put her hand on his arm as he went to move past her, stopping him. "I'm sorry. If I had known it would upset you, I'd—"

"Look, Kathryn..." He sighed and raked a hand through his

hair. "They've got problems out at the Abbott spread, and I've been inoculating cattle and horses for the past seventeen hours. Tomorrow promises to be more of the same. I've been stepped on, kicked, bitten and butted. I'm tired, I'm dirty and not in the best of moods, so let's just drop it. Okay? It's too late to do anything about it now, anyway." He shook off her hand and climbed the remainder of the steps without another word, the set of his shoulders and his stiff carriage telegraphing his anger.

Kathryn gazed after him, feeling guilty and hurt and disappointed. The wooden stair tread was cold beneath her bare feet and coated with a fine layer of grit from the day's activities. She had turned the heat down before retiring, and the chill raised gooseflesh over her arms and shoulders. She noticed neither. She turned her head and studied the littered floor and the ugly stripped walls, and her spirits plummeted lower. Too late she realized that she should have discussed her plan with Dan before putting it into action, should have at least asked his opinion. "That's what comes of being single so long and making all your own decisions," she muttered to herself glumly as she turned and trudged up the stairs.

When Dan awoke the next morning and glanced at Kathryn sleeping peacefully beside him, he felt guilty for the sharp way he had spoken to her. He wasn't happy about the house being torn apart, especially now, with the holidays coming up, but to be fair, he *had* told her to do whatever she wanted with it.

Bracing himself on one elbow, Dan studied his wife in the weak predawn light, his expression growing tender as his gaze traced the incredibly fragile eyelids and the sweep of dark lashes that lay against her cheeks like feathery fans. Her skin was scrubbed clean and silky soft, her pink lips sweetly curved, slightly parted in slumber and very inviting. With a grimace, he resisted the urge to kiss her and instead smoothed a dark lock of hair off her cheek.

It struck him there in the quiet stillness of early morning that Kathryn was the most utterly feminine woman he had ever known. Soft. Nurturing. Without an ounce of guile or coyness. It was part of what had drawn him to her over the years. He found it infinitely more appealing and arousing than overt sexuality.

And beneath that tranquil surface were secret depths that fascinated him more each day.

With a sigh, Dan eased from the bed and headed for the bathroom. When he was shaved and dressed he paused beside the bed, debating whether or not to wake her and apologize. He ran a callused forefinger over the elegant curve of her cheek and smiled foolishly when she made a sleepy sound and shifted away from the feathery touch. No, he'd let her sleep, he decided finally and bent to brush her forehead with a kiss. He'd talk to her when he came home.

But the day turned out to be a repeat of the previous one. The situation at the Abbott ranch was critical, and it was after midnight when Dan arrived home. Kathryn was asleep when he tiptoed into the bedroom and asleep when he left the following morning before dawn. It took almost four days to finish inoculating the Abbott stock and complete treatment on the ailing animals, but when he was done he headed his pickup for home.

It was a little after noon when he turned into his driveway. He was tired, hungry and needed a shower, but that wasn't the reason he was there. He wouldn't lie to himself. He was there because he couldn't stay away a minute longer. The admission brought a wry twist to Dan's mouth as he killed the engine and climbed from the pickup. Turning up the collar of his sheepskin coat against the blustery wind, he hurried toward the house, anticipation building in his chest.

Kathryn was running something through the food processor and didn't hear him step into the kitchen. He leaned back against the door and watched her, his expression softening into tenderness.

He hadn't expected this fierce attraction, this deep yearning to see her. Touch her. Be near her all the time. He had expected peace with this marriage, that their lives would settle, become routine. Wasn't the familiarity of marriage supposed to create, if not boredom, exactly, then a sort of comfortable complacency?

Hell. Since he'd married Kath life had been anything but comfortable. He was forty-two years old, but she made him feel about twenty—eager and hot and lusty and able to take on the world. He felt foolish admitting it, but he was becoming ob-sessed with his wife. A woman he'd known all his life, for heaven's sake!

But foolish or not, it excited him to know that beneath that calm exterior was a sultry passion that could burn a man right to his soul—and that it was all for him.

Still, it wasn't enough. Sex with her was fantastic. It was bet-ter than fantastic; it surpassed anything he had ever known. Yet he sensed that there was a part of herself she was holding back. Despite all those years that bound them in friendship, and despite the new physical intimacy and sweet sensual awareness between them, there were times when she retreated from him behind those gentle smiles. And the longer they were married, the more it bothered him. He wanted it all. Everything Kath had to give.

She turned off the food processor, and into the silence he said softly, "Hi. Remember me?"

Kathryn gasped and spun around, a spatula in her upraised hand. "Dan!" She closed her eyes and sagged against the counter. "You scared the life out of me."

"Sorry." He looked around. "Where's Jake?"

"He had a dental appointment, so he could only work half a day."

Dan crossed the room and stopped in front of her. In silence, his gaze roamed her upturned face. Then his big hand curved around the side of her neck, his thumb beneath her chin, fingers tunneling under the fall of dark hair as he lowered his mouth to hers. The kiss was soft and hot and hungry, his lips rocking over hers with a slow, sweet passion. Beneath his hand, Dan felt the quiver that ran through Kathryn, felt the throbbing beat of her pulse that so exactly matched his own.

When the kiss ended their lips clung, parting slowly. He raised his head, his hazel eyes intent and filled with male satisfaction as he studied her dazed expression. He rubbed his thumb back and forth across her chin and smiled when her lips trembled. "I missed you," he whispered.

"I missed you, too," Kathryn managed in a breathless little voice.

He bent to kiss her again, then stopped and drew back, a rueful smile kicking up one corner of his mouth as he glanced down at his soiled chambray work shirt. "As enjoyable as this is, I think I'd better hit the shower. I'm not exactly socially acceptable at the moment." He touched her cheek with his forefinger and winked. "I'll be right back."

Kathryn leaned against the sink and watched him go, her heart in her eyes. She would not have cared had he been covered in mud; he looked wonderful to her.

With trembling fingers she touched her lips. The last time they had spoken he had been angry, but there had been nothing angry about that kiss. Hope burgeoned inside Kathryn, thrusting up within her breast with the fragile insistence of a flower unfolding. Surely, *surely,* he couldn't kiss her that way unless he was beginning to love her. Just a little.

A short while later Dan returned, bringing with him the fresh, woodsy scent of the soap he used, and when Kathryn turned to greet him her throat went dry. He was barefoot and wearing a pair of snug jeans. He had pulled on a shirt but neglected to tuck it in or button it, and it hung loose and open. His hair was wet, the tawny strands darkened to brown and hanging in soft tendrils across his forehead. Moisture beaded the mat of gold curls that covered his chest and arrowed downward to swirl around his navel and disappear beneath the low-slung waistband of the faded jeans. He looked big and bold and impossibly virile.

With an effort, Kathryn dragged her gaze away from his body and found that he was watching her intently. She squirmed and fluttered a hand toward the table. "Would you, uh…would you like some lunch?"

"Yes. I'm starving." His unwavering gaze remained fixed on her.

"Would you like a sandwich?"

"No."

"Then how about some soup? I made some yesterday." She stepped toward the refrigerator, reaching for the handle. "It won't take but a minute to warm it."

"No."

"Oh." Kathryn stopped and blinked at his flat refusal, then brightened. "I know, how about a salad?"

"No."

"Then what do you want?" she demanded with faint exasperation.

Dan moved toward her with that slow, sexy, loose-limbed saunter, his bare feet silent against the tile floor, and Kathryn's heart began to thump as she watched his eyes grow heavy-lidded and hot. He stopped in front of her and smiled. In a low, dark voice that vibrated with need and sent fire streaking through her, he said, "I want you."

Chapter 5

Much later, they lay in the jumbled bed, luxuriating in the quiet aftermath. Even with their passion spent, Dan kept her beneath him, their intimate embrace unbroken. A feeling of utter contentment filled Kathryn as she gazed dreamily at the ceiling and stroked his back. Outside, the November day was gray and cold. A fine mist was falling, like a gossamer veil, giving the bleak winter landscape the look of an impressionistic painting. In the shadowy room Kathryn felt warm and secure, wrapped in Dan's arms. She loved the feel of his skin against hers, the heavy weight of him crushing her into the mattress. Over the years, when she had dreamed of them together, it had been like this— a storm of passion, then this lovely, quiet closeness, a blending of souls. For the moment she almost felt loved.

Dan nuzzled her neck, inhaling the sweet fragrance of her skin, her hair. "Kath?" he murmured as he mouthed her earlobe.

"Hmm?"

"About the other night...I'm sorry."

Her hands stopped their absent rotation, then started up again. "That's okay. You were right."

"No. No, I wasn't. You were just doing what I'd told you to do. My only excuse for being such a sorehead is that I was beat and out of sorts. Forgive me?"

"Of course." There was a smile in her voice, and her arms

tightened around his back. Though briefly she wondered if the exquisite loving they had just shared had simply been an apology, she quickly thrust the thought away. Even if it were true it wouldn't matter, she admitted to herself with a touch of sadness; she would always forgive him anything—everything—so deep and abiding was her love for him.

"Mmm, my sweet Kath," Dan murmured sleepily as he slid lower. With lazy satisfaction, he kissed her nipples and cupped his hands around her breasts before settling his head against her soft flesh.

A moment later he fell asleep, his moist breath eddying against her skin, warming it. Kathryn sifted her hands through his tawny hair, ran them over his strong back and shoulders, traced a thick silky eyebrow with her forefinger, relishing the freedom to touch him, hold him close. In the peaceful quiet of the dim afternoon she felt happy and cosseted, and after a while she, too, slept.

Over an hour later, Kathryn awoke. She blinked at the clock on the bedside table and gave a startled cry, her eyes growing round with panic.

"Dan! Dan, wake up!" she said, shaking his shoulder. "The children will be home from school any minute."

He raised his head and gave her a crooked grin, his sleepy, sexy smile teasing. "There's no need to panic, Kath. The kids know we sleep together."

"Dan!"

She shoved harder and squirmed from beneath him. As she pawed through the jumble of clothing scattered on the floor, she glanced back at the bed and blushed when she discovered him eyeing her nakedness with possessive satisfaction, a lascivious, purely male gleam in his eyes.

"Dan, will you *hurry!*" Kathryn admonished as she scrambled into her clothes and swiped at her tangled hair with a brush.

Finally, chuckling, he climbed from the bed.

They'd barely made it to the landing when Carla burst through the front door. It hit the wall with a crash as the girl ran for the stairs, sobbing as though her heart would break.

"What the devil—" Dan loped down to meet her, with Kathryn at his heels, but they might as well have been invisible. The distraught girl took the steps two at a time and passed them without a glance, heading for her room.

The two adults exchanged bewildered glances, and at the same time Susan and Joey ambled in through the open door.

Joey's face lit up at the sight of them. "Hi, Mommie! Daddy!" he called with innocent enthusiasm.

After glancing at her sister's retreating form, Susan looked at her father and stepmother, grimaced, rolled her eyes and shut the door behind them.

"What's wrong with Carla?" Dan demanded.

"I think she's crying over some dumb boy," the younger girl said with patent disgust.

"Yeah," Joey agreed. He hooked his satchel over the newel post and took off for the kitchen at a run, calling over his shoulder, "She's silly!"

"Oh, Lord. I should have known," Dan muttered. He heaved a sigh, then turned to Kathryn and smiled tightly. "Well, honey," he announced, sweeping his hand toward his daughter's room with a flourish. "She's all yours."

"Oh, but—"

"No, no. You wanted to deal with Carla's problems your way, so here's your chance. But don't worry. I guarantee you'll handle this situation better than I could."

Kathryn had serious doubts on that score. In the two weeks since the wedding her relationship with Carla had not improved one iota. Still…she had made an issue of accepting her share of the responsibility, so she had to at least try.

As she drew near Carla's room the heartrending sounds coming from inside banished Kathryn's reluctance. When her tap on the door brought no response she opened it partway and stuck her head inside. "Carla? May I come in?"

"G-go…a-away. J-just…go away," Carla wailed between broken sobs.

But one glimpse of those heaving shoulders made that impossible for Kathryn. Carla lay huddled on her side in the middle of her bed, her body drawn up in a tight ball, a clenched fist jammed against her mouth. Anguish contorted her features, and her cheeks were slick with tears. Beneath her head they formed a dark blotch on the aqua bedspread.

Kathryn sat down on the bed and touched Carla's shoulder, but the girl flinched away. "Leave m-me alone!"

"Carla, won't you tell me what's wrong?" Kathryn asked gently. "I'd like to help you if I can."

"No one can help me. N-no one! I'm...f-fat and...and ugly... a-and no boy is...e-ever going to notice m-m-me."

The statement brought on another burst of tears, and Kathryn let her cry it out. When the sobs finally abated she said quietly, "I'm sorry you feel that way, but you're wrong, you know."

Carla gave her a sullen glare and swiped at her nose with the back of her hand. "Oh, yeah, sure," she sneered, though her attempt at belligerence was spoiled by the pathetic quiver of her chin.

"I mean it. You're a bit overweight, yes, but that's not an irreversible problem."

"H-how would you know?" Carla demanded resentfully. "You're as s-slender as a model."

"Only because I eat right and exercise." Kathryn reached out and touched a pale curl at Carla's temple. "You have lovely hair and a pretty face. If you lost weight, maybe got a new hairstyle, you'd be every bit as pretty as your mother was."

Carla sucked in a quavering breath and eyed her suspiciously. "You...you thought my mother was pretty?"

"Very. And you can be, too. If you're willing to make the effort, I'll help you with your diet. I'll even exercise with you."

"Why?" Sitting up, Carla scrubbed her cheeks with the backs of her hands and swiped at her nose again. "Why would you do that?"

"Several reasons." Kathryn rose and crossed the room. "Regardless of what you think, I like you. And I'd like for us to be friends." She snatched a wad of tissues from the box on the dresser, walked back and handed it to Carla. "But most of all, I want you to be happy with yourself."

"And you really think it will make a difference?"

"Yes, I do. But I'm warning you, dieting won't be easy, especially with the holidays coming up, because I don't intend to stint on the goodies I make for the rest of the family. It's going to take a lot of willpower and hard work, but if you're willing to give it a try, I'll help you all I can. Okay?''

Carla plucked at a bump in the nubby bedspread and stared at it, her expression sulky. Finally, she dabbed at her swollen eyes and gave a bored shrug. "Sure. Why not?''

The next few weeks were busy, frantic, exhausting...and the happiest of Kathryn's life. Rising an hour earlier than usual, she dragged a sleepy Carla from her bed and took her jogging, each day gradually increasing the distance they covered. Then it was home to make breakfast. About the time everyone was leaving for work and school, Jake arrived, and after getting him started on the current project, Kathryn spent the remainder of each morning at the shop.

Because of the remodeling mess, they had Thanksgiving at Kathryn's house. Carried away by the holiday spirit and the special joy of having a family, she invited not only Dan's parents but also his brother and his family and assorted aunts, uncles and cousins to share the feast. Then she panicked at the thought of feeding so many and spent every afternoon for a week prior to the holiday frantically cooking.

''Good grief, Kath,'' Dan complained in amused exasperation when he dropped by the house one afternoon and found her baking yet another batch of pies. "You're not feeding an army, you know.''

But to Kathryn, thirty people was an army, and at the last minute she decided to bake a ham as well as a turkey. Just in case.

They ended up freezing half the enormous spread, but everyone seemed to enjoy the meal, even Carla, for whom Kathryn had cooked special low-calorie dishes.

Afterward, the men groaned their accolades, then, rubbing full stomachs, gravitated toward the den to watch football on television. The women exchanged recipes and gossip as they tackled the cleanup, while small squealing children darted among them, playing games only they understood. Susan and two cousins her age commandeered Kathryn's old room for a game of Monopoly.

Teenagers gathered in the living room to listen to music. For the first time in Kathryn's memory the rambling old house rang with voices and laughter. Life.

The boisterous Westwood clan gathered Kathryn into their midst with the ease and firmness of a mother hen tucking a stray chick under her wing. By the time they all left she was bone tired but gratified beyond measure, and when Dan hugged her close against his side and said, "You did great, Kath," she felt so ridiculously happy that tears sprang into her eyes.

The Christmas shopping season started in earnest the day after Thanksgiving. That meant Kathryn had to put in more hours at the shop, but she always made it a point to be home when the children got back from school, even if it meant returning to work later, in which case she always took Joey, and sometimes Susan, with her. After a while Carla began coming along, too.

If Kathryn showed enthusiasm for Thanksgiving, she pulled out all the stops for Christmas. She was determined that this first Christmas with her new family was going to be as beautiful and as perfect as she could make it.

She bought dozens of gifts, giving each a lot of thought, wrapping them with care and hiding them away in the attic as soon as she brought them home. She sent out Christmas cards to everyone they knew, thrilling each time she signed her name along with Dan's and the children's.

Kathryn drew the children into the festivities by enlisting their help for a marathon of baking. She put Joey to work shelling nuts and snipping candied fruit and taught Carla and Susan to measure, mix and stir. Together they made Christmas cookies, which the children cut out and decorated themselves, popcorn balls, pumpkin bread, pies and more than a dozen fruitcakes, which they wrapped in brandy-soaked cheesecloth and packed in tins to be given to friends and family.

She worked like a demon to get the house ready for Christmas. A search of the attic turned up a treasure trove of decorations and ornaments, to which Kathryn added the best from her own collection. She hung a huge wreath on the front door, strung colored lights in the shrubs in the front yard and evergreen and holly garlands from the banisters. The scent of bayberry candles filled the house, mistletoe hung over every doorway, and the Nativity scene Susan had made in art class occupied the mantel. In between, Kathryn helped with homework, put on a Christmas party for Susan's class, nursed Joey through a cold and attended aerobics class with Carla two evenings a week.

Though she was bone weary most of the time, it seemed to Kathryn that the closer Christmas loomed, the more things improved at home. Joey, though he was still affectionate, grew secure enough that he no longer clung to her like a limpet, nor did he suck his thumb or whine. He was a happy child and the joy of her life.

Susan spent less and less time holed up in her room and more with the family, often chattering freely to Kathryn as they worked in the kitchen.

The hectic pace of the holidays kept Kathryn from seeing much of Dan, but her nights were spent blissfully wrapped in his arms. Though she cautioned herself against wishful thinking, it seemed to her that his lovemaking became more intense, more ardent, by the day, and a small flicker of hope burned inside her like an eternal flame.

Even Carla was coming around.

To her credit, she stuck to the diet and the rigid routine of jogging and aerobics Kathryn had instigated, and in the first month she lost seventeen pounds and two dress sizes.

To celebrate, Kathryn took her to the shop and told her to select any outfit she wanted.

"You mean it?" Carla squealed, darting from one rack of clothes to another.

"Yes I mean it," Kathryn said, laughing.

Carla tried on one outfit after another, and while Kathryn waited for her to make a choice she helped wait on customers. By the time they left the shop she was so tired that she suggested they stop by the City Café for hot chocolate.

Carla looked at her sharply. "Are you feeling bad again?"

"Just a bit woozy, that's all."

"That's what you said yesterday when we went to aerobics. And this morning you were dizzy while we were jogging."

"I'm just tired." At Carla's skeptical expression she said,

"Look, it's nothing. But if it'll make you feel better, as soon as we have some hot chocolate we'll buy a Christmas tree and go home. Okay?"

"We could go home now. Dad and I can come back for the tree."

"Are you kidding?" The bell over the door of the City Café tinkled as she took Carla's elbow and shepherded her inside. "Let a man pick out a Christmas tree? Never!" They settled into a booth in the corner. As Kathryn stripped off her gloves she leaned across the Formica table and whispered in a confiding tone, "Sweetheart, it takes a woman's discerning eye to handle these things. Let a man pick out a tree, and every time he'll come dragging in a monstrosity that's flat on one side, has gaps you couldn't fill with an ornament the side of a basketball and is so tall it overshoots the ceiling by four feet."

Amusement danced in Carla's brown eyes, and the corners of her mouth twitched. "That sounds like the one we had last year."

"Which, no doubt, your father picked."

"Uh-huh," Carla confirmed, and promptly burst out laughing. "Oh, Kathryn, you should have seen it. It was *awful*."

"Well, don't worry. As soon as we've had our chocolate you and I will go over to Floyd Tully's lot and pick out a beautiful tree."

Five minutes later, as they were sipping their warm drinks and discussing where to put the tree, a man stopped beside the booth.

"Hello, Kathryn," he said, and she looked up, a pleased smile lighting her eyes.

"Greg! How nice to see you." She scooted over and patted the padded bench beside her. "Won't you join us?"

Carla scowled as he slid onto the seat.

"I'm sure you know Mr. Richards, Carla," Kathryn said. "He's the new football coach at your school. Greg, this is Carla Westwood, my stepdaughter."

Greg acknowledged the introduction with a smile and a polite, "Hello. It's nice to meet you," to which Carla mumbled a barely civil reply.

Ignoring the sullen girl, Greg turned to Kathryn. "I was surprised to hear that you had married," he said softly. Unspoken, but clear all the same, were the additional words, *especially since you turned me down.* It was there in his hurt look, in the hint of accusation in his voice.

Regret and pity created a heaviness in Kathryn's chest, but she refused to feel guilty. She had told him from the beginning that she didn't want to get serious. To start with, he was too young for her. But Greg had not heeded her warning, and when he'd proposed she'd had to explain that she didn't love him, would never love him in the way he wanted. He was a nice man, good-looking, pleasant. But he wasn't Dan.

"It happened very suddenly," she said with a gentle smile.

His sad eyes searched hers. "Are you happy, Kathryn?"

Kathryn sighed. She was beginning to regret asking him to join them. She stole a glance at Carla and saw that the girl was glaring daggers. "Yes. I'm very happy," she assured him and steered the conversation onto safer ground.

They talked about inconsequential things for several minutes, until Greg noticed their empty cups.

"Here, let me buy you both another round." He started to raise his hand to signal the waitress but Kathryn stopped him.

"No, really. We must be going. Carla and I have to stop and buy a Christmas tree before we go home."

They slid out of the booth, and Greg held Kathryn's coat as she slipped her arms into it. "That sounds like fun. Why don't I come along with you? I can carry it to your car for you."

She was about to refuse when Carla jumped in.

"Floyd will do that. Besides, picking out Christmas trees is a job for women. C'mon, Kathryn. Let's go." She threw Greg another challenging glare. "My Dad's probably waiting at home. He worries when Kathryn's late coming home."

Why, she's warning him off! Kathryn realized as she stared at the girl's black scowl and aggressive stance. She was both stunned and warmed…and a bit amused at the display of jealousy and possessiveness.

Reading the signs of imminent eruption in Carla's eyes, Kathryn excused them as quickly as possible and, with an arm around her shoulders, guided the girl from the café.

* * *

Dan wasn't home when they arrived, and Kathryn was too weary to drag the tree into the house, so they left it in the garage, propped in a corner, the trunk in a pail of water. When she went upstairs to change clothes before dinner she sat down on the edge of the bed to remove her shoes and gave in to the temptation to lay her head on the pillow for just a minute.

The next thing she knew Dan was bending over her, unbuttoning her blouse.

"Wha-what? What is it?"

"Shh. Lie still," he said, going to work on the waistband of her slacks. "You fell asleep with your clothes on. I'm trying to make you more comfortable."

"What time is it? Oh, my Lord!" she exclaimed when she glanced at the clock. "Look at the time! And I haven't even started dinner!" She struggled to sit up, but her puny strength was no match for Dan, and he pushed her back down.

"Don't worry about it. Carla's making soup and sandwiches." He finished undressing her, slipped a gown over her head and tucked her beneath the covers. Kathryn was too exhausted to even protest. He sat down beside her and tenderly caressed her cheek with the backs of his knuckles. "She tells me you haven't been feeling well for a couple of days now."

"No, no. I'm fine. Just a bit tired."

"You're overdoing it, Kath. Pushing yourself too hard. You don't have to be supermom, you know."

"Dan, I'm okay. Really."

He studied her in silence, then bent and kissed her forehead. "All right, then, you rest while I go get you something to eat. I'll be right back."

"Okay," Kathryn agreed, giving in to the awful lethargy. With a sigh, she allowed her heavy eyelids to drift shut and snuggled her cheek into the pillow.

When she next opened her eyes sunlight was pouring in through the curtains at the window. Amazement and guilt were her first reactions. Kathryn couldn't believe that she'd left Dan and the kids to fend for themselves, or that she'd slept like a stone for over twelve straight hours. Even so, she still felt exhausted. It was all she could do to crawl from the bed and dress for work.

"You can't be coming down with something, Kathryn," she told her pale reflection in the mirror as she applied extra blusher to her cheeks. "Not five days before Christmas!"

Fearful that she was doing just that, Kathryn wheedled her way in to see the doctor that afternoon. She hoped he would tell her that the problem was a simple one and that he could give her something to at least stave off the malady for a few days. Instead, his diagnosis knocked her for a loop.

"Pregnant?" Dazed, Kathryn stared across the desk at Dr. Fisher's kindly face, her mouth hanging open. Her heart was booming, and her body tingled all over. "I'm really pregnant?"

Chapter 6

Kathryn sat glassy-eyed through Dr. Fisher's lecture on prenatal care and the precautions recommended for a first-time mother of her age, taking in only bits and pieces. When he finished she accepted his congratulations and the prescription for vitamins, made an appointment for the following month and walked out like a robot.

She didn't remember driving home, but fifteen minutes later she was turning into the driveway. By then, however, the numbness was beginning to give way to excitement and burgeoning joy. Kathryn parked the car in the garage, but when she shut off the engine she simply sat there, gripping the steering wheel with both hands.

A baby. A child of her own. She couldn't believe it. She was forty years old and had long ago given up hope of ever becoming a mother. And now…Kathryn placed her palm against her flat stomach. Her throat ached. Her nose burned. She was going to have a baby! Dan's baby.

Overcome, she closed her eyes against the sting of tears and pressed her quivering lips together.

But a moment later she scrambled from the car and dashed through the freezing cold toward the back door, so excited that she was halfway across the yard before she realized it was snowing. She stopped and raised her face. Icy crystals stuck to her lashes and melted on her skin. She caught one on the tip of her tongue and laughed, her heart as light as the feathery flakes that drifted down from the leaden sky.

Dan was not in the best of moods. He stared straight ahead through the falling snow, his jaw clenched. The steady *thump-thump* of the wipers brushing aside the accumulating flakes seemed magnified in the silence.

From the corner of his eye he saw his father take out his pipe and fill it. Since retiring two years before, the elder Westwood occasionally went along on calls just to get out of the house. Dan didn't mind; he enjoyed the company and often welcomed an extra pair of hands to help with a fractious animal. But today he almost wished his father had not come along.

They hadn't spoken a word since leaving the Mason farm, but Dan knew they were both thinking about the same thing.

Damn the woman! In a town the size of Boley very little went unnoticed, and discussing other people's business was the favorite pastime, but Clodine Mason was the biggest gossip of all. They had barely stepped down from the pickup when she sidled up, clapped Dan on the back and—with great delight, it seemed—informed him and everyone within earshot that Kath and Greg Richards had met for a cozy discussion at the café the previous evening.

"Saw 'em myself," she'd bellowed in that foghorn voice of hers. "Sittin' side by side in one of them booths with their heads together." She'd poked him in the ribs then and cackled gleefully, "You'd better watch it, Dan. That there's a mighty good-lookin' young fella, and he's been sweet on Kathryn ever since he hit town. And from the looks he was givin' her, he ain't give up yet."

Malicious old busybody, Dan thought as he reached out and turned on the radio. The country-western lament about cheating love that poured from the speakers made him grind his teeth, and he snapped the radio off, giving the knob a furious twist.

"I heard talk that he asked her to marry him," Charles said out of the blue.

Dan shot his father a hard look. "Who? What are you talking about?"

"Richards. I heard he proposed to Kathryn."

"That's ridiculous. He must be five years younger than Kath."

"Seven. But what's that got to do with anything? Kathryn is a wonderful woman. Anyway, she obviously turned him down." Charles puffed thoughtfully on his pipe for a few seconds, then added, "Of course, that doesn't mean he's stopped loving her."

Dan scowled. He trusted Kath completely. If she'd had coffee with Richards, he knew it had been perfectly innocent. But he didn't like the idea of a man—any man—mooning around after his wife. Kath was *his,* dammit!

After dropping his father off, Dan headed the pickup toward home. Two miles from the house the left front tire blew out, and when he got out the spare it was flat, too. By the time he hitched a ride back into town, bought another tire and hitched a ride back, it was dark and snowing harder. He scraped three knuckles and nearly froze to death putting the new tire on the truck, and when he finally climbed back inside and started for home again, his dark mood had worsened.

Kathryn was wound as tight as a spring by the time Dan arrived. When his mother had dropped the children off she'd been tempted to blurt out her news, but she wanted to tell Dan first. The hours of waiting for him to come home had seemed interminable.

She met him at the back door, her face alight with eagerness. "Dan, we have to talk. I—"

"Not now, Kath," he snapped, tossing his coat over the back of a kitchen chair.

"Dan, I have something to—"

"I said, not now." He strode past her and pushed through the swinging door. On the other side he bumped into a sawhorse sitting in the middle of the hall and cursed fluently. "What the devil is this doing here? Don't tell me Jake isn't finished yet."

"He promised me he would be tomorrow. He only has a few little things left to do."

"Where are the kids?"

"Susan and Joey are watching TV, and Carla went to a matinee with Julie Crenshaw. Mrs. Crenshaw will bring her home," she told him quickly. "But, Dan, listen to me. There's something—"

At that moment, Carla stormed in and slammed the door. She raced for the stairs, her distraught face blotchy and streaked with tears.

Concern for the girl wiped every other thought from Kathryn's mind, and she stepped toward her, her hands outstretched. "Carla, darling, what is it? What's wrong?"

Carla stopped with one foot on the bottom stair and glared. "I starved for weeks and did all that exercising just so Jason would like me, but he hasn't even noticed. And today he was at the movie with another girl," she wailed. "All your so-called advice was worthless! I hate you!"

"Carla, dear, listen to—"

"No! I won't!"

"All right, that's enough! Quiet! Both of you!"

Kathryn jumped at Dan's angry shout. Carla turned reproachful eyes on him, let out an anguished cry and raced up the stairs, her feet pounding the treads like hammerblows.

"Dammit!" Dan thundered. "I don't know where I ever got the idea that marriage to you would solve anything." He swung on Kathryn, glaring fiercely, and flung his arm out in a sweeping arc. "You promptly tore apart my house. My daughter bawls more than ever. Hell, I've hardly had a moment's peace since you moved in."

Kathryn was too stunned and hurt to reply, and after a moment he made an aggravated sound and took the stairs three a time.

Squeezing her eyes shut, Kathryn stood rooted to the spot, rigid, as though afraid she would shatter at the slightest movement. She listened to his footsteps recede along the upstairs hall, heard the bedroom door bang with an awful sound of finality. Inside she quivered with pain and utter desolation. She had been such a fool. Such a hopeless, romantic fool. Despair welled up inside her, so intense it wrung a silent cry of agony from her soul, and in an unconscious, protective gesture, she hunched her shoulders and folded her arms over her abdomen. Her chin trembled and her throat worked as she fought to hold back tears. One after another they seeped through her tightly closed eyelids and trickled down her cheeks.

"Mommie, Mommie! Come watch TV with us," Joey called from the living room. "They're gonna show 'The Grinch That Stole Christmas'!"

Kathryn's eyes snapped open and darted around. She had to get out of there! She couldn't cope with the children right now. She had to be alone.

Panicked, she snatched her coat from the hall closet and ran. Thrusting her arms into the garment, she grabbed the car keys from the peg beside the back door and raced out into a world of blackness and blowing snow.

In less than a minute she was speeding away, with no thought to where she was headed or the worsening weather conditions. All she could think of was the mess she'd made of everything. You were a fool to be happy about this baby, she told herself scathingly. Dan married you to help raise the children he has, not saddle him with more. And face it, you're not doing a very good job of that.

It occurred to her that he might not even have intended for the marriage to last forever but only until the children were grown and gone. In which case he'll probably be horrified to learn about the baby and that he's inextricably tied to you. And the kids will probably hate the idea, resent the baby. Tears blurred her vision, and she swiped at them impatiently with the back of her hand as she leaned forward to peer through the swirling clouds of white. Oh, Lord, Kathryn, why don't you face it? You don't belong in this family. You're nothing but an intruder. And you're a complete failure as a wife and mother.

It was the last semicoherent thought she had, for at that instant the car hit a patch of ice, slid sideways and nose-dived into a ditch. Kathryn's instinctive scream ended with startling quickness as the world suddenly went black.

Dan's temper cooled before he finished his shower, and when he thought about the things he'd said to Kathryn, guilt and remorse riddled him. "God, what a dumbass you are, Westwood," he muttered to himself as he hurriedly dressed and went in search of her. "Kath doesn't deserve that kind of treatment."

She wasn't in Carla's room, as he had half expected. When he didn't find her downstairs he stopped at the door to the living room, where Susan and Joey were sprawled on the floor watching television. "Does anyone know where Kathryn is?"

Susan spared him a distracted glance. "She may have gone out. I thought I heard the back door slam a few minutes ago."

Out? A chill of unease gripped Dan as he headed for the kitchen. When he saw that her keys were missing from the peg beside the door, his gaze went to the swirl of white beyond the window, and his uneasiness became real fear.

He darted back down the hall, shouted up the stairs for Carla to look after her brother and sister, then took off, grabbing his coat on the way out.

Less than a quarter of a mile from the house he spotted the rear end of Kathryn's car jutting up out of the ditch. Dan's heart lurched. He slammed on the brakes, threw the gearshift into park and bolted from the pickup almost before it stopped rolling.

He leaped into the ditch and tore open the car door. Fear clawed at him when he saw she was slumped over the steering wheel. "Kath. Oh, Kath, sweetheart. I'm sorry. I'm so sorry," he murmured over and over as he frantically searched for a pulse. His relief was so great when he found one that he almost sagged to his knees.

Quickly, he ran his hands over her. There was a bump on her head and the sticky wetness of blood on her temple, but there didn't appear to be any broken bones. As carefully as possible, he pulled her from the car. With her limp body cradled against his chest, he staggered up out of the ditch and carried her to the idling pickup.

An hour later, Dan was counting endless minutes in the hospital waiting room. He sat on a vinyl-covered bench, leaning forward with his elbows resting on his knees, his hands clasped in a fisted prayer. *Oh, God, please let her be all right. Please.*

In that first instant when he'd seen her car sticking up obscenely from that ditch, it had hit him that he loved Kathryn.

More than he had ever loved anything or anyone in his life. If he lost her now, he didn't know how he would bear it.

The casual, undemanding love he'd always felt for Kathryn had deepened and grown into something vital and all-consuming without his knowing quite how or when, though he suspected it had begun long before he'd asked her to marry him.

The sound of footsteps brought his head up. Dan was hoping it would be the doctor, but he wasn't surprised when his father sat down beside him on the bench. He had called his parents the moment the attendants wheeled Kathryn away.

Charles Westwood put a hand on his son's shoulder. "How is she?"

Dan shook his head, his eyes bleak. "There's been no word yet."

"I took your mother over to stay with the children. She said to tell you not to worry and to call her the minute we know something."

"Thanks."

Propping his elbows on his spread knees, Charles assumed the same posture as his son. "So what happened?"

"I yelled at her. Blew up because I was tired and angry—"

"And jealous."

Dan turned his head and met his father's steady gaze. His mouth twisted. "And jealous. And like a fool, I let fly at Kath. I shouldn't have, I know, but...dammit, Dad, I just don't understand. Lots of husbands get angry and say things they don't mean without their wives running off into a snowstorm."

"Maybe so." Charles filled his pipe from a leather pouch and tamped down the aromatic tobacco with his thumb. "But then, most wives have the security of knowing that they're loved."

Dan's skin paled even more, and he hung his head. "And I've never said those words to Kath," he murmured guiltily. He wondered if he would ever get the chance, now.

Dr. Fisher appeared in the doorway, and Dan lurched to his feet. "How is she? Will she be all right?"

"Calm down, Dan. She has a nasty bump on her head and a colorful assortment of bruises, but nothing a few days' rest won't cure."

"Thank God." Dan closed his eyes and released a long breath as a shudder rippled through him.

"And equally important," Dr. Fisher continued, "no harm came to the baby."

"Baby?" At first Dan looked confused; then his eyes widened, and his face went comically slack. His knees buckled, and he dropped down hard onto the bench.

"Well, I'll be!" his father whooped, thumping him on the back, but Dan paid no attention.

"Kathryn's pregnant?"

"Yes. Six weeks. She didn't tell you?"

"No, she—" He stopped, remembering her eagerness when she'd met him at the back door.

Dan, we have to talk.

"Oh, God." His expression stricken, he slapped his forehead and slid his hand down over his face wearily. "No. No, she didn't tell me," he said in a voice weighted with self-recrimination. Then his head jerked up, his eyes filled with sudden panic. "Is she all right? I mean, at her age, is it safe?"

"She's fine," Dr. Fisher assured him. "Naturally, we'll take all necessary precautions and monitor her closely, but Kathryn should breeze through this with no problems." He gave his best benign smile. "She's going to be a wonderful mother."

"She *is* a wonderful mother," Dan replied staunchly, and his father's hand tightened on his shoulder in silent approval.

When Dan was finally allowed into Kathryn's room, his heart reeled at the sight of her, so small and still in the hospital bed. She lay with her eyes closed, her hands folded over her abdomen atop the covers. A bandage covered most of her forehead. Her hair seemed darker against the pillow, its sterile whiteness almost matching her pale face.

Dan swallowed hard, love swelling in his chest as he stared at her. With an unsteady hand, he reached out and tenderly stroked her cheek.

Kathryn's eyes fluttered open. "D-Dan."

Gently, he slipped his hand beneath one of hers and brought it to his mouth. He kissed each fingertip and pressed his lips to the center of her palm. Kathryn watched him, bewilderment in her eyes, but when she opened her mouth to speak Dan placed two fingers against her lips.

"Shh. Before you say anything, there's something I have to tell you." He pressed her hand to his cheek. "I love you, Kath," he said softly. "I love you more than anything in this world. More than life itself."

The astounding statement seemed to set off an explosion in the region of Kathryn's heart, and she caught her breath, her eyes widening.

"I should have told you before this," Dan continued as she stared at him in wonder. "But, fool that I am, I didn't realize it myself until I thought I had lost you."

Two diamond-bright tears welled up in Kathryn's eyes and spilled over. "Oh, Dan," she managed in a small choked voice that quavered with emotion. "Do you really mean that?"

"I mean it."

"Oh, Dan." Her chin wobbled, and more tears followed, streaming down her cheeks, unheeded. She lifted her other hand and framed his face between her trembling palms. "I love you, too," she declared tearfully. "So very much. I always have."

Dan bent over and kissed her with such tenderness that Kathryn thought her heart would surely burst. For long, breathless moments his lips caressed hers lovingly, sweetly, while her heart thrummed and the world seemed to spin away.

When at last he raised his head to look at her, his hazel eyes were dark with love and concern. "Forgive me for the things I said, Kath. And for not letting you tell me about the baby."

Alarm flared in her eyes. "You know?"

He nodded. "The doctor told me."

"Do...do you mind very much?"

"I was surprised." He gave a little laugh and shook his head. "No, *surprised* isn't the word; I was stunned." He sat down beside her on the bed and, bending forward, laid his head on her stomach. "But mind? No." He rocked his head against her, and she felt him smile. "Knowing that you're having my baby is the best Christmas present I've ever received." He slid his hand up over her rib cage to cup her breast. "And you? How do you feel about it? Do you mind? Are you worried about having children now?''

Kathryn ran her hands through his hair and smiled, luxuriating in the weight of his head against her, the moist warmth of his breath filtering through the cotton hospital gown, dewing her skin. "I've loved you, wanted you, wanted to have your babies since I was sixteen. How could I be anything but happy?''

Dan raised his head and looked at her, his stunned expression filled with wonder. "Oh, Kath,'' he whispered as he reached out and touched her cheek with his fingertips. "My Kath.''

On Christmas Eve Dan brought Kathryn home. With the second snowfall of the season fluttering around them, he carried her from the car as though she were made of glass.

The instant his footsteps sounded on the porch the front door opened to reveal three anxious faces.

"Mommie! Mommie!'' Joey cried, bouncing up and down as though trying to jump into Kathryn's lap.

"Joey, stop that,'' Carla commanded, dragging him out of the way. "At least let Dad put her down before you pounce on her.'' Taking charge, she led the way to the living room, shooing the other two children ahead as she called over her shoulder, "This way, Dad We have a place all set up for her on the sofa.''

"But close your eyes, Kathryn,'' Susan instructed excitedly. "And don't open them until we tell you.''

"Yeah,'' Joey chimed in. "'Cause we got a surprise for you!''

"Don't peek! Don't peek! Keep 'em closed,'' they all chorused as Dan carried her into the room and set her down.

"I won't. I promise,'' Kathryn said, laughing.

When she was finally settled, there was silence; then Carla said, "Okay. You can look now.''

Slowly, Kathryn opened her eyes, and gasped, joy lighting her face as she looked around. "Oh, kids,'' she whispered in an awed tone. "It's *beautiful!*''

This part of the house was exactly as Kathryn had always pictured it. The new lighter colors opened it up, giving it a fresh look. Gone was the shabby furniture and the heavy old swags of velvet at the windows. In their place were the graceful period pieces from Kathryn's home, and crisp linen draperies in pale blue and eggshell stripes that blended with the blue-and-cream wallpaper and cream-painted woodwork. The Oriental rug that had been her mother's most prized possession was centered on the polished oak floor before the sofa, which faced the fireplace. Flanking it were her father's red leather easy chair and ottoman and two Queen Anne wing chairs in a beige, blue and cream floral print. Visible through the arched entrance to the dining room was her great-grandmother's rosewood Duncan Phyfe table, bearing a centerpiece of thick red candles, pinecones, nuts, berries and greenery.

Five knit stockings hung from the mantel, and there in the corner of the room, twinkling with hundreds of lights and glittering ornaments, with dozens of gaily wrapped presents spilling outward from its base, was the Christmas tree that had been propped in the garage the last time Kathryn had seen it.

For a moment she was too overcome to speak. She looked at the children and found them standing in a tight little group, watching her. "Do you really like it, Kathryn?" Susan ventured doubtfully. "We didn't know where you wanted the furniture, so we can move it if you want us to."

"No. Everything is perfect. Just perfect." Dan sat beside her on the sofa, and she squeezed his hand as she gazed up at them, touched beyond words. "You all did a marvelous job. It's beautiful. All of it."

The children looked at one another and shifted restlessly, still oddly constrained, even Joey. Eyeing Kathryn's bandage, he asked, "Does your bump still hurt, Mommie?"

"It wouldn't if I could have a hug," Kathryn said, holding her arms out to him.

With a muffled little cry, Joey flung himself into her lap and burrowed close.

Then suddenly, to her surprise, the girls knelt on the floor on either side of her knees. "Kathryn," Carla began hesitantly. "We just want you to know that…well…we're glad to have you home. And…and we're real happy about the new baby."

"When it gets here, we're going to help you take care of it,"

Susan said earnestly. "We'll feed it and change it and everything."

"Why, thank you, girls." Kathryn squeezed Carla's hand and smoothed a loose tendril of hair away from Susan's face. "I appreciate that."

"And," Carla added, watching Kathryn cautiously, "since the baby will be our brother or sister, we talked it over and... well...we decided it would be best if we all called you Mom."

Dan's arms tightened around Kathryn's shoulders, but she didn't dare look at him or she would break down and cry. Her chest grew so tight that she could barely breathe, and her lips trembled as she murmured over the lump in her throat, "I would love that. Truly."

As though uncomfortable with the emotion-charged atmosphere, Carla jumped up, announcing as she took off for the kitchen that she had dinner ready and would serve Kathryn's on a tray.

It turned out that they all ate from TV trays in the living room. Afterward, Dan and Kathryn gave in to the children's wheedling and allowed them to open one present apiece. As they tore at the gay ribbons and foil wrappings, Dan pulled Kathryn closer against his side and whispered in her ear, "Merry Christmas, my love."

With her heart in her eyes, she reached up and kissed him softly. "Merry Christmas."

The faint peal of church bells sounded in the distance. Outside, snow fell with silent insistence, piling in drifts about the old house. Inside, a fire crackled in the hearth, and children laughed and bantered, while in the background the soft strains of "O Little Town of Bethlehem" flowed from the stereo.

Her heart overflowing, Kathryn snuggled against Dan's chest and gazed at the tree, but its lights became mere blurry spots of color through the wall of tears banked against her eyelids.

Christmas. It really was the season of miracles.

*   *   *   *   *

HOLIDAY HOMECOMING
Joan Hohl

Dear Reader,

Happy holidays!

Whether written in a card, or called aloud, that greeting always lifts my spirits; the goodwill implied is as warming to me as a hot chocolate drink on a bitter cold night.

The holiday season has always been a special time for me and my family, even when we feel fractured from seemingly running around in different directions, both excited and frantic, certain we won't get everything done. Somehow we always finish in time: the shopping, the wrapping, the decorating, the cleaning (ugh), the preparation of special foods and goodies.

And...speaking of goodies (how's that for a segue?), I'm including herein one of our traditional Christmas cookie recipes. It is one of my particular favorites, and my way of wishing you "Happy holidays."

SAND TARTS

Preheat oven to 375°F.

1 lb butter	*4 cups flour—sifted*
2 cups sugar	*1 tsp baking powder*
3 eggs	*pinch of salt*

Cream butter and sugar. Slowly add eggs, flour, baking powder and salt. Batter will be sticky.

Topping: *1 egg*
cinnamon
chopped walnuts or pecans (optional)

Using a tablespoon, spoon batter into a log shape, about 2 inches in diameter, onto sheets of plastic wrap, leaving space on each side to turn in—I usually get two logs. Turn in ends and roll logs to the end of the wrap.

Place in freezer until log is solid—I generally leave it in overnight.

Remove from freezer, unwrap log and cut into fairly thin slices. Place on ungreased cookie sheet, about 1 1/2 inches apart. Lightly beat one egg and brush over cookie. Sprinkle cinnamon on top. If desired, garnish top with chopped walnuts or pecans.

Bake approximately 10 minutes, or until golden brown around the edges. Cool completely.

There you go, dear friends. I hope you enjoy the cookies, and your holiday...whatever it may be named.

Chapter 1

Snow!

Diana Blair stood entranced outside the narrow four-story office building, by the sign that read Blair & Daughter, Architects, Specializing in Historic Preservation and Interior Design.

When had it begun snowing? she mused, staring in wonder at the swirling white flakes glittering in the soft glow of the turn-of-the-century-style street lamps.

How beautiful, she thought, how like a scene from a Victorian Christmas card. Her mind filled with a sense of wonder as she ran a glance up and down the narrow street, taking in the tall, stately buildings that lined it. Her father, Henry, and then Diana in company with him, had restored most of the buildings to their original splendor, as they had many of the other businesses— and many of the private homes—in the small city of Riverview. And yet, for all the familiarity of the scene, at the first snowfall of the season, Di always experienced the same sense of surprised wonder.

Di had reached the conclusion years ago that her ever-renewed delight in the wintry scene could be attributed more to the city than to the snow itself.

Situated along the Schuylkill River, less than an hour's drive from the modern and bustling city of Philadelphia, Riverview had been named a national historic site. The entire city had a special ambience, the look and feel of a time gone by. The dedicated citizens of Riverview worked hard at maintaining the quaint and unique appearance of the city.

Diana loved her hometown at all times, particularly during the holiday season, and most especially when it snowed.

The last time Di had glanced through one of the office windows, around noon, watery, cloud-filtered sunlight had illuminated the mid-December day. Now, nearing seven-thirty in the evening, large snowflakes pirouetted before capricious gusts of stinging wind.

Perfect, Di thought, quickly surveying the area for witnesses before sticking out her tongue to capture a delicate flake. She laughed to herself as the snow melted on her tongue. A perfect ending to an exciting day.

An exciting day, but a long day, she reflected, judging the depth of the accumulated snow with a measuring stare. About an inch, she decided as she stepped gingerly in her three-inch heels from beneath the awning above the entranceway.

Di's toes were wet before she had traversed half the short distance to the tiny company parking lot situated next to the century-old building.

Once inside her car, Di immediately fired the engine, then flicked on the heater. Warmth began curling around her ankles as she pulled the car off the lot to join the procession crawling along the street.

Simply keeping the car moving in a straight line required all of Di's concentration, but when she inched to a stop at a red light, her thoughts flew back to the phone call she'd received earlier that morning. A smile curved her lips as she recalled the bubbly sound of her stepmother's voice on the other end of the line.

"Oh, Di, it's so wonderful!" Miriam Blair had exclaimed in a gushing rush.

"That's nice," Di had answered, smiling for whatever had infused Miriam with such enthusiasm. "But exactly what is so wonderful?"

"Oh!" Miriam's burst of laughter had held the tinkling sound of a young girl's giggle. "How silly of me. I just had a phone call from your brother—that's what's so wonderful. Now Terry's coming home for Christmas, too.''

Terry. Her baby brother. Di's smile grew into a grin. Terry always claimed to hate it when she referred to him as her baby brother. His claim was a pretense; she knew it, and he knew she knew it.

The light turned to green, and Di slowly moved forward, careful to keep a comfortable distance between her car and the vehicle in front of her.

Of course, Miriam's news was wonderful and exciting—the icing on their Christmas cake, so to speak, coming as it had so soon after hearing that the others would be home for the holidays, as well.

For the first time in years, all the assorted yours, mine and ours—all the members of the Blair and Turner families—would be together for the holidays.

Well, no, not *all* of them, Di reminded herself, reflexively tightening her grip on the steering wheel.

Matt would be noticeably among the missing.

A chill unrelated to the plunging temperature feathered the length of Di's stiffened spine.

Matt.

Thinking of her stepbrother, the eldest child of the combined families—an indulgence Di rarely allowed herself—brought his image to mind, an image undimmed by the nine years since she had last seen him.

Unfortunately for Diana, the love she kept secreted in her heart and soul for him was equally undimmed.

Diana could see Matt, sense him, as if he were seated in the bucket seat beside her. His image was as clear as a sun-spangled summer day, and more biting than the December storm raging outside.

At age twenty-five, Matthew Turner had stood six foot one and a half and had been reed-slim. Matt's shock of jet-black hair—so similar to Di's own as to convince strangers of a blood connection that in fact did not exist—shimmered with a healthy gleam and vitality. His strong, sharply defined facial features were a perfect setting for his cool, remote, incisive-looking gray eyes. Even at such a comparatively early age, Matt had possessed a mature and formidable appearance. And yet, in contrast, offsetting the stern look of him, his white teeth had frequently flashed in a thoroughly engaging smile that gave insight into the devilish facets of his character.

Matt had been a force to be reckoned with for any female. For Diana, the reckoning had come at the impressionable age of four, on the day her father had first brought Matt, along with his mother and younger sister, Bethany, to meet Di and her younger sister, Melissa.

Even at the gangly, cracked-voiced age of twelve, Matt had been a charmer. Giving Diana a secret wink, he had grinned conspiratorially at her and bestowed upon her the nickname Di. She had promptly fallen headlong into a state of absolute adoration for him.

Against her will, Diana recalled those early years after her father and Miriam had joined forces in marriage. Their love for each other had always been obvious, deep, abiding, and wide enough to encompass their respective offspring, knitting the separate units into a whole, creating a loving family. Henry had gained a beloved and trusted son; Miriam had gained two more daughters to fuss over and spoil with caring mothering.

Diana's growing up years had been filled to overflowing. The house had rung with the sounds of laughter, offset only rarely by the discordant sound of tears. And through it all she had remained in a state of adoration for her "big brother," Matt.

It was a state from which Diana knew she would never escape; it had merely shifted and changed from childhood adoration to unqualified love. A forbidden love, a love that had driven Matt away from home and family.

A heartfelt sigh escaped Di's usually rigid guard. Hearing it, the longing sound of it, shook her into full awareness of where she was, what she was supposed to be doing.

Not now! Di ordered her errant consciousness. *Pay attention to the traffic, the weather conditions, your driving.*

The images dissolved, and Di sighed again, this time in sheer relief. It hurt too much to think about him, to stir up memories, to recall that night of sheer madness.

With ruthless determination, Di applied every ounce of mental capacity and every bit of driving skill she possessed to getting the car, and herself, home in one piece.

Miriam was waiting for Diana in the festively decorated foyer of the big old Victorian house. Like nearly every other household in Riverview, the Blair family commenced decking the halls, and every room, the day after Thanksgiving. It had become a tradition in the city, in part because everyone seemed to enjoy getting an early start on the holidays, and in part because of the influx of tourist traffic, which increased yearly.

"I was beginning to worry," Miriam fussed, helping Di out of her coat, then hanging it in the wrap closet off the foyer. "Your father has been home for over two hours. What kept you?"

"I had some work I wanted to finish," Di explained, flexing fingers cramped and stiff from gripping the wheel. "And traffic's moving at a snail's pace."

"Well, at least you're home now, safe and sound," Miriam said on a relieved sigh. "And the snow is so pretty."

"Yes, it is," Di agreed, dry-voiced. "Wet, too."

"So I see." Miriam frowned as she eyed Di's soaked shoes. "You'd better go have a shower and get changed," she ordered. "Are you hungry?"

"Starved," Di admitted, obediently heading for the curving staircase. "Anything left?"

"Really, Diana," Miriam said, in a scolding tone. "We haven't eaten. We were waiting for you."

"That wasn't necessary." Di protested over her shoulder. "But I'm glad you did. Where's Dad?"

"He's on the phone with Terry." Miriam's expression softened, as it always did at the mention of her youngest child's name. "You know your father," she went on, smiling at Diana. "He wanted to know exactly when Terry would be arriving."

"Didn't Terry tell you all that when he called earlier?" Di asked, pausing at the foot of the stairs.

"No, he—" Miriam broke off, making an impatient face. "Diana, you're going to be chilled to the bone if you don't get out of those wet things. Now get moving. We can talk over dinner.''

"I'm going, I'm going," she said, laughing, as she started up the stairs. "Give me twenty minutes."

Seventeen minutes later, warm from a stinging-hot shower, comfortable in soft wool slacks, an oversize sweater and velvet house slippers, Di, with her hair pulled back in a ponytail that made her look more a teenager than a young woman of twenty-six, strolled into the dining room.

"Oh, my great-aunt Matilda," she said, deeply inhaling the aromatic steam rising from the soup tureen set on the long, intricately carved mahogany table. "Whatever that is, it smells absolutely wonderful."

Henry Blair chuckled indulgently and strode over to Di to plant a kiss on her cheek. "Yes, doesn't it?"

"That, my dears, is the latest concoction from our priceless cook," Miriam informed them. "Janet felt creative today, and the soup is the result of her inspiration." She sniffed delicately. "And it does smell delicious."

"So, let's dig in," Di said, circling to her accustomed place at the table. "I'm famished."

The soup lived up to its fragrant promise, and the entrée and the assorted side dishes were equally successful. Conversation was kept to a minimum until coffee and a lemon sponge cake were served.

Declining the cake, Di sighed and relaxed against the needle-point-flowered material covering the padding on the back of the roomy, curved-armed chair. "That was delicious." She smiled pointedly at her father. "And now that I feel like I'll probably survive, are you going to tell me about Terry?"

"That's not all I'm going to tell you." His lips tilted in a secretive smile, his bright eyes reflecting some inner excitement, Henry shifted an expectant glance between his wife and daughter, both of whom were clearly puzzled.

"Henry, what are you up to?" Miriam asked, her own eyes beginning to glow. Miriam always loved a surprise.

"Yes, Dad, what informational bomb are you about to toss at

us?'' Di demanded, not immune herself to an occasional sneak attack of good news.

"In a moment," Henry said, deliberately drawing out the suspense. "But first, Terry's plans. He's booked on a flight into Philly on the twenty-third.''

"Oh, how wonderful!" Miriam exclaimed. "How long can he stay? When must he be back to work?''

"The third of January," Henry answered. "His return flight to Taos is scheduled for late in the afternoon on the second.''

"That is wonderful news," Di concurred with her stepmother. "With Beth and Lissa and Terry all here, it will be like a real family holiday homecoming.''

"More than you know." Henry had a positively enigmatic expression and a smug smile.

"Dad!" Di protested, laughing. "What have you got cooking in that mysterious mind of yours?''

"Enough teasing, Henry," Miriam said in a gently scolding tone. "Tell us.''

Still he hesitated, drawing out the moment of tense anticipation. "It's a very special surprise for all of us," Henry finally relented. "But most especially for you, Miriam," he said, smiling at his wife. "It's going to be a real, complete family gathering this year.''

Leaning forward in their chairs, Miriam and Diana hung on the expectation of his next words. He drew a deep breath and smiled on the exhalation.

"Matt's coming home for Christmas.''

Henry's informational bomb had contained the power of a forty-megaton explosive device. Hours after the blast, Diana was still shivering from reverberating reaction.

The house was quiet. The century-old grandfather clock in the foyer declared the hour of three. Diana lay rigid on her bed, her eyes wide, listening to the deep-throated tolling. Sleep eluded her, banished by shock-activated memories, good and bad.

Matt was coming home for Christmas.

With her mind's eye, Di reviewed the scene in the dining room following her father's announcement.

After an instant's disbelieving silence, Miriam had sprung from her chair. Laughing and weeping, she had rushed to her husband, at the end of the long table. His expression tender with love and understanding, Henry had risen and enfolded her in a gentle embrace.

"Henry, is it true?" she cried on a broken sob. "Matt's really coming home?"

Shell-shocked, feeling the bite of emotional shrapnel, Di remained in her chair, clinging to the stability of the solid wooden armrests, staring at the happy tableau being played out by her father and stepmother.

"Yes, dear, I promise you it is true," Henry assured his wife of twenty-two years. "Matt is coming home."

"But—how?" Miriam sputtered, unmindful of the tears of joy spilling onto her cheeks.

And why now? After all these years spent living outside the country, as far away as he could get from home. Di didn't voice her questions, but continued to sit quietly, certain she'd eventually hear the answers.

"How?" Henry repeated, chuckling. "By plane, of course."

"Henry, really, that's not what I meant, and you know it." Regaining control, Miriam stepped back, out of his arms. Accepting the neatly folded white handkerchief he offered, she dabbed at her eyes before going on. "I spoke to Matt just two days ago, and he didn't say a word, didn't as much as hint that he was thinking of coming home for the holidays." She frowned. "When did he decide to do so?"

Henry's smile held a wealth of self-mockery. "When I called him this afternoon to extend a verbal olive branch."

Miriam stared at him in astonishment. "You called Matt?"

Diana shared her stepmother's amazement; her father had not spoken to his stepson since the night Matt stormed away from his house. Staring at her father, Di waited with bated breath for his response.

"Yes," he answered. "I called him right after you rang me to tell me that Terry was coming." His smile was rueful, and his eyes were gentle on his wife's glowing face. "I decided that since you, my dear, were the one suffering the most for our masculine show of stiff-necked pride, it was time—long past time—to end this dissension between us. Fortunately, Matt agreed.'' He shrugged. ''It's as simple as that.''

Now, hours later, wakeful and restless, Diana decided that there was absolutely nothing simple about it. In fact, she was very much afraid that Matt's return would prove to be very difficult—at least for her, if not for the other assorted members of the family.

Maybe she should arrange to be among the missing this holiday, Di thought, clenching her fingers against the conflicting feelings of anticipation and trepidation waging a battle inside her. Since she was the only family member who had never been away from home during the holidays, she had every right to skip this particular homecoming—didn't she?

Wishful thinking. Diana rolled onto her side and curled into a self-protective ball. She knew full well that her wishful thinking would come to nothing. She wouldn't find, or even look for, somewhere else to spend the holidays. She didn't have it in her to disappoint her father and Miriam in that way. They were so obviously looking forward to having every one of their children with them this year.

The clock standing sentinel in the foyer struck the half hour, telling the silent house that it was 2:30 in the morning of December the sixteenth. And Henry had said that Matt would try to arrange his schedule to make it home in time for Christmas Eve.

One week and two days, Diana thought, panic uncoiling in her stomach.

You can get through it, she told herself, grateful for the sudden weighty tug on her eyelids. You're an adult now, no longer an uncertain teenager. They were all grown-ups—she and Lissa and Beth and Terry and—   He had turned thirty-four last summer.

Had he changed?

Well, of course he had changed.

So had she.

She was a woman, mature, confident.

Diana's rapid-fire thoughts came to an abrupt halt when a

vision of a tall, slender, formidable young man with a wicked smile rose to torment her mind and her senses.

Oh, Matt...

"This is rather sudden, isn't it?"

"Yes." Matt smiled at the woman seated opposite him at the intimate table in the fashionable restaurant. "I decided to fly to the States for the holidays yesterday afternoon, when I spoke to my stepfather."

The woman, who was really quite beautiful, worked her lips into a strained smile. "But I had thought, hoped, that you would accept my invitation to spend the Christmas holidays with me and my family in London."

He very likely would have accepted, Matt silently acknowledged, if not for that astounding call from Henry. Fortunately, Henry's call had come before he accepted Allyson Carruthers's invitation.

"Sorry," he murmured, meaning it, even though he was still feeling euphoric from the unexpected call. "But I couldn't refuse my stepfather's invitation. It has been nine years since I spent the holidays with my family."

Besides that, he added silently, Henry said it was snowing at home.

Home. Matt suppressed a sigh. Where was home? During his self-imposed exile, he had moved around Europe, staying here, then there, calling no one place home, while establishing himself as a management consultant.

Allyson sighed; the sound held a faint but unmistakable tinge of sadness. "When will you return?" Her soft voice, her intonation, indicated her acceptance of the inevitable.

Matt absorbed a flashing sensation of regret; he had never wanted to hurt her, or any of the women he had shared time and intimacy with over the years. His relationships with Allyson and the others had all been open-ended. From the very beginning, by mutual agreement, the parameters had been set for the affairs—first and foremost of which was that there would be no strings attached.

Matt genuinely liked Allyson. She was wealthy, sophisticated, intelligent and amusing; she was also good in bed. But then, Matt reflected, if the endorsements of his partners could be taken into account, so was he.

Come to that, Matt could lay claim to all of Allyson's other attractions, except one—he wasn't quite as wealthy as she, at least not yet. But he was working on it, not only with his consultancy business and various other interests, but also with the flair he had discovered he had for successfully playing the stock market, and he was gaining on her with each new client, each new acquisition, each new market coup.

Not that any of it mattered to Matt. He had arrived at a comfortable position—financially, at any rate. But emotionally? Well...

"Matt?" The gentle nudge in Allyson's voice snagged his distracted attention. "I asked when you would be back."

"Sorry...again. My thoughts were wandering." Matt's smile was self-mocking. "I'm not sure, so I requested an open return flight."

"I see." Her tone now revealed resignation and acceptance. "It's over for us, isn't it?"

Matt could only match her bluntness. "Yes, Allyson, it's over. I'm—"

"Please, don't," she said, interrupting him. "Don't say you're sorry again."

"But I am," he insisted, feeling very much the cad, and hating the feeling. "I never meant to hurt you."

"I know." She shrugged; it didn't quite come off as careless. "If I'm hurt, it's my own fault. I knew your emotions were never engaged." She put a bright smile on her sad face. "But we did have some good times together, didn't we?"

"No." Matt shook his head. "We had some wonderful times together."

"Thank you for that." Allyson's voice betrayed the emotion gathering in her throat. "You were—are—a gentleman, Matt." She smiled. "A gentleman and, as they say in your country, a straight shooter."

Matt laughed through the stab of remorse he was experiencing. He didn't feel like a straight shooter; he felt like a jerk. Damn, he thought, she deserved better. Why hadn't he been able to fall in love with her? he asked himself. Or any of the others, for that matter?

Matt knew the answer, had always known the answer. He just always refused to acknowledge it. And he wasn't about to do so now, either.

Mentally avoiding a confrontation with his inner conflict, Matt raised his wineglass to Allyson. ''Merry Christmas, and health, happiness and love in the New Year.''

''The same to you,'' she murmured, raising her glass and sipping from it. ''Will you tell me something, Matt?'' she asked hesitantly.

''Of course.''

Allyson wet her lips, then quickly asked, ''Is there another woman? Someone I might know?''

Matt shook his head. ''No.''

It wasn't until hours later, when he was alone, that Matt reconsidered Allyson's questions. His answer had been truthful, as far as it went. But in actual fact, there was another woman, had always been another woman. A woman who haunted him, lived inside his mind wherever he happened to be. A woman he had not set eyes on for nine long years. A woman who had then been no more than a child. A child he had adored. A child who had grown into a beautiful teenager, with a woman's mature body and long, silky, enticing legs.

A teenager Matt had not been able to resist. A teenager he had, through his weakness, cruelly betrayed.

Matt shuddered and paced the confines of his bedroom, the Spartan furnishings of which reflected the barrenness of his existence.

But Matt could not outpace the feelings generated inside him by the startling call he had received from his stepfather. The man he had loved as much as a natural father. The man Matt had also betrayed.

Muttering a curse of self-condemnation, Matt stalked to the window to stare sightlessly into the diamond-studded, black-velvet night sky.

By the means of a transatlantic telephone line, Henry had in effect extended an offer of peace and forgiveness, tacitly inviting Matt, not only home for the holidays, but also back into the family fold.

The stars Matt was staring at grew fuzzy around the edges. He blinked against the moist film blurring his vision.

He was going home.

Anticipation and excitement simmered inside him. This time, *this* holiday, he had to make it right, because if he didn't, his future didn't bear thinking about.

Memory crouched, waiting to pounce on Matt the instant he lowered his guard. The stinging memory of another holiday season, and a bitter New Year's Eve.

Cursing aloud, Matt held the memory at bay by allowing himself to speculate on the intervening years.

What kind of person had that child-woman grown into? Matt wondered, swinging away from the window to resume his restless pacing. From the sparse bits of information he had gleaned from his mother and sister over the years, via telephone calls and the meetings he'd had with them in New York and Washington during his few brief visits to the States, he'd learned that she had matured into a lovely and intelligent young woman.

Matt felt the tingle of excitement and anticipation intensify, dance along his spine, at the realization that he would see for himself, judge for himself, in a little over a week.

Tired and keyed-up from the building inner tension, Matt felt his guard sag, just a bit. Her name rushed into the breach, filling his mind, his senses, his desolate soul.

Diana.

Chapter 2

Six days and counting.

The recurring thought ran through Diana's mind as she searched the faces of the deplaning passengers streaming along the concourse. If the flight from Chicago had arrived on schedule, Di's sister, Melissa, should be among the horde of humanity surging toward her.

Six days had passed—passed with excruciating slowness—since the night Diana had learned of Matt's intention to return home for the holidays. Six days, during which she had experienced mood swings from eager anticipation of his arrival to flat-out fear of facing him again.

Now, with only a few days remaining until Christmas Eve, Diana was more than a mite edgy. Her nerves were twanging like a guitar being thrummed by a musician caught up in a frenzy. Appearing calm required every ounce of control she possessed. Yet, so far, she had somehow managed it.

Two down and two to go, Di reflected, grinning and waving as she spied her sister's smiling face. Bethany had pulled in late yesterday afternoon, having driven through a fitful snowfall from New York City. Terry was booked on the red-eye flight from New Mexico, scheduled to arrive early in the morning of the twenty-fourth. That left Matt, who had said he would try to get home for Christmas Eve—just three days away.

"Okay, Di, what's up?" Melissa asked, after the greetings and hugs were exchanged.

"Up?" Diana repeated, smiling despite the clenching of the muscles in her midsection. Linking her arm with Lissa's, she matched her sister's stride as they joined the throng heading for the baggage claim area. "What do you mean?"

"The surprise Miriam said we're getting." Melissa arched her delicate dark eyebrows. "What sort of surprise has she got in store for us?"

"Assuming I knew, it wouldn't be much of a surprise if I told you," Diana replied. "Now would it?"

Melissa snatched her large suitcase from the carousel, grunted, and shot Diana a sour look. "I am assuming you know what it is, and unlike you and Miriam, I can live without surprises, thank you." Lugging the case, she trailed after Diana through the automatic swing doors. "Especially if that surprise concerns the announcement of your engagement," she went on, panting from the exertion.

"My engagement!" Diana stopped dead in her tracks; Lissa crashed into her, nearly sending both of them tumbling. "What engagement? I mean, to whom?"

"That dorky CPA you've been seeing." Lissa set down the case and drew a deep breath. "Who else?"

"Melissa, Mike Styer is not a dork," Diana said, even though she secretly agreed with her sister's assessment. "Besides, we are merely friends. Our relationship is not and never has been a romantic one."

"I should hope not." Lissa made a face. "I also hope the car's not too far away." She stumbled after Di when she stalked away. "This thing weighs a ton."

"Loaded with Christmas presents, is it?" Diana inquired, deliberately changing the subject.

"Yeah," Melissa admitted. "Scads of things."

"Hmm…" Diana murmured, slanting a taunting look at her. "But I thought you didn't like surprises."

"Get bent," Lissa retorted, grinning.

"Tsk, tsk." Diana made a clicking noise with her tongue. "I'm afraid that living in Chicago is corrupting you." Reaching out, she curled her fingers around the suitcase handle, relieving Lissa of her burden. "Wow!" she exclaimed when she felt the sudden dragging weight on her arm. "Did you buy everyone gifts made of cast iron?"

Lissa flexed her fingers and smiled disdainfully. "I do have a few things of my own in there, you know."

"Like what?" Di shot back, sighing with relief as they approached her car. "The kitchen sink?"

Lissa laughed, and enfolded Diana in another quick hug after she set the bag down at the rear of the car. "I have my blow-dryer, my curling iron, my garment steamer, my—"

"Lissa!" Diana exploded. "You didn't need to lug all that stuff. You could have used mine."

Lissa shrugged and helped Di heft the large case into the trunk. "Well, I remembered how you always used to yell at me to keep my hands off of your things when we were kids, and—"

"I absolutely do not believe you," Diana again interrupted her younger sister. "We *were* kids at the time," she reminded her, slamming the trunk shut. "And, as I recall, you had a positive talent for ruining every single thing of mine you got your sticky little hands on."

"Yeah." Lissa's eyes and smile were softened by remembrance. "We've both grown some since then."

"Yes." Her own eyes misty, Diana unlocked the door and slid behind the wheel. She turned to give her sister a more thorough examination after Lissa settled into the passenger seat. "You look terrific. I love that new hairstyle on you." Lissa's sable-brown tresses were now cut in a sleek, swingy bob.

"Thanks." Lissa shook her head. Her gleaming hair swirled, then settled neatly back into place. "You're not exactly looking like dog meat yourself. Your hair's really getting long. I like it."

"Thank you." Grinning, Diana raised her hand to smooth her shoulder-length mane of shiny black spiral curls. "Do you suppose we should adjourn this mutual-admiration-society meeting and head for home?"

"Home," Lissa repeated, her eyes growing bright. "Lord, it seems like forever since I was home last summer." She heaved a contented-sounding sigh as Diana set the car in motion. "I'm as excited as a kid. I can't wait. It's going to be like old times, with Terry and Beth coming.''

''Beth got in yesterday.''

''Great.'' Lissa laughed. ''It's going to be fun—I mean, all of us home for the holidays this year.'' She grew quiet, then sighed again. ''Well, almost all of us,'' she murmured.

Like it or not, little sister, you're in for a big surprise, Diana silently informed Lissa, who had also adored her big, forever teasing older stepbrother.

''Oh, it's snowing!'' Lissa cried as Diana drove the car from beneath the protective covering of the parking deck.

''Again,'' Diana said, tensing behind the wheel. ''The last couple of years, we've had hardly any snow at all. And now winter has barely begun, and this is the third snowfall.'' She sighed. ''I'll be glad when we're home.''

''Oh, doesn't everything look pretty!'' Lissa cried as they drove through the streets of Riverview. ''I can't wait to see the house.''

The house, their home, glowed from within, the candlelight flickering in the windows glittered on the snow blanketing the front lawn, and cast halos around the deep green holly draping the windows and the front door.

Lissa flung the car door open and leaped out the instant Diana brought the vehicle to a stop in the driveway. An understanding smile curving her lips, Diana followed a short distance behind her sister.

As she had been the week before, Miriam was waiting in the foyer. But she was not alone in her vigil.

Diana's smile widened when she heard Lissa let out a whoop of delight. But her smile faded when she saw the reason for her sister's exclamation of joy. While Di's father, Miriam and Bethany stood watching with obvious pleasure, Lissa was being swung off her feet, caught up in the embrace of her grinning stepbrother.

Matt.

''Oh, Matt! Oh, Matt!'' Lissa kept repeating, as if unable to believe he was real, and there.

"Oh, Lissa, oh, Lissa," Matt echoed teasingly. "As gorgeous and spontaneous as ever."

Frozen with shock, her breath shallow and constricted, Diana stood just inside the door, staring hungrily at this tall, handsome man she had not seen in nearly nine years—the only man she had ever loved.

Matt looked the same, and yet he appeared different, more handsome, more imposing, more forbidding, even with his face alight with laughter and love for Lissa. Maturity stamped his sharply delineated features; lines radiated from the corners of his deep-set dark brown eyes and bracketed his sensuous mouth. Silver streaked the short black hair at his temples, and the shock of hair that had tumbled onto his forehead.

Diana's gaze drifted to his body. A shiver of awareness, blatantly sexual, skittered up her spine. His slender hips, flat belly and long straight legs were encased in tight black jeans. His broad shoulders and flatly muscled chest were displayed to advantage in a white cableknit sweater. The slimness of youth was gone. At thirty-four, Matt had the lean, long-muscled look of a man at his physical peak.

Diana experienced an immediate response to the magnetic allure of his body. Her senses reeled, her skin grew warm, her insides quivered. Shaken by her reaction, physical and emotional, she dragged her gaze back to his smiling face.

"Are you the surprise Miriam promised me?" Lissa demanded when he set her back on her feet.

"Yes," Matt replied, his smile gentle, as he raised a hand to smooth a tear away from her cheek. "I'm the designated Christmas surprise for you and Terry and Beth." He turned his head to glance at his grinning sister, and went still when he caught sight of Diana.

There was a momentary hush. Or was the hush only inside her? Diana wondered, unable to breathe or move, ensnared by the intensity of his dark-eyed stare. The hush obviously wasn't felt by the rest of the group, for the laughing Lissa spun out of Matt's arms to rush forward to bestow hugs and kisses on Henry, Miriam and Beth.

"Hello." Matt's low-voiced greeting shattered the inner hush—and every one of Diana's nerves.

"Hel—hello, Matt." Diana hated, but couldn't control, the tremor in her voice. She couldn't tear her riveted gaze from his beloved face, either.

Matt's eyes flickered, and in that instant Diana knew memories were flooding his mind, the same memories that were flooding through hers, washing away the present, her chattering family members, sweeping her back in time to that New Year's Eve, nine long years before.

The house was ablaze with lights, from chandeliers, lamps, candles, and the sparkling twelve-foot Christmas tree rising majestically from the floor to the ceiling in front of one window. Laughter and animated conversation rang through the living room, foyer and dining room from the throats of the thirty-odd guests gathered to celebrate the arrival of the New Year at the traditional Blair family party.

Dressed in a long black velvet skirt and a chic, clingy gold silk blouse, Diana felt like Cinderella attending her first ball. Her short, shiny black curls bounced with her every light step, her dark eyes glowed from within with happiness. Matt had told her she looked beautiful—and sexy.

A shiver trembled through her. No one had ever before said that she either looked or was sexy. Had Matt meant it? Or had he been indulging in his usual pastime of wicked teasing?

A new sensation, strange yet exciting, held Diana in thrall. Matt had appeared serious, his eyes dark and intense, the light of deviltry smothered. If he had meant what he said...

Sexy. She shivered again. The possibilities implied by his comment sent her heartbeat into overdrive and constricted her breathing. How could she find out? Diana mused, smiling absently at a guest as she glided by a laughing group of celebrants.

Did she dare to test the sensuous waters of Matt's murmured remark? The shiver intensified along Diana's spine. But what manner of test could she apply? she asked herself. Other than a few moist, fumbling kisses from boys her own age, Diana's experience of the opposite sex was nil.

Perhaps if she were to employ the wiles displayed by the actress playing a seductress in a movie she had recently seen, Diana mused.

But where was Matt? Diana wondered, smiling as she sailed by another animated group of guests on her way to the kitchen to replenish an empty canapé tray. She could hardly experiment, run a test, without the presence of the object of her foray into experimentation.

Come to think of it, she hadn't seen Matt for over an hour, ever since he had gently but firmly disentangled his arm from the clinging grip of his current lady friend.

Diana grimaced. In her estimation, Sondra Taylor—not Sandra, but *Sondra*—was a real piece of work. Snooty, condescending, supercilious. And grasping. Sondra wanted Matt in the worst way, as was evidenced by her cloying possessiveness.

What did Matt see in the woman? Diana had been puzzling over that question since the first time Matt had brought the rarefied Sondra to the house to meet his mother, his stepfather, and his assorted siblings.

It wasn't that she was jealous or anything, Diana had repeatedly assured herself, all the while knowing full well that she was positively green from that demeaning emotion. But, darn it, Matt could do so much better than the nose-in-the-air Sondra—Diana herself, for example.

And, over the past month, Sondra had given clear indications that she intended to have Matt—to own him. She had even confided to Diana her belief that an engagement ring might be coming for Christmas.

To the other woman's obvious chagrin, and Diana's intense relief, the expected ring hadn't materialized. Still, the relationship between Matt and Sondra appeared to be as solid as before.

So why did Matt seem to be hiding out now, when the party, and his lady, were in full swing?

Her curiosity aroused, Diana went searching for Matt after refilling the canapé tray, as well as the nut, potato chip and pretzel bowls. She found him ensconced in the roomy wingback chair in her father's dimly lit office.

"Got a headache?" Diana asked, quietly closing the door, shutting out the sounds of revelry.

"No." Matt drew his gaze from the flames leaping in the fireplace and settled a brooding look on her. "What are you doing in here?"

Startled by the underlying harshness in his soft voice, Diana forced a faint laugh, and an even fainter shrug. "Looking for you. Why did you cut out of the party?" she asked ingenuously, hoping to hear him admit that he was fed up with Lady Sondra's clutching hands and devouring glances.

"To get away from you," he muttered, pushing out of the chair to stand taut and rigid, his face set into harsh lines, his eyes dark and unfathomable.

Diana stared at him in bewilderment, devastated, not only by his cruel words, but also by his cutting tone of voice. What had she done to warrant this kind of treatment from him? Diana asked herself, racking her brain for some infraction, real or imagined. The only answer that came to her shocked mind was in connection to his earlier comment on her appearance.

Looking more closely at him, Diana felt amazement sweep through her; unless she was greatly misreading his expression, Matt gave every indication of being afraid of her!

Diana thrilled at a never-before-experienced feeling of feminine power. Trying on a copy of the seductive actress's method, she walked slowly toward him. The tingling thrill expanded inside her at the wary, uncertain expression that flashed across Matt's face.

Matt was never uncertain!

Watching him, watching his eyes, she took another slow step. His eyes flickered, lowered to her breasts, then quickly lifted to stare, stark and fierce, into hers.

Diana was young, and she was innocent, but she was by no means stupid or dense. She could feel the silky gold material of her blouse gliding over her breasts, could imagine how sensuous it might appear to Matt, to any man.

She moved her shoulders, just a bit. The silk caressed her flesh, igniting a spark of budding passion deep inside her. She took another step.

Matt raised a hand, palm out, as if to halt her progress. "Diana, don't—" The tight strain in his low voice struck her like a blow to the heart.

Diana's bravado deserted her. She couldn't go through with it. She simply didn't have whatever it took to play the role of the temptress. Not with Matt. She loved him, and for her, loving precluded role-playing.

Raising her own hand, Diana pressed her palm to his. "Oh, Matt, I'm sorry… I… I…"

"You have nothing to be sorry for," he said, interrupting her, staring intently at their fused palms. "It's me. I'm the one in the wrong here." He frowned as his fingers moved between hers, as if of their own volition. A defeated-sounding sigh whispered through his lips as his fingers lowered between hers, lacing their hands together.

"But why?" Diana cried in confusion, clasping his hand in a grip of desperation. "How— What have you done wrong?"

"Thought of you." His voice was even lower, barely a whisper. "In all the ways I should not think of you."

Diana knew. Of course she knew, every living part of her being quivered with the knowing. Yet she had to ask, had to hear it from his lips. "What ways, Matt?" she asked softly, taking another hesitant step.

Suddenly loosening his fingers, Matt pulled his hand from hers. "In the ways of a man with a woman—his woman." His voice was a strangled rasp. "But you're not a woman, Di. You're still little more than a child." Inhaling a ragged breath, he stepped back, away from her.

That heady sensation of feminine power swept over Diana again, washing away all thoughts of caution, all consideration of consequences. In so many words, Matt had just confessed to wanting her—her, not Sondra, *her*. Obeying impulse, she moved toward him, hands raised imploringly.

"I am not a child, Matt. In a few months I will be eighteen, an adult under the law, old enough to vote. A woman in the eyes of the world." Her fingertips brushed the soft material of his shirt, tingled in response to the firm flesh beneath the smooth cotton. She moistened her lips with a quick glide of her tongue before finishing, "I know what I want, Matt."

A light flared to life in the depths of his eyes, almost frightening in its fierceness. "How do you know?" he demanded with unconcealed fury. "Who have you been with? Who taught you?"

"Matt, you don't under—" That was as far as she got before his raw voice cut through her attempt to clarify.

"I'll kill the—"

"Matt, no!" Diana grasped his shirt. "There has been no one. I want you. Only you."

"You don't know what you're saying." His hands shot up to clasp her upper arms. "This isn't a game, Di."

"I know," she whispered. "Games don't hurt, not like I'm hurting now."

Matt's eyes flashed a warning, and his fingers tightened on her tender flesh. Diana expected to be shaken by his hard, rough hands, and she was thoroughly confused, thrown off balance, by the gentleness of his touch, the careful way he drew her close to the warmth of his body.

"Oh, Di, help me," he pleaded on a rough groan. "Tell me to let you go, please." His fingers flexed, as if to release her, then convulsed once more around her arms. "Di, please, get the hell out of here, away from me, while I still have the strength to let you go." It was a cry from the heart.

"I can't. I won't. I don't want to." She flattened her palms against the rock-hard wall of his chest. Even through the soft material of his shirt, Matt's body heat shocked her system, aroused her senses, caused a deep inner ache for…something.

Without conscious thought, she stroked his chest.

Matt's low groan of pleasure drenched her senses. "Di, don't." He shook his head. "No, please, do," he said in a strangled, pleading tone. "Unbutton my shirt, then touch me, stroke me."

Sheer exhilaration froze Diana for a second. Then a rush of wild excitement sent her trembling fingers to the buttons on his shirt, fumbling them free. Her avid gaze fixed on his face, she slid her hands beneath the soft material, thrilling to the sensation of caressing his hot, hair-roughened skin.

Matt shuddered. An expression of near-pain flickered across his face. "Oh, dammit, Di, that feels so good." He closed his eyes, as if savoring the feeling. "Your hands are so soft, so exciting, so arousing."

Her hands, *her* touch, held the power to excite him! Elation shot through Diana, overpowering the lingering traces of trepidation, releasing her inhibitions. Obeying an urgent inner command, she leaned forward and pressed her parted lips to his now-moist flesh.

Matt drew in a sharp breath, and his body jerked, as if it had been prodded by a live electrical wire. "Diana, Diana..." As he groaned her name, he released his grasp on her arms and clasped her head with his unsteady hands. Lifting her head from his chest, he tilted her face up to his.

Diana trembled at the look of him. His face was stark. His eyes were open, and their nearly black depths were alight with a leaping flame of unbridled desire.

"Diana, I must kiss you." Matt lowered his eyes to her trembling lips. "Let me, love..." He moved his mouth closer, to within a breath of hers. "May I?"

He needed to kiss *her*. Diana's mind boggled at the very thought. May I? *May I?* Her mind laughed; Diana didn't. She stared into the inciting fire in his eyes and knew she could happily burn to a crisp from the merest brush of his beautiful mouth against hers.

"Diana," he whispered when she didn't respond. "Let me. I need... I need..." His voice faded into a wisp of warm, wine-scented breath that bathed her lips and intoxicated her rioting senses.

"I...I need, too," she whispered in a faint little cry, lifting her mouth in invitation.

Matt made a sound that was half sigh, half groan, then closed the scant space between them. The touch of his mouth on hers was feather-light, tender, sweet. Diana felt it to the soles of her feet, the depths of her soul. It made her hungry for more. Gliding her palms up his chest, she curled her arms around his taut neck, urging him closer.

Matt's reaction was swift and stunning. His strong arms enfolded her quivering form, drawing her into a fiercely possessive embrace. His mouth hardened, claiming hers. His tongue probed at the barrier of her closed lips.

Diana knew what he was silently demanding of her, and yet she hesitated, unsure of herself, of her ability to please him.

A ragged growl of frustration rumbling from his throat, Matt lifted his mouth a fraction from hers. "Part your lips for me, love," he ordered. "Let me in. Give me your sweetness."

She parted her lips...a bit.

"Wider." Matt's raw tone conveyed urgency. "I want to fill you with a part of me."

His words drew a picture in Diana's mind, an erotic vision that sent a bolt of sensation ricocheting from her head to the depths of her femininity and back to her lips, setting them on fire...for the feel of him.

Diana parted her lips.

Matt's tongue surged inside, filling her mouth, swamping her senses. His hands moved with restless intent, molding her soft curves to the hard, angular planes of his muscular body.

Passion exploded inside Diana. Guided by impulse, she arched into the taut form curved over hers. Her hips made contact with his. Diana gasped at the urgent nudging of his manhood against the mound at the apex of her weak and trembling thighs.

Matt released her mouth to kiss her cheeks, her eyelids, her temples. His tongue outlined the curve of her ear, then delicately dipped into the opening.

Diana shuddered in response to his erotic play.

"Do you like that?" His voice was low.

"Y-yes."

"So do I, but it's not enough," Matt murmured seductively. "Filling your sweet mouth, your pretty ear, only makes me hungry for more." His hands clasped her bottom, pulling her body tightly to the fullness of his. "I want to fill you completely. Feel your body throb, tight and hot around mine. I want to make you wild with desire for me, only me. I'm damn near crazy with the need to make love to you until you shatter for me, while I explode inside you.''

His soft voice drew images in her imagination, images that lit a raging fire in the core of her being. The blood coursed sweet and hot in her veins, and massed in a molten flow around her aching femininity.

Still Diana teetered on the edge of decision, wanting, yet fearful of the initiation into womanhood.

''Diana...'' Whispering her name, Matt covered her lips with his, ending her uncertainty with the evocative rhythm of his thrusting tongue.

Without conscious direction, Diana's body moved against his. His mouth fused to hers, Matt moved, taking her with him as he crossed the room to the long leather couch set at an angle to the fireplace. Diana moaned a soft protest when the rhythm ceased, and gasped when his deft fingers released the fastening on her skirt, sending the garment to the floor in a pool of black velvet around her ankles.

''Lord, Diana, you have the longest, sexiest legs,'' Matt said in a husky whisper. ''Your legs have been driving me out of my mind for almost a year.''

Diana blinked, both thrilled and startled by his confession. ''My legs?'' she said, unable to believe she had heard him correctly.

''Your legs,'' he assured her, reaching out to stroke one thigh encased in sheer black nylon. ''I ache to feel them curled around my waist.'' Matt's fingers trailed up her leg to the juncture of her thighs. One long finger stroked the dark down unconcealed by the filmy panty hose. ''I burn to feel your long legs contract, drawing me deeper and deeper into the moist heat of your body.'' His stroking finger probed, testing the nylon barrier to the portal of his desire.

His intimate caress completely swept away Diana's inhibitions. Extending her hands, she cupped the fullness straining against the material of his trousers. Matt's body jerked in reaction; she felt a responsive spasm beneath her palm.

''Let me show you, Diana.'' Matt's harsh voice betrayed the

need driving him. "Make love with me. Here—" A movement
of his head indicated the couch. "Now."

"Yes," she answered without hesitation.

Matt's eyes blazed, seeming to shoot sparks of fire to the heart
of Diana's desire. She murmured a protest when he drew his
hand and tormenting fingers away from her body, but sighed
with satisfaction when he lowered her to the butter-soft leather
cushions and settled his length between her thighs.

Recalling his earlier confession, Diana coiled her legs around
his slim waist. Matt responded by arching his body, thrusting it
against hers, tormenting them both with a preview of the delights
in store when the barriers of their clothing were at last torn away
and discarded.

Gasping at the fiery sensations his movements sent through
her, Diana fullfilled his fantasy by tightening her legs and arching high into his rhythm.

"Diana..." Matt crushed her mouth with his, and then his
tongue began moving in time with his body.

"Good grief! Diana!"

"Matthew! How could you?"

The shocked voices of her father and Matt's mother pierced
the sensual haze clouding Diana's mind. Muttering a vicious
curse into her mouth, Matt pulled his head back, and angled it
to glare at the open doorway. Henry and Miriam stood in the
opening, while Bethany, Melissa, Terry, and a number of their
guests—Sondra included—crowded around in the hallway.

Horrified at being caught in such a blatantly humiliating position, Diana buried her face and a muffled sob in the curve of
Matt's neck. She could feel the waning warmth of his passion,
the growing heat of his fury.

"Shut the damn door."

Chapter 3

"Diana, did you hear me? I asked if you would you please shut the door."

The sound of her father's voice dammed the flow of memory in Diana's mind. Moving like a sleepwalker, she reached behind her to pull the door shut, Matt's angry voice of nine years before still echoing in her mind.

Shut the damn door.

Blinking, she focused on the man standing, silent and watchful, across the foyer from her.

The memories, *their* memories, were still reflected in Matt's dark eyes.

How much time had expired while she and Matt stared at each other, reliving those memories? Diana wondered, dragging her gaze away from him to skip a glance from her father to Lissa, then to Miriam and Beth. They were still in the process of exchanging hugs and greetings; Lissa was still wearing her coat, as indeed was Diana herself.

Deciding the elapsed time was a matter of mere seconds, rather than the hours it seemed to her, Diana shook her head to reorient herself, and set her fingers to work on the buttons of her own ankle-length wool coat.

Her fingers trembled as much as they had that night, when she fumbled with the buttons on Matt's shirt. The thought brought the memory, that night, close once more, too close, making her feel vulnerable and fragile.

There came a sudden touch on her shoulder, then her nape, at the collar of her coat. Even after nine years, Diana recognized that touch and shivered in response to it.

"The scars inflicted on you that night still haven't healed, have they?" Matt asked, in a hushed voice pitched to reach her ears alone.

Diana went stiff. She was cold outside, yet traitorously warm inside. Fighting an insidious melting sensation and an overwhelming impulse to turn into his arms, she shook her head quickly.

"Liar," he said in a rough whisper. "I could see, read it like print on your face. You were reliving that night, just as I was." His voice went rougher, sounding harsh, bitter. "You are still suffering the shame and humiliation of being found, seen by everyone, with me between your legs."

Diana flinched as though he had struck her. Her eyes closed against a rush of tears from the stabbing pain of the emotional wound. Barely aware of what she was doing, she slipped her arms free of the sleeves when he tugged on the coat. The heavy garment was lifted from her shoulders, but still she felt weighted down.

"I suppose I can't blame you," he murmured, heaving a tired sigh as he made a half turn toward the foyer closet. His lips twisted. "It was not a pretty scene."

Matt's flat statement flung her back in time once more....

"Shut that damn door," Matt ordered in a strangled snarl as he scooped her skirt from the floor. "Diana, I must get up," he whispered, easing away from her.

Mortified by the horrible situation, Diana could do no more than stare up at him with pleading eyes.

Ignoring the babble of voices from the doorway and the hall beyond, Matt slowly backed away from her, drawing the long velvet skirt over her exposed legs as he did so. When the lower half of her body was decently covered, he rose from the couch and turned to face the battery of condemning eyes.

"Oh, Matthew, how could you?" Miriam repeated in an anguished whisper. "Your sister!"

"She is not my sister," Matt shot back.

"No, she is my daughter." Henry's voice was choked with rage; his face was red, mottled by fury. "I treated you like a son, trusted you, loved you." Tears escaped to trickle down his flushed cheeks. "And in return you betray me, my love, my trust, by attacking my daughter."

"No!" Diana's cry of denial went unheard, overshadowed by the grating sound of Matt's voice.

"I asked you to shut that door." He stood tall, poised and taut, as if ready for a battle, or a full-scale war. "We don't need an audience."

"What difference does it make now?" Henry shot back, his usual sense of decorum and reserve destroyed by the depth of his pain and shock. "They have all witnessed the extent of your depravity." Nevertheless, he reached back to grasp the door, and slammed it shut in Sondra's face.

For one shameful yet satisfying instant, Diana's humiliation was soothed by a glimpse of Sondra's chagrined expression. Her satisfaction was short-lived.

"Henry, no! Please, no!"

Miriam's cry tore at the jagged edges of the wound inflicted on Diana's heart by the evidence of her father's visible suffering and pain.

"I am not depraved," Matt bit out through clenched teeth. "And Diana is unharmed."

"By God's grace, and our intervention," Henry retorted in tones of utter revulsion. "And not by a sense of conscience, or even caring, in you."

Diana set bolt upright, unable to bear any more. "Dad, I was as much to—"

Matt cut her off, stunning her into silence with his savage tone. "Shut up, Diana. I'll handle this."

"Handle it? Handle it?" Henry shouted, shaking with fury. "No, you will not handle it! I will!" His voice rose by degrees to a deafening roar. "I want you out of my home, now, at once, and I never want to see your face again!"

"Dad!"

"Henry!" Miriam cried, drowning Diana's cry of protest. Rushing to him, she clutched at his rigid arm. "Henry, you can't mean that!"

"Yes, I mean it!" Henry roared. "I want him gone, for good." His tear-filmed eyes pinned Matt. "What's more, if I had the guts, I'd get my shotgun and blow your filthy-minded son off the face of the earth."

"Oh, God! Oh, God, no!" Miriam sobbed in heartbroken supplication.

It's my fault. It's all my fault, Diana cried in silent anguish, thinking that none of this would have happened if she hadn't invaded Matt's privacy in the first place, or had obeyed his plea to her to leave him while he still had the presence of mind to let her go. She accepted the blame without question, knowing instinctively that, even having refused to leave him, she had held the power to stop Matt at any time.

"Blowing me to hell won't be necessary," Matt said, facing Henry unflinchingly. "I will marry Diana."

Silence screamed in the room.

Diana wished only to die to escape the excruciating pain of the insult piled atop the humiliation.

"There, you see, Henry?" poor Miriam exclaimed, clutching at a thread of hope. "Matt will set everything right."

Henry ruthlessly dashed his wife's hopes. "I'll see him dead before I see him wed to my daughter. The trust is gone, Matthew Turner," he said. "The trust, the love, all feeling. Gone. To me and mine, you are dead. I want you gone, as well. Now."

Matt didn't look at Diana. He didn't move as much as a flicker. Then he smiled—a hard, cynical smile of defeat. "As you wish," he said, walking away from the couch, and Diana. "I will call you in a few days, Mother." He paused to kiss Miriam on her tearstained cheek. Then he strode to the door and pulled it open, the cynical smile reappearing as the other family members and guests started and backed away.

"And a happy New Year to all of you, too," he drawled, sardonically, clearing a path through the ranks.

"Matt!" Sondra called after him anxiously. "Wait, I'll go with you."

"I don't think you'd like where I'm going," he tossed over his shoulder, continuing on to the front door.

"But where are you going?" she demanded.

"Straight to hell." Matt gave a short, harsh laugh and quietly shut the door.

Inside her father's office, curled into a ball of sheer misery, Diana shuddered in response to the note of agony she had heard in his laughter.

Banishment. Matt had been banished from the house he had thought of as home since his teens. She had brought him to this, Diana thought, numb to the comforting sound of her father's voice. Driven by inner urgings she couldn't comprehend, she had willfully played with the fire of temptation. And the flames of passion had seared her heart and soul.

Diana knew, intuitively, that she would carry the scars for as long as she drew breath.

"Diana, don't."

The soft, urgent sound of Matt's voice broke the thread of memory unwinding in Diana's mind. Suddenly at loose ends, and feeling vaguely as though she were twisting in the winds of desolation, Diana glanced around in search of something of substance to anchor her to reality.

Her gaze collided with the most solid-looking substance in the foyer—and he was monitoring her every move, every breath, every emotion.

Matt.

Diana felt hollow, and the emptiness inside her yawned wider with each successive moment. Had he said something about scars? Diana swallowed a bubble of hysterical laughter. Emotional scars? She could dash off a degree-worthy dissertation on the subject in minutes.

Dammit, it wasn't fair, Diana railed silently, staring at him, unaware of the pain shadowing her dark eyes. It had taken her the majority of the past nine years to knit the emotional scars—and still the stitches were none too tight.

"Please, don't, Diana." The urgency in Matt's voice was gone, replaced by a whispered plea.

"What?" Diana gave a brief shake of her head in hopes of rattling her thoughts into a semblance of coherency. "Don't... what?"

"Don't look at me like that," he murmured.

"Like what?" Of course, now she was staring at him even more intently.

"With that haunted look," he said in a harsh whisper, slanting a glance at the others to see if they were taking notice—they weren't. "That look of remembering that night, and resenting me, my being here."

"That's not true." Diana was fighting a sense of encroaching unreality again, feeling once more as though she had been standing in the foyer for hours, days, a lifetime, instead of mere minutes.

"Isn't it?" Matt raised one dark, wing-arched brow in a show of patent disbelief.

"No, I—" That was as far as she got, which was fortunate for her, since she had no idea of what to say to him.

"Supper's on the table, folks," Janet called from the dining room.

"And not a minute too soon." Laughing, Lissa crossed the foyer to Matt. "I'm starving," she announced. Her eyes bright with teasing humor, she shrugged out of her coat and offered it to him. "Are you going to stand there holding Diana's coat, or were you thinking of wearing it?"

"I see you haven't changed much, Melissa," Matt drawled, plucking the coat from her hands and turning to hang both garments in the closet. "You always were a flippant, nagging brat."

"I do my best," Lissa retorted, hooking her arm through one of his. "Nagging is my vocation."

"Yeah, well, take a vacation from your vocation." Grinning, Beth strolled over to them and captured Matt's free arm. "I hear enough nagging at work, thank you."

"Come along, children, you can fight it out over dinner." Her face and smile reflecting her contentment, Miriam clasped

Henry's arm and started for the dining room. "Isn't this wonderful? Just like old times."

"Yes, dear, it's wonderful," Henry agreed indulgently, tossing a satisfied look over his shoulder at their assorted offspring. "Just like old times."

The two men's eyes met in silent, forgiving communion. Diana was the sole witness to the masculine reunion. A sigh lodged in her throat, a sigh of relief at the end of the nearly nine-year estrangement.

"Yes," Beth piped up. "Do you remember the time..." she began enthusiastically.

Diana tuned out her stepsister's bubbly voice, feeling left out as the trio trailed after her father and Miriam. It was not just like old times, she thought, slowing following the laughing, chattering group. For, while she rejoiced for the repair to the family breach, she feared things could never again be quite as they once were.

The chatter and laughter continued around the table throughout the meal. Quiet, speaking only when she was directly spoken to, Diana observed her family, concluding that her unvoiced opinion was correct.

For all his display of hearty congeniality, there were faint but definite signs of strain in Henry's tone. And, for all her show of contentment and delight, Miriam's eyes mirrored an underlying anxiety.

No, it was not just like old times, Diana mused, playing with the scant amount of food she'd served herself. Lissa and Beth were trying too hard to appear natural, and it was obvious, at least to Diana. And Matt, though friendly, seemingly relaxed, was watchful and wary, as if he anticipated an ambush.

Diana skimmed a glance over the faces of her table companions. They were all working very hard at maintaining a festive atmosphere. She released a soundless sigh, deciding that the ghost of New Year's Eve nine years past hovered over the table, undermining the holiday spirit.

A roar of laughter penetrated the murky thoughts clouding Diana's mind. The laughter contained the sound of genuine amusement. Forcing a smile, she ran another, clearer-eyed glance around the table. The others, including Matt, appeared to be thoroughly enjoying themselves.

Had she been projecting her own misgivings onto the other members of her family? Perhaps she was the only one experiencing undercurrents of unease. Startled by the consideration, Diana studied each smiling face in turn.

Miriam's still-lovely face was flushed with pleasure.

Beth's eyes were sparkling.

Lissa looked like an eager teenager.

Henry appeared smugly complacent.

And Matt—Diana's thoughts fractured.

Matt was staring intently into her startled eyes.

Feeling suddenly exposed, naked and vulnerable, Diana wrenched her startled gaze away from him. But from the corner of her eye she saw him frown.

What was Matt thinking? she wondered, automatically rising when the others slid their chairs back and stood up. The intensity of his stare unnerved her.

Certain that Matt was blaming her for all the years, all the holidays, he had missed sharing with his family, Diana gave him a wide berth as they all leisurely made their way out of the dining room and into the living room.

"Oh, the tree is magnificent!" Lissa exclaimed, rushing across the room to the majestic blue spruce.

"It certainly is," Matt agreed, sauntering over to her. "Smells good, too."

"Must I wait till Christmas Eve, or may I put my presents beneath it now?" she asked, turning a hopeful look on Henry and Miriam.

"You know we were never allowed to place gifts under the tree before Christmas Eve, Lissa," Beth said chidingly.

Lissa made a face. "That was when we were kids," she reminded Beth. "We're all grown up now."

"Coulda fooled me," Matt drawled, his dark eyes dancing with devilry, his grin wicked.

The evocative and so-familiar sight of his tormenting grin elicited responsive grins from Lissa and Beth, a girlish-sounding giggle from Miriam, and a soft chuckle from Henry. Diana didn't grin, giggle, chuckle, or even smile. She couldn't. His teasing, endearing grin stirred too many precious memories of happier times, when she had loved Matt with childish innocence, before that innocence had blossomed into sensuality, precipitating that dreadful confrontation.

They had been such a close-knit family, regardless of the fact that they had not all shared the same blood ties. And yet, Diana reflected, in one night—no, within little more than one hour— she and Matt had rent the fabric of their family by surrendering to sensuality and need.

She and Matt were both guilty as sin for the years of separation and unhappiness borne by the family. Diana accepted the burden of guilt without question, even as she acknowledged that she would do the same again to experience the thrill and excitement of Matt's embrace, his kiss, his loving.

She loved him. She had always loved him. She would always love him. She sighed. Merely surviving Matt's visit was going to be pure hell, loving and wanting him as she did, concealing her true feelings from the others—and most especially from Matt himself. But she would have to do it. The problem she had to deal with was how she could do it.

Keep busy.

The answer that sprang into Diana's mind mobilized her into determined action. Turning away from the bantering group, she headed for the foyer.

"Diana?" Henry's call halted her in the doorway. "Where are you going?"

"To the car," she replied, moving into the foyer. "I'm going to get Lissa's suitcase."

"Wait, I'll get it," Henry said.

"It's my case," Lissa called. "I'll get it."

"No, both of you stay here." Matt's tone held a note of command. "I'll get it."

Diana didn't pause to see who won the argument. Crossing the foyer, she pulled open the door and walked into the snow-tossed evening.

Dammit. Cursing to himself, Matt strode after Diana. Coming home had been a mistake. If he had had any doubts on that score, they had very effectively been demolished by the shattered expression shadowing Diana's eyes.

She didn't want him here, in her father's house. The realization caused a twisting pain inside Matt. He had waited so long to come back. It had been a deliberate decision on his part to stay away, a decision that had nothing to do with Henry's dictum.

Diana had been so young, and she had been caught up in the throes of first passion. He had forced himself to wait, giving her time and space to grow up, mature, learn something of the world, and the explosive nature of physical attraction.

Matt felt a stab of pure male jealousy. Diana was now twenty-six, and had probably long since been tutored in the act of sensuality. Resentment burned in his mind, in his gut, resentment of the man upon whom she had bestowed the honor of being her guide into the realm of erotic pleasure.

Matt had forced himself to wait, to persevere, and the emotional cost had been exceedingly high.

Throughout the intervening years, existing on the snippets of information he could garner about Diana from his mother and Beth during their brief visits together, Matt had bided his time, denying each urgent impulse to come back and demand that Diana recognize him, not as a teasing brother, not as a sensualist indulging his appetites with an untried girl, but as a man—the man who loved her, the man for her.

But was he in truth the man for her? Matt asked himself, stalking her to the back of the car. As far as his feelings went, there was no longer any question. After nine years of fruitless rationalization and self-denial, telling himself that she was too young, that he had merely been lust-driven and that, in any event, he had blown his chances by giving in to his desires, Matt had finally faced the truth.

He was in love with Diana. Matt grimaced as he crunched through the snow toward her. Hell, the truth was, he had always been in love with her, if in different ways. Coming to a stop beside her at the open trunk of the car, Matt felt the blade of pain twist deeper when Diana flinched and stepped aside, putting a measured distance betweem them.

He loved her—and she couldn't bear to be near him. Diana had made that abundantly clear from the instant she spotted him after she followed her sister into the house. Her eyes had betrayed her, revealing the shock and the remembered pain and humiliation she was experiencing.

"I said I'd get it." Matt's voice was harsh. He couldn't help it; he was feeling his own pain.

Diana didn't respond, but just stood there, staring down at the snow-covered driveway.

Calling to mind every curse he knew, Matt grasped the handle of the suitcase and heaved it from the trunk. Damn, the thing was heavy! What in hell did Lissa have stuffed in there? he wondered, closing the trunk with a slamming *thunk*.

Diana just stood there, staring at the snow.

"You planning to spend the rest of my visit out here?" he asked, slanting a hard look at her.

Her head jerked up, and she transferred her stare to him. "No." Her voice was reedy, barely a whisper. "But I was giving serious consideration to Cancún, Hawaii, maybe Australia."

"Cute." Taking her by the hand, he hefted the case and started back toward the house, literally dragging her along with him. "But I feel I must tell you that Australia isn't far enough away."

Diana gasped and jerked her arm back, trying to free her hand from his.

Stopping in midstride, Matt tightened his hold on her hand and wheeled around to face her. His chest contracted, cutting off his breath. Words weren't needed—Diana's stark expression said it all, and then some, about her feelings. He had flat-out terrified her by telling her she couldn't run far enough for him not to follow, find her and bring her back.

Diana didn't want him to find her, not here or anywhere. Despair settled in Matt's mind. He loved her, and she didn't want him. He was thinking that he might as well return to Europe when his fighting spirit shot through him, zapping the despair. Matt was a success in business not only because he was good at what he did, but also because he relished a challenge. And the biggest challenge of his life was standing before him now, watching him warily, probably wondering why he was staring intently, silently, at her.

He'd meet the challenge Diana presented. Somehow, some-way, he would make her love him.

The tension inside Diana seemed to crackle, sizzling from her to him, jolting him from his reverie. Matt imagined he could feel the seething electricity coiling around him, singeing his body hair. Smoldering, he stared at her, drinking in the sight of her.

Her dark eyes looked huge, bottomless, in the watery light flittering through the curtains on the windows. Snowflakes got tangled in her long lashes, spiking them as they melted. The stinging wind whipped flags of pink in her cheeks. Her long spiral curls glistened with beads of moisture.

She was wet! The realization drew Matt into awareness. His narrowed eyes skimmed the shivering length of her. Dammit! he railed against himself. She was cold!

"We'd better get back inside before you catch pneumonia." Pivoting abruptly, Matt gave a hard, no-nonsense tug on her hand. The weight of the suitcase yanked on his arm. "What in hell does Lissa have in this thing?" he muttered, more to himself than to her.

"Everything she owns, I think," Diana replied, in a rather wry tone.

Surprised that she had bothered to respond, Matt shot a keen glance at her as he strode into the foyer. Diana was actually smiling at him. Strained though it surely was, her smile still had the power to stop Matt in his tracks. The suitcase dropped from his hand, unnoticed.

"Everything she owns?" Matt asked, not caring about the answer, simply wanting to bask a moment longer in the warm glow of her smile. His breath caught when, amazingly, the smile leaped from her red lips to sparkle mischievously in her eyes.

"Well, maybe not everything." She raised her hand to ruffle her damp hair. "But a lot of stuff," she went on. "Including Christmas presents."

Christmas presents! Bells rang in Matt's head, celebrating the birth of an idea. He needed time with Diana, time alone, away from the rest of the family. Time to let her get to know him as a man, not a brother. And he hadn't done any Christmas shopping before leaving for the States. And he had never met a woman who didn't love to shop. A smile began inside Matt and worked its way to his lips.

"That reminds me. I still have shopping to do." Matt infused his voice with a note of chagrin. "And I haven't a clue as to what to get for everyone." He heaved a deep sigh. "Can I impose on you to go with me, help me with my selections?"

Chapter 4

"You want me to go with you?" Diana stared at Matt in sheer astonishment, certain she had misunderstood him. After telling her mere moments ago that she couldn't go far enough away to suit him, she couldn't believe he was now requesting her company on a shopping expedition.

"If you would, I'd appreciate it." Matt shrugged, drawing her eyes to the damp patches on his sweater. "I confess I haven't an inkling of what to buy."

Diana shivered, and not only because of the chill from her own wet sweater, but also from a gnawing uncertainty about the wisdom of spending an extended period of time alone with him. A burst of laughter wafted into the foyer from the living room. She sighed. Still, how could she refuse to accompany him without appearing churlish, if not downright childish? she asked herself, unconsciously revealing her ambivalence by absently tugging at the hem of her sweater with trembling fingers.

"Forget it," Matt said with harsh abruptness when the silence stretched too long between them. "Your reluctance to spend any time at all with me is obvious." His gaze homed in on her fingers, and a derisive smile crooked his lips. "I'll muddle along on my own."

"No." Diana blurted out, already feeling both churlish and

childish. "I'll go with you," she said, the sound of an animated discussion inside the living room reminding her that this holiday visit was supposed to be a time of family peacemaking and healing. "When do you want to go?"

"Well, there are only a few days left until Christmas," Matt replied, his derisive smile changing subtly to one of self-satisfaction. "But, of course, I do realize that you work, and so…"

"And so?" Diana prompted when he paused, made uneasy by his self-satisfied smile, and positive he was about to make a suggestion she wouldn't like.

"How about tomorrow, after work?"

Diana took a moment to consider the idea. How long could it possibly take to buy a few gifts? she mused. If she left the office early, they could zip through the local shops, Matt could make his purchases, and they could still be home in time for dinner. Men hated to shop, anyway, didn't they?

Pleased with her conclusions, Diana smiled—and pondered the sudden taut, alert look on Matt's face. "Tomorrow will be all right," she said, puzzled by the flicker of emotion that briefly altered his watchful expression.

"Fine." Matt nodded, and it seemed to Diana that he was fighting to control a smile, or his feelings, or something. "What time do you usually leave the office?"

"The official closing time is five, but I often stay late." Shrugging off a sense of bafflement about the cause of his fleeting expression, Diana went on to outline her hastily put-together plan. "Since I'm caught up with the current project, I thought I'd leave the office at four. That way we could get an early start. Would that suit you?"

"Perfectly." Matt apparently lost the inner fight, at least against a smile. It curved his lips in a way that sent a tingle skipping up her spine to shiver along the fine hairs at her nape. "Do you ride to the office with Henry?"

"No." Diana frowned at the unexpected question. "As my hours are rather erratic, I drive myself. Why?"

Matt shrugged. "I thought it would save time if I could use your car and pick you up at the office."

Liking the idea of saving time, thus shortening the time she would have to spend with him, Diana pounced on his suggestion. "Yes, that makes sense. I'll drive into the office with Dad tomorrow."

"Good." Matt's tone of voice could only be described as a purr. The sound of it instilled apprehension in Diana. "I'll pick you up at four. We can shop for a while, then take a rest break and have dinner, then finish shopping refreshed."

Suddenly aware that she had good reason for apprehension, Diana opened her mouth to protest. "But—"

"Hey, what are you two doing out there all this time?" Lissa called from the living room doorway. "Are you cooking up Christmas surprises?"

"Yes," Matt admitted, turning to stroll toward the laughing woman. "So mind your own business—or you just might find your present pile short on Christmas morning."

Trapped. Convinced she had made a very big mistake by stupidly falling in with Matt's plans, Diana mentally kicked herself as she watched Matt and Lissa walk arm in arm into the living room to join the family.

Toting a bulging, oversize shopping bag, Matt kept his eyes pinned to Diana's enticing form. He was following in her wake as she adroitly weaved through the crowd of holiday shoppers bustling along the sidewalk.

Over an hour had passed since he had brought her car to a stop in front of the office building to find Diana waiting for him. Expecting to drive to one of the nearby malls, Matt had been surprised when, instead of getting into the car, Diana suggested he park in the office lot, since the restored shopping district was within walking distance.

Slushy snow covered the ground and lay in hard little piles along the curbs in front of the shops, lending an aura of authenticity to the quaint turn-of-the-century look of the area, which was three blocks long and closed to traffic.

Straight out of the pages of *A Christmas Carol,* Matt thought, noting the changes that had been made during his nine-year absence from the town.

Matt decided it would be easy to imagine having been flung back in time, if not for the modern dress of the shoppers, the piped Christmas music filling the crisp air from discreetly placed loudspeakers and the periodic blare of a car horn one block away from the confined area.

It was all very charming, Matt mused, dodging a group of giggling teenagers and extending his stride to catch up to Diana. Or it *would* be charming, he thought, if not for the damp cold seeping into his bones, the jostling of harried shoppers, and the breakneck pace Diana had set from the moment they reached the area.

Of course, Matt allowed, progress had been made—due to her single-minded determination. The bag he was lugging contained gifts for over half the names on his list. But, good God, the price he'd paid—not in currency, but in the wear and tear on his nerves, his patience—and his libido.

And there, four steps in front of him, strode the perpetrator of his activated libido. A grim smile tightened Matt's lips as he ran a slow look over Diana's curvaceous form.

The upper half of her body was concealed beneath a waist-length fake fox jacket. It was the lower half of her that was driving Matt to distraction. When she left the house that morning, Diana had been suitably attired for the office in a crisp white silk shirt and a knee-length wool skirt. Along with her attaché case, she had carried a small bag. The contents of that bag now encased her hips and legs—tight, straight-legged, soft denim jeans.

Heat rushed to converge in a very vulnerable part of Matt's body. No woman should look that appealing in pants, he silently protested. It simply wasn't fair to the male population, especially if that particular woman possessed a compact, neatly rounded tush, and legs that went on forever.

A nine-year-old image filled Matt's mind and senses. An image of those same long legs, encased not in denim, but in tantalizing sheer black nylon.

Matt smothered a groan, and murmured an apology to the elderly gentleman he had absently clipped with his shoulder while striding by. Damn. This was ridiculous, Matt railed, at himself and at the situation he had worked so hard to set up. His plan had been to get Diana away from the house, so that they could talk, one on one. Why hadn't he realized that streets and shops jammed with eleventh-hour holiday shoppers were not conducive to private conversation?

A sigh of undiluted relief whooshed through his lips when he saw Diana come to a stop in front of a brightly decorated jewelry store. When he came to a halt beside her, she took scant notice of him. Her lower lip caught between her teeth, she was intently perusing the glittering contents of the display window.

"I'm parched. Can we break for dinner now?" he asked, his eyes trailing her roving gaze, but getting snared by a small blue-velvet tray of diamond engagement rings. One ring in particular caught his fancy. Nice. Very nice. He imagined how that large, pear-shaped stone would look gracing Diana's finger. Better than nice. It would be perfect.

"I just know your mother would adore that coat pin."

"What?" Shoving the consideration of the ring to the back of his mind, Matt turned to frown at her.

Diana heaved a long-suffering sigh. "I said, I believe your mother would like that coat pin." She pointed to the left side of the case. "The gold unicorn with the pearl-studded horn and tail and the ruby eyes."

"I was hoping we could stop to eat now," Matt muttered, dutifully transferring his gaze to the piece of jewelery. "I'm hungry and thirsty."

"But, Matt, we're almost finished." Diana began ticking off purchases on the fingers of her right hand. "You bought the cashmere jacket for Dad, the leather bomber jacket for Terry, and those absolutely gorgeous, wildly expensive stone-washed silk lounging pajamas and kimono for Beth. That only leaves your mother and Lissa."

And you, Matt thought, shifting his gaze back to the tray of diamond rings.

"Unless you have other names on your list besides the fam- ily..." she went on.

"No." Shaking his head, Matt dragged his gaze from the ring to her face. "But I'm still hungry."

Diana sighed again, more deeply this time. "But we could finish up here," she insisted. "As I said, I know your mother would love that pin, and I'm sure we can find the perfect gift for Lissa in the specialty shop next door." She gave him an overbright smile. "We could finish up all your shopping and still get home in time to have dinner with the family."

Matt clenched his teeth and felt a muscle twitch in his jaw. However nicely, Diana had made it clear that she didn't want to have dinner alone with him. His frustration was nearing the ex- plosion point. But what could he do? There was no way he could force her to have dinner with him. Backing down had never been Matt's style, but, at least for now, he had little choice in the matter.

"Okay," he said, motioning toward the store's entrance. "Let's get it over with."

It was late. The house was quiet. It was so quiet Diana imag- ined she could hear Matt breathing in her father's office down- stairs.

She couldn't sleep. In fact, she was wide awake, alternately prowling the perimeters of her room and plopping down on the side of her bed, refereeing a tug-of-war between her intellect and her emotions.

Battle had been joined after dinner, while the family was gath- ered together in the living room. But Diana had had hints of the brewing inner conflict for some time, ever since the evening her father had announced that he had offered the olive branch of peace in the form of an invitation to Matt, welcoming him back into his house to spend the holidays with the family.

Diana's inner conflict had begun that very evening, escalating by increments with each successive day. Intellectually she knew it was time—long past time—to resolve the anger and resentment that had separated the family for nine years. The strain had taken its toll on all of them, and most especially Diana, who had shouldered the burden of responsibility. And so, intellectually, she acknowledged that it was also time for her to make peace with Matt. And what better time to make peace than at the Christmas season?

That was when Diana's emotions came into play, causing the inner conflict. From an emotional standpoint, she felt unequal to the task of facing Matt, let alone welcoming him home like a long-lost brother.

Diana loved Matt with every cell, molecule and breath in her body. She knew she would always love him—and not as a brother, but as a man.

But, with his cutting remark about Australia not being a great enough distance between them, Matt had made his antipathetic feelings for her abundantly clear.

And yet he had almost immediately made an about-face by not only asking her to help him with his shopping, but also insisting they have dinner alone together.

Why had Matt even wanted to be alone with her? Diana's intellect repeatedly questioned. The answer that sprang to her mind was predictably logical.

Ask Matt. Talk to him. Alone.

The opportunity to have a private discussion with him had presented itself several hours ago, when Matt had asked for and received Henry's permission to use his office for a few hours later that night.

Matt was down there; Diana knew it, for she had identified the others as they passed her door on the way to their bedrooms over an hour ago.

Perched on the edge of the mattress, Diana heard the grandfather clock in the foyer strike one. The inner conflict raged on. Intellect urging her to seize the opportunity to speak with him alone, to make her peace with him. Emotions cautioning her against exposing herself to the possibility of rejection, more pain, a deeper hurt.

Matt probably wouldn't remain in the office much longer, Diana thought as the clock struck the half hour. To go or not to go, *that* was the question.

Diana absently pleated the soft folds of the full skirt she had changed into for dinner after returning to the house. When she became aware of the nervous action, she frowned at her plucking fingers.

Damn it all! she railed, impatient with herself. Was she a mature adult, or still an impetuous teenager, locked inside a woman's body?

Spurred by the chastising thought, Diana deserted her perch and strode purposefully to the door. Besides making her a nervous wreck, this situation was getting ridiculous. Pushing her emotional fears into the background, she left her room and moved quietly along the hallway and down the stairs.

The office door stood slightly ajar, the light beyond indicating that Matt was still inside. Diana hesitated a moment, drew a steadying breath, then tapped against the panel, pushed the door open and entered the room.

Matt was seated behind her father's desk, a sheaf of papers in front of him, an attaché case open and lying to one side. His expression revealed surprise at her entrance, but was quickly controlled as she came to an uncertain halt a few steps inside the room.

"Well, hello," he said softly, slicing a glance at his wristwatch. "To what do I owe this nocturnal visit?"

His ebony hair was ruffled, as if from the absent raking of his fingers. His shirt collar was open, revealing the strong column of his throat. He looked tired, but so handsome, so appealing, and so blatantly male and sexy.

"I, er…that is…" Diana's surge of courage suddenly deserted her, leaving her feeling tongue-tied, inadequate, gauche, much more the girl than the woman. Hating the feeling, she inhaled a quick breath, then blurted out, "I wanted to talk to you… privately."

"All right." Pushing the chair back, Matt stood and circled the desk. "Come sit down," he said invitingly, giving a negligent wave of his hand to indicate the long sofa set at an angle near the fireplace—the very same sofa of that awful night.

Feeling slightly sick with nerves, Diana slowly crossed the room, moving not toward the sofa, the setting of their downfall, but to one of the overstuffed chairs grouped around it.

"Afraid?" Matt softly taunted her, intersecting her to take her by the arm and redirect her to the sofa. "I give you my word that you have nothing to fear from me, Diana."

Certain he was again, however obliquely, telling her that he wasn't interested enough in her to cause her to fear him, Diana felt a hollow, desolate sensation invade her stomach. Keeping her spine ramrod-straight and her shoulders squared, she sank into one corner of the sofa and kept her eyes fixed forward.

Matt settled his long form next to her, close, too close for her peace of mind, yet carefully not touching her with any part of his body. "Comfortable?"

Comfortable? Diana nodded in response and swallowed a groan of despair. Her taut, stiff posture concealed her senses inner clamoring to touch him, cling to him, beg him to want her again. Her tightly controlled expression betraying nothing of her feelings, she slanted a wary look at him. It was nearly her undoing. Matt's expression was gentle, yet intent. His dark eyes seemed to glow from an inner fire.

"You said you wanted to talk to me," he prompted her in a low, enticing murmur.

"Yes, I…" Diana paused to swallow once more and glide her tongue over her nerve-dried lips.

"Oh, Di, don't do that," Matt muttered, raising a hand to rake his fingers through his already ruffled hair. "We'll never get around to talking if you continue to do that."

"Wh— Don't do what?" she asked in a parched and raspy sounding whisper.

"Wet your lips like that with your tongue," he murmured. "The effect is the same as it was that night, like a silent invitation to me to kiss you." He heaved a sigh, and gave her a self-deprecating smile. "And I've been waiting so long, so very long, for that invitation."

"Waiting?" Diana turned to face him, and caught her breath at the expression of near-desperate longing straining his taut features. Barely breathing, trembling, she unconsciously wet her lips again. "But I thought—"

"Don't think, feel," he muttered, turning to lean over her. Then, giving a fatalistic shrug, he bent his head and brushed his mouth over hers.

Diana's mind fractured. Part of it, a tiny, still-lucid part, insisted that he had to be playing with her, deliberately tormenting her, since he had made a point of telling her she couldn't get far enough away to suit him. But the other part, the larger part, overshadowed the lucid part, shouting a demand that she seize the moment.

The issue was decided by an inner fear that the moment might never come for her again. Surrendering to the rioting demands of her raging senses, the searing need to taste him, she raised her arms and captured his head with her hands, drawing his mouth back to her parted and eager lips.

Matt went rock-still for an instant, as if startled—or shocked, by her blatant advance. Then, with a groan rumbling deep in his throat, he crushed her mouth beneath his.

No longer the tremulous girl, Diana responded with heated fervor, initiating a sensuous play by gliding her tongue along his lower lip while arching her body, pressing her soft curves to the hard angles of his.

Matt didn't hesitate to accept her silent offering. Stroking her tongue with his, he plunged inside, deepening the kiss as he sought her breast with one hand. He stroked the full outer curve before slipping his hand between their bodies to capture the taut tip, teasing it into a tight, throbbing arousal.

Sensations splintered inside Diana, sending shards of desire streaking from her pulsating nipple to every nerve ending in her quivering body. Starved for the feel of him after her nine-year fast, she sent her tingling hands exploring his head, his neck, his shoulders, his back, every inch of him that she could reach with her searching palms and fingers.

"Diana, Diana..." he groaned, releasing her mouth to string

hot, stinging kisses over her cheeks, along her jawline, then down the arched column of her throat. "I want you, I want you. Don't do this unless you want me, too."

"I do," she confessed, kissing his silky eyebrows, his eyelids, the vulnerable hollows beneath his eyes. "I want to be with you, to belong to you."

"But not here." Pulling away from her, Matt skimmed a hard look around the room. "Not here."

"No," she whispered. "Please, not here."

Matt was still for the length of a breath. Then, with a decisive nod of his head, he stood, scooped her up into his arms and strode from the room.

"Where—?" Diana's voice faded as he started up the staircase. Her room? she wondered. His?

Without hesitation, Matt strode to the end of the hallway and mounted the staircase leading to the third floor, and the bedroom that had been his from the day his mother married Diana's father. Locking the door behind him, he carried her to the side of the bed, then gently set her on her feet.

His chest heaving from his exertion, Matt stared into Diana's eyes. "You can still change your mind." His lips twisted into a smile of self-mockery. "But if you're going to, do it now, before I change mine."

Diana didn't hesitate long enough to allow common sense to overrule her emotions. Letting her actions speak for her, she slipped off her shoes, crawled onto the bed and held her arms out to him.

Matt inhaled sharply, then stretched his length next to her on the mattress. They turned as one, each reaching to embrace the other. Their kiss was deep, breathtaking. When they had to break the kiss to breathe, Matt raked his lips down her neck.

"I've waited so long, and I need you so damn much." His breathing strained, ragged, Matt glided his tongue from the wildly beating pulse at the base of her throat to the V of her silk shirt at the valley of her aching breasts. Smoothly, deftly, he undid the shirt buttons and unfastened the front clasp of her lacy bra.

After his remark about Australia not being far enough away for her to go, his claim of intense need succeeded only in confusing Diana. "I— Matt!" She gasped, shuddering, when his tongue gently lashed her nipple. "I don't understand. Just last night you told me that Australia wasn't far enough for me to be away from you. Now you say you need me. It doesn't make sense." She cried out with a quickly drawn breath when his tongue curled around her nipple.

"Then I'll make myself crystal-clear." Lifting his head from her breast, Matt stared into her passion-shadowed eyes. "What I meant last night was that Australia wasn't far enough away for you to run from me. I'll find you, wherever you go." He drew in a harsh breath, then said bluntly, "I ache for you, Diana. I have ached for you from the year you turned seventeen. And the aching has been damn near unbearable the last nine of those years." The flame deep in his dark eyes leaped into a blaze of unleashed desire. "Every woman I've been with throughout those years has been a pale substitute for you." He lowered his head to seize her surprise-widened lips with his own.

Matt's kiss, though brief in duration, was devastating in effect. It drowned her senses, and the questions still nagging at the edges of her mind. But the answers no longer mattered to Diana. Matt wanted her, needed her, if only to appease an unsatisfied hunger.

Lust. It was light-years away from love, but it was an emotion, a driving emotion that Matt felt for her. It was better than the nothing she had lived with for nine years.

Diana was vaguely aware that she would very likely regret this night, but for now, Matt was here, in her arms, needing her, eager to fulfill her own yearning.

"Stay with me. Join with me. Be one with me, Diana," he pleaded, stroking her lips with his teasing tongue, and her breast with his fingers.

"Yes," she whispered in surrender. Then, more urgently: "Oh, Matt, *yes.*"

Murmuring shocking, erotic, exciting words to her, words that described his fantasies about all the ways they could be together,

Matt smoothed the clothing from her body. Then he rolled off the mattress to stand beside the bed, his glittering eyes devouring her nude form while he literally tore away his own clothing, revealing to her the extent of his arousal.

Diana trembled, not in fear, but in anticipation. She knew what to expect, and she didn't care. Like him, she had waited so long, too long to be deterred by the prospect of a moment of discomfort.

"Diana." Matt half growled, half groaned her name as he took the one step needed to bring him to the edge of the bed.

Ready, eager, desperate for him, Diana offered him the ultimate invitation by again holding out her arms, and this time parting her thighs for him.

"It will be good, it will be more than good," Matt promised, bracing his hands on either side of her as he eased his body into the cradle of her thighs. "It will be wonderful."

Lowering his head, he crushed her lips beneath his, and thrust his tongue into her mouth at the same instant he thrust his body into hers.

The tearing pain wrenched a muffled cry from Diana. Her body contracted and stiffened in reaction to the sudden invasion of her flesh by his.

Matt went absolutely still for a heartbeat. Then he pulled his head back to stare at her in blank astonishment and sheer disbelief.

"Diana..." His voice was rough, heavy with self-condemnation. "I hurt you... But I had no idea, never dreamed that you could possibly still be a vir—"

"It's all right," she broke in, grasping his buttocks when he made as if to withdraw. "No, don't move. The pain is gone. Just give me a minute."

Matt watched her, examining her eyes, her face, for evidence of strain, his expression betraying the inner battle he was waging, between his concern for her possible discomfort and his raging desire.

Diana kept a tight grasp on him, holding him deep inside her as her body adjusted to the fullness of his. The stiffness drained from her body, to be replaced immediately by the tension of rising excitement and desire.

"Now," she whispered, digging her nails into his taut flesh and arching into his responsive thrust. *"Now."*

Set free of the constraints of his concern for her, Matt obeyed Diana's ragged command. Unleashing the power of his strong body, he drove himself, and her, mercilessly. Reveling in her uninhibited response to his every move, his body and hers gleaming slickly in the pale moonlight splashing across the bed, he drove them both over the edge, into gasping completion.

Chapter 5

"**W**ake up, Sleeping Beauty."

Diana emerged from the deep sleep of repletion to the feel of a sweet kiss from her own Prince Charming. Thoroughly exhausted, they had slept still coupled, and not from their first joining, but their third, his body buried deeply in hers.

"Ummm..." she murmured, stretching her cramped limbs by flexing her arms, which were circling his neck, and tightening the muscles in her legs, which were clasped around his thighs. "More," she pleaded softly, seeking the smiling lips hovering above her mouth.

"Just one more," Matt whispered, teasing her with quick stabs of his tongue into the corner of her mouth.

"Why?" Diana protested, pushing her lower lip forward in a pout of disappointment.

"Because it will soon be dawn," Matt said, gliding his tongue along her pouting lip. "And I'm cold."

"Pull up the covers."

Matt grinned. "Can't. We kicked them onto the floor sometime during the night."

Covered by his larger form, Diana felt deliciously warm, and was growing warmer by the second. She moved her hips, wriggling and arching to ease the heaviness of his weight, which was pressing her into the firm mattress. She smiled when she felt the leap of renewed life inside her.

Matt drew a sharp breath, then went still, as if savoring the sensation of his quickening arousal. "I mean, my back is cold," he said, moving his hips. "My front is warm, and heating up like crazy." Suddenly he went still, frowning down at her. "Did that hurt? Are you sore?"

"No. And yes." She did have a few twinges of soreness. "But please don't stop." She sighed in response to his gentle, tentative thrust. "It feels so good, and it makes me forget the soreness."

Matt shot a glance at the watch clasped on his naked wrist. "It will have to be a quick one, Beauty." He began moving his body as he murmured the warning. "Or we'll be risking getting caught again, this time with our pants down."

"Off," Diana told him, the sexual tension spiraling inside her negating the anguish usually associated with the memory. "Oh, Matt, hurry…hurry!"

Proving he was only too happy to comply, Matt set a rhythmic pace that hurled them, breathless and mindless, into the heights of shattering release.

Spent, Diana lay entwined with Matt as she slowly descended from the realm of unbelievable ecstasy. Feeling his heart thump in time with her own, listening as his breathing evened and reg-ulated, she smiled and stroked her fingers through the sweat-dampened strands of his glistening black hair.

"For all your lack of experience," he whispered, his chest expanding in a sigh of contentment, "you are fantastic." He raised his hand to a long, jet-black spiral curl coiled on her shoulder and slowly wound it around his finger, as if binding her to him. "You're even more exciting as a lover than I ever dreamed you'd be."

Feeling inordinately complimented by his praise, Diana rushed to admit to her fears. "I…I was afraid you'd be disap-pointed…in comparison to your other…er—" she hesitated, groping for another word for *lover* "—partners." She blurted out the final word artlessly.

Matt raised his head from her breast to gaze at her with eyes alight with amusement. "There haven't been all that many, Di."

His voice, though quiet, rang with sincerity. "And, as I told you, they were all merely subtitutes, shadows of the one lover I always wanted."

"Me?" Diana asked, her tone betraying both her amazement and her aching desire to believe him.

"You." Matt smiled the smile of a self-satisfied conqueror. "And to think I was the first." He shook his head, as if unable to believe his good fortune. "All I can say is, being first with you is the best Christmas present I ever received."

Diana didn't respond, couldn't respond, for while her emotional self grew flushed with his expressed pleasure, her intellectual side rejected the importance of virginity.

Matt lowered his eyes to her cheeks, noting the evidence of her blush, thus missing the cloud of conflict in her eyes. Then, sighing again, he buried his face in the curve of her neck. "It must be nearly five now," he murmured regretfully, pressing his lips to the side of her throat. "We've got to move."

"I know." Diana agreed. "But I'm not even sure I can move. I'm so, so..."

"Satisfied?" Matt finished for her, pushing himself up and back to stare down into her still-flushed face.

"Yes," she admitted, telling herself she had moved far beyond dissimulation. "And so sleepy." She yawned and turned her head to peer at his watch. "I'd better get to bed. To my *own* bed. As it is, I'll only get about two hours' sleep."

Grunting, Matt heaved himself up, away from her and off the bed. Then he proceeded to steal her restored breath by raising his arms and stretching luxuriously, flexing the tendons and long muscles in his fit, magnificent body. "I feel great," he declared, bending to collect their clothes. "Better than I have for—" He paused, absently stroking her shirt. "Forever," he finished, smiling, as he stepped into his briefs.

Her uncertainty, soreness and sleepiness aside, Diana felt pretty good herself. The loss of her physical innocence seemed to lend an added measure of maturity to her perceptions. Although Matt had confessed to lusting for her, not loving her, he had made love with her, not merely had sex with her, and had rejoiced in her innocence and her pleasure. And if Matt's offering was less than she desired in her heart of hearts, it still was more than she had ever hoped to have of him.

"Why don't you take the day off?" he suggested, holding her shirt for her, then raising a hand to lift her long hair from beneath the collar. "Sleep in."

"Can't." Diana fastened her skirt, then gathered up her bra, panty hose and shoes. "The office closes at noon today for the duration of the holidays." She gave him a faint smile as she slowly walked to the door. "Dad and I take the office staff to lunch after closing. I have to be there." She paused at the door to look back at him with unabashed longing. "I'll be home early, and I'll catch a nap before it's time to leave for the airport to pick up Terry."

"Wait till I pull on my pants, and I'll walk you to your room," he said when she unlocked the door and grasped the knob.

Diana gave him a chiding look. "And risk being seen together?" She arched her brows. "With you half-dressed and me carrying my underwear?"

Matt heaved an impatient sigh. "I don't care anymore, Di," he said, walking to her and pulling her into his arms. "You're a woman now, an adult. You said you wanted to belong to me, and now you do." His mouth claimed hers in a quick, hard, possessive kiss. "And I don't care who knows it."

"Matt, please, think." Diana gazed at him imploringly. "Do you really want to chance disrupting another holiday? Do you want to insult Dad after he extended an offer of peace to you?"

Matt's expression revealed his conflicting feelings. "No, of course not." He shook his head. "But, dammit…"

Diana effectively silenced him with her mouth, gently pressed to his complaining lips. "I'll be quite safe," she promised, teasing him. "There are no muggers in the hallway."

Matt favored her with a wry smile, and another satisfying kiss. "Okay, you win—this time."

"Thank you. Now I must run." She raised a hand to cover another yawn. "Have a good day, Matt."

"Oh, I intend to." Matt's expression was oddly enigmatic. "Sleep well, Beauty."

* * *

"Hey, Di, are you alive in there?" Lissa's shout followed a loud rap on the bedroom door. "Dad, Matt and Terry have gone downstairs already."

"In a minute," Diana called, grimacing at herself in the mirror as she gave one last tug of her hairbrush through her sleep-tossed riot of curls. She belted her robe securely around her waist as she headed for the door, declaring herself ready to face the traditional Blair-Turner family Christmas-morning activities.

Ever since the two separate families had combined forces to form one family unit, a Christmas-morning ritual had been observed, a ritual that had been adhered to with only slight variations to the present.

Since both the four-year-old Diana and the two-year-old Melissa naturally still believed in Santa Claus—and Miriam had doubts about the nine-year-old Bethany's professed disbelief— Miriam, Henry and Matt, then in his teens, had kept up the game of Christmas-morning wonder and surprise by trooping downstairs at the crack of dawn with the excited girls, who were too eager and impatient to wait for anyone to dress.

Then, after the gifts had all been opened and exclaimed over, and the living room looked as if it had been hit by a tornado, everyone had pitched in to clear away the wrapping paper, ribbons, bows, gift cards and other debris before trooping into the dining room for breakfast. After breakfast, everyone had then returned to their rooms to dress for church.

Of course, the game had continued after Terry's birth. By the time the youngest member of the combined families no longer believed in the largess of a jolly fat man in a red suit, a family ritual had been established.

But this was the first Christmas morning in nine years when every member of the family would be there to take part in and enjoy the gift-giving ritual.

"Di-a-na!" Lissa yelled.

"Yes, yes, I'm coming." Diana reached for the doorknob, sighed, and let her hand fall to her side.

And this was the first Christmas morning ever that she'd wanted to absent herself from the ritual.

Diana's reasons for wanting to remain in her room, hiding behind a contrived migraine, or a sore throat, or some other debilitating illness, were many—and every one of them bore the name Matt.

Matt. Diana sighed and shifted a longing gaze from the bedroom door to her bed. The soreness in her body had dissipated over the past two days. But, in direct response to Matt's baffling demeanor, the uncertainty plaguing her mind had intensified.

Not that Diana had expected Matt to betray to the rest of the family the intimacy they had shared in his bedroom, in his bed. Absolutely the last thing she wanted was a replay of that terrible scene of nearly nine years ago.

In retrospect, Diana really didn't know exactly what she had expected from him, but it certainly hadn't been the odd looks and contemplative expression Matt had worn in the course of the past two days.

What were his thoughts, his feelings? she had found herself wondering. On her return to the house the day after their night in bed together, Diana had nervously anticipated their first meeting. She'd been tired, not only from the exercise of repeated wild lovemaking, but also from a lack of sleep, the employees' luncheon, and dashing around to find the one gift she had not yet purchased—a present for Matt.

More than a little uncertain about the gift she had finally selected, she had entered the house feeling heavy with misgivings about how the gift would be construed, and not at all anxious to face the prospective recipient of her offering.

She might as well have saved herself the hours of angst. Matt hadn't even been in the house. In passing, Miriam had casually mentioned that he'd gone out to do some eleventh-hour shopping of his own. Grateful for the reprieve, and claiming exhaustion, Diana had dropped like a stone onto her bed, sleeping through dinner and straight up to a few hours before it was time to drive to the airport to collect Terry.

The day and evening before Christmas had been jam-packed with last-minute activities that allowed not a single opportunity for so much as a few private words between Diana and Matt.

But she had several times caught him staring at her with that strange, reflective expression.

When the seemingly endless day came to a close with the family all bringing their gifts into the living room to arrange around the base of the tree, Diana had held back the gift she had bought for Matt, and then, against her better judgment, had thrust it to the very back of the pile.

Now, at an ungodly hour on Christmas morning, Diana hesitated, a step away from her bedroom door, wishing the small gift was safely back in her dresser drawer.

"Diana, you'd better get a move on," Beth called in a tone of voice edged with impatience. "Lissa's threatening to go downstairs without you."

What else is new? Diana thought, smiling despite her trepidation. Beside herself with excitement, Lissa had always threatened to go downstairs alone on Christmas morning. Keeping her smile firmly in place, Diana opened the door and left the room. Her smile tilting to one of apology in response to the long-suffering expressions aimed at her by Lissa, Beth and Miriam, she stifled a sigh and trailed behind the trio, down the stairs and into the living room.

"Well, at last," Terry said teasingly. "Don't tell me, let me guess. Diana held up the parade—right?"

His good-natured remark was met with affirmative nods from the women, an indulgent chuckle from her father, and an enigmatic smile from Matt.

Deciding she was getting pretty tired of his enigmatic and musing looks, Diana ignored the bunch of them as she walked to the chair farthest from the tree. Clasping her hands in her lap to keep them from trembling, she sat quietly, watching as Miriam and Lissa handed out the gifts, whittling away at the pile around the tree. Then, just as quietly, she opened the presents handed to her, softly murmuring her thanks and declaring her pleasure with each successive gift, while observing the reactions of the others, and most especially Matt.

"Hey, thanks, Matt!" Terry hooted, jumping up to try on the leather bomber jacket.

"Hmm, smells sexy," Matt said, shooting a devilish look and

a grin at Lissa as he sniffed at the expensive cologne she had chosen for him. "Thank you."

"Matt, this really wasn't necessary," her father murmured, stroking the cashmere jacket. "I don't know what to say."

"Then don't say anything," Matt replied, shifting a soft gaze to his mother. "I only hope you like it as much as I like this," he went on, holding an imported Irish sweater up to his chest.

"Darling, this is absolutely fabulous!" Miriam cried, displaying the coat pin for everyone's perusal.

And so it went, Beth delighting in the silk pajamas and kimono, Lissa in transports over the small beaded evening bag Diana had spied in the specialty shop, and Matt obviously touched by the symbolism in the gift of a new front-door key from Henry.

When she opened her gift from Matt, Diana prayed she was successful in concealing the disappointment and hurt she felt about the lovely but ordinary scarf he had chosen for her. Reminding herself that her gift was every bit as ordinary, even if it did convey her deepest feelings, she waited, growing more nervous by the second for him to get to it. Hers was the last gift he opened.

Matt drew out the moment, carefully tugging the wrapping loose before lifting her gift from the paper. He held the book in his hands for long seconds, staring down at the title. When, finally, he raised his head to stare at Diana, the enigmatic, reflective expression was gone, and his eyes were soft, glowing with some strong inner emotion.

"What is the title, Matt?" Miriam asked curiously.

"Come Home to Love," Matt said quietly, reading from the book's cover.

"Oh, how clever of you, Diana!" Lissa exclaimed. "Perfect for the occasion."

"More than you know," Matt said, glancing around at everyone in turn, pausing an instant to share a secret, mysterious smile with Henry.

"Yeah, terrific, Di," Terry interjected into the brief silence that ensued. "Now, how about breakfast?" He sprang up from his sprawled position on the floor. "I'm starving."

"If all of you will be patient for a few more minutes," Matt said, bringing the rustle of movement to a halt, "I have something I want to say."

Diana had set her gifts to one side in preparation to rise, but she settled back in her chair to hear Matt out, convinced by his expression, the emotion shining from his dark eyes, that he planned to voice his appreciation to all of them for their warm and generous homecoming welcome.

"I have discussed this with Henry, and have received both his permission and his blessing."

Matt's opening statement startled and confused Diana. Her father's permission and blessing? she repeated to herself. For what possible reason... Her thoughts were scattered by a sudden leap of hope as Matt began speaking again.

"In deference to the man I had come to love, respect and regard as a father," he said, slowly glancing at the attentive faces around him, "I exiled myself from this house and frequent personal contact with the members of my family, most particularly one member." His gaze came to rest on Diana. "The one person I love, have always loved above all others."

Diana drew in a sharp breath; it blended in with the chorus of surprised gasps from the others. Her eyes wide, unconsciously pleading with him to be telling the truth, she watched him rise and slowly walk toward where she sat, riveted to the chair at the far corner of the room.

"I denied my right to that love for nine long years, paying the price for my loss of control and self-indulgence on that ill-fated New Year's Eve." He slid a hand into the pocket of his cardigan sweater as he came to a stop in front of Diana. "But, no matter how much I denied myself, I never stopped loving," he said, staring deeply into her eyes, as if attempting to see into her soul. "I knew the moment Diana walked into the house the day I arrived that I had been in love with her, am still in love with her, and will always be in love with her."

Diana's eyes were stinging from tears she couldn't hold back. She didn't notice. All she saw was Matt's beloved face as he dropped to his knees before her.

"You have given me the most precious gift a woman can give

to a man,'' he murmured, in a heart-wrenchingly tender tone. Removing his hand from his pocket, he opened it to reveal a small black-velvet jeweler's box. ''In comparison to the gift of your innocence, my offering is paltry,'' he whispered for her ears alone. ''But I love you, and pray with all my heart that you will accept it.'' His hands unsteady, his fingers shaking, Matt lifted the lid of the box.

''Oh, Matt!'' Diana breathed, staring in disbelief and delight at the beautiful pear-shaped diamond engagement ring winking up at her from the satin lining of the box. ''It's...it's...so very beautiful.''

''I know.'' Matt smiled with loving tenderness. ''But will you accept it...and me?''

''Yes,'' she answered in a reedy whisper. Then, exultantly: ''Yes, yes, yes!''

Matt's waist pressed against Diana's knees as he leaned forward, bringing his mouth close to hers. His lips were within a fleeting thought of touching hers. Her own lips were tingling in anticipation. Then his breath was exhaled into her mouth in a moist *whoosh* followed by a chuckle at the confused sound of his stepbrother's voice.

''What did he say to her?'' Terry asked as the other members of the family discreetly headed for the doorway.

''You mean you can't figure it out for yourself?'' Beth drawled, laughing, as she slipped from the room.

Lissa taunted him, following Beth. ''What a brain trust.''

''It's all right, Terry,'' Miriam said soothingly. ''Your time will come, and then you'll understand.''

''My time for what?'' Terry demanded. ''And where are you all going?''

''Your time for love, Terry,'' Henry answered, draping one arm around his son's shoulders to steer him in the wake of the others. ''And we're all going in to breakfast.''

''Love?'' Terry repeated, rather as if it were an unsavory word. ''Matt and Diana are in love?''

''From the way they are looking at each other now,'' Henry replied, his voice drifting back to the couple from the foyer, ''I would say that they are.''

"Are they?" Matt murmured against Diana's lips. "Are they *both* in love?"

"They are," Diana whispered, straining forward to coax his mouth into contact with hers.

Matt pulled his head back, just far enough that he could gaze into her misty dark eyes. "Then say it, Beauty. I said it. Now I want, need, am dying to hear you say it, too."

"I love you, Matt Turner." Diana's voice was strong with conviction. "I have always loved you. I will always love you." A teasing smile tilted her lips. "And don't ever even think about running away from me, because there is no place on this entire planet far enough away that I won't find you." She gave him a smug smile. "So, what do you say to that?"

Matt answered her silently first, in the form of a long, sweet, satisfying kiss. When he raised his head, his dark eyes were bright, and his verbal answer came accompanied by a wicked smile.

"Merry Christmas, Diana."

* * * * *

SANTA'S SPECIAL MIRACLE

Ann Major

Dear Reader,

Christmas has always been a favorite season in my life.
Luckily. I come from a large, loving family, and we
always get together. We cook. We party. We share stories
and open gifts beneath the tree. We gain weight, too.

This past year my daughter-in-law brought her Scottish
terrier, Scootie, to the festivities. While I cooked the
Christmas turkey, Scootie slept on top of my foot. Scootie
stayed nearly two weeks, and everybody but my four cats
fell in love with her. Not a single cat purred until the
holidays were over and Scootie was gone.

My spoiled cats aside—what better season than Christmas
is there to find true love?

New beginnings. New love. A new family. That's what
Christmas and life are all about.

Merry Christmas to you all!

Ann Major

Chapter 1

Oh, why had she let Sara and Jim and their children talk her into driving with them into San Antonio to shop?

Lights and red and gold velvet streamers sparkled from the ceiling of San Antonio's River Center Mall. A festive, last-minute mania infected the shoppers and salespeople who hustled and bustled everywhere.

But Noreen Black couldn't get into the Christmas spirit. Instead she felt a quiet desperation, an aching loneliness. Oh, sure, she'd bought half a dozen gifts. Sure, she was being jostled along in the crowd like everybody else during the holiday season. And right now she was struggling to keep a tight grip on Darius's little hand as well as manage her huge shopping sacks. But unlike everyone else who seemed in a joyful mood, Noreen felt only despair.

Suddenly through the crowd Noreen saw a tall man with broad shoulders and darkly handsome good looks threading his way toward her.

It couldn't be! No! Not Grant! Not after all these years. Not when she had Darius clinging tightly to her fingers.

She wanted to run, to cry out. Instead her panic overwhelmed her, and she did the most foolish thing of all. She simply froze.

Then, right before he headed into a luxurious lingerie shop, the man turned and saw her. She felt an instant sensation of doom. For a fleeting second he studied her with one of those quick, assessing, male glances. He saw a beautiful woman in her early thirties who was tall and delicate of feature. A woman who had enormous, dark, frightened eyes. A woman with a shocking mass of jet-black hair bound untidily in a lopsided knot. A woman who wore a bright animal-print scarf and baggy sweater and had a Bohemian air about her. But she was not someone he knew. He smiled briefly and vanished inside the shop.

He was just a stranger. A stranger with gray eyes instead of Grant's vivid, beautiful blue ones. A stranger who probably thought her too dull in her unfashionable clothes, or too skinny. He wasn't Grant. Wasn't even remotely like Grant. Still, it took a second for Noreen's shock to subside.

Just being in San Antonio was enough to make Noreen as nervous as a cat, and today, despite her cheery pretenses, had been no different. San Antonio was part of her past, part of that other life that she had deliberately walked away from five years ago, part of Grant. Even the briefest visit to the city could fill her with an intense sensation of loss and loneliness and leave her depressed for days. A part of her had died here, and she had never recovered.

Of course, living as she did only fifty miles away in a Texas town so small and so poor that it had no doctor or shopping facilities, she had to come into the city from time to time. Never once had she run into Grant or his mother, but the threat of that happening had always been in her mind. She found herself looking around with a strange mixture of excitement and dread in the pit of her stomach, as if she were unconsciously searching the crowd for Grant's black head, for his tall, wide-shouldered form.

Darius suddenly yanked free of his mother's grip, and Noreen felt close to panic again. Then she saw that he was racing for the line of children waiting to talk to Santa. Darius loped ahead of her as eagerly and trustingly as a puppy, his short quick legs spraddling everywhere, shoestrings snapping in all directions, sure his mother would follow at her proper adult pace.

Watching him, she smiled fondly. Instead of Velcro fasteners, he insisted on shoelaces because his best friend's teenage brother, Raymond Liska, had laces. It did no good to tell Darius that big brothers could have laces because they were able to tie them.

There was an empty bench right in front of Santa's Workshop, and Noreen sank down on it, piling her bundles beside her. Her feet ached all the way up her calves to her knees. She loosened her scarf. It wasn't even noon yet, and she was exhausted from shopping and from chasing Darius—two jobs she vowed long ago never to take on simultaneously.

But Christmas was coming soon, and all four-year-old boys had to talk to Santa at least once. Darius had talked to five Santas since Thanksgiving. Every time he had done so, his big blue eyes had grown huge as he'd leaned into Santa's ear and whispered. When she'd asked him what he wanted he'd refused to tell her.

"Santa knows," he would say wisely.

Today Noreen had dragged him to every toy store in the mall. With huge shining eyes, Darius had handled the toys, at first with exuberant enthusiasm, until she'd asked him, "What do you want?" Then he had reluctantly set the toys back at cockeyed angles on the shelf. His darling baby-plump face had become still, and his answer had been reverent and enigmatic.

"Santa knows."

"You must tell Mommy."

"Why?"

Little did he know that she had almost nothing for him under the tree. That was the main reason she had let the Liskas persuade her to come into San Antonio.

As Noreen watched Darius jump joyfully into Santa's plump red velvet lap she thought, *At least he'll sit still for a second and I can catch my breath.*

"Silent Night," her favorite Christmas carol, was being piped over the sound system. For the first time since seven that morning when she'd climbed into the Liskas' Suburban, she relaxed. She glanced down at her wristwatch. She and Darius still had an hour to shop before they were to rendezvous with the Liskas and their four children for lunch on the river at Casa Rio.

Noreen groaned inwardly as she watched Darius unwrap the

peppermint candy cane that Santa had given him and whisper into Santa's ear at the same time. Santa was going to have sticky ears. Sugar made Darius absolutely hyper. He wouldn't eat lunch, and he probably wouldn't nap on the way home.

"So what special present do you want Santa to bring you this year, young man?" Santa asked.

"Special?" The word was new. Darius licked his candy cane thoughtfully.

"The best present you've ever gotten?" Santa prompted.

Darius whispered again, but Santa couldn't make out the whisper and told him so.

Darius's eager, piping voice rang through the store. "The best present ever? A daddy that's even better than Leo's, that's what!"

Noreen looked up sharply at her son, all the old sorrow upon her. Her brown eyes grew bleak. She had tried to explain so many times to Darius that his father was in Heaven. She'd framed her favorite picture of Larry and kept it in Darius's room.

Noreen scarcely heard Santa's low rumble. But she heard her son's matter-of-fact reply. "Nope. Just a daddy."

"What about a toy truck or a car?"

Darius shook his black head as stubbornly as his father would have. As stubbornly as any Hale.

Santa was setting the child down, helping him get his balance as Noreen came over and gently took Darius's hand.

"You could have told me what you wanted," she said softly to her son, her voice immeasurably sad.

"Do you think Santa can really bring me a daddy?"

"Honey, I told you how your father died. You have his picture on that little table by your bed."

Darius's big blue eyes, so like his father's and his Uncle Grant's, grew solemn at that memory. "But I need a real live daddy, too."

She rumpled Darius's black hair. "A daddy is…well… er…That's a very complicated present."

"That's why I asked Santa, Mom. 'Cause he's magic."

Noreen remained silent. She turned helplessly back to Santa, who had been eavesdropping. But Santa was no help. With a merry jingling of tiny bells, he just tipped his hat and gave her an audacious wink.

For a moment she remembered her marriage, Larry's death, Grant, the bitter loss of it all. And suddenly she was so cold inside that she could feel nothing else.

Noreen was in a hurry now, a hurry to leave the mall and make it to the Casa Rio by one-thirty to meet Sara and Jim and their brood. She had shopped in a frenzy ever since she'd found out what Darius really wanted for Christmas. She couldn't provide the father he wanted, but she could get him other things. Now she was so loaded down with bags that she could no longer hold them all, and Darius was even carrying the two he'd bought for Leo and another friend.

They were on the escalator when the nightmare she had dreaded for five long years became a reality.

There was no time to prepare. No time to run. She and Darius were trapped on that gliding silver stairway.

They were going down.

Her ex brother-in-law was going up.

Fortunately, Grant wasn't looking in her direction when she saw him. She went rigid with shock, turned her head away, and lifted her shaking hand to cover her features. But not before his harsh, set face had etched itself into her brain, and into her heart and soul, as well.

He looked tired. Tired and haggard in a way that wrenched her heart.

But he was as handsome as ever. He was taller than other men, and broader through the shoulders. So tall he dwarfed her in comparison. His face was lean and dark, his hair as thick and black and unruly as her own, his eyes the same dazzling blue she remembered, his mouth still as beautifully shaped.

As if she could have forgotten him.

As if any woman could.

Her heart was beating like a mad thing gone wild. She was almost safe. They were gliding past each other. She would probably never see him again. Why would she? He was a Hale and, no doubt, by now one of the most powerful lawyers in San Antonio. She was a nobody, a small-town librarian.

How many nights had she dreamed of him? He had probably never given her another thought.

A fatal impulse possessed her. Forgetting her fears for Darius, forgetting she was risking her new life in doing so, she couldn't resist glancing over her shoulder for one last glimpse of him.

She did so just when Grant was looking back.

Their eyes met.

And so did their souls. One fleeting instant of mutual longing bound them before other, darker emotions stormed to the surface.

Slowly his black brows drew together—in a smoldering rage or in hate, she did not know which. Terror welled up in her.

Fortunately, the moving escalators were crowded. Fortunately, the railing was high, and Grant couldn't see that she was with a child.

"Norie!"

The husky sound of his voice crying her name cut her like a knife.

Grant shouted a second time as she scrambled to get off the escalator, pulling Darius, juggling packages.

One of her packages fell. She looked back. Her new pair of sparkly red high heels had tumbled out of their box. But she raced on, into the nearest store where she grabbed a wild assortment of jeans and tops and took Darius with her into a tiny dressing room.

There she stayed for an hour, reading to Darius in a whispery voice from one of the storybooks she had bought for the school library.

A long time later, a saleslady called to them. "Does anything fit?"

She heard male voices in the next fitting room, saw a pair of male legs on the other side of the divider of her stall. It was only then that Noreen noticed she'd grabbed men's jeans, and she and Darius were hiding in the men's fitting room.

She began to laugh silently, a little hysterically, and Darius watched her with huge worried eyes.

* * *

When Noreen and Darius were a breathless thirty minutes late to the Casa Rio, the Liskas were too dear to criticize.

They were a handsome couple. Jim was tall and dark, gentle and strong. His wife had soft brown hair, brown eyes, and a sweet face. They'd been high school sweethearts and had one of the happiest marriages Noreen had ever seen.

Noreen sank down beside them, offering neither excuses nor explanations, and let Jim order her lunch. Sara, who'd grown up in a small town and simply adored gossip, studied Noreen's white face with avid curiosity.

Fortunately, before Sara could start quizzing her, the children took over. First Leo knocked over his soda. Then Darius tried to feed a chip dipped in hot sauce to a pigeon, leaned back too far in his chair, and nearly fell into the river.

At last the chaos of lunch was over and the Liskas had bribed Raymond to take his younger siblings and Darius off to ride the paddleboats.

The table was set in a cool and shady spot. Mariachi music was being played softly in the background. Sunlight sparkled on the river and shimmered in the golden leaves overhead. Jim, who worked as a science teacher at the same school Noreen did, was finishing the last of his beer. Sara was holding his hand. Noreen sipped her cup of tea.

"We'd better enjoy this before the kids come back," Sara said. "Noreen, the kids were terrible in the mall. I guess it's just that they're all so excited. Leo wanted everything in sight. Raymond kept teasing him, telling him he'd been so bad Santa was bringing switches this year. How was Darius?"

"He told Santa that he wants a daddy."

Jim put down his beer bottle. His dark eyes lit with humor. "That's certainly going to set the town on its edge. I can just see the headline now: Town's Mystery Librarian Gets Son A Daddy!"

Noreen didn't smile. "Darius is getting older. He wants things that I can't always give him. I'm not quite sure what to do about him anymore."

"No parent ever is," Sara said.

A devilish half smile curved Jim's mouth as he pulled his hand free of Sara's and leaned toward Noreen. "I think Darius has a good point. He does need a daddy. But no more than you need a husband."

"What? If ever I heard a chauvinistic remark—"

"Jim's full of them," Sara said placidly.

"You've practically buried yourself alive these past five years," Jim continued.

"Why, that's not true. I stay very busy with my job and with Darius. You know I'm as involved as anybody in civic projects."

"You're still the town mystery," Jim persisted. "You came to town five years ago—pregnant and single."

"That sounds so deliciously sinful," Sara said, "like a soap opera or something. You know it wasn't like that."

"I was a widow," Noreen replied tautly.

"Who still wears her wedding band, but goes by her maiden name. People know just what you want them to know. They know you're the school librarian."

"And a good one," Sara said, still trying to make peace.

"They know you moved in with Miss Maddie, that you inherited her farmhouse last year after she died. Not that anyone thinks you shouldn't have. Not after the way you took care of her after she went blind. They know that in the summers you hold the best story hour in the county every Wednesday morning at 10:00 sharp. They know you're a woman without pretensions. You're as plain as earth. As simple as water."

"Thanks." Noreen still wasn't smiling.

"I meant it as a compliment."

"Don't be mad, Norie," Sara said, folding her hand over Jim's again. "That's the way he compliments me, too."

"If I'm so ordinary, then why can't people be satisfied that there's nothing to know?"

"Because you don't talk about your past. You're running away from something or someone. And everyone wants to know who or what."

"Why—why, that's nonsense." But Noreen's slim fingers were so tensely clenched around her teacup that every vein stood out.

Jim leaned over and gently unclenched her hand. "Is it? Then why don't you accept a date with Mike Yanta the next time he asks you out?''

''Because...''

She looked at Jim and then looked away. Her dark eyes grew luminous with a pain she could neither share nor explain.

Her two dear friends would never understand. They didn't know she was a Hale by marriage. They knew nothing of her wealthy background. They wouldn't understand if she tried to explain.

People like them would have considered the Hale wealth and power a blessing. They wouldn't know that money could be the cruelest of weapons. It could be used to destroy love, to wield power, to sever the closest bonds that could exist between a man and a woman.

Noreen had learned all about money and its misuse by bitter experience. First she had lost the man she loved. Then she had lost her husband. She was determined not to lose her son.

Unbidden came the memory of Grant Hale on the escalator.... Of his arrogant tanned face... Of his husky voice calling her name...

Chapter 2

Noreen was shivering as she gripped the steering wheel of her truck and strained forward to see through her fogging windshield. The last lights of the town were growing dimmer in her rearview mirror. The sky ahead was black; the narrow, curving road that led to her farmhouse treacherously slick with ice. And it was still sleeting.

Texas weather. Yesterday San Antonio had been sunny and warm, so warm it had been impossible to believe that today could be this dark and wintry with cold.

Because she didn't like driving the lonely road by herself, Mike Yanta had offered to follow her home. But she had known he would have expected an invitation to come in, so she had refused.

It was nearly midnight, and Noreen was tired. She hadn't slept much the night before. Instead she'd lain awake in her icy bedroom, listening to all the eerie creaks her farmhouse made as the norther howled. And she'd been thinking of Grant. Thinking of how his face had seemed leaner and harsher. Remembering how his eyes had pierced through her. Today had been no better. The past had seemed very near, all the old conflicts as deeply troubling as before.

Although she was off for the school holidays, she'd spent the day sewing Darius's cow costume for the school's annual Christmas pageant. Darius had stood by the sewing machine "to help." He had helped by losing pattern pieces and stabbing a stray pin into his bare toe.

She was on her way home from the Liskas where she'd left Darius to spend the weekend with Leo. Sara and Jim had invited her to dinner, and they'd had Mike Yanta over, too.

Darius's cow costume was neatly folded in the passenger side of the cab. Tonight's pageant had been a success, with Leo and Darius both starring as cows in Jesus's manger.

She was nearly to the bridge and the gate that led to the road to her house. Suddenly a blur of red and white lights up ahead and off to the right dazzled her. With a mitten, she wiped at the cloudy windshield.

Taillights jutted out of the ditch beyond the bridge. A pair of headlights shone like twin cones cocked at a crazy angle. A black Cadillac had skidded off the bridge and was stuck in the ditch.

Carefully, she drove across the bridge. When she came alongside the car, her truck slid to a halt with a hush of wet tires. She leaned across her passenger side and rolled down the window. Icy air blasted inside the truck. Dear God. She couldn't see any sign of life. Suddenly she was afraid of the dark and the unknown. Never had the road seemed more abandoned or forlorn. Just for a second, she toyed with the idea of driving on to her house where she could call for help. But the thought of leaving someone seriously injured in this cold stopped her.

The road had no shoulder, but she pulled off anyway, turned on her hazard lights, and set the emergency brake. She fumbled blindly under the seat for her flashlight and a crowbar, found them and jumped out.

Frigid gusts tore at her white woolen poncho and whipped her flimsy skirt. Her white boots sank into mud as she stepped off the road. When she reached the Cadillac, the mud was oozing over her ankles.

Frantically, she banged on the tinted window on the driver's side with her crowbar and shouted. Precious seconds were ticking past.

Then there was a feeble sound from inside. She caught her breath.

She made out a man's voice. "Help me open the door."

She struggled with the handle, tugging upward against the heavy door with every ounce of her strength until it gradually yielded. A man's strong hands were pushing at it from the inside.

"Get your keys and turn off your lights," she yelled.

The man could be dying and she was worrying about his battery.

But he obeyed.

"Can you hold the door by yourself, so I can get out?" a huskily pitched male voice asked from the depths of the Cadillac.

"I—I think so."

It took all her strength, but she managed the door just long enough for him to climb outside. The night was so dark she could only make out the shape of him. Once he was free, the door slipped out of her grasp and slammed with a thud.

"Sorry," she murmured in breathless apology.

"Hey, listen, honey, there's nothing to be sorry about. I was trapped till you came along."

His deep voice was muted and weak, but it was achingly familiar. "Grant?" Just for a second she flashed her light on his face.

"Damn."

He closed his eyes and ducked his head, but not before she recognized the high chest, the carved jaw and strong cheekbones, the jutting chin and the aquiline nose. Dear God. There was blood on his dark brow, in his hair.

"Merry Christmas, Norie," he muttered. "I didn't mean to land my Cadillac in your ditch."

"You're hurt," she whispered, tearing off her mitten, touching his face gently, even the sticky bloody place, smoothing his inky hair before she remembered he was the last man she should ever touch in such a familiar way.

She jerked her hand away. "What are you doing here?"

"I knew the welcome wouldn't last long." His voice was filled with the same bitter, insolent arrogance she remembered. "I was coming to see you. It's colder than hell. Can we get in your truck?"

Noreen stumbled backward, away from him, her white poncho

billowing in the crisp, cold air, and when he tried to follow her, he staggered.

She moved toward him, not wanting to touch him, knowing she had to. Wordlessly she gave him her hand and he clasped it tightly. Although his fingers were icy, her flesh burned from his touch. She began to tremble. He put his arm around her and leaned on her heavily as she helped him pull himself out of the ditch.

He was so weak she had to open the truck door for him. Her groping hand found Darius's cow costume and tossed it behind the seat. Grant heaved himself inside and collapsed.

When Noreen climbed behind the wheel, she was instantly aware of how big and male and virile Grant was beside her. As always he was wearing a flawlessly cut three-piece suit. His lawyer uniform, he'd once jokingly told her. The cuffs of the pants were as muddy as the hem of her white skirt.

"Why did you want to see me?" she whispered, her breathing as rapid and uneven as his.

His mouth curled contemptuously. "It was crazy, I know. But then, our relationship always was a little crazy."

The conventional Hales had thought her too uninhibited.

"More than a little."

His fathomless eyes were boring holes into her. "Yeah. More than a little."

"You should have stayed away."

"Maybe you're right," he muttered thickly. "I tried to talk myself out of coming a dozen times." But he reached for her hand, and with the last reserves of his strength, he pulled her hard against him. As his muscular body pressed into hers, she began to tremble all over again.

Anger flared in his eyes. "But then maybe you're wrong."

"Grant, please, let me go," she begged in a small voice. "It's been five years. We're strangers now."

"Whose fault is that? You ran away."

That old familiar undercurrent of electricity was flowing between them, even more strongly than ever before.

"Because I had to," she said desperately.

She felt the heat of his gaze on her mouth, and the emotion

in his eyes was as hot as the night was cold. With a light finger he gently touched her red lips, traced the lush, full curve of them.

Her own eyes traveled languorously to his hard handsome face, and she felt the old forbidden hunger for his strength, for his wildness, for the feel of his powerful body on hers.

A long tremulous silence hung between them.

"It's wrong, Grant." She gasped out the first coherent words that came to mind. "So wrong."

"Maybe so, but whatever it is, it's lasted five hellish years."

"You should be out with one of your beautiful women."

"Yeah, I probably should be."

He let go of her, and she jumped free.

He fell weakly back against his seat as she started the truck.

Grant lay woozily with his head against the cold glass. No telling what he'd done to his Cadillac. No telling when he'd get to Houston to check on his apartment projects, but at the moment, he didn't much care. His right knee throbbed, and so did his chest where he'd banged it hard into the steering wheel. Every bump in the road made the pain worse, but he said nothing. He was too aware of this woman, too aware of how she still stirred him.

Tonight when he'd stepped free of his car, she'd seemed like an angel, a Christmas angel, in her white swirling clothes and gypsylike looped earrings. Funny, because he'd never really cared much for Christmas. As a child he'd thought it the loneliest season of the year. His wealthy mother had been too busy socializing to pay much attention to him or Larry, and Grant had never known his real father or even his real father's name.

The truck skidded, and Grant watched Noreen struggle with the wheel to maintain control. She was such a fragile, delicate thing. She was the kind of woman that made a man feel protective. He didn't like the idea of her driving this lonely road at night.

The fragile scent of her perfume enveloped him, tantalized him. She was as sweet as roses. And as prickly, too.

Five years. To remember. To want. To do without. And he

wasn't a man used to doing without. At least not where women were concerned.

She'd thrown that up at him once.

You only want me because I belong to your brother.

Well, she'd been wrong. Larry had been dead five years, and here was Grant. He was such a fool for her, he'd come the minute he'd found out where she was.

Why? Norie wasn't the traffic-stopping kind of glamorous beauty Grant usually dated. But she was lovely in her own way. It wasn't her black hair, her red lips, her breasts, not her slim body—none of the things he had wanted from other women. It was her, her personality, something inside her that captivated him. Something that was quiet and powerful and completely honest.

He loved the way she liked to read quietly. The way there was always an aura of contentment around her. The way she was so gentle with children. The way she'd almost tamed Larry. Even the bright, offbeat styles she dressed in appealed to him. Norie didn't try to pretend to be something she wasn't.

Grant had gotten off to a bad start with her. He hadn't met her until Larry had written to their mother that he was seriously interested in her. Georgia had become hysterical. "This girl's different, Grant! Smarter! Larry's going to marry her if you don't drive up and stop him!"

"Maybe she's okay."

"No, she's a gold digger like all the others who've tried to trap him before."

It had never occurred to either Grant or his mother that Larry might be trying to stir her up and get some maternal attention.

Bad start. That was the understatement of the year. That first night in Austin had been a disaster.

Just like tonight, Grant thought coldly, suddenly furious with himself for coming. Why the hell had he bothered? She was as unfriendly as ever. He'd driven all this way, wrecked his car, and she'd hardly had a single kind thought.

"So, how long are you here for?" she asked.

"That depends on you," he replied grimly.

"There's no motel in town, and I don't feel like driving

twenty-five miles to get you a room and then back again. It's nearly Christmas, but I—I can't very well put you in the stable.''

He knew she didn't want him anywhere near her. But the mere thought of sleeping in the same house with her made him shiver with agonizing need.

''Cold?'' she whispered.

''Thanks for the invitation,'' he muttered, getting a grip on himself.

She started nervously twisting knobs on the dashboard, adjusting the heater. ''We'll call the wrecker in the morning.''

A gust of hot air rushed across his face. His hand covered hers on the knob, and he felt her pulse quicken. ''Hey, there's no reason to be so flustered. Honey, it's just one night.''

She pulled her hand away and let him fix the heater.

''Right. It's just one night,'' she murmured, with an air of false bravado.

''I hope I'm not putting you out,'' he said softly. Without touching her again, he swept his gaze over her body.

The silence in the cab was breathlessly still.

''Oh, I have a spare bedroom.''

''Then you live alone?''

There was another long moment's silence, and he wondered if there was a new man in her life. He thought she blushed.

''Y-yes.''

She was lying. He felt it. ''What a shame,'' he murmured, pretending to believe her.

But she didn't hear him. She was leaning on the steering wheel, turning the truck, braking in front of a locked gate.

She got out and unlocked it. The least he could do was slide across the seat and drive the truck through. So he did. She relocked the gate and climbed back inside.

''So, do you do this often?'' he demanded, the mere thought making him angry all over again.

''What?''

''Drive home alone? Get out and struggle with that damned gate in all kinds of weather?''

''As often as I have to.''

''You need a man.''

"So I've been told."

That rankled.

"But I don't want a man."

His taunt was silky smooth. "Then you've changed."

And that made her good and mad.

She stomped a muddy white boot to the accelerator so hard his head snapped back. A sudden blaze of pain exploded somewhere in the middle of his brain.

"Ouch!"

"Sorry," she said.

But he knew she wasn't.

He rubbed his head. At least she wasn't indifferent. But then, she never had been. Neither had he. That had been the problem.

Chapter 3

So this was where Norie had been for five damn years. This was what she preferred to the kind of life a Hale could have given her, the kind of life *he* could have given her.

As she drove, Grant stared in wonder at the small farm, the falling-down picket fence, the white, two-story, frame house built on a scant rise beneath towering pecan trees. The windmill. Why had she chosen this instead of him? Instead of everything he could give her?

The house was probably eighty or ninety years old. He'd been in old houses like this one before, houses that were built so they would catch the summer breezes and the windmill would be driven. In the winter such shabby structures were too vulnerable to the cold north winds.

A screened-in porch was on either side of the building and there was a veranda across the front. A solitary yellow bulb by the front door was the only source of light. He noted the tumbledown cistern in the backyard and the large flowerbeds where she could grow flowers in spring and summer. A clothesline was strung from the corner of the house to the back gatepost. There was a small enclosed yard.

She parked the truck in front of the house. Everything seemed so bleak and cold to him—so remote. He was used to living in the middle of town, in a beautiful home, surrounded by beautiful things—antiques, carpets, tapestry, crystal.

"It's not the Hale mansion," she whispered.

Was he so obvious? "You ran from all that."

"I never belonged."

"You could have."

"No." The tortured word was torn from her throat.

For a second longer she stayed beside him, so close he could almost feel the heat of her body. Then she threw open her door and ran up to the house. He followed at a much slower pace.

He felt almost sure there was no man in her life. Even though it was dark, he saw that the grass was too high. There wasn't much firewood left. The gate latch needed fixing. He stumbled and nearly fell when the bottom two steps gave beneath his weight because the wood was rotten. A splintering pain centered in his hurt knee, and he had to stop for a second.

"You okay?" she whispered.

"Great."

She was fumbling with the key when he caught up to her.

"The lock keeps sticking."

"That's because your hands are shaking. Let me help you, Norie."

She handed him the key, dropping it into his open palm, careful not to touch him. "A lot of things are broken around here."

His knee throbbed. "I noticed."

He opened the door, and she led him inside, into an icy living room with high ceilings and tall windows. She pulled the chain of an ancient Tiffany lamp. There were wooden rocking chairs and a battered upright piano. The atmosphere was homey, but everything—the furniture, the paint, the curtains—had a faded, much-scrubbed look. There was no central heat. He saw a single gas space heater at one end of the room. It was an old-fashioned house, the type kindly grandmothers were supposed to live in.

"Like I said, it's not the Hale mansion," Norie apologized again. "But would you mind taking off your shoes?"

She was about to lean down and remove her own muddy boots, but he grabbed her arm. At his touch a sudden tremor shook her. He felt a strange pull from her, and he couldn't let her go.

"Do you really think I give a damn about your house?" His voice was rasping, unsteady. "I came to see you."

For a moment longer he held her. She didn't struggle. He almost wished she had, because he probably would have pulled her into his arms. Her expression was blank; her dark glittering eyes were enormous. He could think of nothing except how beautiful she was. Unconsciously she caught her lower lip with her teeth, and that slight nervous movement drew his gaze to her mouth.

They were alone, in the middle of nowhere. It had been five years. Five long years. He wanted to kiss her, to taste her. But he had made that mistake before—twice—the first night he'd met her, and on her wedding day.

He swallowed hard. "Thank you...for letting me stay."

He saw intense emotion in her eyes.

Although it was the most difficult thing he'd ever done, instead of drawing her closer, he released her. She leaned down and pulled her boots off. As he bent over to do the same, the shock of pain that raced from his knee up his thigh made him gasp.

"You're hurt," she said, kneeling before him. "I'll do it."

Standing, he could see nothing but the gypsy-thick waves of her dark hair glistening in the honey-gold glow of the lamp as they spilled over her delicate shoulders. Her loop earrings glittered brightly. He felt her quick, sure hands on his ankles. He caught the dizzying scent of her sensuous perfume. No other woman had such drowsy dark eyes; no other woman possessed this air of purity and enduring innocence that mingled with something so free, so giving.

He had always wanted her. From the first moment he'd seen her angel-sweet face and known the beauty of her smile.

He'd only meant to stop by and see her on his way from San Antonio to Houston, to inform her that Larry had not left her penniless. Grant had intended to take no more than an hour from his busy life. He had a big case to prepare for next week and his Houston project was a mess.

He hadn't expected all his old feelings for her to be stronger than before. It was only one night, he'd told her. One night alone together. Nothing to get flustered over. But his hands were shaking.

Right, he thought grimly. One night. Alone. Together.

The time stretched before him like an eternity. Every slowly kindling nerve in his body burned for her. He clenched his hands into fists.

"There." She was done.

Smiling up at him, she placed his shoes neatly beside her boots and led him through a series of icy rooms. Since the house had no halls on the lower floor, each room opened into the next. To get to the kitchen and the stairs that led to the upper story, they had to walk through her bedroom. It was large and airy—too airy on a night as cold as this one. As they passed through it, he saw a large four-poster bed, a library table full of books and magazines, and a television set. A large Christmas tree decorated with handmade red and gold ornaments stood in the corner. He caught the crisp aromatic odor of fresh spruce. There was a nativity scene sandwiched in between the books on her table.

"Why is the Christmas tree in your bedroom?" he asked.

"Because we—"

"We?" he demanded. Grant gazed at her for a long moment. "I thought you lived alone."

Norie's breath caught in her throat. "I—I do. What I meant to say is that I spend most of my time there." She flushed under his hard scrutiny. "I don't like to heat up the whole house." She lowered her gaze to avoid his unfaltering one.

He hadn't practiced law for fifteen years without developing an almost uncanny sense about people. She was lying—covering something up. But what? Scanning the room again, he found no trace that a man might share it with her.

He shrugged. The best way to find out was to leave it alone—for now.

The stairs were difficult. His knee hurt so badly he could barely climb the steps, and he felt weak again when he had struggled to the top. He followed her from the dark hallway into a charming bedroom with frilly curtains and yellow flowered paper. The room was as icy as the rest of the house.

She knelt on the faded carpet and lit a fire in the space heater, then rose and went to the bed to find the cord and controls to the electric blanket. He crossed the room to help her.

Together they located the switch, pulled the covers back, and plumped the pillows. It seemed an intimate activity suddenly, unmaking the bed, and he stopped before she was through. For a moment he stood without moving, watching her, enjoying the simple beauty of her doing this simple thing for him.

"There," she said softly, smoothing the blanket. "The bathroom is right next door. I'll put out fresh towels. If you're still the same size you were, there are some boxes of Larry's clothes under the bed." Her eyes darkened. "I—I never got rid of them."

"I haven't put on an ounce."

He felt the heat of her eyes move swiftly over his body, mutely confirming his statement. And then she smiled in her unutterably charming way and blushed rosy pink before she glanced down at the carpet in front of his toes.

"I'll leave you to settle in, but I'll be back...with something hot to eat." Her tone was light and a little breathless. "You're probably starving."

"Oh, I am." His own voice when he answered was oddly hoarse. He gave her a look that told her it wasn't only food he was hungry for.

She backed away, stumbled against the doorjamb, blushed again, and was gone.

Damn. She was afraid of him.

The jeans Grant found in the box under the bed fit his muscled body like a snug second skin. The black turtleneck sweater molded every hard muscle in his torso, shoulders, and biceps. Well, maybe he'd put on an ounce. Or maybe as he'd gotten older he'd gotten into the habit of wearing looser-fitting clothes. Comforting thought.

As soon as he finished dressing he climbed into the bed to get warm. He lay beneath the toasty electric blanket, listening to the sounds of Norie bustling about in the kitchen beneath him. Outside, the wind was swishing around the corners of the house and whistling under the eaves. But his pillow was soft, the electric blanket warm. The room was beginning to seem almost cozy. He felt a baffling contentment, to be here, alone with Norie, so far from his own exciting but hectic life.

It was odd, Norie choosing this ice-cold house on a remote farm outside of a dying town, as opposed to the life she could have had.

Why?

He had never understood her.

Not from the first.

Maybe that was why he'd made so many mistakes.

His thoughts drifted back in time. Back to the first night when his mother had sent him to Austin to save his little brother from a scheming older woman.

"Noreen Black is a penniless little nobody. Some sort of Bohemian—an intellectual! An orphan who was raised in north Texas on a dirt farm. She's twenty-seven to Larry's twenty-three. I'm sure she's out to catch him," Georgia Hale had shrieked before Grant left for Austin. "Do you want the same thing to happen to your little brother that happened to you?"

Grant had been making vast monthly payments on a settlement to the beautiful young woman who'd deliberately married him so she could take him to the cleaners. Remembering the bitter consequences of his own mistake, he'd driven off to Austin determined to pay off Noreen Black before she had Larry completely in her clutches.

When Grant had knocked on the door of Miss Black's little apartment a couple of blocks west of the UT campus, a soft welcoming voice had answered. "Larry?"

"Larry's brother."

She'd thrown open the door. "Grant! Larry's told me all about you."

The "scheming older woman" was a slim girl with enormous dark eyes. Her cloud of dark hair was tied back with a green scarf, and huge silver loops danced at her ears. She didn't look twenty, much less twenty-seven. There were books scattered untidily on the dilapidated couch, red plastic dinette chairs and table. She had a pencil tucked behind one ear and had padded barefoot to the door in a pink and black leotard and tights. Tendrils of damp curls clung to her forehead. Her smile was the sweetest he'd ever seen.

His gaze roved the length of her body, passing downward over a flawless neck and shoulders, gently rounded breasts, a narrow waist, and long, shapely legs.

"Lovely," he said in a low voice.

Unconsciously Norie drew back, crossing her hands over her breasts.

"I—I was studying, but I stopped to exercise. To get the oxygen flowing again. I—I wasn't expecting company..." She trailed off uncertainly.

He couldn't tear his gaze away from the curve of her thighs, and Norie's color deepened.

"Are you looking for Larry?"

"No, I came to see you."

"I don't want to be rude, but I do have a big test tomorrow."

She was giving him, Grant Hale, the brush-off. Anger coiled in him as tight as a spring. Of course she was. She was after Larry. Somehow Grant managed to keep his voice calm. "Surely you have time for a quick dinner. I drove all this way just to meet you."

"I—I'm on a very limited budget."

"I'm buying."

That seemed to settle it.

"Well...since you drove all this way..."

She smiled so disarmingly that a shiver of unwanted male excitement darted through him. She was good, really good, at working a man with her charm, he thought cynically. He could see why Larry had fallen for her.

"It'll only take me a minute to dress. Make yourself at home. There's soda in the refrigerator."

While he waited for her, he rummaged about in the kitchen. There was, as she'd said, one soda in her tiny refrigerator. He saw milk, eggs, hamburger meat, canned goods, a few plastic dishes. A tight budget, she'd said.

Not for long, not after she caught Larry.

She returned wearing a red embroidered Mexican smock, red painted earrings, and silver jewelry. Grant complimented her on the outfit and drove her to an elegant restaurant on Town Lake.

She ordered the least expensive thing on the menu.

A trick, Grant thought.

To his amazement, he began to enjoy himself. In the candlelight, with her shining eyes and her pretty, sweet smile that seemed to be for him alone, she was beautiful. Larry was forgotten.

Grant began to drink, rather too much. He never got around to offering her money to leave Larry alone. Instead he talked about himself, about his secret dreams. He told her about Susan, their divorce, the hurt of it all. He told her things he'd never told anyone else. How as a child he'd secretly wished to know his own father. How he'd wanted love, how he'd grown up without it, how it was something he no longer believed in.

Then she'd told him about herself, about her loving parents, about their wonderful life together on their small farm until her parents had died in a car accident.

"I want all that again," she whispered. "You see, I do believe in love. More than anything, I want a home, children. I even know what I'll name them."

"What?"

"The boys will be Darius and Homer. The girls Galatea and Electra."

Grant laughed. Her fingers were toying with the tips of her silverware, and his hand brushed against them accidentally. He felt a warm tingle at the touch of her flesh. She drew her hand away and looked at him, her beautiful face still and silent and tender.

"I—I got those names out of books," she said in a rush. "I always loved to read, even as a child. Especially after Mother and Daddy died. I have a master's in English, and I've taught for three years. I'm studying to be a librarian. And now...I really do need to get home. That test..."

She was lovely, lovelier than any woman he had ever known. She drove. Because she knew Austin better, and because she hadn't drunk any alcohol. On the way back into town, he was grimly silent.

She parked in the dark in front of her apartment building.

"I had a wonderful time," she whispered. Her face lit with a guileless, naive happiness. Her eyes were sparkling in the darkness.

"So did I." Grant ran his hand up the pale smoothness of her bare arm.

"You're not like Larry."

At her mention of his brother, Grant's mood turned grim. "No?"

"Not at all."

"I came because Larry wrote that he was serious about you."

"What?"

"Don't pretend you don't know," Grant murmured in a coaxing, cynical rasp.

"I'm not pretending. He's just a good friend."

The wine and the hard liquor Grant had consumed made his thoughts swim. She was so soft and lovely, this gypsy girl, so totally different, she mesmerized him. His emotions were in turmoil. "You're poor. He's rich."

"I had no idea." Her voice was a tender whisper. "He seemed so young and so mixed-up. I felt sorry for him."

"I told you not to pretend with me."

"Grant..." She looked lost.

He swore under his breath. "You're good, girl. Very good. Maybe you can fool Larry with your angel face and your innocent, sweet Bohemian act, but you can't fool me. All night you've tantalized me, smiled at me, beckoned me with your beauty. You don't love my brother."

"No, I don't."

Silver bracelets jingled. She reached for the door handle, but his larger hand closed over hers. The minute he touched her, he was lost.

She was warm satin flesh. Her pulse raced beneath his fingertips. He was on fire. His gaze rested on her soft lush red mouth for one second only. Then his lips covered hers. He circled her with his arms. She tried to cry out, but his hot, ravaging mouth stifled all utterance. She was trembling with fear, and with some other emotion that more than matched the power of his own blind passion.

She was warm and sweet like heated honey. An angel who was erotic as no wanton could ever be. Shock waves of desire surged through every aching nerve in his body. He wanted her, as he had never wanted another. This funny, seemingly innocent woman-child who was poor, who was a gypsy girl.

Her slim body was crushed beneath the power of his weight, and the hands that had been pushing against his chest stopped pushing. He felt them curl weakly around his neck, and she pulled him closer, returning his kisses with guiltless wonder, sighing softly in rapture. So there was fire in her, too. Fire for him as well as for his brother.

At last Grant let her go.

"I want you," he said. "I'll give you everything Larry would have given you and more. Except a wedding ring. Like I told you, I made that mistake once before."

Her lovely face changed subtly, quickly, from the soft glowing expression of a woman newly in love to that of a woman who'd lost everything.

"You really think that I..." A sob caught in her throat.

His expression was harsh.

Her luscious, passionate mouth, swollen from his kisses, quivered. Her face was very pale. He saw the sparkle of new tears spill over her long lashes. Her beautiful neck was taut, her head proudly poised and erect.

"I've made mistakes, too," she said softly in a small, brave voice that didn't quite mask her utter despair. "And tonight...you, Grant Hale, were one of them."

He tried to stop her when she tried to go.

"I'm not what you think," she whispered. "And you're not what I thought."

He was forcibly struck by the sorrow in her pain-glazed eyes. She got out of the car and ran all the way to her door where she dropped her keys and struggled with the lock for a long time. He knew she was weeping so hard she couldn't see.

Flushed with anger and frustrated desire, he watched her fumble about, thinking he should help her, thinking he should go, thinking he would forget her, and knowing deep down he never could. When she vanished into the gloom of her apartment building, he started the car and burned rubber in his wildness to get away.

But he'd never forgotten her stricken, tear-streaked face. Not even after she'd married his brother on the rebound. Not in the five years since Larry's death.

Chapter 4

There was a whisper from the doorway that had nothing to do with the wind.

Grant opened his eyes and saw Norie standing there, holding a plastic tray with two cups of steaming hot tea, milk, and Christmas cookies. She'd removed her poncho and was wearing a white sweater that clung to her slender body, and a soft woolen skirt. She seemed to hesitate on the threshold, as if she had doubts about the wisdom of joining him in his bedroom.

Her hair fell in dark spirals, framing her lovely face and neck. Her dark eyes were immense and luminous. Just the sight of her looking so gently innocent and vulnerable made his own body feel hard and hot with wild ravening need.

The wind whistled, and the house shuddered from a particularly strong blast.

"Come in," he murmured.

"I was afraid I'd wake you," she replied breathlessly.

He watched her set the tray down on the table by the bed. She handed him a cup of tea and a plate of homemade cookies. Neither spoke for a while, and the silence seemed awkward and heavy to both of them.

"It seems funny...you being here...in this house," she said at last.

"What do you mean?"

"You're used to more glamorous settings—New York, Europe. You've been all over the world."

"I feel at home here…with you."

She stared into her teacup. "We're nothing alike."

"In a way that's true. But there's an old cliché. Opposites attract."

"You never liked me." Her voice was low, whispery.

The knowledge that she had run away and hidden from him for five years weighed heavily on his heart. "I liked you too much," he said through gritted teeth.

Her teacup rattled precariously in its saucer, and she looked up. "Can we talk about something else?"

"Fine. What?"

"I—I don't know. What can two people as different as we are find to talk about?"

Hard pellets of ice pinged on a piece of tin nailed to the roof. "Maybe the weather." His tone was derisive. "Bad night."

"Yes, it is."

That was all either of them could think of for a very long time. He was too aware of her beauty, too conscious of his need to run his hands through her black hair, to kiss her lush red lips. He felt white-hot with need. There was an awful, passionate, unbreakable tension in that silent room that was tearing them both to pieces. What was going on here? Suave, sophisticated Grant Hale never had trouble talking to a woman.

Desperate for distraction, he forced himself to remember the past. Norie had always been different, unconventional. She'd been an enormous amount of trouble to him. First he'd tried to stop her from marrying his brother. The problem was, she hadn't even known Larry was that interested in her until Grant had told her. Larry had written that letter to his mother when he'd been drunk, in the hopes of stirring her up. Hales were like that. Stirring was in their blood. Larry liked to be the center of a family drama.

Norie had been so upset about what happened between herself and Grant that night in Austin that she'd begun to see Larry in a more favorable light. She'd felt sorry for him for having such a materialistic mother and brother; she'd believed that was why he was so wild and unhappy. In the end she'd acted on impulse for the first time in her life and married Larry. But the marriage had never been a happy one. Not with Georgia's continual interference. Not with her threats to disinherit Larry because he'd chosen such an unsuitable bride. Not with Larry's weak, wavering nature.

They were married for two years. A month before he died, Larry had left Norie to please his mother.

It was the most horrible irony to Grant that he'd driven the only woman he'd ever loved straight into the arms of his brother who had never really cared for her.

Then, right after Larry had killed himself on his motorcycle, Norie had run off for no reason at all.

Norie didn't care about success or money. In fact, Grant wouldn't blame her if she was terrified of money and how it could twist people. She didn't care about knowing the right people, or traveling to the right places. She didn't have a single status-seeking cell in her body. She didn't know anything about fashion or fads. There was no way she could ever fit into his life. Their values were nothing alike. He needed a woman who could shine at cocktail parties, a woman who knew how to be an elegant hostess. A woman his mother could brag about to her friends.

He had had all that.

And it was empty as hell.

He wanted *this* woman. And he didn't care if it cost him everything he had, everything he was.

Maybe they could talk about the cookies.

The Christmas cookies really were quite interesting. Some of them were expertly painted. There were green Christmas trees with silver balls and red-and-white Santa Clauses. But some of the cookies were painted with a violent, primitive awkwardness. Grant picked up a particularly brilliant, clumsily painted cookie.

''Who painted this?''

She shut her eyes. Her voice was trembly. ''A—a little friend.''

He remembered Larry telling him about all the neighborhood

children that flocked to their house whenever Norie was home. She'd baked for them. Larry had been bored by children.

Norie's teacup rattled again in its saucer, and she quickly changed the subject. "How did you find me?"

"Yesterday morning, I was reading the paper. There was a mention of a UIL meet in Karnes City. I read through the students' names and the names of the teachers and school personnel accompanying them. I saw Noreen Black. I'd been looking for Noreen Hale. After that all it took was a few phone calls. Imagine my amazement when I found out that you were living only fifty miles away. If you hadn't run from me yesterday, we could have settled everything then."

"Settled what?"

"Larry left you an estate, of course. Did you imagine you were penniless?"

"I don't want Larry's money." Her dark eyes flashed. "I never cared...about his money. Anyway, we were separated when he died."

"It's yours, nevertheless. I've been managing it for you ever since."

"I'm sorry to have put you to so much trouble."

His voice was velvet soft. "I didn't mind. I liked knowing I was helping you, Norie."

"I don't want your help."

His gaze roamed her shapely length as heatedly as if he touched her. She began to tremble. Then she stiffened.

"You're afraid of me," he said gently. "Why?"

"I'm not afraid." But her voice was a slender thread of sound.

"Then why did you run from me in San Antonio?"

"Grant, I..." Her throat constricted.

"I came here to help you, Norie."

"I'm perfectly fine. I—I don't need your help."

"I know that I wasn't always your friend. In the beginning Mother and I—"

"I don't need either of you," Norie pleaded desperately.

He felt just as desperate. "Did it ever occur to you that maybe we, that maybe *I*, need you."

"No. No…" She set the teacup down, her hands fluttering in protest. She got up and was slowly backing away from him.

"Norie…"

"You need to go to sleep now. I'll be back to turn off the heater later."

"Norie!"

But she was gone.

Norie was in her bed in a warm flannel nightgown, removing her heavy earrings. She picked up a book review of a children's story. But the black print blurred when she tried to read. She kept thinking of Grant. She felt a throbbing weakness in the center of her being. He seemed so hard and tough, so masculine. So sexy with every muscle rippling against the soft black cloth of that sweater. She'd always been both fascinated and disturbed by him. She still was—and he knew it.

But he was a Hale, and even if he wasn't the weakling Larry had been, he was still Georgia Hale's son.

Grant was so smooth with women, so experienced. And Norie knew next to nothing about men, especially men like him.

What did he really want with her?

One thing she knew. She had to get him out of her life before Darius returned on Sunday.

Darius! A shiver of apprehension raced coldly over her flesh.

Why hadn't she thought? She remembered the way Georgia had used her money to turn Larry against her. Georgia could be subtle; she could be ingratiating. But she liked to control everything and everybody. Especially Larry, her favorite son. If she found out that Larry had had a child, what might she do to get control of Darius? Would she use her money to destroy Norie's relationship with her own son as she had used it to destroy her marriage to Larry? What if Georgia found some way to take Darius away?

In a flash Norie threw back her covers and got up. In her bare feet she scampered across the cold floors, removing every trace of Darius—his Christmas stocking laid out in front of the tree, his gifts, his tennis shoes and socks that he'd taken off by her bed. She dashed upstairs, hid these things in his room under his bed, and pulled the door tightly shut.

And to think that after Larry's death Grant had been so grief-stricken she'd almost told him that she was pregnant.

On her way downstairs she saw the pale thread of golden light under Grant's door. The door creaked when she opened it, but Grant didn't stir. For a second longer she studied him. He was beautiful with his long inky lashes, his tanned skin, his dark unruly hair, his powerful body. He had thrown off some of his covers. She watched the steady rise and fall of his powerful shoulders. Hesitantly she tiptoed to the heater and turned the knob at the wall.

The room melted into darkness.

The room would cool down quickly, so she went to Grant's bed to arrange his covers.

She was about to go when suddenly his warm hand closed tightly over hers.

She was caught in a viselike grip.

"I—I thought you were asleep," she murmured breathlessly. "I didn't mean to wake you."

"I'm glad you did." His voice was like a hot caress. "What have you been doing? Your hand is as cold as ice."

His concern made her pulse leap. "A few household chores downstairs."

"It's a shame for a woman as lovely as you to live out here all by yourself. To have to do everything by yourself."

She couldn't answer. She felt all choked-up inside, and she was too aware of his nearness, of his warm callused hand imprisoning hers.

There was a long moment of charged silence. She caught the musky scent of him, felt the warmth of his body heat.

"Why did you run away?" he murmured. She felt his finger-tips stirring her hair. "Was it because of the way I felt about you?"

"What are you saying, Grant?"

His fingers were smoothing her hair down around her neck, and she wanted nothing more than to be pulled into his arms.

"I wanted you from the first minute I saw you," he murmured

huskily. "I thought you belonged to my brother. Not even that mattered."

"I was a challenge."

"Once I might have agreed with you. Mother sent me to end your relationship with Larry, but the minute I saw you, I had my own reasons for wanting to end it. I wanted you even when you belonged to my brother. That's why I was always so nasty the few times I saw you after your marriage. I couldn't deal with those feelings." Grant's hand kept moving against her scalp in a slow circular motion that was mesmerizingly sensuous. "I've persecuted myself with guilt because I drove you away. I haven't always been the kind of man a woman like you could admire."

No... She remembered the holidays they'd been forced to share when she'd been Larry's wife. Georgia had been coldly polite, but Grant had been unforgiveably rude.

If only he hadn't been touching her and holding her, Norie might have fought him. But she felt his pain and she had to relieve it. "Georgia wanted me out of Larry's life. When he left me, I felt completely rejected by all the Hales. After he died, I thought you wanted me gone, Grant. That's why I left," she admitted softly.

"What?" His hand had stilled in the tangled silk of her hair.

"I overheard your family talking after the funeral. Your mother had worked so hard to break up my marriage. She said Larry never would have died if he hadn't married me, that I'd made him unhappy. You can't imagine how terrible that made me feel. It was clear everyone wanted me gone. Everyone. I thought I heard your voice."

"The Hales can be a crazy bunch. Maybe they did say those things, but I didn't. After the funeral I had to get off by myself. I felt so bad about Larry. He was so spoiled, so young. He died before he ever knew who he was or what he wanted. He couldn't stand up to Mother. I left the house for the rest of the day. When I came back, you were gone."

"It doesn't matter now."

"It does to me." Grant's voice was hard and grim, determined. "I should never have left you alone with them."

He pulled her closer, so close she was quivering from his heated nearness. So close her pulse throbbed unevenly.

"What are you doing?"

His lips touched hers, gently at first. A gasp of heady pleasure caught in her throat.

"Honey, I think it's obvious. For seven years I've wanted you more than I've ever wanted anything. Or any woman. You thought I didn't. I should have done everything in my power to stop you from marrying Larry. After the wedding I couldn't admit to those feelings, not even to myself. We've always been at cross purposes. For five years I've searched for you. Now there is nothing to keep me from claiming you."

Nothing but her own common sense and her will to preserve the placid life she'd made here for herself and Darius. Her heart raced in panic.

"Grant, no—" Norie twisted to evade the plundering fire of his mouth.

He covered her parted lips with his, and with heated kisses teased them to open wider. His hands ran over her body and lifted her gown. She felt dizzy. Uncertain.

"Please, don't do this," she murmured helplessly. "We're all wrong for each other."

"I know." There was the hint of cynicism in his tone of voice, but his eyes were dark with passion.

"But—"

"I don't care. Not anymore. I just want you, Norie. And if I can have you—even if it's only for one night—I will."

"Your family—"

"To hell with my family. If I can have you, I don't want anything else."

"You're a Hale."

His breath drew in sharply. "Not really, gypsy girl. I told you that my real father deserted Mother shortly after I was born. When Mother married Edward Hale, she forced him to adopt me. She wanted both her sons to share the same name so people would think of us as real brothers instead of half brothers."

Norie had heard all that before. To her he was a Hale, and

that was that. She tried to pull away, but Grant held her fast, with hard, powerful arms. And he kissed her.

She tasted him. Her tongue quivered wetly against his. A thousand diamonds burst behind her closed eyelids. She drew a breath. It was more like a tiny gasp. Suddenly she was clinging to him with quaking rapture. His male attraction was something she could no longer fight. He ripped back the covers and pulled her down against the solid wall of his chest.

"Norie. Norie…"

Her name was sweet as honey from his lips.

Inexpertly, she caressed his rough, hard jawline with trembling fingertips. Her dark eyes met the smoldering blue fire of his gaze.

"You're mine," he said inexorably. "Mine."

Then he began to kiss her, his mouth following every curve, dipping into every secret female place, lubricating her with the silky wet warmth of his rasping tongue until she was whimpering from his burning hot kisses.

Her dark eyes flamed voluptuously, and she was as breathless as he in a mad swirling world of darkness and passion and wildness that was theirs alone.

She wanted him more than anything in the world.

And yet…

"I—I can't," she pleaded desperately, placing her fingertips between her lips and his. "I want to, but I just can't."

His grip tightened around her.

A sob came from her throat.

On a shudder that was half anger, half desperation, he let her go.

For a long moment she hesitated.

"Go," he commanded, a faintly ragged edge to his breathing. "Go, before I change my mind."

Then she fled, away from Grant's warmth, out into the cold, empty darkness of the house.

Chapter 5

Norie lay in her icy room, in her bed, her nerves and muscles wound so tightly she jumped with every blast of the norther outside. At last she drifted into fitful sleep, only to be plagued by dreams of Grant. She would then awaken with her pulse throbbing unevenly and lie listening to the wind. Yet it wasn't the storm outside that was battering her heart and soul, but the one within her.

Her slim fingers curled and uncurled like nervous talons, twisting and untwisting the sheets. She wanted Grant. More than she ever had.

His presence made her aware of the emptiness of the past five years. She had accomplished nothing by running away. If she didn't send him packing soon, she knew she would be lost. There was only one thing to do—call the wrecker first thing in the morning. The sooner Grant left, the sooner she could start all over again to try to forget him.

But the next morning when she picked up the phone, it was dead.

No sound came from upstairs, so she assumed Grant was still asleep. She dressed quickly in the dark, cold house, ate a bowl of bran with a banana, and went out to her truck.

The road into town was glazed over with ice, and she went only a quarter of a mile before deciding to turn back. Better to spend the day with Grant, than to kill herself trying to get rid of him.

Only when she got back to the house and found him in her kitchen scrambling eggs, she wasn't so sure. There he was, large and male, making himself at home, dominating the room with his virile presence. He was watching her. His blue eyes flamed in a way that told her he was remembering last night. Treacherous, delicious shivers danced over her skin, and she blushed uneasily. That made him smile.

"The phone's dead," he murmured without the faintest note of regret in his voice.

She was toying with her woolen scarf nervously. "That's why I thought I'd try to make it into town to try and get a wrecker, but the road's too icy."

"I'm glad you had the sense to come back." There was a quiet, intimate note in his low-toned remark.

She was pulling off her coat and scarf, and he was watching her again. His intent, hot gaze savored the beauty of her flushed face and the soft curve of her breasts.

"You'd better keep an eye on those eggs." She pivoted sharply and hung her things on a peg by the door.

"Looks like you're stuck with me for another night," he said mockingly. "I've got one more day...and one more night to change your mind." His voice was a honeyed caress.

She gasped uneasily. "That's not going to happen."

His eyes darkened to midnight blue as he stared at her thoughtfully. "Something tells me you're not so sure."

She felt another treacherous blush creep up her neck and saw his quick smirk of male triumph. What was he, a mind reader? "You think you know so much!" she snapped, exasperated. "Those eggs are going to be dry as dust."

He turned off the stove. "I never was much good at talking and cooking at the same time. I get distracted easily." His voice grew huskier. "The eggs didn't have a chance against a distraction as lovely as you." He grinned in an impish, teasing way that made him even more incredibly handsome.

She was horrified by the pleasure she felt at his compliment, horrified at the warm, wonderful confusion that was totally enveloping her, leaving her defenseless.

She stared at him, speechless for at least a minute. She wanted to think of something to say that would be so spiteful he would leave her alone, but words failed her. All she could do was sweep haughtily out of the kitchen into her bedroom. She slammed the door on the low rumble of his male chuckle.

He was seducing her, teasing her, laughing at her for her weakness where he was concerned. As experienced with women as he was, he probably considered her an easy conquest. Somehow she had to summon the strength to fight him. But as she made her bed and picked up her things, she was aware of every sound that came from the kitchen. He sang and he clattered plates. Pots banged on the stove.

She decided her only option was to ignore him, to try to stay as far away from him as she could possibly get. So she went into the living room to dust. But wherever she went, he allowed her no peace. He called her into the kitchen saying he didn't know what plate to use or where the salt and pepper shakers were. And when she was reaching up to get the objects he wanted, he was right behind her, his body so close, so warm, that it was all she could do to resist the fatal impulse to step back into his arms. The rest of the morning and the afternoon he pestered her in the same way.

Later that night, after dinner and the dishes, he went up to bathe, and she thought she was safe. But while she was cleaning the pantry, he called down to her from his bedroom.

At first she ignored him, but he wouldn't stop calling to her. Surely he was the most stubborn man on earth.

When she trudged up the stairs at last, she found him standing in the middle of his bedroom trying to look hurt and helpless. He said his shoulders were so sore from the wreck that it hurt him to lift his arms and button his shirt. It took only a second for her senses to register his physically disturbing state. His unbuttoned blue shirt contrasted with the dark bronze of his damp skin. He smelled clean and male. She caught the sensual scent of his aftershave. His black hair was jet dark, wet and curly.

They were alone. This was their last night together. Her last chance. She should run back downstairs at once.

But she could only stare at him, thinking he was as darkly beautiful as a muscled pagan god. She could only feel dizzy and weak with a sickening longing to touch him and caress him.

His blue gaze was electric. "Come here, Norie," he commanded gently.

She began to tremble, but she lacked the strength to move either toward him or away from him. It was he who closed the gap between them with two swift silent strides.

His shirt swung open further. He stood so close she could feel the heat from his body, see the wetness that glistened on his bare chest.

He had asked her to button his shirt. In that moment it was as if she had no mind of her own. Very slowly she reached toward him, intending to bring the edges of his shirt together. Instead her fingertips slid beneath the soft blue fabric to touch the hard curves of his muscular chest and torso. She felt bone and muscle. His skin was like warm, polished bronze. Her slim fingers tangled in the hair on his chest and then splayed in wonder over the place where his heart pounded with excitement.

He sucked his breath in sharply as her soft hands moved on, wandering in sensuous exploration, lovingly pushing his shirt aside, over his shoulders, then more urgently wrenching it off, and tossing it to the floor. Gently, her lips followed the path of her hands, kissing him first in the spot that concealed his violently thudding heart, then following every curve of his hard muscles.

She would have stopped touching him and kissing him, if only she could. But she was hot, as hot as he was. At last she lifted her head helplessly, and found that his blazing eyes were upon her radiant face. His gaze studied every inch of her face with such tenderness that she almost stopped breathing. Very slowly he leaned down and kissed the black shining curls at her temples. Then her cheek. Then her throat. She felt his breath falling warmly against her skin like heated velvet whispers. Only the tumultuous drumming of his heartbeat betrayed his restraint.

"Don't fight it," he whispered. "You can't." He balled his

hands into fists. "I know, because I can't, either." His voice was a ragged, hoarse sound.

Very gently he drew her into his arms and toward the bed. And she let him.

He was right. She couldn't fight him. She was weak. She wanted him too much.

His hand curved along her slender throat. His finger wound a strand of silken black hair into a sausage curl and released it, letting it bounce against her satin throat.

"Open your lips," he instructed huskily.

He brushed a soft, sweet kiss across her mouth, and then he, too, was lost. All of his careful control was disintegrating. He was shaking against her. His breath drew in sharply, loudly, fiercely. He kissed her again, harder and hotter than before. He held her so tightly she felt that her own body was fused into his. His mouth moved against hers, his tongue moist and urgent as it slid between her parted lips to taste the warm, sweet wetness within. She let her tongue touch his.

Norie's knees became weak, but it didn't matter because he was lifting her into his arms and carrying her to the bed.

Her lashes fluttered lazily, hopelessly shut as he stirred her with his lips and hands to erotic, feverish, passionate ecstasy.

Outside, the flat Texas landscape was bleak and barren and frozen. The wind was howling wildly. It was going to be another stormy night.

Inside, the two lovers were lost to the world and conscious only of each other. For them, there was only the wonder of their passionate extravagant present. For Noreen, only the wonder of having Grant at last.

He was still forbidden.

He was still a Hale, no matter how he denied it.

Tomorrow she would probably be sorry.

But tonight, as she lay enfolded in his crushing embrace beneath crisp cotton sheets, he was hers. Recklessly, gloriously, completely hers.

She abandoned herself heedlessly to the night, to the mounting passion of her lover, to her own wildness that had lain dormant until now. At last, she discovered the ecstasy that she had read about in books and always wanted but never known, not even during the brief unhappy years of her marriage.

After it was over—their fierce, molten mating—he buried his lips in her silken hair and breathed in the sweet, clean smell. She ran her hands over his magnificent body that glistened with sweat, and she reveled in the beautiful strength of his hard, muscular physique.

Tears of joy flooded her eyes.

She felt vulnerable, soft.

Gently he brushed her wet cheek. "Forgive me," he murmured quietly.

"For what?"

"For all the wasted years." He clasped her tightly. "For that first night in Austin, all those years ago. For your wedding day when I insulted you with the kind of kiss no brother-in-law should ever give a bride."

"Don't," she whispered shudderingly. She put a fingertip to his lips.

"I was wrong, Norie. So wrong. I thought…I thought I was protecting Larry."

"I know."

"I always loved you, but I couldn't admit I was wild with jealousy when you married Larry. I couldn't admit that you might love him. I treated you badly. I stood by and watched Larry pit you against Mother. He always loved to be fought over." Grant ran a light finger down her belly. "No more. At last you are mine."

Noreen let him stroke her hair, let him kiss her again. She even let him remove the wedding ring she'd continued to wear for Darius's sake. Yes, tonight she belonged to Grant. Tonight was their dream. Tomorrow would be soon enough to awaken to reality.

His black head lowered and his parted lips moved over hers tenderly, nibbling for a time, forcing her mouth open again, slowly, teasingly, while his hands traced over her body and then pulled her closer. She could feel his heat beginning to flame all over again.

"I thought you were hurt."

He laughed softly. "I have miraculous recuperative powers."

Noreen's hand slid down his hair-roughened chest, stroking his flat muscled stomach, hesitating, then moving lower. She touched that hot, warm part of him that told her just how fully aroused he was.

"Indeed you do," she whispered on a wanton giggle.

"And you're one sexy...librarian."

"Oh, Grant," she breathed against his lips and threw her arms about him. "I thought things like this only happened in books."

"So you like this better than reading?"

"Much...much better."

He chuckled huskily.

And that was the last thing either of them said for a very long time.

When Grant awoke the next morning, he was alone. Outside, everything was covered with a layer of frost and the sky was white and wintry. Inside, the room was cozily warm. Norie must have turned on the heater before she'd left him and gone downstairs.

If only she'd stayed in bed, it would have been so much easier to face her. He got up quickly and began to dress. The hall outside was icy as was every other room in the house except his and the kitchen.

Norie was in the kitchen bending over the stove. She looked pretty in her looped earrings and a pale yellow dress that emphasized her slim waist and the curve of her breasts. The sight of her made him remember last night. His heart gave a leap of pure happiness.

He smelled bacon and eggs, freshly brewed coffee and baking biscuits. The wooden table in the middle of the room was set with handmade red place mats and blue china. Everything was so charming, so perfect, and the most perfect thing of all was Norie.

He shut the door, and she turned, and he watched the flush on her cheeks rise in a warm blush of color. Their glances met. He smiled, and she set the spatula down, hesitating, but only briefly, before she stepped joyfully into his open arms.

He kissed her gently, on the brow first, and then her mouth, and she surrendered heedlessly to his lips. He thought, this is how marriage would feel. He would wake up, and she would be there—every day.

"I feel very lazy, very spoiled," he said. "Can I do anything?"

"I wanted to spoil you. Did you sleep all right?"

"Perfectly."

"And your knee?"

"Much better."

"Everything's almost ready. Nothing fancy."

"I don't want fancy." He reached out to touch her cheek.

"The phone's back on," she said quietly.

Her eyes, meeting his, were intense and thoughtful. She turned back to the eggs, and Grant opened the refrigerator out of old habit just to inspect its contents. Inside, he saw a turkey.

"So you're going to cook a turkey for yourself out here, all alone?"

Her face changed. "I—I cook Christmas dinner every year."

"For anybody special?" he demanded, sounding both stiff and disconcerted.

The room grew hushed.

She wouldn't look at him, but he saw the color rise and ebb in her cheeks. She seemed to hesitate. "If you're asking about another man, there isn't one."

His stomach tightened. What was she hiding? In some indefinable way, she had erected a barrier. He felt shut out of her life again and angry about it. But what right did he have to say anything?

"How long till breakfast?" His voice came out harsh and loud from the strain of controlling both his curiosity and his temper.

She had turned away and was stirring something on the stove. The spatula was clanging rather too loudly. "Six or seven minutes."

"I think I'll walk down to my car." His words, his manner, were a careful insult.

"Fine."

At the door he turned. "Norie..."

She drew a sharp breath. "Just go."

He jerked open the screen door and stomped out, his footsteps crunching into ice and shattering the frozen stillness of the morning.

A wan sun shone through the thin white clouds and made the layer of frost on his black Cadillac sparkle. It was going to take a wrecker, all right, to get it out of the ditch. Grant wouldn't know till then if he would be able to drive it or if it would have to be towed. But his mind wasn't really on the car. It was on Norie.

Last night, she'd been sweet and warm and loving. This morning she couldn't wait until he drove himself and his car out of her life.

Why?

Impatiently, he grabbed Norie's rolled-up newspaper and pulled it from her mailbox. Then he headed briskly back to the house.

Six minutes, she had said. He stopped in the middle of the road to think. Okay, so she had managed without him for five years. She was independent and proud. It was stupid to think he could storm into her life and take over in the first forty-eight hours. His gaze wandered over the farm. Not bad. For a woman alone, she had a lot to be proud of.

Sure, the house could stand some paint, but in the sunlight with every window pane glimmering, it wasn't nearly as bad as he'd thought in the darkness the other night. A magnificent spiderweb hung on a low branch. In the frozen sunlight, it seemed to be spun out of crystal gossamer lace. Along a fence a line of bare trees stood out sheer and black. The farm and its isolation appeared peaceful, almost beautiful this morning. He remembered how she liked to grow things. Maybe she was afraid he would want to take her away from all this. Maybe there were people here, friends who mattered as much to her, or more, than he ever could.

Grant felt on edge. He'd never liked going slow, waiting. Hell, they'd already lost seven years.

He started back to the house. He was barging around the back of it when his ankle caught on a handlebar, and he fell against a low shrub. He barely managed to catch himself.

"What the..."

At his feet he saw a tangle of shiny red metal and wire wheels.

A tricycle. He pulled the thing out of the hedge and set it upright on all three wheels. For some reason he remembered the clumsily hand-painted cookies. Her little friend must have left it.

He remembered how she'd always loved children, and it seemed a shame that she had to content herself with little friends she had over to paint cookies, a shame that she didn't have any of her own. She would make a wonderful mother; she would be nothing like his own unmaternal, socialite mother. He could give Norie marriage, children.

"Grant!"

He looked up.

She was in the doorway looking soft and lovely and calling him to breakfast.

Over breakfast the barrier between them was still there. But he tried to enjoy himself, anyway. The food was perfect, but he hardly tasted the biscuits and the bacon and the coffee. All that mattered was Norie. He tried to concentrate on her. She was telling him as she had on that first night about her childhood in north Texas, about her parents. Soon she had him talking about himself, telling her how he'd always wanted to know his real father but his mother was ashamed of that early marriage and would never allow it. But all the time Grant was talking, he kept wondering what was wrong.

"So how did you end up here?" he asked at last, switching the conversation back to her.

"The very same day Larry was buried, after I got home to Austin, Mike Yanta, the school superintendent here, called me and offered me a job. It seemed like the perfect solution."

"And was it?"

"In a way. I love the school, the children, the story hours. I know everybody in town, and everybody knows me."

"The perfect life." His voice was unduly grim.

"More or less. For me anyway."

"But are you fulfilled?"

He wanted just one word from her, one word to show that she cared. But even before she answered, he knew she wouldn't give it.

"Are you?" she whispered.

"I used to think so. I was a success. That's all I considered. Until I met you."

"I probably make a tenth of your income, but it's all I need." She was twisting her napkin nervously.

Her *all I need* certainly didn't include him. A little muscle jumped convulsively in his jaw. "I told you part of the reason I came was business. Larry named you as his only beneficiary."

"But I thought..."

"Mother controlled most of the money, and she still does. But Larry had a sizable trust all his own. I've managed that trust for you for the last five years and more than tripled the original amount. You are not a poor woman."

Norie was very pale, and she was shredding the napkin into pieces. "I told you I don't want it."

"But it's yours," he said harshly.

"I—I don't feel that it is. Georgia wouldn't want me to have it."

"Mother changed her mind about you a long time ago."

"I don't believe you!"

"When you ran away, when you never came back to claim your inheritance, Mother came to realize that you hadn't married Larry for his money after all. She wanted me to come here. She even told me to tell you that she's sorry. I was wrong about you, too. In the beginning I thought you were after Larry's money. Hell, you weren't even after Larry."

"Not till you came and your coming made Larry so mad he wanted to show you and Georgia he could live his own life. But he failed. We both failed."

"It took me a while to figure out that's how it happened. I was a fool not to see the truth the minute I met you. You're the most honest woman I've ever known, and the most loving."

Her eyes grew enormous and she gripped the table. "Grant... You're just as wrong about me now as you were then. I'm not the saint you seem to think I am."

"To me you are. You shouldn't be living alone. You should be married."

"I've been married."

"You should have children this time. Do you remember telling me that you wanted a big house with four children? You even knew what their names would be."

She turned white. "Homer, Electra, Galatea, and...Darius," she whispered, rising slowly from the table.

He laughed. "So you still remember?"

She seemed uneasy suddenly. "I used to be such a bookworm. Those names appealed to me when I was a child."

"You planned a big family. Aren't you waiting a little long to get started?"

A burning color washed back into her face, and she said quickly, "Life doesn't always work out the way we plan it."

"It's not too late."

She looked at his face for a long time, and then she looked away. "I—I wish I could believe that, but I can't." Methodically she began to stack the dishes. "This is real life. You and I—we're so different. I'm what I am. I like flowers, kids, friends, wide-open places. You're a Hale."

"I'm a man. You're a woman."

"It's not that simple. We can't just erase what happened. I can remember dozens of beautiful women on your arm. How long could you be happy with me?"

"Forever."

"Do you think Georgia would ever allow that?"

His stomach went tight and hard, as if Norie had punched him there. "Do you think I'm like Larry? Do you think I would allow anyone, even my mother, to come between me and the woman I love?"

"If not her, then her money." Norie's voice was a bitter, tormented whisper. She walked to the sink with the dishes and shoved the handle of the faucet. Water splashed loudly. "You've accomplished what you came here to accomplish...and more." She flushed. "We've got to get your car pulled out of that ditch. Then you can go."

At the terrible finality in her low voice, Grant felt something inside himself break and die. It was as if his heart was being twisted and wrenched, and the agony was unbearable.

He hardly knew what he was doing as he sprang blindly to his feet. His chair crashed behind him to the floor.

"Grant!"

He moved toward her and jerked her hard against his body. A dish fell and shattered in the sink.

"So you think money, any amount of money, could change what I feel for you?" His hard gaze flicked over her pale face. She seemed small and defenseless against his enormous body. "What did last night mean to you anyway?" he demanded roughly.

"I—I don't know. I don't know. I just know I've got my life and you've got yours."

"Is that really all we've got?" Grant studied her, straining to read her expression. But she seemed a very long way away. "Damn it. I can't let you go."

"You don't have a choice."

"There's always a choice, Norie. Always. That's all life is."

She began to struggle, fighting him silently to escape, but she was like a child in his grasp.

His mouth took hers. He held her against him until she stilled, crushed until she did nothing more to stop his hands as they molded her curves to fit the tough contours of his body.

When she fought him no more, when she became smooth and warm, when he could feel her quickening response, only then did the stubborn will to conquer her with the force of his own passion subside.

Tenderly, he kissed away the salty tears that had spilled down her cheeks. At last he withdrew his mouth, his hands. Norie drew a long breath and opened her eyes. Then she pulled herself free of him and stumbled shakily backward toward the kitchen door, one of her hands clutching her throat. For a numb moment she could only stare at him.

"Norie, please…"

For a second longer those big, scared eyes were upon him.

Then she broke and ran.

Chapter 6

The icy morning air was biting cold as it seeped through her jean jacket and her thin yellow dress. Noreen was pale and shivering, and her unhappy dark gaze was fixed on Jimmy Pargman and his wrecker and the muddy black Cadillac he had just pulled out of the ditch. In his car, Grant was coolly ignoring Norie as he tried to start the engine. His lean face was set and hard. He had not spoken to her once since he'd kissed her and she'd run out of the kitchen. He was now just as anxious to be gone as she was to be rid of him.

Her heart beat jerkily. In another minute Grant would drive away, this time forever, unless she did something to stop him—and that was something she would never do. Because of Darius. Because she was too afraid of the Hale money and of what Georgia might try to do if she found out about Darius.

But as Norie looked at Grant, she felt a terrible stab of longing. More than anything she wanted to cross the road, to fling herself into his arms. To forget how different they were. To hold him, to touch him, to smooth that black tumbling lock out of his face…just one last time. Her eyes swam with unshed tears. And this weakness made her despise herself.

Fragments from last night kept replaying in her mind like newly edited film clippings. She remembered the way his fingers had unbuttoned her gown, the way his hands and mouth had roamed everywhere until she was as thoroughly and wantonly aroused as he.

How could she have let him? How could she have been so totally unlike herself, so shamelessly forward? She was the one who had gone to him when he'd called, to his room, to his bed, knowing what might happen.

She had forgotten Darius, forgotten everything that really mattered to her. Nights like that were probably commonplace to a man like Grant, to a man who could have any beautiful woman he desired.

The Cadillac's engine purred, and Norie felt a hopeless, sinking sensation in the pit of her stomach. She closed her eyes. She had to forget him! To go on as if last night had never happened. To go on as if her feelings for him didn't exist.

When she opened her eyes again, she saw the Liskas' familiar blue Suburban coming toward her.

Sara was bringing Darius home! Dear God!

Grant opened the door of the Cadillac just as Sara braked alongside Norie and rolled down the windows on her side.

"Hey, Mom!" Darius's blue eyes were wide with curiosity as he looked first at her, and then at the Cadillac across the road. "Guess what? Raymond let Leo and me play his Nintendo, and we didn't even break it."

For a paralyzed, horrified moment Noreen couldn't speak. Then she managed a weak, "That's great, hon."

Grant was paying Jimmy, so he didn't notice Darius.

Noreen touched Sara's arm. "Why don't you drive on to the house? I'm almost through here. We'll have tea while the kids play."

"Who's he?" Suddenly Sara saw the tears in her friend's eyes. "Hey..."

"Later, Sara," she whispered chokily. "I'll tell you everything."

"Why do I know you really won't?"

"Please..." The sudden huge knot in Norie's throat made it impossible for her to explain.

Sara's brown eyes softened with compassion. She stepped on

the gas just as Jimmy did the same. The Suburban turned off to head toward Norie's house. The wrecker headed back into town.

Noreen and Grant were left alone, standing on opposite sides of that desolate bit of asphalt in that wide-open landscape that seemed to stretch away forever. Noreen stole a glance at him. He was looking at her, too. And they were as mute and awkward with one another as if they were strangers.

Grant opened his trunk and pulled a shoebox and briefcase from it. He opened the shoebox and dangled a pair of sparkly red shoes from the tips of two lean fingers.

Her heart was pounding with fright. She had no choice but to cross the road and retrieve them.

She came so close to him, their steamy breaths mingled. Her hands touched his briefly. Warm skin against warm skin. They both tensed in acute awareness of one another. Then she was snatching her shoes from him and replacing them noisily into their tissue paper and box. He was briskly unsnapping his brief-case and pulling out a thick sheaf of legal documents.

She raised her eyebrows.

"These papers deal with your inheritance." His voice was harsh and loud.

"I told you I don't want money, Grant."

"That may be, but getting rid of it is going to be a little bit more complicated than that." His dark face was as stern as death, his blue eyes unreadable.

He handed her his card. It was so crisp and sharp it cut her fingers.

"Call my secretary and make an appointment. I'll have her help you do whatever you decide to do about it."

He was so coldly formal Norie's blood seemed to freeze in her veins. He was killing her. She almost broke down. Instead she met his chilling blue gaze.

Not a muscle moved in her beautiful face. Nor did she allow even the glimmer of a tear. She held herself as rigidly as he.

"All right," she managed, forcing herself to speak, surprising herself by sounding calmly unconcerned.

For a moment longer he stared at her. His mouth hardened. "So, it's goodbye? This time for good?"

When she said nothing to break the frozen silence, he opened the door of his car and hurled his great body angrily inside. "Have it your way. It's not even goodbye." He twisted the keys viciously in the ignition. "Merry Christmas, Norie."

As his big car zoomed away from her, the tears she had held back slipped down her cheeks in a scalding flow.

She watched his car until it vanished into the big empty landscape, and the knowledge that she was doing the right thing didn't help her at all.

"I'm sorry, Grant." Her voice was low and muffled by her sobs. "So sorry."

But he was too far away to hear her. Too far away to know of the desperate pain in her heart that his leaving caused her.

Norie sat at the same table where she'd shared breakfast with Grant only an hour earlier. On the surface, everything was just as before. Except for the fact that it was Sara who was seated at the table with her.

There was no visible trace of Grant in the kitchen. No visible trace of him anywhere except in her heart.

The farmhouse was cozily warm. Sara had lit several of the space heaters, both upstairs and downstairs. The two women were in the kitchen dipping their tea bags into their cups. Leo and Darius were in Norie's bedroom looking at the ornaments and presents.

"So who was he, Norie?" Sara demanded quietly. Her soft brown eyes were aglow with curiosity and concern.

Norie sipped her tea, too upset to reply. She wondered if her life would ever be the same without him. Instead of answering her friend, she listened to their sons in the next room.

"Yeah, Leo, I made this one."

"I could tell 'cause you forgot to paint the reindeer's hoof."

"And I popped the popcorn and stringed it. Mom made most of the good things though."

"You don't have as many presents as me under your tree."

"That's 'cause I want something special. See, Santa's gotta bring it all the way from the North Pole. And it could smother in his bag."

"What do you want?"

"Santa knows."

"I bet it's a dog."

"It's sorta like a dog. Only better."

The boys began to whisper conspiratorially.

But Norie couldn't hear them. Her own heart was pounding too hard.

"Mom!" Darius yelled from the doorway.

"Darius, that's your outside voice," she murmured softly, correcting him out of maternal habit.

His impatient tone was only a fraction softer. "Where's all my stuff?"

"In your room."

"Everything?" He cocked his four-year-old brows as arrogantly as any Hale.

She nodded.

"Mom, I had things out where I wanted them."

She smiled. "Out is where you want everything." But she was talking to an empty doorway. The boys were racing each other up the stairs like a pair of rough-and-tumble puppies.

"Boys! Leo! No running!" Sara called.

They pretended not to hear. The wild footsteps careened up the stairs and down the hall overhead.

"They sound like a herd of stampeding elephants." Sara giggled.

Norie cringed when doors opened and slammed. "So much for minding."

"They're just excited over Christmas," Sara said.

Norie sipped her tea.

"So who was that very attractive man?" Sara repeated her earlier question.

Norie had dreaded this. "My brother-in-law."

"What happened to his car?" Sara eyed the plump stack of legal papers in their blue folders that Norie had placed on the edge of the table. "Why was he here?"

"Sara, it's something I can't talk about, not even to you."

"Jim's right about you being mysterious."

Galloping footsteps crashed down the stairs, and a breathless

Darius flung himself into the kitchen. "Hey, Mom, who slept in the guest bed upstairs?"

Sara arched her brows knowingly, and Noreen turned red.

"Can we play in there, Mom? The fire's on, and it's real warm."

"No!" The single word was too sharp, and Darius, who was not used to such sternness from her, looked hurt. More gently she said, "You bring your things down here where we can watch you."

"But we want to play up there by ourselves."

"No."

"You never let us."

"Darius!"

Mother and son stared at one another across the kitchen. Darius's lower lip swelled mutinously.

"Darius, remember about Santa. He rewards good little boys."

Darius gulped in a big breath.

Then Leo said, "Can we build a house by the tree with blankets and cushions?"

"Of course, but try not to make too big a mess."

Sara laughed. "You don't mind asking the impossible."

Leo was running back up the stairs, and Darius was right behind him.

The showdown was over. At least the one between mother and son. Norie knew that Sara was more determined.

"So your brother-in-law spent the weekend here?" Sara asked softly. "With you? Alone?"

Norie got up to pour more water into the kettle. Then she went to the stove. Her back was to Sara. "He skidded into the ditch. I couldn't very well leave him there."

"Something tells me you didn't want to leave him there."

"Much as I love you, Sara, I'm just not ready to talk about Grant."

"Well, I'll be here when you are."

"I know. You have always been my dear, dear friend."

It was a long time before Norie could turn around and pretend to Sara that everything was normal.

*   *   *

The next few days were the bleakest and loneliest Norie had ever known. They were even worse than when she had come to town pregnant and alone to live with Miss Maddie. No matter what she did or where she went, Norie couldn't quit thinking of Grant.

When she was Christmas shopping, she would see things she wanted to buy for him. She'd even bought one gift—a beautiful blue silk dress shirt that would look wonderful on him because of his blue eyes. It had seemed so stupid and silly, buying a present for a man she would never see again.

When she got home, she hid the gift under her bed. But sometimes she took it out to admire it secretly and dream of really being able to give it to him.

At night she lay awake thinking about him, seeing in her mind his every gesture, his every smile, remembering the exact things he'd said to her. Most of all, she remembered the way he'd gently, tenderly, brought her again and again to shuddering heights of ecstasy.

And every time she looked at Darius, she saw Grant. With his black hair and dazzling blue eyes, Darius was almost a miniature replica of his handsome uncle. Darius did not mention the special gift he had asked Santa for again, but every time Norie looked at him she knew that he was silently longing for a father—as once Grant had longed for his father. She felt Darius's special excitement, his expectancy, and these things only made her sadder.

Somehow she got through the days and the nights.

It was Christmas Eve, the night her church held a beautiful candlelight service. Norie was sitting alone on a wooden pew watching Darius, who was in the children's choir. Her black dress was tied at the waist with a handmade lavender sash. As always, large loops dangled from her ears.

Darius and Leo were wearing white choir robes with huge red satin bows tied beneath their scrubbed chins. They looked like angels, and they sounded like them too, as their voices and those of the other children filled the sanctuary with the lovely familiar melodies of sacred Christmas carols.

The service was an hour long, and it was a time of beauty and peace for Norie. All too soon the lights of the sanctuary were put out. For a moment there was darkness except for a single candle. Then the candles of the congregation were lit one by one. A hush filled the church, and Norie whispered a prayer that made her own candle flutter gently. *Merry Christmas, Grant. Be happy. Wherever you are.*

"Silent Night" was played, and so many candles were lit that the church became more brilliant than she'd ever seen it.

She felt an arm brush her waist possessively, and she turned.

Grant was there beside her.

For a moment he stood without moving, just looking down at her. Then he smiled at her boyishly, charmingly. His eyes were filled with tenderness and warmth, and some powerful emotion she couldn't be sure of.

She could barely see him for the mist of emotion that rushed at her.

"Grant..." A radiant smile broke across her face.

Black hair, blue eyes. He was movie-star handsome in a dark, conventional suit and tie as he towered beside her.

Her pulse stirred with a thrilling joy.

His hand closed over hers, and suddenly she knew how much she loved him. It didn't matter that she could never be as socially correct as his mother or the other women he had dated. Norie was still scared, scared of loving him, but in all her life she had never felt the swell of love that she felt for this man. The past— Larry, the Hales, their money and its misuse, all the grief, the rejection, and the heartbreak—no longer mattered so much.

"Merry Christmas," she whispered, her voice warm and light and happy.

"I had to come, gypsy girl," he said quietly.

His low, raspy voice was the most beautiful sound she had ever heard; more beautiful even than the sound of the angels. Gently he touched one of her gold loop earrings.

Her lashes, strangely heavy, fluttered down, but she felt the warmth of his caring in every cell of her body.

For her the world held promise once again.

Shyly, she squeezed his strong hand.

She was wrapped in happiness as she listened to the haunting loveliness of the last verse of "Silent Night."

For the first time in years Christmas really seemed a time of love and renewal and rebirth. Then she glanced up and beneath the glimmering jewel-bright stained glass windows, she saw two angelic-looking little boys in white robes and red bows. Darius's big blue eyes were wide and curious as he studied Grant. Then he smiled happily, knowingly, and he sang so joyously that Norie imagined she could hear his voice soaring above all the others in the choir and congregation. It was Christmas Eve, and Darius believed very firmly in the magic of Christmas.

Darius!

Grant still didn't know about Darius!

Dear God. She made a quick, silent prayer.

After the hymn was over, and the lights came back on, Norie managed to slip away from Grant and ask Sara to keep Darius for an hour or two, so she could be alone with Grant and explain.

Then she rushed out of the church and found Grant waiting for her by her truck.

Chapter 7

Norie's eyes kept flicking apprehensively to the bright reflection of Grant's headlights in her rearview mirror. What would he say? What would he do when she told him about Darius? Grant had always believed in her honesty.

Never before had the drive home seemed so long. How in the world would she go about explaining?

There's something I haven't told you...

A little something I have to explain...

I wanted to tell you, Grant, but...

How could she make him understand why she had run away? Why she'd been so afraid of the Hales and what their money might do?

Larry had married her because she was different, and he'd wanted to defy his mother. Norie had been caught in the middle of their troubled relationship. She'd been too naive to pick up on the secret machinations that were weakening her marriage until it was too late. Larry's incessant extravagances had made it all too tempting to him to go to Georgia for the money he needed, and all too easy for Georgia to use this as a weapon to destroy Larry's fragile new loyalty to Norie.

After Larry's death Norie had felt utterly rejected. She'd been afraid that she might still be too naive to prevent Georgia from using her money to divide her from her son. No, Grant would never understand.

The high-ceilinged rooms glowed with rosy, welcoming light and warmth and smelled sweetly of fir and spruce. Norie was in the kitchen nervously making tea. Darius's things were everywhere, but Grant hadn't seemed to notice. He'd been too busy lighting the heaters and laying out his presents for her in front of the Christmas tree.

He had taken off his jacket and was kneeling by the tree. From where she stood, Norie watched him with a longing that was so intense it bordered on pain. She marveled at the play of powerful muscles in his back beneath the fine fabric of his shirt every time he moved, at the way the light shimmered iridescently on his blue-black hair.

Finally he became aware of her and met her gaze with a hungry, flushed look that made her cheeks glow even brighter than his. As she moved toward him, he picked up a small green present wrapped with a golden bow. "I want you to open this one first, gypsy girl," he said in a deep, husky voice.

"Now?"

"Now," he said softly.

She remembered the blue silk shirt hidden beneath her bed. "I bought you something, too."

"Did you?" He grinned at her. "I wasn't sure whether you'd be glad to see me or whether you'd throw me out."

She nuzzled her face against his shoulder. "It's a good thing you didn't call. I would have told you not to come. But now that you're here…" She slid her pale hands upward across the broad expanse of his chest until they found the knot of his tie, but she was so clumsy at loosening it that he had to help her. Unbuttoning the first three buttons, she slid her fingers inside and touched his hot, warm skin. "I'm glad you came," she whispered in a hushed voice. "So very glad." With her lips she began to explore the hollow at the base of his throat.

"I kept thinking about your turkey. It seemed a shame for you to be out here all alone, eating by yourself," he said in a low, hoarse tone, pulling her closer.

"You better not have come back just because of my turkey."

He gave her the small present. "I want you to open this one first. It will explain everything."

Her fingers shook as she tore into the glittering ribbon and then the green paper. Inside was a white cardboard box, and inside it, a smaller black velvet one. She snapped the inner box open instantly.

A solitaire diamond engagement ring winked at her from black velvet.

Her breath caught. She stared at the ring for a long moment, then looked back up at him.

"Well?" he whispered. "Do you like it?"

Gingerly she touched it, tracing the finely cut stone, the gleaming band with her fingertip. Her gaze blurred. "It's beautiful, Grant. The most beautiful ring in all the world."

"For the most beautiful woman."

"But are you sure?"

He smiled down at her. "I love you, Norie. Marry me."

She ought to tell him. About Darius. Now.

But she was too dazzled by Grant's words, by the tenderness shining in his eyes. So she just stood quietly and let him slide the ring onto her finger and twist it so they could both watch it catch the light and shimmer.

"There, it's a perfect fit," he said, pleased.

"Grant, I'm not the right kind of woman…"

"Hush." His hands were in her black silky hair. He pressed her face against his chest and smoothed her hair. Softly he said, "You're so beautiful, Norie. The whole time I was gone, every day, every hour, I was thinking of you."

"So was I."

"I nearly picked up the phone to call you a thousand times. But I knew what you'd say. I needed you so much. I felt so hopeless, so lost."

"So did I."

"No more, gypsy girl."

"What about Georgia?"

"She will accept you. I swear to you she will."

Then he lifted Norie's face toward his, and he bent slightly to cover her lips with his. He kissed her ever so gently. She moaned and raised her arms to encircle his neck. Her heart had begun to thump erratically. Waves of desire pulsed through her, and she knew she had to stop him.

Finally she got the words out. "Grant, there's something terribly important I have to tell you."

"What could be that important?" His hand cupped her chin and he lifted her face again so he could resume kissing her. "More important than this?"

Their lips met. His tongue dipped into her mouth again just as the front door flew open with a bang. Norie scarcely heard the eager footsteps as her child ran inside, the door slamming behind him. She was too aware of Grant tensing in surprise.

"Mom! Hey, Mom, I'm home!"

Suddenly Darius stopped and stared in disbelief at the vision of his mother in a man's arms, the two of them framed in the doorway with the lights of the Christmas tree twinkling behind them.

Norie withdrew slowly. Still holding her hand, Grant stepped back a single step to stare at the diminutive replica of himself.

Darius was still in his "church clothes," but just barely. His shirttails were wrinkled and hung loosely out of his slacks, his tie was crooked, and his shoelaces were dragging. Norie was sure that in all his life, Darius had never stood so absolutely still for so long without being told to. His blue eyes were open wide with wonder.

"Santa is awesome!" Darius shouted in his outdoor voice, using his idol, Ray Liska's, favorite word. Then Darius ran happily toward them, never doubting for a moment that he would be a welcome addition in the big man's arms.

Grant knelt slowly to the child's level.

"Santa really did bring me a daddy." Darius let out a big sigh. Then he touched Grant's sapphire tie tack. "You are real! Boy! You even look a little like me."

"What's your name, son?"

"It's Darius."

"Darius?" Grant looked up at Norie. His face was dark, unreadable.

"Hey, can you play football?"

"I played in high school," Grant told him almost absently.

"Awesome."

Darius didn't usually hug people he'd just met. But he made an exception with Grant and laid his cheek against Grant's trustingly just for a second before pulling himself free and dashing eagerly toward the kitchen.

"Hey, come on. I gotta lot of things upstairs I want to show you."

Grant stood up slowly. As Darius dashed up the stairs, Norie's soulful eyes sought Grant's and silently pleaded with him to understand. But he looked past her, his expression closed and hard. Without a word he left the room and followed Darius.

Norie stayed downstairs, her heart filled with an agony of doubt and regret. She could hear their voices—Grant's deep baritone mingling with Darius's overly excited shouts.

Why was her life always like this? Just when she was sure she loved Grant, she'd ruined everything. She wouldn't blame him if he hated her.

An hour passed before Grant came down again. Norie was in the kitchen, sitting silently at the table. The tea she had made for herself had gone cold while she'd waited nervously, hopelessly.

He sank down heavily across from her, his jaw rigid, his eyes dark. "That kid's got energy. He was so excited, I had to bribe him to get him down for the night."

"We have to talk," Noreen said.

"That's the understatement of the year."

"Grant, I was going to tell you."

"When? Did you ever stop to think what the past five years have been like for me? I cared about you. After Larry died, I wanted to help you. I would have done anything in the world to try to make you happy. But what were your feelings for me? My only brother died. Knowing where you were, knowing about Darius would have meant everything to me. Not only to me. But to Mother. Larry was her favorite child. I was very little comfort to her."

"I want to explain."

"It's too late for that. I'm going."

"Grant, no."

He looked up. "Don't you understand? I believed in you. I believed that deep down you cared something for us, for me. You think the Hales rejected you. Honey, by keeping Darius from us, you rejected us. The one thing I never expected from you was dishonesty of this magnitude."

"I wanted to tell you," she said softly, each word carefully enunciated. "I almost did, the day of Larry's funeral. But then I heard all the Hales talking, and I thought you felt the same way."

"Norie, none of it matters anymore. You're free of me and the Hales. If you're so afraid of us, you don't need to be anymore." Slowly he got up. "I'm going. I won't tell Mother. Be happy. You're finally really, truly free of us all."

Norie went to him and put her arms around him. "But you know that's not what I want anymore." She was speaking rapidly, desperately.

At her touch, everything in him went as still as death. He released her gradually, slowly pushing her away, all the time staring into the shadowy depths of her eyes.

"Grant, please—" Her lips barely moved as she whispered. But he wouldn't let her finish.

"Tell Darius... Tell him, Merry Christmas from me tomorrow, will you? Tell him...maybe next Christmas Santa will do the job right, and he'll get a daddy who'll teach him how to play football. I'm not the right guy."

Then without speaking to her again, Grant turned and strode out of the house, letting the door close behind him on a whisper of icy air.

Tears pooled in Norie's eyes, but she didn't chase after Grant. He had decided to go, and no matter how much she wanted him to stay, she knew that no amount of pleading could persuade him.

The house seemed frigid and empty, as frigid and empty as her own heart.

She heard a slight sound on the stairs, and knew that Darius had not gone to bed after all. He came into the kitchen, his eyes as big and sad as hers. He was dragging his favorite red teddy bear.

"Where's Grant?"

"I don't know."

"Will he come back?"

"I don't know that, either," she admitted.

"But he's my special present from Santa."

She took him into her arms and ruffled his black hair. "Mine, too, darling," she murmured softly. "Mine, too. But he's your uncle, and you'll see him from time to time."

Darius sat on her lap and sucked his thumb.

"You're a big boy now, Darius. Big boys don't suck their thumbs."

He pulled his thumb out reluctantly. His face was very serious. "I didn't ask for an uncle. I asked for a daddy."

"Well, it isn't Christmas yet. Maybe, just maybe, Santa realized he'd delivered our special present too early. Go back to bed. Santa doesn't come until little boys are asleep."

"Do you really think he'll send Grant back?"

"Maybe, if we both pray very hard."

"Mom, do you really believe in magic?"

Behind them the Christmas tree lights were softly aglow. Grant's ring was still on her finger. His other gifts were still under the tree. Her gaze stole to the manger scene that she and Darius had built together, to the tiny figure of the baby Jesus.

"Yes, in a way," she replied gently. "You see, when it's Christmas, I believe in miracles."

Chapter 8

Norie sat up in bed, her heart beating expectantly, not knowing what it was that had awakened her.

And then she knew.

It was Christmas Day.

She fell back against her soft cool pillow in a daze of happiness.

Her bedroom was cozily warm. Someone had come in earlier and lit the space heater. From the kitchen wafted the aroma of coffee and bacon and biscuits. A man's deep husky voice was accompanying a radio that was playing "Joy to the World."

Grant had come back to her as she and Darius had prayed he would.

She listened to Grant sing with her eyes closed, his baritone washing over her, caressing her.

At last she got up, pulled on her robe and stumbled barefoot across the cold floors into the kitchen.

"Grant?" His name was a broken cry across her lips.

His dark gaze smoldered with love for her.

"I thought it was you," she managed to utter dreamily. Then she was flying across the kitchen into his arms. "You did come back."

Tenderly, he enfolded her into his strong arms and lowered his black head to the long pale curve of her beautiful neck. She felt his hands smoothing the snarls from her sleep-tangled, silken curls.

"I had no choice. I know from experience that life without you holds nothing but emptiness. I love you, gypsy girl. I always have and I always will."

"Enough to forgive me?"

His dark eyes moved over her face, and his expression grew momentarily soft. "There's nothing to forgive."

"Last night I was afraid you despised me."

"I was angry. But after I calmed down, I understood why you did what you did."

"I should have told you about Darius years ago. Instead I ran away."

"We drove you away," he said gravely.

"After Larry died and I heard your family saying they didn't want me, I felt completely alone. The only thing I had was my unborn child. When Mike Yanta called and offered me this job, I took it. I came here and made a life for myself, but because I never resolved my conflict with you and your family, there was always something incomplete in my life. You see, I wanted to belong to your family, to be a real Hale, for Darius's sake as well as my own. I knew I was keeping your mother's only grandchild from her. But I was afraid of her, afraid that she might try to dominate my child the way she had dominated Larry. I was afraid she might use her money to alienate Darius from me. But I couldn't forget you, Grant. No matter how hard I tried."

"Mother won't use her money like that again. She knows she made a terrible mistake." Grant's tone grew gentler, lower. "But I was as guilty as she. From the first, I was insensitive to you. To the person you really were. I hurt you. I promise I'll be more careful in the future."

"Oh, Grant…" She could scarcely speak. "My values were so wrong. I was so mixed-up about the power of money that I attached more importance to it than I should have. I should have believed in you, in myself." She winced as she thought of all the hurt she had caused everyone. "I'm always going to wonder what would have happened if I'd been stronger and hadn't run away in the first place."

Grant took her anguished face between his hands and tilted it back. "That's something we'll never know. Maybe we needed these years so we'd know how much we nearly lost."

"And how much we really love each other." She had never dreamed that he loved her so much, that money and its powers no longer could seem frightening.

She pulled away a little from him then, smiling up at him, but he drew her back and kissed her. His hand wrapped around the back of her shoulders. His hard mouth slanted over hers in fierce possession.

A long time later they pulled apart, breathless.

"Darling," he murmured. "How do you think Darius would feel about Santa bringing him a grandmother and a grandfather for Christmas as well as a daddy? You can say no..."

She smiled up at him mistily and placed two fingertips over his mouth. "Hush... I don't want to say no. I want you to call them and invite both of them for Christmas dinner. It's a little late, I know. Georgia usually has so many invitations. They'll have to drive fifty miles."

"They'll come."

Grant sought her lips again. Then he rained hot urgent, kisses over her forehead, her brow, her throat, before stopping to cradle her face in his hands and peer into her eyes.

"It looks like Santa brought all of us a lot more than Darius asked for." Grant kept holding her. "If I didn't know better, I'd say today is the next best thing to a miracle."

"Santa's special miracle," she breathed.

"And mine," Grant said. His dark face grew solemn. "Darling, I—I have a confession to make." For the first time his confidence seemed to desert him.

"If it's about other women...don't..."

"It's even worse than that."

Her black brows arched quizzically.

"It was because of me, that the phone went dead that morning. I tampered with it that night, you see. I had to have you by fair means or foul."

For a long moment, she stared at him in stunned surprise.

Then her expression grew radiant. "I guess you were just helping Santa work his miracle."

"I love you," he whispered.

She took his hand and squeezed it. "Let's go upstairs and tell Darius."

The kitchen door by the stairway banged against the wall. "I'm right here, Mom!" Darius shouted exuberantly right before he burst into the room dragging his blanket and his teddy.

Norie put her fingers to her lips.

"I know, Mom. My outdoor voice..." In a softer, more tentative tone, the child whispered, "Right here...Dad."

Grant knelt down and folded the little boy into his arms. "Right here...son." Very gently he lifted him from the ground.

"Are you really going to stay?" Darius demanded eagerly.

"Forever."

Norie drew a deep breath of pure happiness.

"Merry Christmas, Norie," Grant whispered, his blue eyes dazzling bright, as he drew her closer into the warm circle of love.

Holding Darius tightly, Grant bent his head and kissed her.

*   *   *   *   *

THE COLTONS

invite you to a thrilling holiday wedding in

A Colton Family Christmas

Meet the Oklahoma Coltons—a proud, passionate clan who will risk everything for love and honor. As the two Colton dynasties reunite this Christmas, new romances are sparked by a near-tragic event!

This 3-in-1 holiday collection includes:

"The Diplomat's Daughter" by Judy Christenberry

"Take No Prisoners" by Linda Turner

"Juliet of the Night" by Carolyn Zane

And be sure to watch for **SKY FULL OF PROMISE** by Teresa Southwick this November from Silhouette Romance (#1624), the next installment in the Colton family saga.

Silhouette®
Where love comes alive ™

Don't miss these unforgettable romances… available at your favorite retail outlet.

LONE STAR
LS&CC
COUNTRY CLUB
EST. 1923

Where Texas society reigns supreme—and appearances are *everything*.

On sale...

June 2002
Stroke of Fortune
Christine Rimmer

July 2002
Texas Rose
Marie Ferrarella

August 2002
The Rebel's Return
Beverly Barton

September 2002
Heartbreaker
Laurie Paige

October 2002
Promised to a Sheik
Carla Cassidy

November 2002
The Quiet Seduction
Dixie Browning

December 2002
An Arranged Marriage
Peggy Moreland

January 2003
The Mercenary
Allison Leigh

February 2003
The Last Bachelor
Judy Christenberry

March 2003
Lone Wolf
Sheri WhiteFeather

April 2003
The Marriage Profile
Metsy Hingle

May 2003
Texas...Now and Forever
Merline Lovelace

Only from

Silhouette®
Where love comes alive™

**Available wherever
Silhouette books are sold.**

AVAILABLE IN OCTOBER FROM SILHOUETTE BOOKS!

THE
HEART'S
COMMAND

THREE BRAND-NEW STORIES BY THREE
USA TODAY BESTSELLING AUTHORS!

RACHEL LEE
"The Dream Marine"

Marine sergeant Joe Yates came home to Conard County ready
to give up military life. Until spirited Diana Rutledge forced him
to remember the stuff true heroes—and true love—are made of....

MERLINE LOVELACE
"Undercover Operations"

She was the colonel's daughter, and he was the Special
Operations pilot who would do anything for her. But once
under deep cover as Danielle Flynn's husband, Jack Buchanan
battled hard to keep hold of his heart!

LINDSAY McKENNA
"To Love and Protect"

Reunited on a mission for Morgan Trayhern, lieutenants
Niall Ward and Brie Phillips found themselves stranded at sea—
with only each other to cling to. Would the power of love give
them the strength to carry on until rescue—and beyond?

Available at your favorite retail outlet.

Silhouette®
Where love comes alive™